# PRAISE FOR
# THE MYRTLE WAND

"Audiences familiar with the general outline of *Giselle* will find Porter's narrative naturally engaging, but she's taken care to keep other readers involved as well . . . An absorbing and touching tale . . . a fully realized, moving portrait of the storied court of Louis XIV."

—*Kirkus Reviews*

"Main characters are fictional, but powered by the real-world experiences of minor players . . . Readers are immersed in a world of court and commoner. A powerful story, highly recommended for its realistic quandaries and strong female characters."

—*Midwest Book Review*

"Lushly atmospheric . . . rich with historical detail. Porter imagines the story behind the iconic *Giselle*, transporting us to France during the early reign of the Sun King. Betrayal and redemption, magic and religion all cross paths in dangerous *pas de deux*—and Princess Bathilde finally gets her opportunity to take center stage."

—*Leslie Carroll*
***Royal Romances: Titillating Tales of Passion
and Power in the Palaces of Europe***

PRAISE FOR
# A PLEDGE OF BETTER TIMES

"Porter's ambitious novel of 17th-century England is brimming with vivid historical figures and events . . . rigorously researched and faithfully portrayed."

*—Publishers Weekly*

"A true delight for fans of monarchy . . . Porter does a sensational job portraying the time period."

*—The Examiner*

"Porter winningly captures both the dramatic societal upheavals and the sparkling wit and court life of the time . . . A very rewarding reading experience—I highly recommend it."

*—Historical Novels Review*

PRAISE FOR
# THE LIMITS OF LIMELIGHT

"An engrossing glimpse into a bygone era and the forces affecting a young woman's evolution into her own abilities and adulthood . . . vigorous and involving to the end."

—*Midwest Book Review*

"Based on a true story . . . a witty and meticulously researched treat."

—*Kirkus Reviews*

"A biographical novel as bright as the Golden Era . . . A lovely tribute to the larger-than-life celebrities of early Hollywood . . . a glitz and glamour novel that shines brighter the deeper you go."

—*Independent Book Review*

"A captivating novel about Hollywood . . . providing a more realistic and multifaceted view of the era . . ."

—*Historical Novels Review (Editors' Choice)*

# Praise for
# BEAUTIFUL INVENTION:
# A NOVEL OF HEDY LAMARR

"Hedy Lamarr is feted as much for her intellect as for her beauty in this captivating novel . . . Porter's insightful account of a gifted yet often misunderstood inventor and movie star makes for a winning novel."

*—Publishers Weekly*

"Fast, fun, fascinating, enjoyable, intriguing, and recommended."

*—Historical Novels Review*

"The terror felt by Lamarr . . . is brilliantly conveyed by Porter, whose empathy for Lamarr and historical knowledge brings danger to the plot . . . A revealing look at Lamarr's life . . ."

*—The Lady Magazine (UK)*

# THE
# MYRTLE
# WAND

*The Myrtle Wand*/Margaret Porter—1st Edition

ISBN 13: 979-8-9856734-9-4

# THE
# MYRTLE
# WAND

## A NOVEL

# MARGARET PORTER

GALLICA PRESS

*To my beloved partner in the dance of life.*

# ⚜FRANCE⚜

•Paris
Fontainebleau •  •Vaux-le-Vicomte

•Nantes

•Poitiers
Château des Vignes• •Niort
•
Château Clément

•St. Jean de Luz

*Une vive clarté se répand,—et l'on doute*
*Si le jour, qui renaît dans son éclat vermeil,*
*Vient de votre présence ou s'il vient du soleil!*

From the magic forest illuminating the vault,
A bright light spreads,—and one doubts
Whether the day, which is reborn
in its vermilion radiance,
Comes from your presence or whether
it comes from the sun!

—Théophile Gautier, *À la Princesse Bathilde*

# Part I: Myrte

## 1649-1654

*Mon âme est une soeur pour ces ombres si belles.*
*La vie et le tombeau pour nous n'ont plus de loi.*
*Tantôt j'aide leurs pas, tantôt je prends leurs ailes*
*Vision ineffable où je suis mort comme elles . . .*

My soul is a sister to these shades so beautiful.
Life and the grave for us no longer have any law
Sometimes I help their steps,
sometimes I take their wings.
Ineffable vision where I am dead like them . . .

—Victor Hugo, *Fantomes*

# CHAPTER 1

*Convent of the Ursulines, Niort, 1649*

The bell within the stone tower clanged ten times, marking the end of mid-morning lessons and the start of a welcome half-hour of leisure. In her first weeks at the school, Bathilde had timidly trailed the sedate procession of pupils as it moved to the courtyard. Nowadays she was among the first to escape her classroom, fighting the impulse to race to the cloister where her friend would be waiting.

She found Myrte on their favorite bench, the one facing the stone arch that framed a section of garden and grass.

"You must have been in a great hurry. You didn't fasten your cloak." Myrte settled Bathilde's garment more evenly over her shoulders, and with fingers whitened by the January chill, she tied its ribbons.

"This is the day she's supposed to arrive. Do you suppose she'll come before we sit down to dinner?" Bathilde breathed, each word hanging as a cloud. The days and nights here offered scant variation, and her unhappy experience as a newcomer fostered her determination to befriend the unknown *demoiselle* who was expected to enter the academy that day.

"Perhaps," Myrte responded. She brushed away snowflakes that had fallen onto Bathilde's russet head and pulled up her hood. "Before nightfall, surely."

"I wonder if she's nearer to my age, or yours." Bathilde was eight, and Myrte was five years her senior.

"Enough about her. Did you provide correct answers to the multiplication questions I helped you with last evening?"

She nodded. "Soeur Marie praised me for it, too. A little."

"I shall praise you a great deal." Myrte leaned over to embrace her. "They strive to instill humility in us. You suffer from an excess."

Perplexed, Bathilde gazed into her friend's lovely face, framed by the little black curls that resisted all efforts at restraint. "I'm not sure what you mean."

"Although unacquainted with any other princesses, I've always regarded them as excessively proud and haughty. You've improved my opinion."

"Maman wasn't like that." Her voice broke, as it always did when speaking of the parent who had died last summer, entombed in the cathedral at Poitiers, with the brother Bathilde never saw.

"Tell me about her." Myrte guided her to the stone bench against the inner wall. "It's important to remember. That is how she can remain with you always."

"She was pretty. She played the harpsichord and sang to me. She had a sweet voice, like yours. She sat me on a stool and showed me the notes of the keyboard. And she let me try on her favorite shoes. Red velvet, with green vines and blue flowers embroidered all over. She held my hand so I wouldn't stumble as I tottered across the floor. We lived at the large château, the one near the sea."

"Aren't they all large?"

Bathilde considered the question. "Château Clément, where I was born, is the larger one. Château des Vignes, older and not as grand, has the forest where Maman and Papa went hunting. It lies close to the River Sèvre, not very far from here." Glancing upwards, she said, "If the new girl is also a princess, I hope she's a nice one."

Myrte smiled. "So do I. But you'll forever be my favorite. I promise."

This assurance sent a warm flow of pleasure and relief coursing from her head to her toes.

Hoofbeats and the creak of coach wheels broke through the courtyard chatter.

"She's here!"

They joined the girls running towards the wall with a lack of decorum the sisters would deplore. Peering over the top layer of rough stone, they saw a fine carriage, its dark body splashed with mud.

"Drawn by six horses," Myrte observed. "Perhaps she really is a princess."

A formal procession of the highest members of the convent's hierarchy moved across the courtyard. Mother Superior, her authority in no way diminished by her lack of inches, was accompanied by her under-prioress, her sacristan, her cellarer, and the leading choir nun. The wind, stronger now, battered the long, full habits and toyed with the veils, and snowflakes stuck to the heavy, black fabric. Their every step caused the long rosaries dangling from their waists to swing back and forth. According to Myrte, nuns who descended from the well-born families moved with a certain grace, whereas those of common stock tended to amble. The daughter of a wealthy merchant, she could point to the class distinctions within their small universe. But until that comment about haughty princesses, she'd never offered negative criticism about those whose status was below or above hers.

"I wonder if she's as eager to meet us as we are to meet her."

"That depends on whether she comes willingly or not."

This reply revived Bathilde's stark memory of her own reception when Papa brought her here. He'd assured her that she would benefit from the education the sisters could provide and enjoy the companionship of nearly thirty resident pupils. Their separation, only a few months after he'd placed Maman in the family vault in Poitiers Cathedral, left her as desolate as that permanent loss. It also meant parting from her doting nurse and her only playmate, little Giselle from the village.

Pleasing Papa was her primary purpose in life, and until that day it had never been difficult. On trembling legs, she'd passed through the portal, doubtful that she could ever be happy in this strange place.

The constant activity of the château—bustling servants on stairs and in the passages, the noisy laborers trooping past on their way to the vineyard, and the playfulness of the grooms in the stables—hadn't prepared her for the Ursulines' soft voices and their faint tread in the chilly stone-paved passages. By far the youngest of the girls, and thus the smallest in size, she became known as "little squirrel" because of her reddish hair. This term was never uttered in the nuns' presence, so she knew it wasn't complimentary. She joined a class of ten pupils considered the least intelligent, and even though she swiftly caught up to them, and surpassed several, there she remained until an unexpected intervention. Myrte Vernier, whose beauty and vivacity and cleverness set her apart from their schoolmates, befriended her.

"I never saw a creature as scared and shy as you were during your first days," Myrte said. "I decided to prove to you that this isn't a bad place."

"It seemed so. Before I knew you."

Whenever sad thoughts surfaced, the older girl dried her tears and offered a consoling embrace. Myrte sat with her at mass, prayers, meals, and vespers. She'd penned an eloquent request to Mother Superior with the result that they were allowed to sleep in adjacent dormitory beds. By some mysterious persuasion she convinced her class regent to admit the princess to the same class she attended, even though Bathilde was years younger than the rest of the girls.

As a manservant helped a handsome, fashionably gowned woman descend from the coach, they glimpsed several layers of lacy underskirt flounces. The breeze toyed with the curling feathers of her broad-brimmed hat. Head held high, she approached the gate and addressed Mother Superior. Bathilde couldn't make out the words, but the tone was, as Myrte described it, condescending.

"She seems like a princess," Bathilde whispered. "The proud kind."

"If I had a mother like that," Myrte commented, "I'd be glad to escape her."

The girl who emerged from the carriage looked nothing like the woman, in looks or in attire. The hair beneath her plain linen cap was an enviable dark shade of auburn, simply arranged, and too-short skirts revealed frayed stockings and worn shoes.

"Not the daughter," Myrte surmised. "She must be a poor relation."

The portress unlocked the gate and opened it.

"We welcome you, Madame de Neuillant," Mother Superior said, "and gladly receive Mademoiselle d'Aubigné."

The woman placed a gloved hand on the girl's shoulder, pressing hard. "Make your curtsy, Françoise." With an apologetic smile, she added, "You must excuse her lack of manners. Her years in the jungles of the West Indies, with her pitiable mother and older brothers, turned the child into a little savage. On their return, they placed her with a Protestant aunt, who indoctrinated her in heretical beliefs."

Glancing at Mother Superior, the girl shook her head as though to refute this statement.

"In your letter, requesting admission, you informed us that she was christened in the true faith."

"Indeed, it is so. I wasn't present, but her mother can write an attestation if you require it. As will my own daughter, for she is Françoise's godmother. To prevent Madame Villette's scheme to turn her niece into a complete Huguenot, I felt it necessary to remove her from Château de Mursay. The Queen of France not only permitted me to do so, she provided an official *lettre de cachet*. Unfortunately, despite my stringent efforts, the girl's time in my household failed to refine her manners or deportment. That responsibility now falls to you and the good sisters."

"We shall do our best, *madame la baronne*. To what extent has mademoiselle been educated?"

"She's had no time for study. I've relied on her to perform all manner of tasks—feeding and tending the poultry, watching the goats in the pasture. Her mother permitted her to read books of all kinds. That, of course, is no preparation for entering genteel society."

Myrte muttered, "Neither is farm labor."

The servant removed small, scarred leather *coffre* from the vehicle with ease, so it wasn't very full—and placed it near Françoise's muddied wooden clogs. White flakes, pelting rapidly down, covered the dark surface.

"Will you both come into the parlor and warm yourselves at the fire?" Mother Superior invited them. "It will be more comfortable for bidding one another farewell."

"I cannot stay." With a flick of her fingers, the baroness added, "You need not send me reports of her progress. I trust you to direct your new charge back into the Catholic fold, by whatever means are necessary. Instill in her a proper submission to authority." With that, she returned to her coach, without waiting for the blessing departing visitors received.

Mother Superior inclined her head, saying to her newest charge, "Enter, my child. We must all get out of this cold and wet weather, for none of us can risk getting chilled."

Françoise, Bathilde noticed, did not cast a backward glance as the vehicle proceeded along rue Crémault. Her face was blank, devoid of any emotion—neither sorrow or relief or fear. She appeared to be completely resigned to whatever fate she would meet within the convent walls, and her fortitude, whether feigned or genuine, impressed Bathilde.

Soeur Céleste, the youngest and prettiest of the teaching nuns, came over—not to address Bathilde, but her companion.

"Myrte Vernier, Mother Superior wishes to see you in her study before the summoning bell rings for dinner."

"What infraction have I committed?"

With her gentle smile, the sister replied, "None to my knowledge. Although if you wish to confess something, you should certainly do so. There's a particular duty she wishes you to perform. And you, I feel sure, will acquiesce with the obedience that she deserves from you. From us all."

Bathilde didn't see Myrte again until everyone had taken their place in the refectory. Mother Superior and those who carried out lesser administrative responsibilities were arranged on either side of her at a high table. The other sisters sat together, and the lay sisters had their own section. Boarders occupied wooden benches running parallel to the long tables. Breakfast followed morning mass, and a midday dinner consisted of three wholesome dishes and a dessert. Supper of soup and brioche was served at the conclusion of vespers, and cheese and fruit were available between the last catechism class of the day and the bedtime hour.

Bathilde had just knelt on the hard stone floor when Myrte slipped into the vacant place beside her. Her friend's heavy sigh indicated dissatisfaction with the allotted task. All heads, coifed or capped, bowed low while Mother Superior offered up a thanksgiving for the simple food they were about to consume.

When she and Bathilde sat down together on their bench, Myrte whispered, "I'm not in trouble. I didn't receive a lecture."

Although not badly behaved, at times she proved herself to be somewhat spoiled. Her father was as wealthy as any nobleman, and she was the only daughter in a family of many sons.

"What did Mother Superior ask of you?"

"Martyrdom."

Bathilde gazed curiously back at her confidante, whose deep blue eyes appeared darker in the dim light.

"I've been instructed to devote myself to Françoise d'Aubigné. I must teach her about convent life, what's expected and how to conduct herself. Explain the lessons, if she has difficulty following them. And most importantly, draw her away from her Protestant leanings and lead her onto the righteous path. She will sit by me and sleep near me. As you do." Myrte handed a spoon to Bathilde. "This soup smells wonderful, and it's hot. After staying so long outdoors in the cold, we need it."

"She's taking my place. You'll be with her all the time instead of with me."

"Of course not, *petite*. I shan't abandon you, as I told Mother Superior. These responsibilities she imposes on me require the sacrifice of my attention and my time. But nothing and no one can break my bond with you. True friendship cannot be compelled, it resides in the heart. And mine is not large enough to accommodate mademoiselle."

# CHAPTER 2

"Your name is quite unusual. Why did your parents choose it?"

Myrte answered Françoise's question. "Bathilde was a Queen of France, married to the second King Clovis. And a saint."

Bathilde overcame her shyness to expand upon this cursory explanation. "During her journey from Paris to Poitiers, to be married, my mother prayed at Chelles Abbey, where Saint Bathilde is buried. She vowed that if she gave birth to a son, he would be christened Clovis, and that her first daughter would bear the sainted queen's name."

"Have you a brother?"

"Not any longer. He lived only a few days after his baptism. He and Maman were buried together, last summer. In autumn, Cardinal Mazarin and the queen asked Papa to help fight the war. He brought me here to be cared for and taught by the sisters."

"You know why I had to come. But the plan to transform me into a devout Catholic is destined to fail." Turning away, Françoise gazed towards the rooftop cross.

"Surrounded by them as you are, it shouldn't be too

difficult," Myrte said. "The baroness who brought you said a priest baptized you."

"My mother was devout, and she insisted. My father, who holds the title of baron, wasn't religious at all. He descends from a respectable Calvinist family, but you'd never know it. He murdered his first wife, for infidelity, but his father saved him from prosecution. He later betrayed the English Protestants who sought to capture La Rochelle. He was repeatedly cast into prison and always won his release, I know not how. After capture for his role in a traitorous conspiracy against Cardinal Richelieu, he landed in the Niort *conciergerie*. My mother joined him, and that's where she gave birth to me."

The older girl's frank recitation roused enough pity in Bathilde to quell her distress at losing Myrte's undivided attention.

"Mother placed me in the care of my father's sister, my Tante Louise, at Château de Mursay, a short distance from this town. At Richelieu's death, the king issued a general release to all prisoners—my father among them. He got himself appointed governor of Marie-Galante, and we set out across the ocean. During the voyage I fell ill of a fever and sickened unto the point of being declared dead. They shrouded me, but just as I was being cast into the sea, I revived."

Myrte eyed her with evident suspicion. "That sounds like a miracle tale from a saint's life."

"It's true," she insisted. "On Martinique we lived with the Governor of Guadeloupe, for a long while, until my father settled us on his island, inhabited with natives and Irishmen, quite ungovernable. He traveled back and forth to France—or England—as he pleased, involved in schemes he dared not reveal. Danger to us increased, so we fled back to Martinique, where we had a lovely house. Until it burned. Mother succeeded in saving her precious books, but the flames destroyed my favorite doll. Our next home was in Basseterre, with the governor of Sainte-Christophe, but he grew to dislike us. That's when we sailed back to this country. During the voyage, a pirate ship attempted to overtake our vessel. If you think I'm telling lies, or exaggerating, ask the abbess to let you read the letter my mother wrote, relating our difficulties. I can show you the rosary I held, while we prayed for our lives to be spared."

Bathilde whispered, "I believe you."

"In La Rochelle, we lived as paupers. With my brothers, Constant and Charles, I went begging from door to door, pleading for scraps of food to keep us alive."

Myrte looked up from her needlework. "How humiliating. Could you not go to your father?"

"We've had no news of him. He might be in prison again. Or dead. Mother is in Paris, mounting lawsuits to obtain certain properties he was supposed to inherit. My brother Constant drowned himself in the moat at Mursay, he was so despondent after our experiences in the islands and his lack of prospects here. Charles was sent to Poitiers to serve as a nobleman's page. I remained with Tante Louise, who let me roam the fields and woods and share lessons with my Cousin Philippe. And worship as a Protestant—which I prefer."

"Yet here you are," Myrte commented, not looking up.

"I was forced to come," Françoise replied. "Baronne de Neuillant took it upon herself to compel my conversion. She petitioned my mother—and the Queen Regent—for guardianship. The *lettre de cachet* allowed her to take me away from de Mursay, where I was happy. By turning me into a servant, she meant to weaken my resolve. Failing to do so, she sought the nuns' assistance. And yours." She cast an accusing glance at Myrte.

"I do as I'm instructed," Myrte said mildly.

Their chatter drew Soeur Céleste to their bench. *"Demoiselles,* tongues should keep still while needles are moving. Your thoughts should be prayerful. Bathilde, how do you get on with your hemming?"

She held up the linen square to display her stitchery.

"Better," the nun approved. "You see, as I've been telling you, tiny fingers can work as precisely as bigger ones."

"It won't be long before she's embroidering chasubles like this one." Myrte indicated the velvet garment spread across her lap, destined to be worn by a priest—or possibly a bishop.

Françoise, so talkative all the morning, kept silent. Her pink lips contracted in a pout as she stabbed at the fabric.

"Mademoiselle d'Aubigné." Soeur Céleste spoke with particular softness when addressing the new pupil. "If you promise to attend mass tomorrow morning, you will not be obliged to sew in the afternoon."

"Thank you, but I had rather do this all day than spend a single minute kneeling and chanting hymns."

Myrte untied her white lace cap to tuck in loose strands of black hair. "I promised her that if she comes with us, I'd give her my beautiful image of the Blessed Virgin that hangs above my bed."

"What use have I for such a thing?" Françoise retorted.

Bathilde held her breath, expecting the black-garbed figure to issue an admonition. None was forthcoming.

Soeur Céleste placed a hand upon Françoise's head covering. "All your companions pray constantly for the opening of your heart and mind."

As their prefect turned her back, Françoise muttered, "It will do no good whatsoever. My mind is firmly closed, as securely locked as the convent gate will be tonight after the portress inserts her key. No entreaty or bribe can ever win me over."

Myrte smiled. "I've been here long enough to witness a change in more than one stubborn *pensionnaire*. Families thrust their girls into the convent to be rid of them, either because they're too ill-featured to catch a husband, or have a small dowry, or after they've been orphaned. They didn't want to be here, either. Over time, they succumbed to a yearning, an overpowering desire to become a bride of Christ. Some are novices, others postulants. Several have become choir nuns."

"They had the misfortune to be brought up in the Catholic faith to begin with."

"Acknowledging a vocation," Myrte responded, "is far from easy. It means professing vows of poverty, obedience, and chastity. And a commitment to the education and improvement of thankless, insubordinate creatures like you. Spoiled, worldly ones like me." Her arm curled around Bathilde's waist, drawing her closer. "And, occasionally, a sweet, shy princess."

"I didn't realize we're in the presence of royalty."

The derision in her companion's tone made Bathilde squirm. "My papa isn't a Prince of the Blood, though he does have royal ancestry. He inherited a principality, but I'll never be a queen." Maman had explained this to her last summer, during their last days together.

With a soft laugh, Myrte said, "That's not a certainty. You're of suitable age for our King Louis—he's only two years older than you. And very handsome, I've heard."

"You shouldn't encourage foolish hopes," Françoise objected.

"She teases," Bathilde clarified. Myrte's whimsy was among her most endearing traits.

During the night she dreamed of standing on a ship's

deck, helpless in an attack by saber-wielding brigands. Her hands gripped the rail, and she prepared to leap overboard into the roiling waves.

"Wake up." Myrte, reaching across the narrow gap between their beds, tugged her arm.

Opening her eyes, she found herself in the familiar darkness of the dormitory. Her heart raced and her breath came in sharp gasps.

"You were mewling like a lost puppy."

"I had a nightmare. I was in danger of being killed."

"Don't dwell on it, or you'll be wakeful the rest of the night. In your mind, sing the *Angelus,* or recite a section of the catechism. In no time you'll drift back into sleep."

Françoise was a constant presence—at prayers, while dining, during indoor or outdoor recreation. Even if she didn't treat Bathilde unkindly, she made no secret of the fact that she regarded the younger girl as a nuisance, someone to be tolerated and occasionally disdained. Wounded by this treatment, Bathilde ceased to follow Myrte about as often as she had previously. The loneliness of her early days at the convent returned, stronger than after several months of experiencing true affection from her special friend.

Adding to her dismay, Françoise appeared quite indifferent to the privilege of being Myrte's frequent companion. One day, while Soeur Céleste was guiding Bathilde through a recitation of the catechism, she voiced a complaint about it.

"Mademoiselle d'Aubigné has rarely spent time with girls her age," the nun explained. "Being a good companion is something else we must all teach her, as well as offering instruction in languages and arithmetic and history and geography."

"She thinks she knows more than the regents do."

"In some instances, that may be true. None of the teaching sisters has twice crossed the ocean or lived in foreign places. Her mother, I understand, is a learned woman, who allowed her to read from all sorts of books. Perhaps you might benefit from whatever knowledge she brought here."

Bathilde suspected Françoise would find this suggestion as unwelcome as she did.

"Strive not to compare yourself to others," Soeur Céleste advised. "Or judge their actions. You and Mademoiselle Vernier and Mademoiselle d'Aubigné are different in almost every way, and that is a good thing. God loves us each as we were created, for the purpose we are meant to serve here on earth."

"Françoise says it's better to be Protestant than Catholic. Myrte hasn't converted her."

"It is early days. If ever you're conscious of unkind reflections about her, say a prayer for the joyful result we all hope for. Can you do that?"

"I will try," Bathilde replied, and meant it. "Is it all right if I also pray for her to like me?"

"Certainly, if at the same time you are behaving in a way that makes it possible."

Midwinter, she discovered, was far less comfortable in a convent than a château. Morning in the open and drafty *penssionnaires'* dormitory meant steeling herself to leave her bed after the older students had risen and dressed and washed. Teeth chattering, she shivered as a lay sister helped her put on shift and bodice and petticoats and gown. From her *coffre* she removed the lace-edged cap that covered her ears, and the linen neckerchief that she tied across her goose-pimpled chest. After breakfast, in the common room, the girls lined up before the fireplace, taking turns at warming their hands. At night, layers of clothing were removed and replaced with a woolen nightshift. Bathilde secured the ribbons of her bedcap and climbed under the covers, hoping she'd soon be warm enough to fall asleep.

Françoise, accustomed to the balmy, humid conditions of the West Indies islands, was miserable. Her meager collection of light garments had to be augmented with more substantial ones left behind by former pupils. Shabby and showing signs of frequent mending, they made her conspicuous in a classroom of better-dressed students. Myrte supplied her with a heavier shawl, and offered a pair of thick stockings, which were gratefully accepted.

"But your generosity won't turn me Catholic," Françoise warned.

Myrte smiled. "I know. But I'm determined to keep you alive. If you freeze to death, I can't fulfill my mission."

"You might as well accept that it's a lost cause."

Looking down at Bathilde, seated between them on the bench, Myrte asked, "Which of us is more determined, would you say?"

"Quiet at the back, please," the regent called out. "Be attentive to your ledgers."

Their lesson in household finance and accounting was largely beyond Bathilde's comprehension. She had a vague sense that her father's receiver-general paid the wages of dozens of indoor and outdoor servants and provided money for the purchase of food and linens and any necessities not grown or made on the estate. He also paid her school fees, to the nun in charge of the convent's bursary, when they came due.

The day pupils, unlike the girls who boarded, paid nothing for their education. Each morning they were admitted to their separate section of the school through a different entrance than the one Françoise had arrived at weeks ago. These daughters of town laborers and artisans and domestic workers learned simple household skills required for a life in service. Those who showed aptitude received instruction in reading and writing. Like the *pensionnaires*, they also studied the catechism in preparation for their first communion. Bathilde envied their freedom to come and go, and liked to imagine them at home with their families, describing their daily activities.

Although she and her fellow pupils were not informed about ongoing events in the kingdom, Papa's letters told of upheavals in places distant and near. At the first of the year, Protestant malcontents over in England had executed their King Charles, whose exiled son of that name was a powerless, uncrowned monarch. Her father had met him at the royal palace at Saint-Germain. He mentioned the Fronde revolt, an uprising of the princes of the royal blood and the nobles of the Paris Parlement who pitted themselves against the powerful and unpopular Cardinal Mazarin, the Queen Regent's chief advisor. Lately, a compromise about taxation ended the rioting and skirmishes and blockades of the capital city.

He wrote to her every few weeks but discouraged her from replying, for the movement of the court or the King's army determined his location—he went wherever he was needed. Myrte, with whom she shared her letters, observed that the Queen Regent must value him greatly, as he reported often being in her presence since his return from the field of war.

"She's interested in your secular and your religious education." Glancing up from the most recent missive, Myrte added, "Perhaps she's considering you as a bride for her son. If someday you become Queen Bathilde, the king's consort, Françoise and I can serve as your *filles d'honneur*."

"Not I," Françoise objected, eyes fixed on her drawing paper. "The Queen Regent won't care to associate with a Huguenot. Or permit her son to do so."

"Ah, by the time Bathilde is of marriageable age, you'll be the most devout Catholic in the realm."

Their companion's head shook repeatedly, causing her glossy auburn curls to tumble loose from her cap. "That is a fantasy."

Each day, the pupils received the white cloths they turned into the nuns' coifs, aprons, and undergarments, or white veils that distinguished the novices from postulants, choir nuns, and prioresses. Because Myrte was particularly skilled in embroidery, she was responsible for decorating priestly vestments and was therefore trusted with the costly gold and silver thread.

"Such luxury." Françoise's tone was scathing. "The vast wealth of the Catholic church would be better spent assisting the poor than on adornment and ostentation. I could respect your priests and bishops if they dressed in plain robes, as the monks do."

Bathilde could tell by the thinning of Myrte's lips that she struggled to reign in her temper.

"If you examine my design for this chasuble, Françoise, you'll see that it consists of grapes and vines, frequently mentioned in the testaments. My stitches imprint symbols of my faith upon this fabric."

"We would do better to bestow real grapes on those who hunger."

"The Ursulines, like the nuns of all religious communities, are committed to perform acts of charity. They likewise teach us to be charitable, as good Catholic wives and mothers, whatever our birth or fortune. The day school pupils pay nothing for their education."

Prickly Françoise had a tiresome habit of criticizing. But her harsh comparison of the church's wealth and the contrasting poverty of too many faithful led Bathilde to a recognition of an inherent truth. It also inspired a desire to seek out and serve those less fortunate after she left the convent and entered the greater, more complicated world beyond its stone walls.

With spring's approach, provisions laid in for the winter had decreased. A line of concern etched itself into the area of forehead exposed by the cellarer's coif, and at mealtimes she conferred with Mother Superior in a tone of distress. Prayers for fortitude in a season of abstinence were inserted into the grace offered before food and drink were served.

On a day bright and mild enough for outdoor exercise, the portress opened the great door in the wall. Bathilde, recognizing the occupants of the horse-drawn wagon, dropped the leather ball Myrte had tossed and rushed to greet them. Pascal, who managed the château vineyard, was accompanied by his sister and niece.

"See, Giselle," Berthe Durand said, "here's our princess."

Beaming, the child extended a tiny hand.

"The prince informed Monsieur Jousson that the abbess has a need of wine. We had more than enough workers for the day's vine pruning, so I've brought it myself. Giselle asked to come with us, she misses you so. Tell Princess Bathilde your age, *petite*."

The little girl splayed her fingers. "Five."

"In a few years," Bathilde said, "she'll be old enough for the day school."

Berthe climbed down from the cart and set her daughter on the ground. "I won't be able to spare her. Every pair of hands is needed for the spinning and weaving, and in our *potager* and your father's vineyard." To her brother, she added, "Be quick with the unloading. The clouds have thickened, and I can smell rain in the breeze."

Curiosity drew Myrte and Françoise close to the activity in the courtyard. With pride, Bathilde explained that the de Sevreau grapes had produced the contents of the wooden wine casks Pascal heaved down from his cart and shoved through the gate. Convent servants drew up their skirts, tucked them into their girdles, and rolled the casks towards the cellar door.

"Mother Superior and the sisters will be grateful," Françoise remarked. "And the visiting priest. But how does this benefit us?"

Myrte replied, "Wine isn't only drunk at meals, or blessed during mass. It's also used medicinally."

Newly conscious of her power to provide, Bathilde thought of a way to please her schoolmates. "Tell me what you wish for, Françoise, and I'll send a request to the château."

"I miss sweet things. I'd sell my very soul, which you value so highly, for a spoonful of confiture. Or honey. John the Baptist dined on that. As you'd know, if you Catholics were given the Bible to read and study." Françoise cocked her head. "Do you think we'd be allowed such treats?"

Myrte responded, "Anything created from fruits of the earth and from flowers of the fields are gifts from God."

Bathilde turned pleading eyes towards Berthe and Pascal. "Will you stay while I write a note to Monsieur Jousson?"

She raced back to the schoolroom to carry out her task. She passed her quill over the paper, shaping her letters with great care. On finishing, she carried the letter into the passage and waved it in front of the fire to dry the ink.

Berthe Durand's prediction of a change in the weather had been fulfilled, and the cart's occupants huddled under a length of protective canvas to shield themselves from the raindrops. Mother Superior, standing with the cellarer in the arched entrance on the nuns' side, bestowed her blessing from a distance, drawing a cross in the air.

Bathilde trotted across the courtyard and handed her note to Berthe, who tucked it inside her bodice to keep it dry.

Mother Superior beckoned. Placing a hand on Bathilde's head, she intoned, "At evening prayers, we will give thanks to Our Father for the prince's generosity. I can guess who informed him about our privation."

Flushing at this display of favor, she returned the older woman's smile.

"Hurry out of the wet, my children, and be sure to dry yourselves well."

She and Myrte made their way towards the cloister, but Françoise hung back.

"Don't linger," Myrte called over her shoulder.

Standing her ground, Françoise declared, "I don't mind the rain. On the islands, I welcomed the storms that came. I'd run outside and stay until I was drenched."

Myrte could barely contain her frustration. "Then do as you please. Remember, you're in the tropics no longer. And if you muddy your clothes, you make more work for the laundresses." Taking Bathilde by the hand, she led her inside. "That creature tries my patience like no other," she muttered. "She is defiance personified."

They didn't encounter her again until supper. Dressed in a fresh gown and cap, she slid into her usual place on the refectory bench. Seated next to Françoise, Bathilde could feel her entire body shivering and saw the fire in her cheek.

"How long did you remain in the courtyard?"

"As long as I could bear being pelted. On Martinique, the rain felt delightfully mild, almost warm. Here, it's cold like ice."

Late in the night, persistent coughing from the bed on the far side of Myrte's woke the dormitory's occupants. At dawn, a novice summoned the sister from the infirmary, and Françoise, too weak to walk without support, was taken away.

Myrte turned onto her side, facing Bathilde. "Soeur Elise has great skill. She'll cure whatever ails our stubborn little savage."

# CHAPTER 3

For more than a week, daily prayers for the sick included Françoise d'Aubigné. Her fever lingered, and her lungs were dangerously congested.

"If only she'd heeded Mother Superior," Bathilde commented to Myrte.

"A harsh punishment for her willfulness. Let us hope it teaches her to be more biddable."

"She might die," Bathilde pointed out. "Soeur Céleste, who is often with her, says she's extremely ill."

"They haven't yet sent for the priest to give her the last rites. Though I daresay if offered, she'd refuse them."

An altered Françoise emerged from the sickroom. Whether her new desire to please resulted from her schoolmates' fervent intercessions to the Blessed Virgin or from Soeur Céleste's Christian kindness was a matter of debate.

Myrte, again summoned to Mother Superior's study, was relieved to be informed that her duties as guide and exemplar had devolved upon the young nun. Once more, Bathilde possessed her dearest friend's undivided attention.

"Will Françoise take communion?" she asked.

"Soeur Céleste lets her read the psalms instead of

studying the catechism," Myrte reported. "And she won't attend mass at all, if she doesn't want to."

A servant from Château des Vignes delivered sealed jars of honey and fruit jam in a straw-filled cart pulled by a shaggy Poitevin donkey. Françoise, who had yearned for the treats, proved her devotion to her preceptress by giving her share of the fig conserve to Soeur Céleste. Myrte and Bathilde marveled at her acceptance of the most menial tasks—mending and ironing and plain sewing. She exerted herself to help the younger girls with washing, dressing, and preparing for bed. To everyone's surprise, she no longer refused to appear at early morning mass. And she voluntarily witnessed a postulant's final profession of the Ursuline vows of poverty, chastity, obedience, and commitment to the education of young girls.

Another welcome development, from Bathilde's viewpoint, was the softening of Françoise's temperament. She no longer made pointed references to the variance in their status or criticized aristocratic privileges familiar to Bathilde from birth. Instead, she spoke of their common experiences of château life: the contentment Françoise had known with her beloved Tante Louise at Château de Mursay on one side of the River Sèvre and Bathilde's similarly comfortable existence at Château des Vignes on the opposite side

"If I had a little sister," the older girl said one day, "I'd want her to be like you."

During the latter part of Lent, Françoise was elevated to the role of *dizainière*. These select individuals, older pupils deemed the cleverest and most capable, instructed ten younger *demoiselles,* with a teaching nun assigned as advisor. Bathilde found herself in Françoise's group.

"Here's a fine turnabout," Myrte told her. "You were sad because I had to devote myself to Françoise. And you spend so much of your time with her that I've grown jealous."

"You needn't be. I like her more than I ever thought I could, but I love only you. Although Françoise is nicer now than she used to be, she really only cares for Soeur Céleste."

Lent, the penitential season, concluded in the early days of April. After the Holy Week observances, the convent celebrated Easter. Springtime was on full display in the garden, where the boarders who were so inclined helped the nun in charge and a lay sister with digging and planting and picking. During recreation time, Bathilde eagerly deserted the courtyard and cloister for the enclosure where herbs, fruits, and vegetables were green with vibrant life, and flowers bloomed, and rose bushes formed tiny buds. The supervising nun reminded her that God's purpose in providing the array of plants was two-fold.

"We appreciate their utility, for seasoning food and distilling medicines and cordials. But we also cherish them for their beauty and scent, which lifts our spirits and awakens our appreciation of the marvels of nature. And as we pray for them to flourish, we also express thanks to Our Father for the blessing that they are."

Because the pupils were permitted to pursue their interests, when beneficial to the community, Bathilde assisted Amalie, the lay sister responsible for planting, weeding, and harvesting. When the bell forced her to remove her grass-stained apron and return to the classroom, she always promised to return the next day.

The history and background of the professed nuns, postulants, and novices were a mystery to their pupils, for they were prohibited from speaking about their worldly lives before being cloistered. As far as Bathilde could tell, the *converses,* women who lived in and served the community without taking vows, had fewer restrictions imposed upon them. If they had any, Amalie wasn't especially observant.

A native of Strasbourg, with craggy face, lopsided mouth, and hunched back, she spoke with an accent peculiar to her region, flavored by her residence in foreign lands. A hard worker, and a talkative, confiding one, she told Bathilde that her father and grandfather had been gardeners at a bishop's palace. For years she served in the kitchen of a diplomatic family sent by Cardinal Mazarin to Pressburg, not far from Vienna. Upon their return to Niort, unsympathetic to her increasing infirmity and advancing years, they cast her aside. Like other women in direst circumstances, she sought refuge with the Ursulines. Her initial labors took place in the distillery, until her stated preference for outdoor tasks was honored.

Françoise, enfeebled from her illness, didn't assist with physical work, but Myrte occasionally deigned to pluck weeds with Bathilde.

Seated on a bench in the shade cast by a pear tree in full bloom, they observed Amalie patting the ground and murmuring to herself.

"Is that a special prayer?"

"No, Mademoiselle Myrte. I offer comforting words to all the poor *samovili,* unloved and forgotten."

"What are they?" Bathilde wondered.

Amalie's halting gait brought her closer to the bench. "I learned of them from the Slovak and Czech people. A *samovila* is the spirit of a dead girl betrayed by an unfaithful lover. In the nighttime, groups of the *vili* rise from the forest floor or grassy places or the water. Their eyes flash with fire as they dance and do dark deeds. They seek out any man who has ill-treated his lady and chase him, and capture him, and force him to dance unto death."

The girls exchanged glances. Credence in folk superstitions was supposed to be sinful.

"Your *vili* wouldn't choose a convent garden for a resting place," said Myrte.

Amalie rubbed her curved spine to soothe an ache. "Spirits of the dead don't confine themselves to a particular place. Whether buried in a churchyard or in unconsecrated ground, at night they will roam wherever they please. And woe to them who caused their heartbreak."

Bathilde, conscious of inexplicable coldness prickling her flesh, stood up and stepped into a patch of sunshine. Seeing the starry blossoms that had opened on a green shrub growing in a pot, she plucked a spray and offered it to Myrte.

"The herb *myrtus*—myrtle. Its leaves have a pleasant scent, sharp and fresh."

Her friend held the frond to her face and inhaled. "Does it have medicinal properties?"

"Lungs and stomach," Amalie said. "It's also favored by brides, who carry it when they're wed. Later in the year, you'll see it covered with dark berries."

Myrte held the green spike high, waving it back and forth. "Which of us will be the first to carry the myrtle?"

"You will," Bathilde predicted. "You're the loveliest girl in the school."

"And the richest," Françoise commented.

In subsequent days, she appeared much less cheerful than she'd been since her dismissal from the infirmary, seldom smiling and often falling into abstraction in the midst of lessons. Several times she made her way to Mother Superior's parlor, causing heated speculation.

"It can't be for discipline," Myrte said. "Her behavior has been exemplary."

"Maybe she realized she has a vocation," Bathilde suggested, "and wants to take the veil."

Myrte was dubious. "Unlikely. She isn't studying the catechism and still hasn't expressed a desire to take holy communion. She's given no sign of wanting to become a bride of Christ. Besides, she hasn't any dowry. She wouldn't be accepted into the novitiate without one."

With typical frankness, Françoise offered an explanation.

"Madame de Neuillant never paid my boarding fees and refuses to do so. She's not a blood relation, she says, and therefore bears no responsibility for my upkeep. She forwarded the bursar's request to my Tante Louise. Despite her fondness for me, she's too firm a Protestant to fund my education in a Catholic academy. Mother Superior and the under-prioress have been soliciting aid from the convent's local benefactors. But my father's reputation for criminality, and his imprisonment in Niort, is too well known. No one will help."

"You can become a day pupil. They don't pay at all," Myrte pointed out.

"But I've got nowhere to live. Any family that took me into their household would expect me to work for my keep, not spend my days in the convent school."

A letter from the baroness decided her fate. Madame de Neuillant informed Mother Superior of her decision to resume her guardianship of the orphan girl. Her son, who had succeeded his father as governor of Niort Castle, had daughters of similar age. Moreover, she resolved to bring about the delayed conversion by any means necessary— an ominous proclamation.

On a breathtakingly lovely morning when the orchard blossoms were falling, floating in the light breeze, Madame de Neuillant's fine coach returned—empty, as it had not been on the snowy day earlier in the year. A tearful Soeur Céleste, a heartsore Bathilde, and a stoic Myrte accompanied Françoise, weeping profusely, to the gate.

Occasional letters contained unsettling descriptions of Françoise's days with Madame de Neuillant's household.

In ill-fitting dresses, wearing wooden clogs like a servant or a common laborer, she performed menial tasks and tended the animals.

"What a sad waste of intelligence and learning," was Myrte's response.

"I miss her," Bathilde confessed. "She promised to compose birthday verses in my honor and offered to read them in class."

A *demoiselle's* birthday was acknowledged with a special prayer at dinner. On the day Bathilde turned eight, self-consciousness alternated with pleasure at the recognition. For the first time she was invited to meet privately with Mother Superior. All the pupils regarded the tiny woman with respect and affection, but to Bathilde, she was also an object of veneration because her size didn't limit her effectiveness as spiritual leader, administrator, and substitute parent.

"You have a letter," Mother Superior announced, her black-clad arm reaching out to present it.

Always happy to see Papa's flowing script, Bathilde quickly scanned the lines, which made her lightheaded with joy. "I'm to have music lessons," she breathed. "He says Maman would have wanted me to become proficient on the harpsichord. And the Queen Regent wants to receive reports of my progress."

"In our eyes, as in God's, all the girls entrusted to our care are equals. But we also have a duty to prepare them for the lives they will lead after their departure. Yours, my child, will be different to that of your companions. After leaving us, you will carry our teachings and example and guidance with you into the royal court. I'm certain that you'll do us much credit there, and admirably fulfill your father's wishes."

Daunted by the prospect, and the responsibility, Bathilde replied, "But not for a long, long time."

# CHAPTER 4

*Poitiers, November, 1650*

With relief, Bathilde eyed the tall gatehouses at either end of the ancient bridge spanning the breadth of the River Clain. After a long and exhausting eighteen-league journey from Niort, she was eager to escape this swaying, creaking coach and recover from the headache brought on by the constant pounding of horses' hooves. She'd boarded it in the chill of dawn, when its interior was so dim that she could barely make out the three de Sevreau scallop shells painted on the panels. And now the lengthening shadows foretold the coming of dusk.

The students of the *pensionnat* rarely visited their families, typically remaining at the Niort convent from their entry to their exit, unless they joined the novitiate and were forever cloistered. News of births and marriages and illness and deaths came to them in parental letters. But a royal request must be granted. Bathilde received immediate dispensation to join her father at his *hôtel particulier*, where Her Majesty recovered from an infirmity.

Stepping down from the coach on wobbly legs, she gazed at a façade more modern than either of their châteaux. This wasn't an inherited property, but one acquired from the wealthy banker who had built it. In the fading light, she could glimpse the river on the other side of the fortifying wall that surrounded the city.

Papa received her in an elegantly furnished *salle de compagnie*. Tall windows overlooked a garden, and the sections of wall between them were hung with allegorical tapestries. She hurried across the parquet floor, remembering to curtsy before she flung her arms around him.

"How often I've thought about you, these two tumultuous years," he said during their embrace. "Show me your face."

Reluctantly she raised her head, not wanting him to see her tears.

"So like your mother's."

They crossed themselves.

He towered above her, sturdy and broad-shouldered. A brown moustache and a pointed beard lessened the squareness of his face, sun bronzed from years as a cavalry commander. Standing beside him, Maman had looked as pale and fragile as a fairy.

"She would've taken pride in your progress under the sisters' tutelage. I've seen for myself that you can write a neat hand and a sensible letter. I've been informed that you excel in Latin. Though what use it will be to you in the future, I can't conceive. While here, you must demonstrate to me—and Her Majesty—your abilities on the harpsichord."

"How long does she remain?" she asked.

"Another day or two, perhaps. It's not for me to inquire about her plans, only to ensure that she's comfortable and adequately fed. In Bordeaux she attended a ball, where she succumbed to a cold, and chose to travel from there by horse, which worsened her condition. Her women say she makes no complaint, apart from expressing her longing for Fontainebleau. Because you often figure in our conversations, she insisted on your being presented to her without delay. She stands in need of diversion," he added. "In addition to her ill-health, she has numerous concerns."

As nervousness crept in, Bathilde said, "At the convent, we aren't taught how to conduct ourselves in the presence of royalty. I might embarrass you."

Before he could reply, a handsome young woman swept in with a rustle of rich fabric. "Her Majesty has retired already and prefers to take her evening meal in her chamber. She says she'll send for the princess tomorrow."

"Duchesse de Navailles, I present my daughter Bathilde, recently arrived from the convent school in Niort."

Bathilde sank into a curtsy, careful to hold her balance.

"My goddaughter spent several months there," said the duchess. "You must have known Françoise d'Aubigné."

"We slept near one another, *madame*. During her time as a *dizainière*, I belonged to her group of ten pupils. I've had no news of her in over a year. Is she well?"

"As far as I know. She lives in my uncle's house in Paris with my mother, Baronne de Neuillant, and my sister Angélique. All efforts to marry her off have failed— hardly surprising, as she hasn't any dowry or fortune. We had expectations of a chevalier, though he's rather old for a girl of fifteen. But we succeeded in breaking her allegiance to the Protestant religion, and she has at last embraced the faith into which she was born and baptized. The Ursuline sisters of Paris prevailed where the ones of Niort could not."

Bathilde regarded this as a slight against the nuns who had patiently dealt with Françoise, nursing her through illness and placing her in the charge of her adored Soeur

Céleste. Concealing her resentment, she murmured, "I'm glad."

Papa waited for the duchess to depart before saying, "This house is large enough to accommodate several members of Her Majesty's retinue. As it's filled to the garrets with ladies and lackeys, you'll share our cousin's bedchamber."

She smiled up at him. "It will be no hardship. In the school dormitory, I sleep surrounded by more than two dozen girls."

An older female came into the room, her silk skirts whispering with her movement. Neither plain nor pretty, she had regular, unremarkable features, and neatly arranged hair of faded blonde and incipient gray.

"Suzanne de Navailles told me she'd arrived." Approaching Bathilde, she said, "No, you needn't curtsy to me, child. I bear no title, I'm merely Madame de Sevreau. But I hope you'll call me Cousin Sophie." She reached beneath Bathilde's hat to stroke a strand of hair. "How like your Marie she is, Gerard. You must see it, too."

"I do. More than ever." To Bathilde, he said, "My grandfather had a wastrel of a brother, whose son turned out better than anyone expected. He had the wisdom to marry Madame and died far too soon, at which time she left Château Clément for Paris."

"Only because my widowed sister needed me, for companionship during her mourning period. On her return to society, she found a second husband and set about providing him with heirs. Gerard very kindly offered me refuge from that ménage. Henceforth, I'll have the pleasure of residing at Château des Vignes, close enough to call upon you at the convent school. Come with me," Sophie invited. "Like the queen, you can have your supper in private, and I'll put you to bed right after."

Hand in hand, they ascended a curving stair and

followed a broad passage to a corner chamber. A servant had removed Bathilde's nightshift and bed cap from her *coffre* and placed them on the blanket chest. Steam rose from the water in the washbasin, and a fire had been kindled.

While waiting for food to arrive, Sophie examined gowns and chemises, choosing what Bathilde should wear when the Queen Regent received her.

"How well did you know Maman?"

"My husband and I lived at Château Clément after Gerard—your father—returned with his bride, whom I was honored to serve as *dame de compagnie*. I never saw an aristocratic pair that much in love, or so devoted. How we rejoiced the day you were born. And wept over the loss of Marie and her newborn son. I was never blessed with children. I cannot replace the mother you lost, but I shall make sure you grow into the accomplished young lady she would have wanted you to become."

# CHAPTER 5

"Come forward, my child, so I may see you better."
Bathilde approached Anne of Austria, an imposing figure in a high-backed parlor chair. Having performed three curtsies—one for each member of the royal family—she faced the fresh challenge of moving gracefully across a gleaming wood floor.

The Queen Regent was flanked by her two sons. King Louis was a very attractive boy with a complexion as fair as any girl's, golden-brown curls tumbling over his shoulders, and the dark eyes bequeathed by his Spanish and Italian forbears. His exceptionally pretty brother had rosy lips and pointed chin, feminine in their delicacy.

"My sons, here is the daughter of our great friend and supporter, the Prince de Coulon." She spoke French with perfect fluency and only the slightest accent of her native Spain. "Prior to the Siege of La Rochelle, he welcomed your father to Château Clément. There they prepared their strategy for the great battle. Since then, he has often led our troops into victory. Unlike several others with whom he served, he never turned against Cardinal Mazarin. We can always rely on his loyalty to the crown."

Papa, wearing a sober expression, inclined his head at this recognition.

"Take Princess Bathilde into the next room," the queen went on, "while the prince and I discuss military matters and state business. We will join you in a little while, to hear her play the harpsichord."

Bathilde stepped aside, aware that she must let the king and his brother precede her. Following the pair to the antechamber, she marveled at this encounter with the person Myrte had teasingly designated as her future husband.

"Have you made your first communion?" Louis wanted to know.

"At Easter I will," she replied.

"I did last Christmas. You look to be near the same age as Philippe. He's ten."

"I am nine, Your Majesty."

The younger boy said, "The Duchesse de Navailles told us you live with the nuns, in a convent. I suppose they make you pray all day long."

"We attend early mass and have prayers in the morning and at meals and before going to bed. The rest of the time we're busy with lessons or needlework. My friend Myrte is a singer, and I spend a great deal of time at the keyboard, as her accompanist. And I enjoy helping Amalie, a lay sister, tend the plants."

"I like gardens, too," Louis confided. "One day you should see the grounds at the Palais du Luxembourg. Our grandmother, Marie de Medici, demanded that they be arranged in the Italian style, with tree-lined walks and a fountain. The one at the Palais Royal is beautiful also."

His brother's slender fingers grasped the flounce of her sleeve. "Your lace is very fine."

"A postulant made it."

The young king commented, "I hope you don't mean to become one yourself. You're too pretty to spend the rest of your life in a black habit and veil. Do you dance?"

"I've learned the *menuet.*"

"He likes dancing more than anything," Philippe volunteered.

"Would you care to dance with me?"

Uncertain of how she ought to respond, she thought for a moment. "If you wish me to, I will."

With all the dignity of one who had inherited a kingdom before his fifth birthday, he extended his hand. "Ready?"

Together they moved forwards and backwards, poised on their toes for each series of three steps, dipping down again in unison. Bathilde, silently counting out the measures, followed as best she could. At one point she turned away instead of facing him. Louis abruptly reversed his position, making the situation worse. For a moment they spun about in confusion, and Philippe's giggles were so infectious that they joined in his laughter.

They were breathless from merriment when Papa and the Queen Regent joined them.

"Refreshing—comforting, I should say, to see our young people enjoying themselves. What amuses you, my children?"

"Louis and Princess Bathilde danced," Philippe piped up. "They almost fell down."

Grinning, Louis declared, "We will do better next time. With music."

"I am ready," said his mother, "to hear the princess play."

Earlier in the day, Bathilde had practiced a tune neither too simple nor overly complex. Standing before the instrument, she clasped her hands and offered up a brief prayer to Saint Cecelia, the patroness of musicians. Inhaling slowly, she placed her fingertips on the cool ivory keys. The thickness of the sturdy wooden case brought forth a richer tone than she produced on the convent harpsichord. She missed Myrte, whose clear soprano could match or harmonize with her notes.

"Impressive," the Queen stated, "for a girl your age. My dear prince, your daughter must certainly continue with instruction—I insist upon it. In fact, I will write to the Mother Superior myself, and send a sum of money to convey my pleasure with Princess Bathilde's progress. Within a few years, she'll be old enough to join my household as a *demoiselle d'honneur.*"

With characteristic grace, Louis bowed to Bathilde. "As I said, we shall dance together again. Many times."

The harsh winter of frequent illnesses in the school came to an end at the same time the Fronde rebellion subsided. Spring delivered gentle showers and clouds of gold where the *jonquilles* in the convent garden bloomed, and with each passing week, the unfolding tulips added new colors. Bathilde was torn between joy at the nature's awakening and dread of the day she would lose the companionship of her dearest friend. For Myrte Vernier would soon observe her fifteenth birthday, the age when a *demoiselle* left the *pensionnat.*

"Perhaps Mother Superior will let you stay on," she said hopefully, as they sat on a bench in the cloister.

"Even if she agreed to it, my parents would not. I'm supposed to return home in the summer, before my birthday. But the distance between us won't be great. My family's new mansion will soon be completed, and it's close enough for me to attend mass in the chapel whenever I please. Our stables will be quite large, and I'll have my own horse. I can ride over to visit you every week."

Bathilde responded with a feeble smile. "You might wish to, but I expect you'll be far too busy. Admirers will flock to your door, and before long one will become your sweetheart. And then your husband. You'll forget about me."

"That's nonsense. I want to see as much of you as possible before you leave the school to join the Queen Regent's household. In Paris, dancing with the king, you won't remember your friend in Niort."

Bathilde's brief experience with Louis as her partner had fostered greater application during her dance lessons. She concentrated on perfecting her arm movements and performing the intricate steps with precision. She enjoyed the sprightly simplicity of the *allemande*. The bouncing *gavotte* was a lively contrast to the stately *menuet*. A *sarabande* required graceful gliding and bending the knees with the back held very straight, to avoid any appearance of awkwardness.

The class bell rang, summoning them to the schoolroom, but a prefect stopped them before they could enter.

"*Demoiselles,* you have a visitor in the *parloir.* The regent says you need not be present for this lesson and gives you leave to go to her."

"It must be Cousin Sophie," Bathilde said. Her relative, established at Château des Vignes, occasionally came to Niort to shop, and sometimes she attended mass in the convent chapel.

After smoothing their skirts and ensuring that their caps and neckerchiefs were straight, they entered the small chamber in which pupils and lay sisters were permitted to meet their guests, with supervision by a nun on the other side of the grille.

When they entered, Françoise d'Aubigné skipped towards them, a bright smile lighting her face.

# CHAPTER 6

"Here's a surprise," Myrte greeted their former schoolmate. "Your godmother told Bathilde you were living in Paris."

"Madame de Neuillant remains my guardian, so I must go anywhere she chooses to take me. Social activity in the capital city wanes at this season, and she likes to play the grand lady here in Niort, as the governor's mother." To Bathilde, Françoise said, "Suzanne de Navailles told me how you charmed the Queen Regent when you were in Poitiers. And her sons."

"Her Majesty received me kindly," Bathilde replied, "and has been generous to the convent. Do you enjoy living in Paris? What is it like?"

"Enormous. Busy. Dirt and filth everywhere. Unending noise. Carriages and carts clog every thoroughfare. Hordes of pedestrians. The citizens are brusque and often rude and given to street fights and rioting. Dwellings and shops are ancient and in poor repair. The river looks nice, if viewed from a distance, but the water smells. All the churches and abbeys are beautiful, as are the palaces of the aristocrats and the grand residences of the wealthy bourgeoisie."

"You have a suitor, your godmother said."

Françoise said dismissively, "The Chevalier de Méré is more like a tutor. He professes his admiration eloquently in correspondence. Only he hasn't any money. And I've got none. Besides, he's at least thirty years older."

Myrte sliced the air with her hand. "That's no cause for refusal. You'd surely outlive him, and what a pretty young widow you'll be."

"I see you haven't lost your habit of jesting. I hope you find a husband who appreciates your lively wit and attempts to amuse."

"So do I."

Bathilde, glancing from one friend to the other, wondered whether she would ever exhibit the ease and assurance afforded by attractiveness and intelligence. She excelled in several subjects and had grown increasingly confident at the keyboard. She'd begun composing brief pieces. But her appearance troubled her. Her hair showed no sign of darkening to a deep and flattering chestnut shade like Françoise's, and there was no chance at all that it would become as attractively black as Myrte's. Their figures had developed womanly curves in the bosom and hips, whereas Bathilde's had yet to blossom. For two and half years, the nuns had warned her about the unseemliness of placing importance on physical attributes, which should never take precedence over moral and spiritual ones. But she couldn't help wishing for a portion of the beauty her mother had possessed.

Guiding her thoughts towards religion, she said, "Tell us about your first communion."

"When the baroness thrust me into a convent outside Paris, nothing like this one, I spoke not a word to anyone. They assumed I was a mute, until Madame de Neuillant refuted this. I therefore stopped eating altogether, but they regarded my strict fast as a sign of incipient holiness. I quickly wearied of being hungry all the time. I bargained with the nuns, and their priest. I demanded to know whether their church would consign my dear Tante Louise and my Huguenot cousins to eternal damnation and torture in the fires of hell. If I obtained the desired response, I said, I'd agree to be confirmed and take the sacrament. And that's exactly what happened. Madame, satisfied at long last, took me to live at her brother's house, near the Palais d'Orléans."

Myrte commented wryly, "You proved your cleverness, not your contrition."

"I can't help that I haven't a pious nature," Françoise retorted. "I doubt whether Madame de Neuillant truly cares, as long as she receives credit for my so-called conversion. And nor does it matter what prayers I utter, aloud or in my mind. Freedom from constant lecturing and private sermons and harsh punishments became more necessary to me than holding fast to Protestant teachings."

This admission troubled Bathilde, and it drew a sharp laugh from Myrte.

"I understand now. Like King Henri IV, you decided that possessing Paris is well worth a mass."

Françoise nodded. "In my place, you'd have done the same. Instead of starving in a convent cell and kneeling on cold floors, I receive ample sustenance and sleep in a comfortable bedchamber. Baron de Saint-Hermant, Madame's brother, holds a position in the royal household. His daughter is my age, and we get on very well. At night we visit a famous, very fashionable salon where intellectuals and literary people gather for food and brilliant conversation."

"About what?" Bathilde inquired.

"Books. Poetry. Romance. Religion. Politics. It's wonderfully stimulating, and so amusing to observe the sophisticated debates. And the flirtations. Our host, Monsieur Scarron, is an unusual gentleman. A scholar and an author with only one good hand to write with. What's more, he cannot walk at all, but is pushed about in a wheeled chair. His body is woefully deformed, thin and twisted, and he cannot raise his head at all. One must bend low to address him. His face is swollen and ill-featured, and he's missing several teeth. I didn't think he'd noticed me, unless it was because I dress badly. But while I've been in Niort, I've received extremely soulful letters and some flattering verses from him."

"Do you reply?" Bathilde wondered.

"Oh, yes. We're practically strangers, yet he is quite infatuated—from a distance. He says his heart is troubled because of his deep feelings for me."

"If I were you, I'd pin my hopes on that chevalier," Myrte advised. "Despite his age. Unless this Scarron is extremely rich."

"Not at all. He relies on his guests to bring meals, as well as wine and wood for the fire. They say he lives on an annual pension of five hundred *écus* from Her Majesty. He calls himself 'the Honorable Invalid to the Queen.' He's even older than Méré, by ten years at least."

"You've described an ogre from a folk tale, blighted by a witch's curse. On your return to Paris, you must kiss him and transform him into a handsome nobleman."

Françoise retorted, "Your mockery is evidence of your envy. You're stuck behind these walls with only women about you, and you envy the social opportunities I've enjoyed. And will again."

"Don't quarrel," Bathilde pleaded.

Myrte said mildly, "Let her think I'm envious, if that consoles her."

In a tight voice, Françoise said, "Would you please find Soeur Céleste and tell her I wish to see her, if she's at leisure. I've missed her."

Thankful for a means of escaping an increasingly tense conversation, Bathilde replied, "I'll go."

Myrte followed her from the parlor and along the passage. "Françoise will present herself as humble and devout, wholly indifferent to worldly things. Which she demonstrably is not. Living with Madame de Neuillant, and exchanging letters with that repulsive Scarron creature, has corrupted her."

"How can you say that? She's restored to the one true faith."

"Very well. I won't judge the condition of her soul—I'll leave that to the Lord. At my next confession, I will admit to mocking her. And mistrusting her."

They didn't encounter Françoise again until Easter, the day of Bathilde's first communion.

Myrte helped her put on a pure white gown, arranging the lace veil that flowed all the way to her feet, and carefully set the circlet of cherry blossoms in place. On legs that ached after hours of being bent in prayer, she followed her fellow confirmands into the chapel, clutching her silver rosary—a gift from the Queen Regent.

All the girls of the school attended the service. Cousin Sophie de Sevreau, present for the momentous occasion, promised to describe it in a letter to Papa. Françoise was there, accompanied by her guardian and Niort's governor and his daughter.

As the officiant approached the row of kneeling girls, Bathilde recognized Myrte's exquisite needlework on his episcopal vestments. Before the laying on of hands, with quivering fingers she removed her floral wreath. For the moment the bishop's palms rested against her head, she sensed heat surging through her entire body, as though his touch had kindled a flame inside her, and it lasted throughout the eucharist. She received the consecrated host, light and dry, on her tongue. A priest held the cool rim of the silver chalice against her lips, and for an instant she detected the wine's aroma before it was taken away.

The flock of newly confirmed proceeded to the courtyard to receive felicitations from their relatives and friends.

The significance of this spiritual birthday overshadowed the tenth anniversary of her actual birth. Myrte presented her with a handful of the fragrant, bell-shaped *muguet de bois* that sprouted in the shady spots beneath the convent orchard's aged fruit trees. During morning prayers, Mother Superior offered an intercession on her behalf, imploring the Lord to bestow on His servant wisdom, virtue, sincerity, a forgiving heart, and an enduring belief in the promise of eternal life.

Six weeks later, on a warm summer morning, she sought a few minutes alone with Myrte for a private farewell.

"You told me you wouldn't cry," her friend reminded her.

"I said I'd try not to," Bathilde corrected, eyes welling.

"We will write. And I'll visit as often as I'm able."

She handed over a sheaf of papers. "I composed an aria for you. I've written the notes and the words. I wasn't sure whether you would want to sing them in French or Italian. I've given you both versions." Glancing up, she saw moisture gathering at the corners of Myrte's blue eyes, dimming them. "It's light and cheerful. I hope you'll like it."

"The nicest present I've ever received. I depend upon you to complete the chasuble I couldn't finish," Myrte said. "There's nobody else whose embroidery matches mine, and it pleases me to know our stitches will be combined. I shall think of you, helping dear old Amalie in the garden, and listening to her strange tales of the ghostly *samovili* who pursue their betrayers through the forest."

Their fingers were entwined when Soeur Céleste appeared.

"The Vernier coach is waiting, *demoiselles.*"

Myrte drew her hand away. "Come with me to the gate. If my brothers are fetching me, perhaps you'll take a fancy to one of them."

This remark, typical of her, prompted a fond smile. For the last time, she and her friend walked to the courtyard together.

During afternoon catechism class, which Bathilde no longer needed, she worked on a fresh composition, slow and mournful.

# CHAPTER 7

*October, 1651*

Although it had no effect on the nuns or their *pensionnaires,* news of Cardinal Mazarin's departure from France penetrated the convent's solid stone walls. The anti-Mazarins, resenting what they viewed as their enemy's pernicious influence over France's queen, insisted that his exile must be permanent.

In early September, King Louis turned thirteen. His majority, proclaimed by royal decree, had been celebrated in Paris with great pomp, and Bathilde's father was a participant.

> We departed from the Palais Royal. The trumpeters went first, with hundreds of people following behind—soldiers, the nobility, provincial governors, officials in the king's household, and heralds. As I've recently had the honor of being designated a Marshal of France, I rode with the military leaders. We were two abreast, our steeds richly dressed, their silken cloths decorated with gold and silver embroidery. (Perhaps you and your schoolmates should

undertake this style of needlework, although I doubt the war horses would be as appreciative as the priests and bishops for whom you sew!) Behind us came the Grand Equerry of France on his charger, bearing the sovereign's sword. He was followed by pages and footmen. Our young king was magnificently dressed. The crowd shouted exuberantly, causing his white horse to rear, and his skillful handling impressed his people all the more. He attended mass in the chapel and addressed the Parlement. All day the city fountains spouted wine in place of water, and throughout the evening fireworks lit up the sky. The memory of these events will remain with me to my last day. My one regret is that my beloved daughter could not enjoy them, but I am confident, dearest Bathilde, that you will be present at future ceremonials.

Believing him to be firmly established in Paris, Bathilde was surprised when he arrived at the convent, an event as delightful as it was unexpected. Almost a year had passed since their parting in Poitiers.

"Momentous events have occurred since I posted my last letter. The Frondeurs continue plaguing Paris with their anarchy and acts of violence and destruction. The parliament of nobles repudiated Cardinal Mazarin's authority, before he fled, and the queen's. Last winter the malcontents started rumors that she would abscond with her sons and flee the city, which provoked the common folk to the point of storming the Palais Royal. After declaring the king's majority, she took him and his brother and their chief ministers and her favorite courtiers to the palace of Fontainebleau. But its nearness to the capital was deemed unsafe, and my soldiers and I escorted them to Bourges. From there we proceeded to Poitiers."

"Will you have to fight in a battle?" she asked.

"Not immediately. I'm responsible for enlisting more soldiers from Poitou who are faithful to the crown and willing to oppose the Frondeurs. I was therefore able to be present for our grape harvest at Château des Vignes, and the start of the wine-pressing, and I've conferred with Pascal about clearing land to plant and stake new vines. Today I shall inform Mother Superior that you will accompany me on my return to Poitiers."

For her second journey to that city, she had Papa and Sophie as companions, and being in adult company for long hours fostered a welcome sense of maturity. She'd been provided with a gray traveling habit, a smaller version of the one her cousin wore, and strapped behind the coach was a trunk containing a collection of pretty new gowns, quite unlike the plain dress of a *pensionnaire*.

This, she told herself, as they rattled along the icy roadways, is a foretaste of the life I'll lead after leaving the convent.

Because the royal retinue was too large to fit into Papa's *hôtel particulier,* she didn't share Sophie's chamber but had a spacious and airy one of her own and a dressing room. The servants, less harried than they had been last autumn, bustled about, performing their duties with brisk efficiency.

"While the housekeeper and I were in the marketplace this morning, I met an acquaintance of ours," Sophie revealed to Bathilde. "The Duchesse de Navailles promenaded there with her mother, the baroness. And her sister, one of the Queen's *demoiselles d'honneur.* Perhaps we might invite them to dine here, if Her Majesty can spare the duchess."

The invitation, made with all formality, was accepted.

Sophie and Bathilde received their guests in the *salle de compagnie*. Initially, the duchess and the baroness treated their hostess with chilly condescension. They thawed slightly on realizing that Madame de Sevreau, after marrying into the Prince de Coulon's family, had resided at Château Clément.

"But we never see you at court," the baroness remarked. "Of course, not anyone is admitted."

Faintly smiling, Sophie replied, "Long before your daughters entered Her Majesty's service, I was frequently there. The late king often boasted of matching my sister with her second husband, the Comte d'Erignac. One of his blood relations."

"How well you know the royal pedigree."

"I was also acquainted with your brother, Baron de Saint-Hermant. Does he still hold a position in the royal household?"

The baroness seemed startled by the question. "He does."

"Pray give him my regards. And his wife."

Bathilde admired Sophie's neat parry of the older woman's attempts to belittle.

The duchess intervened, saying, "My sister Angélique regrets her inability to meet you, but the queen required her presence."

"Perhaps Princess Bathilde will see her tomorrow," said Sophie, "when she has an audience with Her Majesty. The king will also be present. They became acquainted last year, during his stay in this house. Does Mademoiselle Angélique have a suitor?"

With evident reluctance, the baroness replied, "Not yet."

Voicing the question uppermost in Bathilde's mind, Sophie asked, "And what of Mademoiselle Françoise d'Aubigné? We were so pleased that she—and you—attended Princess Bathilde's confirmation."

Madame de Neuillant shook her head dolefully. "I confess, she continues to be a burden to me. Having drawn her back to the Catholic faith, I dare not return her to those Huguenot relations. Her mother is too impoverished to do anything for her, in addition to being unwell and worn down by futile lawsuits. I'll marry the girl to whomever I can, as swiftly as I can, you may be sure."

This callous vow infuriated Bathilde.

The young duchess nodded in agreement. "Poor little Françoise. She has become rather a pet of the *philosophes* and *salonnières,* though I cannot understand what they find so captivating. I'm of the opinion, Maman, that it might be best to encourage a match with that monstrosity Scarron. Before one of his acolytes seduces and ruins her."

Later, Bathilde revealed to Sophie everything Françoise had confided about her miserable existence in her guardian's household.

"I don't know how she endures being treated as a servant and a farm laborer. She bears it with surprising patience. She's frank, and often stubborn, yet I grew fond of her when she was my teacher. I wish the *baronne* would consider her happiness when choosing her husband."

"It's shameful," Sophie responded, "that people who believe themselves to be charitable often disdain the recipients of their charity."

The blue silk bodice felt tight in the chest, and the sensitive tips of her breasts rubbed uncomfortably against the fabric of her shift. A lace fall bordered her gown's curving neckline, and its full skirt parted in front to reveal a petticoat of ivory silk. Thick, russet curls hung down to her waist, proclaiming her youthful status. Her joints often ached, possibly a sign that she was gaining inches. A pink spot had risen on her chin, and she'd tried to conceal it with rice powder.

Papa presented her with a pair of teardrop pearl earrings.

Their cousin came forward, holding up a pearl necklace. "This belonged to your mother."

Bathilde felt a surge of emotion as Sophie placed it around her neck and tied the ribbons at her nape to fasten it. She inspected her reflection in a looking glass—an item unavailable to her at the convent—heartened to discover that her hair appeared less fiery.

They traveled to the royal lodgings by coach, a brief trip through the heart of a city dominated by towering church spires and the great bulk of the former palace of the Dukes of Aquitaine, where justice was dispensed. Even after proclaiming her son's majority, the Queen retained her position as ruler in his stead. And, according to Papa, they both continued to rely upon Cardinal Mazarin, who offered advice from afar.

"Her correspondence with him is constant, the letters fly back and forth from Poitiers to Brühl, his place of exile. She pleads and plans for his return. Now that the great Turenne has transferred his allegiance from the Prince de Condé and the Frondeurs, and has joined the fight against them, the cardinal's path back to France becomes smoother. She and the king require a devoted minister, as he has proved himself to be. But she fears he'll suffer harm if he returns before the rebellion is put down. Which my comrades and I are determined to accomplish, though it may well take months."

An equerry ushered them into the royal presence. Anne of Austria, seated at an ornate desk, put down her quill. Was she penning another of those letters to the banished cardinal? Her only companion, a *demoiselle d'honneur,* appeared to be slightly older than Bathilde.

"This is Mademoiselle Angélique de Baudéan, Madame de Neuillant's other daughter," the Queen announced. "The Duchesse de Navailles, with whom you are acquainted, is her older sister. Child, go to the king and bid him come to me. His brother, too, if you can find him. You need not return." To Bathilde she said, "My son has expressed his eagerness to welcome the girl who danced with him last year. You are quite the young lady, I see."

King Louis and his brother Phillipe had grown taller than they'd been at their memorable first encounter. She curtsied to them, and each stepped forward to kiss her hand, making her feel even more mature than her tight bodice and fashionable blue-and-cream gown.

"My children, you may take the princess into the gallery and show her the pictures while I confer with the prince."

The king led the way, as usual. Pausing, he turned to Bathilde and asked, "Do you care about paintings?"

Unsure whether he would prefer an answer in the affirmative or the negative, she replied, "I enjoy looking at portraits of my family. And yours," she added quickly.

"A dull business, sitting to a painter," he complained.

"I don't mind," Philippe declared. "It means dressing up. I used to wear girls' clothes most of the time, and I liked it. We always look our best when draped in velvet robes and silken breeches and lots of lovely lace."

"I prefer my armor. I have command of a militia troop now. Your father the prince has been teaching me how to drill the men. He's one of our finest officers—and deservedly a *maréchal* of France. Very nearly Turenne's equal."

"Your praise would please him," she said.

With a winning smile, Louis went on, "Come to the stables, and I'll show you my favorite charger. And Philippe's horse, too."

The boys descended the staircase with ease, unhampered by long skirts and new, smooth-soled satin slippers. She followed them through a warren of passages and a creaking door that opened onto a courtyard. Judging from their high spirits and conspiratorial air, this was a forbidden excursion.

On the other side of the *basse-court,* horses were housed in a long, high-ceilinged building that smelled of sweet hay and pungent manure. The pair of grooms polishing silver-studded bridles bounded up from their work bench and bowed low. Their lack of astonishment indicated that the king and the duke had a habit of entering the stables.

Louis nodded to them and strode along the row of stalls where the tethered animals snorted and stamped their hooves. He halted at the one occupied by a horse that had a creamy coat, a long wavy mane, and a switching tail.

Watching France's uncrowned king as he patted the creature's muzzle, Bathilde asked, "Is this the one that carried you in the grand procession?"

"How did you know?"

"Papa wrote to tell me of it."

Philippe said excitedly, "Louis wore a coat so covered with embroidery that it was impossible to tell the color of the fabric underneath."

"It was heavy. And hot. You may touch him," he assured Bathilde. "He's gentle."

She reached up to stroke the velvety nose.

"Do you ride?"

"No horses at the convent."

"We could teach you, Philippe and I. You must let us

make a horsewoman of you—repayment to your father, who instructs us in military matters. He wouldn't mind, would he?"

"He's a skilled rider. My mother was also. They were fond of hunting and hawking, in the forest near Château des Vignes."

"Is that your home?"

"Before going to school, that's where I lived. I was born at Château Clément, near La Rochelle, but I've not been there for a very long time."

"With our help, you'll be able to ride with the prince's staghounds next year."

"I'll still be at school," she said regretfully. "For five years more."

"Don't stay too long," Philippe warned, "or they'll turn you into a nun."

The king's dark brown head bobbed in agreement. "If they try, my mother and I will stop them. I promise."

Bathilde knew plenty of girls who had no choice. Abandoned by their families, deemed unmarriageable for any number of reasons, they passed through their novitiate and postulancy, eventually to professing vows that required them to remain cloistered for the rest of their lives. Whether or not they began with a true and heartfelt vocation, in time they discovered and embraced it.

Papa didn't want her to become an Ursuline, that was abundantly clear. Throughout their journey from Niort, he and Sophie had talked a great deal about the royal court and its hierarchy. The monarch and his mother and his brother at the top, below them Princes of the Blood and their offspring, then the different levels of aristocracy in order of precedence—duke, marquis, count, viscount, baron, and their spouses. Some wives held titles higher than their husbands'. Nobles could be born, or they could be created, as a reward for service to the crown, or they could purchase properties with seigneurial titles attached. All of this information, she knew, was intended as preparation for her future as a courtier.

As Philippe clamored to introduce her to his glossy black charger, she perceived his desire to assert himself. How trying it must be, she reflected, to live in the shadow of an older brother who was not only revered as monarch, but also attractive and charming. Not that Louis attempted to outshine Philippe, or denigrate him. Their closeness made her wish for a sibling with whom to share joys and sorrows.

But I've got Myrte, she reminded herself.

"Did you ever wish for a sister?" she asked on their way from the stable to their mother's chamber.

"We have a girl cousin," Louis answered. "Anne Marie Louise, La Grande Mademoiselle, more than a decade older than I and the richest young woman in all France. Her father is our Uncle Gaston, Duc d'Orléans, who conspired against Richelieu but was permitted to return from exile. She's an ally of our rebel uncle the Prince de Condé, and his Frondeurs, and isn't received at court."

"But she plans to marry you," Philippe said. "She calls you her little husband."

"I'm not little now," Louis responded defensively. "I want nothing to do with her. She's insolent towards our mother and her antics disrupt the court. Worse, she's a troublemaker, like her father, and will never, ever be Queen of France. Let her cast her lures at our cousin Charles Stuart, the English king. He's closer to her in age, and won't care that she's plain and her face is poxed. What's more, he has a far greater need of her fortune. He could purchase an army large enough to win back his crown from those pestilent Protestants who murdered his father."

"She dislikes him," his brother pointed out. "He barely speaks French, and he hasn't any *élan.*"

"She could smooth his rough edges."

Philippe said brightly, "You're the king, you can designate Princess Bathilde as our sister. Our mother says we're related to her. She must be a cousin of some sort."

"So is nearly everyone we know." The dark eyes narrowed. "Well, princess, what do you say to my brother's suggestion? Do you consent to be our sister in name, if not by blood?"

Deeply touched, Bathilde murmured, "That would be an honor."

He came forward and gently kissed each of her cheeks, then stepped aside for his brother, who copied the gesture.

"Consider it done. When Cardinal Mazarin returns, I'll have him draw up an official document. Or do you prefer to keep it a secret matter, among the three of us?"

"Whatever Your Majesty desires," she replied.

That, according to Papa, was always the correct answer to a question from the sovereign.

# CHAPTER 8

When Bathilde returned alone to the *grande salle* where Papa and the Queen Mother were conferring, her suspicion that they had been talking about her was immediately confirmed.

"Stand by me, child," the Queen Mother invited her, "while we tell you of our decisions."

Bathilde obeyed. Folding her hands, she looked up at the full, fair face.

"We have agreed that this is the proper time for you to leave the Niort *pensionnat*. But I do not want the Mother Superior and the sisters to suffer financially at your early departure. I mean to pay in advance all the fees they would have received, had you remained with them until your fifteenth birthday. Your father and I are also of one mind about making plans for your marriage—your youth need not preclude our doing so. Do you wish to inform her of your choice, Prince?"

Papa, standing at a window, turned to face Bathilde. "Over the recent months I've exchanged letters with the Duc de Rozel, my former comrade-in-arms, concerning an alliance between you and his only son. Her Majesty, who has previously expressed her approval, assures me that the Marquis de Brénoville is amenable. I believe he's a few years older than King Louis, whom he knows well."

I'm going to be a marquise, thought Bathilde in stupefaction. And someday, a duchess.

The Queen added, "On leaving the army, de Rozel returned to Normandy, and has bravely opposed efforts to bring his province into the Fronde. The Bertrands may not be rich, but their pedigree is as long as any in the land. The young marquis, educated at a Jesuit college in Paris, has received a commission in the king's militia. Albin is a fine, promising young man, and I'm happy to provide him with a richly dowered bride, heiress to a vast fortune and properties more substantial than he will inherit."

"He wishes to wed me, even though we've never met?"

Papa cleared his throat. "The marriage will not take place for several years. During that time, you'll have opportunities to become fully acquainted. I've decided to withdraw you from the school, that you may become chatelaine of Château des Vignes—with Sophie's guidance. The marquis will be busy soldiering. After the rebels are subdued, you will meet one another. At court."

"Too many young girls are left in ignorance about their fate," the Queen opined. "You, my dear, have the advantage of knowing what to expect."

"Will I be able to say farewell to the nuns, and my friends?"

Papa took her by the hand, drawing her to her feet. "Naturally. A few weeks from now, Cousin Sophie will deliver you to the convent. Sometime before Christmas she will take you away."

Confronted by these impending changes, she was relieved that she wouldn't be abruptly wrenched from the place that had been her home for years. Like Françoise and Myrte, she would pass through the great doors and the front gate, never again to return as a pupil. She took consolation from the fact that the château's proximity to Niort meant she could attend mass in the chapel, as Myrte sometimes did, and as Françoise had done at Bathilde's confirmation.

Her subsequent days in Poitiers were full. Papa, approving the king's desire to impart his knowledge of horsemanship, purchased a pony and the necessary bridle and sidesaddle. She named him Lune because his coat was as pale and silvery as the moon. For the duration of her stay in the city he would be stabled with the royal horses, and on her departure would be transferred to the château. Her initial lessons consisted of leading him around the courtyard and feeding him a handful of oats and tying ribbons in his mane.

"You'll soon be close companions," Louis said, "and then you can climb onto his back."

After nearly a week of this pleasant but unsatisfying and undemanding activity, he judged it the proper time for her to mount Lune. She settled into the padded and velvet-covered sidesaddle, her right leg supported by the pommel, and her left foot resting in the stirrup. He showed her how to hold the reins firmly while maintaining a lightness in her gloved hands.

"Our mother said to tell you that if you feel unbalanced, you should grasp the pommel for support rather than tugging on his mane, or the reins. You don't want to startle him into running."

"There's much to remember."

"Only at first. You'll soon be guided by instinct. Keep your body facing forward, and hold your back as straight as you can."

He clipped a long tether to Lune's bridle and walked away until it grew taut.

Philippe positioned his shiny black horse in front of

Lune. "Follow me," he called over his shoulder. "Press your heel against the pony's side."

She didn't know whether the pony would feel the movement of her foot, buried within the thick, gray fabric of her habit, but she followed his instruction.

Lune stepped forward in a walk, steady and sure.

"Excellent."

Vaguely aware that Louis praised her, she didn't look away from the space between Lune's ears. As long as they stood upright and didn't flick backwards or flatten, Papa had said, she had nothing to fear.

Phillipe and his horse led Lune in a circle, maintaining a slow and soothing pace. After they completed several circuits, Bathilde became conscious of a twinge in her back. Her thigh ached from pressing against the pommel.

A groom helped her dismount. Her legs shook from the strain on untested muscles, and she grasped the stirrup leather to maintain her footing.

Unhooking the tether, Louis said, "An acceptable first effort."

Shaking her head, she responded, "I didn't do anything, apart from not falling off."

"In a sidesaddle, that counts as an achievement. You'll suffer some soreness, I expect, it's only natural. We shall look for you tomorrow."

She grew familiar with the physical discomfort that followed those initial days in the saddle—her bottom hurt when she sat, and she winced on rising. But she persevered, and eventually her instructors judged her ready to venture beyond the stable yard. Their outing was no simple affair but required the attendance of a pair of equerries—one for the king and one for his brother—and a quartet of guards, two riding in front and two behind. Louis and Philippe were dressed more simply than Bathilde had ever seen them.

"We mustn't be recognized," Louis explained. "I have a dislike of being stared at."

"Aren't you accustomed to it?"

"It's not bad within the walls of a palace or château, among acquaintances who follow the prescribed etiquette. Last winter, Cardinal Mazarin's flight stirred the rumor that he'd taken me with him into exile. The mob of Frondeurs stormed the Palais Royal, looking for me, rousing our mother from her bed. Our Uncle Gaston's messenger had the effrontery to make demands of her—a Spanish princess and the Queen of France. In a gross breach of privacy and protocol, he intruded into our apartments, then came into my bedchamber. His followers shouted and threatened worse violence unless they could see me."

"They didn't mention me at all," Philippe complained.

"Our mother, so very brave and proud and composed, commanded that all the palace doors should be opened to anyone who wished to come into my chamber, provided they kept quiet and didn't disturb my slumber."

"It was too late for that," his brother said. "We were wakened by all the shouting."

"What did you do when they invaded your room?" Bathilde asked.

"Pretended to sleep. The crowd crept all around my bed, silent as could be. Mother pulled away the velvet curtain on one side and let them gaze upon me. They all fell to their knees, while I lay there with eyes firmly shut, scarcely breathing. My heart pounded so violently beneath my nightshirt, I feared they might hear it and guess I was feigning. Which I did—for hours. She stood by me, so dignified, guarding me while those ruffians traipsed in and out. The horrors of those hours return in nightmares which I shall probably have until my dying day."

"Your subjects love and respect you," she comforted him. "They did you no harm."

"Not physically, no. But I can never again be comfortable in Paris. Not at the Palais Royal, or in the Louvre. I prefer to live at Fontainebleau. Or Saint-Germain, my birthplace. Or even here." With a faint smile, he added, "I've talked enough about my past. Let us discuss your future. I've heard that you're going to marry a friend of ours. Albin Bertrand."

Hearing that name, her hands jerked the reins involuntarily. Lune protested with a shake of his head, and she stroked his neck to calm him. "You know him well?"

"Oh, yes. The Comte de Guiche is a closer friend, but our mother regards him as a bad influence and prefers that we bestow our favor on the Marquis de Brénoville."

"The queen mentioned that he's from Normandy, but I know almost nothing else. Can you tell me what he's like?"

Philippe said, "Every bit as handsome as de Guiche. His hair is brown, almost as dark, and it's long and fine. He has beautiful brown eyes, surrounded by long, black lashes. When last we saw him, he'd grown taller than Louis."

The king pursed his lips in displeasure at a comparison that put him at a disadvantage. "Until his father could no longer afford the expense, or chose not to, Albin attended the Jesuits' Collège de Clermont, by the Sorbonne. For all he's a great scholar, he never intended to take his degree from a university and didn't care to enter the priesthood or a monastery. He's accepted a captaincy in the militia under my command."

"He'll look even more magnificent in uniform," Philippe commented.

Ignoring this, Louis continued, "Like you, he belongs to the *noblesse ancienne*. It's therefore a worthy match."

"If you and your brother like him, I'm sure I shall." The facts her companions had shared were cause for optimism but didn't fully satisfy her curiosity about the stranger to whom she was betrothed.

On the Feast of All Saints, she and her father attended mass at the Cathedral of Saint Peter and prayed together at Maman's tomb. It pained her to see tears slide down Papa's cheek and fall onto the marble monument. His enduring love for her departed parent made her wonder whether she could inspire a similar devotion to the marquis whose bride she'd be, whose children she would someday bear.

At age ten, she knew perfectly well that many aristocratic girls never met their intended until shortly before their wedding day. She, at least, had Papa's promise that she would become acquainted with the Marquis de Brénoville. Thus far, her only significant experience of males had been limited to her father, the youthful King of France, and his brother.

Before departing Poitiers, she saw the Queen Regent once more. This time only Sophie went with her, as Papa was setting battle strategy with Comte d'Harcourt.

"The king asked me to offer his farewell," the Queen told her. "We expect hard fighting, when we permit Cardinal Mazarin to cross the border back into France."

According to Louis, the mysterious Marquis de Brénoville served in his troop. Did that mean he was even now in Poitiers?

"These revolts against our royal authority cannot continue forever. From prudence, and for the protection of my son's birthright, I have at times attempted to satisfy the demands of de Condé and d'Orléans. No more. Their soldiers are ill-trained, their cause never became as universally popular as they expected. In truth, the Paris

Parlement regrets the violence and unrest it spawned. We will re-take the city in due course."

"It's what I pray for," Bathilde assured her. "Every day."

"However, my child, I didn't send for you to talk of these troublesome affairs. I had a fancy to hear you perform again on the harpsichord before you return to the Ursulines. Your father tells me you have made great progress over this last year."

"She practices daily," Cousin Sophie declared, "without any urging. For hours at a time."

The instrument was more beautiful than any Bathilde had yet played. Rural landscapes decorated the sides of the case and the inside of the raised lid was edged with gold paint. Its wooden legs were carved like twisted vines. Determined to impress, she embarked on the most complex piece in her repertoire, a *sarabande* by the court composer Chambonnières. Her music was increasingly important to her—necessary, even—as an unbreakable connection to the mother she had lost. Absorption in her performance, whether in private or with an audience, made her forget her cares. And by using the talent she devoted herself to developing, she could give pleasure to others.

"The prince accurately described your improvement," the Queen praised her. "Whoever oversees your instruction must be commended. Give me the name, and I shall pen a letter at once to send back with you."

"Soeur Inès," Bathilde replied. "She plays beautifully. From her speech and her delicate table manners, we suspect she belongs to an aristocratic family. But the nuns don't talk of the lives they led before taking the veil, unless to share a story about an inspiring spiritual awakening or experience."

"I shall make good my promise to send the Mother

Superior the funds to cover the years of tutelage you will not receive."

As the carriage returned them to the de Sevreau *hôtel particulier,* Sophie commented, "Young ladies usually rejoice at leaving school. Will you?"

"I'm glad to return to the château," she admitted. "But I'll miss many of the sisters. I'm fondest of Soeur Céleste, gentle and patient with everyone, and never in a bad humor. Mother Superior can be firm, but she never treats the pupils unkindly or unfairly, not even those who misbehave. I've learned much about plants and flowers from Amalie, the lay sister who tends the garden and orchard. I'll never cease to name them in my prayers. But I've had no close friend during the months since Myrte Vernier left the *pensionnat.* After I go, I'll be able to see her as often as I like."

"You should also ask the d'Aubigné girl to visit—I'm sure she'd welcome an occasional escape from the *baronne.* At your confirmation I formed an unfavorable impression of Madame de Neuillant, which our recent encounters have confirmed. I've never enjoyed the company of ambitious women, especially those who enjoy wealth and privilege but selfishly deprive their poorer relations. In her place, I would strive as hard to provide Mademoiselle Françoise with as good a match as she seeks for her younger daughter."

"Someone like the Marquis de Brénoville."

"No girl of her background, however pretty, can aspire to a duke's son. But I can't imagine a worse husband for an innocent girl that age than Monsieur Scarron, a living, breathing scandal. His wit may be sharp, but he pens the rudest, crudest pamphlets. He draws in those persons who admire clever words more than good deeds, and receives libertines and all the most fashionable—and disreputable—females in Paris. Ninon de l'Enclos and her friends. I don't understand why the pious Madame de Neuillant and the proud Duchesse de Navailles permit their charge to associate with Scarron and his followers."

"She went there once. But he has often written to her since she left Paris."

"I shudder to think what the content of his letters might be."

Wistfully she said, "I wonder whether I'll receive any from the marquis."

"Would you like that?"

Bathilde nodded.

"Perhaps you will, when you're settled at Château des Vignes." Sophie patted her hand, adding, "I look forward to having you with me there during the winter. Those who served your mother will also be glad of your return, and the place will benefit from a youthful presence. That reminds me, I must waste no time in finding a suitable female who can wait upon you, either here or in Poitiers. Someone younger and less set in her ways than the good woman who served Marie throughout her girlhood to her last day."

She regretted parting from Papa, aware that he and his fellow marshals were in readiness for battles yet to be fought—probably quite soon. Although he rarely shared his efforts to fend off the Prince de Condé and his Fondeur adherents, she knew they would place him in danger.

"Will we see you at Christmas or New Year's?" Sophie asked, as he handed them into the traveling coach.

"I imagine I'll be making merry with the royal family." He bent to kiss Bathilde's cheek. "Your pony will soon leave here for the château, to await your arrival. Be sure to pen a letter of thanks to Her Majesty, who has shown you great favor."

"I already did, Papa." Would it be wrong to remind

one of the realm's greatest soldiers to be careful when engaging with the enemy?

He must have read the concern in her face, because he pinched her chin. "Don't fret over me, *petite*. I mean to grow very old in the service of the crown."

# CHAPTER 9

"I'm sure you'll be happier as a marquise than as Queen of France," Myrte declared. "And what a coincidence to hear your news, because I came to tell you that I'm also betrothed."

Bathilde stared in astonishment. "To whom?"

"Monsieur Etienne Lavigne, the lawyer who deals with contracts, deeds, and wills for my family. He and my brothers are friends, and our father is impressed by his acumen. Like any young man beginning to rise in a profession, he seeks a wealthy wife. During the summer, whenever we met each other, we fell into conversation, which I found most pleasant. Evidently, he did as well. Before long, I grew quite enamored."

"I suppose he is, also." How could he not be?

"Oh, yes. It's a love match." Her friend's elation faded as she said, "But we won't be wed until next year, after I turn sixteen. In the meantime, I'm permitted to sit with Etienne in our parlor, alone. We can walk together in the garden. The new house is large enough for us to live with my family, if we choose to, but my dowry allows for the purchase of our own. I intend to become a magnificent hostess—not only renowned in Niort, but in all Poitou. I hope you and your marquis will be our most frequent and favored guests. Forgive me, I've talked your ears off. I want to hear about your suitor."

Bathilde's gaze fell upon old Amalie, creeping across the lawn with her secateurs. "I haven't met him. I've no idea when our marriage will take place—years from now, Papa says. His father's estate is in Normandy. King Louis and his brother admire him and say he's extremely handsome. He received his education from the Jesuits and is now a soldier. Like your Etienne, he wants a rich bride."

"I've no doubt he'll adore you from your very first meeting. What's his name?"

"Albin Maurice Laurent Bertrand, Marquis de Brénoville," she recited. "He's the Duc de Rozel's heir."

"Very grand. Will you live in Normandy?"

"It will be a very long time before I know. I hope not. I'd rather remain in Poitou and Aunis all the time. But Papa says the marquis will eventually receive a position or an office at court. That means we'll reside in Paris a great deal, perhaps with lodgings in a royal palace."

Her friend showed more pleasure over Bathilde's future prospects than she felt herself. Seeking a diversion from uncomfortable thoughts, she joined Amalie, busily cutting pink roses from the sprawling, thorny specimen that spread itself across the garden wall.

Myrte crossed the lawn to ask, "Isn't it late for flowering? Summer is long past."

Bathilde told her, "This is a special variety. It produces blooms throughout the year."

Amalie added, "*Quatre Saisons* has likely grown in this place for a century or more, even before the convent was established."

Bathilde leaned close to inhale the heady fragrance. "I wish I might have such a rose at Château des Vignes."

"Look there, see the tall, straight canes coming up from the ground? Before you leave us, I'll dig them out with their roots and pot them up for you to take away. In the spring, you can plant them in your garden. Within another year or so, they'll be giving you flowers like these."

Amalie's curved back bent lower and she pressed her calloused palms against the earth, muttering to herself. Bathilde, watching her carry out the familiar ritual, wondered whether she prayed or recited an incantation.

Myrte leaned over and stroked the grass with her fingertips. "Poor *vili*, destined to forever dance out their disappointments in the afterlife. If Etienne abandoned me, I vow I'd join that band of unhappy, restless spirits, and haunt him unto death. And every man who betrays a loving, trusting maiden."

"Your lover will remain true," she said. "What a beautiful bride you'll be."

"And you, when your turn comes. Just think, our children will play together. Many, many years from now, we'll be old ladies, reminiscing about long-ago days as *pensionnaires.*"

Bathilde laughed. She couldn't imagine her vivacious friend as an elderly woman, droning on about past events.

Prohibited from talking to pupils or the sisters about her recent experiences in the secular word, she readily shared all that had happened in Poitiers.

Myrte, insatiably curious about her encounters with the royal family, demanded descriptions of the Queen Mother's dresses. "And what is King Louis like?"

"As regal as a ruler should be. Extremely gallant and polite. He and his brother taught me to ride my pony. They treated me as a sister."

"I suppose your wedding will take place in Paris."

Although acknowledging this as a possibility, Bathilde would prefer to marry in the de Sevreau chapel within Château des Vignes, or at the village church with the local priest presiding. Not among aristocratic strangers, who would stare at her and exhibit the disdain she'd received from Madame de Neuillant and her duchess daughter. Most likely the decision rested with Papa—or her bridegroom. Or the queen.

In her final week of schooling, a nun called her to the parlor to receive a visitor, who turned out to be Françoise.

"The last time I wanted to see you, they told me you were in Poitiers. I'm here to bid you farewell before Madame de Neuillant takes me back to Paris."

"I'm glad you came. I didn't know whether you remained in Niort or had already departed."

"I shall be glad to leave this town. When local ladies call upon Madame, or whenever she deigns to go to them, I have to hear her tell how she removed me from the pernicious influence of my Huguenot aunt, praying and agonizing until she turned me into a good Catholic. She says nothing of how she makes me perform household tasks and keeps me in these ugly clothes. At least I won't have to endure the shame of it much longer."

Feeling the press of a shoe against her ankle, Bathilde recognized the signal. Addressing the nun seated at the grill, eyes on her missal, she asked, "Might I show Françoise the rose that still blooms?"

"And I'd like to see Amalie," her friend volunteered.

"I see no harm in it," said the sister. "Like Mademoiselle Vernier, Mademoiselle d'Aubigné used to be a *pensionniare*."

Bathilde led the way from the parlor to the shadowy cloister, and into the deserted garden. "During my time in Poitiers, the queen and my father explained that I'm betrothed to a marquis. And Myrte expects to marry her sweetheart next year."

"I'll probably precede both of you to the altar," Françoise boasted.

"Really? The Duchesse de Navailles didn't mention it."

"She doesn't know. Nobody does—not yet. For months I've listened to Madame declare that she and Suzanne will marry Angélique to an aristocrat. That's why they pleaded with the queen to give her a position in the royal household. But first they mean to be rid of me because I'm prettier—and more popular. Well, I have a means of granting their wish." Françoise reached beneath her neck handkerchief for a thick letter. "I told you about Monsieur Scarron."

"The invalid who is courting you."

Françoise nodded. "We've continued writing to one another all these months since I left Paris. At first, as I told you, he praised my cleverness. Then he sent amorous verses—with scandalous imagery that makes me blush. He wants to see me naked, without my ugly gowns. And he professes to be madly in love with me."

Bathilde stared at her. "How do you respond?"

"I haven't. But I can no longer put it off now that I've received this." She fluttered the folded sheets. "He plans to emigrate to one of the West Indies islands, thinking the tropical Caribbean climate and more healthful food might cure his ailments. He dreads Mazarin's return, because he used to write unflattering, insulting pamphlets against him, full of accusations and foul language. He expects to be punished in some way, and fears the revocation of his pension from the queen. That isn't all. He wants me to leave France with him. As his wife."

Bathilde stroked the pale petals of a fading rose, the only one remaining on the branch. "If you go so far away, we'll never meet again."

"But I shall convince him that those islands aren't the paradise he imagines, nor will he find the residents to his liking. He's accustomed to entertaining the cream of intellectual society, people who are sophisticated and erudite, who can entertain him. I can't imagine him living far from the excitement and activity of Paris. Our letters are flirtatious, yet I never guessed his feelings for me could be serious or directed towards matrimony. I'm considerably younger than he. A nobody."

"Wouldn't you prefer a young and handsome husband, with money enough to indulge you?"

"Scarron must have some tucked away somewhere. He offered to pay my dowry, if I choose to enter a convent instead of becoming his bride."

"Are you considering the religious life?"

Françoise shook her curly head. "As a *dizainière*, I enjoyed teaching, but I'm not devout enough to become a bride of Christ. My life with Scarron would be extremely interesting. He dotes on me and would probably allow me plenty of freedom to do as I please. His health is poor, and his age advanced. I daresay I'll be a widow longer than a wife." Pointing to the flower, she asked, "This is the rose you spoke of?"

She nodded. "Amalie will give me pieces of the plant to take home."

"When do you go?"

"Any day. Cousin Sophie will send a message, and then she'll come in the carriage to collect me. I'll remain with her at the château until I'm old enough to marry the marquis."

"When I'm Madame Scarron, I'll invite him to our salon."

"Have you really made up your mind to wed him? I hope you'll do whatever will make you truly happy."

"If I don't accept him soon, Madame de Neuillant will do it for me. Escaping her toils will be worth any little hardships I might face as an author's wife. At least

I'm acquainted with him. You probably know nothing about your marquis."

"He's a soldier, a valued friend of the king and his brother. They told me how handsome and well-educated he is."

"Naturally. Nobody wants you fretting about a fate you cannot escape."

Until this moment, she hadn't been concerned. Unlike Myrte, effusive and encouraging, Françoise the skeptic had planted an unwelcome seed of uncertainty about the matrimonial partner Papa and the queen had chosen for her.

# CHAPTER 10

## Château des Vignes, May, 1654

On setting out from Paris, Wilfride Mensy heartily wished for an errand of greater significance, one that hadn't brought him to this obscure and remote region to deliver a thirteen-year-old girl's birthday present. His lengthy journey, begun in rain and concluding in sunshine, had sent him across several provinces, to the minor town of Niort and this tributary of the Sèvre-Niortaise river. At least his cousin's future bride had been born in early May, in a season of flowering apple and pear and cherry trees. Gardeners were busy in their neatly planted *potagers*. The carriage rolled past verdant fields of wheat crops, and an extensive vineyard where men and women marched between the long rows of trellised vines, striking the ground with hoes to dig out the weeds.

At a village, the coachman halted to call out a question to a female who pegged sheets to line stretched between two saplings. When he asked how far to the prince's estate, her arm sketched a circle in the air.

"It is here." Pointing towards a square steeple, she added, "And there. The château lies beyond the church and the wood. But the prince is away."

Wilfride knew that, having parted from him several days ago. Since Cardinal Mazarin's return from exile, he and Albin had fought against the Frondeurs with the king's militia, supporting more experienced forces commanded by Turenne, d'Harcourt, and de Coulon—whose daughter would be the recipient of a carved ebony box and its contents. The prince, temporarily in Paris, would soon join the generals in their latest challenge, battling the Prince de Condé and his Spanish allies.

Farther along the road stood a pair of pillars, each surmounted by a carved stone shield containing the three shells of the de Sevreau coat of arms. The smooth carriageway followed the broad bend in the river to a sprawling and partially moated castle. A substantial flat-topped circular tower stood at the water's edge—the original stronghold. Sections of later construction and smaller turrets with pointed roofs were connected to form an inner courtyard. The château didn't match the splendor of the primary royal residences, but its antique grandeur reminded Wilfride of the lesser ones.

The princess would someday inherit this impressive architectural achievement, all the surrounding territory, as well as a larger estate near the western coast and several city properties. And, according to Albin, an immense fortune.

A stone bridge supported by three arches spanned the river, which fed the moat on one side of the castle. On the other, the carriage track continued past a dovecote to an extensive stable block. Adjacent to it was a low-roofed kennel, and beyond it, a massive barn.

The coach's arrival scattered a flock of grayish-brown geese. The man who was currying a pale pony's flowing tail came forward, comb in hand.

Wilfride, clutching the ebony casket, climbed out of the vehicle. His boot heels sank into rain-softened earth. "I am Monsieur Mesny, sent here to pay my lord's respects to your mistress."

"Madame de Sevreau," the groom replied, "has gone to Niort. You likely passed the coach on the road."

"Did her young charge accompany her?"

"Princess Bathilde is in the garden. Follow the path around the outer wall until you see the hedges. If you're staying the night, the *maître d'hotel,* Monsieur Jousson, will arrange for a chamber to be prepared."

Lacking an invitation, he'd been unsure what degree of hospitality would be extended. But a castle this large could easily accommodate a hundred guests. If not more.

He located the garden without difficulty. Espaliered fruit trees grew along the walls that enclosed it on three sides. Graveled walks separated squares edged with low evergreens and decorated with swirls of grass, and in the center of each section, a flowering vine scrambled up its *tuteur.*

A pair of girls shared a bench, their heads—auburn and brown—bent over a book. The elder one's reddish curls were held away from her face by gold combs that glinted in the sunlight, and she wore an amber-colored gown. Her companion was dressed in servant's garb, with a white neckerchief and apron and wooden clogs.

"Princess Bathilde."

Hearing her name, she looked up, revealing a face of remarkable loveliness. He announced, "I come from the Marquis de Brénoville. I am Wilfride Mesny. His *écuyer* and *serviteur.* And cousin."

In a swift yet graceful motion, she left the bench. "He sent you to me? Where is he?"

"In Paris." He held out the casket. "I bring his gift. For your birthday."

"It's tomorrow." Smiling up at him, she asked,

"Might I have it now?" She ran her fingers over the intricate carving. "I shall treasure it."

"Your gift is here." He raised the lid to reveal a miniature portrait, painted on ivory. It was set in an oval frame studded with diamonds and attached to a blue silk ribbon.

Her expression softened as she confronted her future husband's face. "A good likeness?"

"Exceptionally so. Painted from life." Before and after his sitting, Albin had complained mightily.

"How thoughtful of him, to have this made for me."

Wilfride wouldn't spoil her delight or disappoint her by refuting this false assumption. Her father had asked Albin to pose. He'd also paid the artist's fee, as well as the jeweler who created the elaborate setting.

She took the miniature from its velvet nest and held it to her lips, a gesture he found utterly enchanting.

"Pray tell him how grateful I am to be remembered. I often think of him, and wonder where he might be, and what he's doing."

"He spends a great deal of his time with his soldiers. And King Louis. Or your father. Although not a member of the royal household, he's often at the Louvre, as His Majesty's friend and comrade."

Albin lacked the funds for the lavish appearance and extravagance expected of a courtier. Marriage would bring wealth enough to establish himself more prominently in the monarch's circle—if he cared about that. He was two years Wilfride's junior, and his ambitions weren't fully formed.

"The king, and his brother, correctly described him as handsome. I like that he seems to smile, ever so slightly. When I sat to an artist, I wasn't allowed to."

A pity. Her mouth, sweetly curved, was as pink and delicate as a rose petal. He believed Albin would admire the broad forehead, smooth cheeks, and rounded chin, and her gentle, expressive voice. The slight figure wasn't yet womanly, but it had promising proportions.

"When is his birthday?" she wanted to know.

"The tenth of September, five days after the king's. He's three years older, and this year turns eighteen."

"I wish to send my miniature in exchange," she said. "I'll ask the artist from Nantes to come here. It shouldn't take him very long to complete something that small. If it's not inconvenient for you to remain here for a week or so, you could take it to Paris. And in September, give it to the marquis."

His thoughts moved quickly. "I won't impose on you longer than a single night. Tomorrow I can continue on to Normandy to visit my family in the Cotentin." He needn't petition for a long leave, for Albin wouldn't object to his spending time with his parents and siblings. "And I'll return to collect the portrait."

She glanced again at the image, then looked up to ask, "Will the marquis dislike my hair being red?"

"It will delight him," he assured her, as though he knew it to be so. Which he didn't.

Turning away, she called to her young companion, still seated. "Come, Giselle, see what Monsieur Mesny brought me."

He judged her no more than ten, close to his youngest sister's age. Long brown strands streamed over her thin shoulders, and the dominant feature in her elfin face was a pair of large, bright eyes.

Displaying the miniature, the princess said, "The Marquis de Brénoville. We are betrothed."

"He looks kind. I should hurry home now, princess. My mother doesn't like me to be away too long."

"If you visit at the same hour tomorrow, I'll read the rest of the tale."

Skipping away, the child vanished into the adjacent woodland.

"She's our vineyard-keeper's niece. I'm trying to persuade her mother to send her to the Ursuline school in Niort, as a day pupil. Giselle knows her letters now, and I'm teaching her to read." On a sigh, she added, "I want to improve her prospects, but not in a way that her relatives will regard as interference."

That, in Wilfride's judgment, was a mature reflection for a girl of thirteen.

"You must be travel weary," she went on, "and hungry. My cousin had an errand in Niort but will soon return. We rarely receive guests, and she'll be pleased that you're staying overnight. She'd probably appreciate any court news you might have. And I wish to know how the king prospers. He has been very kind to me."

While Bathilde posed, the younger version of herself on the opposite wall returned her gaze. She hadn't felt as self-conscious then as now, knowing this portrait would eventually belong the Marquis de Brénoville. Having outgrown the blue and cream gown of two years ago, she'd chosen one of gold brocade with a flat lace collar. Sophie had provided Maman's pearl and crystal chain and necklace and arranged her hair with meticulous care. The bodice flattened her breasts, their tenderness signifying the return of her monthly flux.

"Eyes upon me, princess."

She sat nearer the artist than she had last time. He permitted her to smile—but not too broadly.

This light and airy chamber served as her *salle de musique*. The front of its great stone chimneypiece was carved with the de Sevreau scallop shells. She'd banished the heavier furniture of her grandparents' era to older parts of the château, replacing it with the elegant *escritoire* and several giltwood chairs Papa sent by carrier from Paris. Maman's harpsichord, her greatest treasure, stood against a wall in a corner of the room, at a safe distance from damaging sunlight.

Despite her youth, she could confidently assert herself as chatelaine, the result of Sophie's tutelage in household management. No stranger to kitchen or larder, where pupils had worked alongside the nuns, she'd familiarized herself with all her servants' tasks. After consulting the receiver-general about revenues, she overruled Monsieur Jousson's policy of parsimony. She requested new liveries for her footmen and page and provided vineyard workers with better implements. Aged retainers like Jeanne, who had waited upon Maman, were given responsibilities better suited to their age or infirmities. Some were granted pensions and allowed to remain in their lodgings. She employed a pair of energetic gardeners who refreshed the gravel in the *parterre* and shaved the evergreens. They determined exactly the right placement of her trio of *Quatre Saisons* roses. Amalie would rejoice to see how they thrived.

Monsieur Jousson and members of his family regularly dined with her and Sophie. Myrte, a frequent visitor, sometimes brought her Etienne, a pleasant and rather reserved young attorney. Their marriage was delayed, for unspecified reasons. In her jesting way, Myrte predicted that even so, there would be a Madame Lavigne long before there was a Marquise de Brénoville.

# CHAPTER 11

Well before her eighteenth birthday, the early promise of Myrte's extraordinary beauty was fulfilled. Glossy black hair, modishly arranged, contrasted with her swan-white complexion. Beside her statuesque friend, Bathilde deplored her own lack of inches.

"I've something to show you." She tugged the blue silk ribbon tied around her neck, drawing the portrait of her betrothed from beneath a billowing lace collar. "My marquis."

Myrte peered at the miniature. "An Adonis, to be sure. He hardly looks real. How did you acquire this?"

"His *écuyer* brought it."

"I imagined a resemblance to the king, as he appears in a painting my mother purchased. But this man is more handsome. His countenance is truly noble."

Unable to resist another glimpse, Bathilde turned the image towards herself. The diamonds surrounding the frame sparkled with the movement. "I'm sending my picture to him. It's finished, if you'd care to see it." From the cabinet she removed the oval disk, larger than the one she'd received from the marquis. She handed it to Myrte.

"His heart will be captured. As yours must have been, on seeing his image."

"I can only judge him by what I've been told. Monsieur Mesny described him as devout and scholarly, from his years among the Jesuits. And brave in battle. Everyone who knows him speaks of his good qualities but not of his faults. I know he lacks wealth. That's why he wishes to marry me."

"You've described how your parents cared for each other, and your father surely wants yours to be a similarly affectionate alliance. I say it's time for this magnificent marquis to come to Poitou and pay court to you."

Bathilde smiled. "He's nearly your age, and a soldier besides. Such a one isn't likely to devote himself to a thirteen-year-old girl."

"Did a letter accompany the portrait?"

She shook her head.

"I told Etienne, before legal business took him to Poitiers, that he must write every day."

"I've perfected a lovely *pavane* that you and he could dance to. When does he return?"

"He'll be away for at least a fortnight, perhaps longer. We must persuade my father to set our wedding day. Even though I'm not yet of age, he sanctioned the match, which means the parish priest won't be required to publish the banns. The details of our marriage contract are agreed, so further delay is quite unnecessary." Myrte's rare despondency seldom lasted. In a brighter tone, she asked, "What do you hear from Madame Scarron, your Paris friend?"

"She's your friend, too," Bathilde responded.

"I wonder. I wasn't very conciliating towards her. But I'm sorry she married such a one as Paul Scarron. At sixteen!"

"Let's go to the garden, and I'll tell you what I know."

She led the way down a curving stair to the wooden door, creaky from age, that opened onto the section of lawn surrounded on five sides by the château walls.

"A few months ago, Françoise and her husband moved into a house in the Marais, also inhabited by a disreputable *comte,* a former Bastille prisoner pardoned for his support of the Frondeurs. They have servants, but their furniture, and the food, and all the firewood are given by the friends who support Monsieur Scarron. She dislikes living on charity, having done so all her life. You know how proud she is."

"He can't walk, or move in any way, can he? I suppose her virginity is preserved. Of necessity and not by choice, poor thing."

"They don't share a bedchamber," Bathilde confided, as they strolled the courtyard's outer perimeter. "Hers is on one floor, his on another. She says he's in such pain at night that she wouldn't be able to sleep if they were to lie together. She's very proud of having one of the most popular salons in all Paris. Everybody goes there. Papa went with Marshal Turenne. In one of his letters, he named the wits and nobles and playwrights and actors and musicians who frequent the Scarron house. Madame de Sévigné. Ninon de l'Enclos, the courtesan. Even members of the royal family. Françoise boasts of receiving La Grande Mademoiselle, the king's cousin."

"Exalted company."

"She's fashionably unfashionable, she says. She sought a pension for her husband from Monsieur Fouquet, the finance minister, and received it. His wife is fond of her."

"Does she attend mass?"

"She never mentions going to confession or to any church."

"If she maintains the façade of piety, professing herself a Catholic without ever receiving the sacrament, that makes her a hypocrite." Myrte paused to run her hand over one of the shrubs growing in a lead planter, its greenery sheared into a ball. "I like your *topiaires.* Myrtle, is it?"

"Yes. I aspire to create a pond, if water can be pumped from the moat or the river. Perhaps a fountain. With a central statue."

"The figure of Adonis would look very fine. Modeled on your marquis, of course."

Bathilde shoved at her. "How would that be possible? I've seen no more than his head and shoulders."

Myrte gripped her hand. "I do hope he won't take you away to Paris. I couldn't bear not having you near."

Touched, Bathilde squeezed her fingers. "I feel the same. But wherever we live, you and Monsieur Lavigne will always be welcome."

On the following day, Monsieur Mesny returned from Normandy. He solemnly declared her portrait to be a masterpiece and assured her that his cousin would value it highly. At Sophie's urging, she performed a selection of tunes on the harpsichord and showed him a chapel altar cloth she was embroidering. She held back a multitude of questions that might make her appear too forward or excessively curious. He stayed but one night, departing with the dawn.

For several weeks, she neither saw Myrte again nor received a letter. An indication, she supposed, that wedding preparations had begun.

Sophie sought her assistance with an inspection of household linens. After determining that everything should be replaced, they set out for Niort to purchase material. They delivered their discards to the convent, for the sisters' use or to be distributed to the poor of the district.

Leaving Sophie to deal with the cloth merchant, Bathilde walked from the center of the town to the Verniers' mansion. Even more surprising than closed shutters and unkempt shrubbery was the fact that nobody had scrubbed the mud marking the front steps.

"Is Mademoiselle receiving today?" she asked the maid who opened the door.

"I can inquire. It's one of her bad days."

Hoping her friend wasn't ill, she waited in the vestibule. The house was unusually silent. She heard none of the chatter and scurrying of the many servants employed by the extravagant Madame Vernier.

Myrte, in a wrinkled gown, stepped onto the landing above. Her black curls, undressed, flowed almost to her waist. Slowly she descended, her hand sliding along the stair rail.

"Have you heard? Is that why you're here? I meant to tell you myself, only I didn't know how."

Bathilde stared at her in confusion. "Cousin Sophie and I had errands in the town. You haven't visited for weeks, and I wished to see you."

"Then news of our misfortunes hasn't reached Château des Vignes."

"What's happened?"

"It's shameful, but quite simple. My father and brothers, through risky speculation, lost our entire fortune. They're bankrupt. Father has enormous debts that he cannot pay, and may land in prison. He's in Poitiers, preparing to face a court. I believe Etienne has taken on his case. My brothers fled Niort, and I know not where they've gone. My mother, who cannot bear the gossip and accusations, went to her relatives in Parthenhay."

"Do you mean to say they've deserted you? You're here alone?"

Myrte nodded.

"You should've written to me. You know I'd have come straightaway."

"I paid off the remaining servants with money I found

in a strongbox and dismissed all but my maid. We make meals from the food the others didn't take. I'm thankful Father has the coach and horses, because I wouldn't be able to provide them with fodder. The chickens and geese can fend for themselves."

"You aren't staying. Sophie and I will take you home with us."

"Etienne might come for me."

"The maid can tell him where you've gone."

"If I leave, she won't stay."

"I can arrange for trustworthy servants, pensioners of mine, to take her place. Go and make ready. Pack a trunk, or more, with your clothing and trinkets." Gazing into her friend's tear-glazed eyes, she said, "You devoted yourself to my care for all the years we were together at the convent. We are as sisters. And I promise I'll help you in whatever way I can, for as long as you need me to."

# CHAPTER 12

Each of Bathilde's Paris correspondents, Papa and Françoise, sent wordy accounts of the king's consecration in Rheims cathedral in June—although only her father had been present at the day-long event. Reading about the ceremony, she wondered whether Louis, her onetime dancing partner, would continue to regard her as friend and sister now that he'd been crowned. But because she had more pressing concerns, she quickly dismissed the matter from her mind.

No communication had arrived from Etienne Lavigne. Myrte's birthday, the following month, went unacknowledged by her family, scattered throughout the province. The Niort house and its contents were sold to pay some—though not all—of Monsieur Vernier's creditors. Her friend bore these various calamities with fortitude, trusting her lawyer lover to fulfill his longstanding pledge to wed her.

"Father's case is complicated," Myrte declared, "and keeping him out of prison must be taking up all of Etienne's attention. There are taxes to be paid as well as the debts. There's no knowing how long they'll remain in Poitiers. I've had no reply to my last two letters."

"Perhaps your father changed his lodgings, and they haven't yet reached him."

Pacing the length of the *salle de musique,* Myrte continued, "I thought of that. I should go there myself and take my jewelry. I doubt I'd get as good a price for it in Niort."

"It seems too soon for such drastic measures," Bathilde told her. "If you're needed, your father or Monsieur Lavigne will send for you."

"It's really my mother who should be there. Not that I'm surprised she ran to her relatives. Her own comfort is always of paramount concern. She cares not at all for mine. And she's exceedingly vain. She feels cursed, having a daughter my age, looking as I do. If the Ursulines allowed their pupils to stay past the age of fifteen, I'd be with them still. She's as eager to marry me to Etienne as I am to be wed."

"What are his parents like? You must have met them."

"Only once. They came to Niort from Lusignan to inspect me. Monsieur Lavigne is a grain merchant, and of course my mother treated them to such embarrassing condescension that I wanted to crawl under the carpet. Asking how many servants they employed, and whether their son could afford to keep a carriage. Which of course he will. My dowry is enormous."

She's fortunate to have a mother, thought Bathilde, acutely conscious of her early loss and saddened by the lack of affection between Myrte and Madame Vernier.

The weeks dragged on with no information from any source, until one of Myrte's brothers wrote to her. Monsieur Lavigne would soon return to Niort, he informed her, to make partial payment of sums owed to local merchants and town officials.

Standing with Bathilde on the moat bridge, Myrte read from her letter.

"'Make every effort to be pleasing to Lavigne. We are in desperate straits and rely on you to hold him to his promise of marriage. But do nothing to impair your virtue or good name. He must not claim you until the vows have been spoken and the union properly recorded in the priest's book.'" Forming a fist, she crumpled the page. "Does he think I'd let myself be seduced? Or that Etienne would attempt it? These cautions are bewildering."

"He's protective of you," Bathilde replied. "As a brother should be."

"'Hold him to his promises.' I can't imagine why that's necessary. Etienne loves me."

"He'll come for you soon," she pointed out. "With permission to marry you at once, which is exactly what you desire."

Without returning her smile, Myrte smoothed creases from the letter and read it once more.

Determined to cheer her, Bathilde added, "I'll send a servant to his lodging with an invitation to join you here. Your wedding can take place in the chapel. We'll decorate it with flowers—and roses, for there must be some on *Quatre Saisons*. I'll make a crown of myrtle for you to wear. None of my gowns will fit, you're taller than I. Sophie has grown fond of you, so I expect she'll let us alter one of hers."

Her cousin, amenable to these hastily formed plans, provided a silvery silk court ensemble she'd had no occasion to wear since taking up residence at the château. Myrte put her sewing skills to good use, taking in the bodice and attaching silver lace flounces to the sleeves. Bathilde consulted Monsieur Jousson about laying in provisions for a banquet. The servant responsible for procuring them from Niort delivered her message and Myrte's letter to Monsieur Lavigne's quarters. She apprised her household chaplain of his role in the proceedings and assured him that the banns had previously been published at Église Notre Dame. If he required confirmation, the parish priest could provide it.

Throughout this period of heightened activity, Bathilde watched Myrte lovingly prepare the gown and imagined what she might wear herself when she became the Marquise de Brénoville.

"You'll have the wedding I want," she confessed. "I wish mine could take place here."

"My circumstances, however, are unenviable," Myrte replied. "This isn't what I dreamed of. Nor does it match my parents' plans. A nuptial mass in the big church, and afterwards lavish and costly celebrations intended to rouse envy of the rich, important Verniers. Well, nobody envies us now. When people gossip about us, it isn't complimentary."

A week of summer showers raised concerns that inclement weather had postponed or hampered Etienne Lavigne's journey from Poitiers to Niort. But the clouds couldn't obscure Myrte's optimism, nor did the deluge wash it away.

"The flowers will be quite spoiled," Bathilde moaned. From a window overlooking her *parterre,* she observed the incremental spread of the puddles filling the paths.

She felt no less concerned about the grapes in her vine-yard and the farm crops in the fields and the meadows of uncut hay. If prolonged storms resulted in flooding, her tenants would suffer considerable losses and muddy, rutted roads would impede the transport of their produce to Niort market.

She'd never been as glad to see the sun as she was the next morning, and ventured out early to discover whether the beds of herbs and flowering plants were intact. Satisfied that they had survived the onslaught, she searched for Myrte and found her in the *grande salle haute,* poring over a letter.

"You must see the sky," she said merrily. "As blue and pure as the Virgin's robe."

Her friend made no reply, merely shaking her head.

She went to the sofa and placed a hand on one rigid shoulder. "Is it from Monsieur Lavigne? When will he come?"

"Never." Myrte's fingers unclenched, and her letter fell to the floor. "He releases me from our betrothal."

Kneeling beside her, Bathilde said, "You must have misread."

"See for yourself," Myrte replied, her voice taut.

She scanned the single page, her dread increasing as she absorbed the import of each line. "Is there really no legal document sealing his commitment to you?"

"Without signatures, it's meaningless. Nothing more than a stack of paper that specifies the amount of my dowry, and the share of my father's estate that I'm entitled to." Myrte drew a ragged breath. "But of course, there's no dowry left. And nothing to inherit. Therefore, he cast me aside."

"He loves you."

"Even if he does, I'm not the rich bride he expected." Her head suddenly came up. "I may not have money, but I've got lots of jewelry. A stomacher studded with dozens of diamonds. A bow brooch set with rubies. My emerald necklace. The set of pale sapphires. Gold and pearl bracelets. Hair combs. Instead of selling them to pay my father's debts, I'll use them to restore my dowry. And if that's not enough to satisfy Etienne, I shall seek employment."

"As what?"

"A seamstress. A dressmaker. In Poitiers, where the trade would be better than Niort and few people would be aware of my family's scandal. If Etienne believes I'm too spoiled to live in modest circumstances, I'll convince him he's mistaken." Her chin jutted outward. "I'm nothing like my mother. Or my father and brothers. My pride is quite different to theirs."

Relieved by this show of spirit, Bathilde said encouragingly, "Write to him now. Your wedding clothes are ready. You can exchange your vows in the chapel, just as we've planned."

Two days passed without any response to Myrte's eloquent, urgent entreaty.

"Let me take you to Niort," Bathilde said. "To Église Notre Dame. You can wear your beautiful gown and myrtle wreath. We'll send for him. The moment he sees you, he will take your hand and lead you to the altar. Afterwards, we'll come back here to celebrate."

Her prediction drew a smile. "I'd rather save my finery for the wedding feast."

This turned out to be a wise decision. Throughout the drive, the raindrops descended with force. In some places the wheels almost became mired in the mud and ruts left by prior storms, but the coachman managed his horses well and skirted the worst stretches. At the conclusion of a protracted journey, the vehicle bore a thick coating of grime, and the boots of driver and footman were similarly filthy.

Myrte told the servant where he'd find Monsieur Lavigne, and Bathilde ordered him to bring the gentleman to the church—without fail.

Before her friend left the coach, she protested, "You mustn't wait for him outside, it's too wet. Stay here."

"I'll keep dry under the arch."

"I'm coming with you."

She assured her coachman, sheltering beneath an oiled canvas, that they would soon return. The shallow overhang of the soaring doorway offered no protection from the wind. Raindrops lashed their faces and dragged down the feathers of their hats, yet even as Myrte shrank from the onslaught, she refused to abandon her position.

Bathilde spied her *serviteur* trotting along the wet paving stones. The lawyer followed, at a slower pace, draped in a cloak.

Myrte whispered a prayer of thanks and hurried to meet the man she loved.

# CHAPTER 13

Near darkness obscured soaring stone buttresses, and the lack of sunlight dimmed the colored glass that formed holy images in the tall windows. Bathilde felt the chill of the silent, sacred space seep through her garments.

Myrte faced the gentleman, saying soberly, "You, a practitioner of the law, insisted on making a contract with my father. But you postponed the signing. Were you aware of his financial difficulties and the extent of his indebtedness?"

"Not when I initially approached him about our marriage. Later, I grew suspicious about the amounts he invested in risky ventures, and expenditures incurred despite his inability to recover his losses. It's clear that I shan't receive any payment for the assistance I've rendered him to date. He's still in Poitiers but intends to flee the country. If he remained, he'd spend the rest of his years in prison. Two of your brothers have already traveled as far as Metz. They may already have crossed the border into a German province."

"What of the others?"

He shrugged. "I've no idea."

"My entire family abandoned me. Why should we care what becomes of them? Let's be married, here and now. Or in the chapel at Château des Vignes. I've been making ready, with help from Princess Bathilde and her cousin. My dowry is nonexistent, but I remember everything the nuns taught me about managing a household. I'm able to cook simple dishes, and I'll learn to make better ones. If I take in fine sewing and embroidery, I can earn money."

"You don't understand." He looked down at his feet. "I've got debts of my own. An impoverished lawyer will never draw a respectable clientele. I haven't concealed from you that a rich marriage is a necessity. As much as it pains me to say so."

"What of your affection for me? The promises we exchanged? You can't dismiss them so easily."

Stiffly he replied, "I consider all verbal pledges to be nullified by your changed circumstances. Our situations are the same. I must seek a wealthy bride, and you a husband of means."

Myrte stepped back, nearly colliding with Bathilde. "Go, then. Find her."

"I am grieved and regretful. Most truly. Please believe that."

She turned away. "I don't care. And I cannot bear to look at you or listen to you any longer. *Adieu, monsieur.*"

Bathilde followed her friend from church to coach, her tears flowing like the rain. Myrte's eyes, wide and staring, were dry, but her entire body quivered as if stricken by palsy.

During their journey to the château, Bathilde could find no sufficiently consoling words for a young women steeped in sorrow.

She left Myrte by the fireplace, warming herself, and hastened upstairs to put away the bridal garments. She ached to see the altered gown and petticoat, and a pristine lace-trimmed chemise sewn in the belief that each precise stitch moved her friend ever closer to happiness. Carrying them to her own room she encountered Sophie, who expressed dismay but no surprise at what had occurred in Niort.

"Most unkind of him to jilt her in the church where she expected to be wed. Despite her poverty, she'll not long remain a spinster. Gentlemen of substance, having no need of money, place a high value on beauty and charm. Eventually we'll join your father in Paris and can take her with us, as your companion. It's a respectable position and a means of providing for her without damaging her pride. Later, you'll have opportunities to introduce her to worthy suitors. And titled ones." Sophie unknotted Bathilde's neckerchief. "Change into dry clothes and see that Mademoiselle Vernier does also. Where is she?"

"In the *salle basse*. I could tell she wished to be alone. Please don't mention Monsieur Lavigne."

"Henceforth, his name will never pass my lips."

"Nor mine," Bathilde vowed.

"You both missed dinner and must be hungry."

"I don't think she'll want food."

"She should have it anyway. We'll offer her something simple and sustaining. *Pain au fromage*."

They followed the passage to the place where Bathilde had left Myrte. No longer seated in the chair before the hearth, she was lying on the floor, unconscious.

Emerging from the chapel after a long session of praying to the saint for whom she'd been named, and many others, Bathilde went to kitchen to find out what was being prepared for the invalid.

Sophie was there, holding a woven basket filled with tiny eggs. "So many this morning. In these mild September days and nights, the doves are more productive than they were in springtime."

"Have you taken them all?"

"I didn't let the boy disturb any nests in the top tiers. Your father is fond of roast squab."

"Perhaps he'll host a hunting party like the ones he and Maman enjoyed. Having company might cheer Myrte."

"How is she this morning?"

"Stronger, I think. But bored, after weeks of being confined to her bed. She wants to go with me to watch the man who draws honey from the beehives. But only if the doctor says she can walk that far without gasping for breath."

The severe chill that struck Myrte on that rainy day in Niort had lasting and worrying effects. Although the physician didn't feel it necessary to visit as often as he had in the early days of her illness, today his expression was grave as she reported his findings to Bathilde and Sophie.

"If she suffers from consumption, as I believe," he told Bathilde and Sophie, "I cannot offer a cure. I recommend that you do all in your power to increase her stamina and improve her mood before winter sets in."

Wishing he could provide a remedy for a broken heart, Bathilde assisted her friend down the stairs and led her into the sunshine. Myrte immediately lifted a pale hand to shield her eyes from the bright light despite the hood hanging low over her forehead.

"Let's go into the wood, where it's shady," Bathilde suggested. As they traversed the *parterre*, she added, "If you walk a little farther each day, it won't be long before you'll be able to ride. The donkey is placid and easy to lead. And Lune's gait is quite smooth."

"My fingers are too weak to hold the reins. See how

they shake? I can't thread a needle, or sew a seam, or embroider a cloth."

"A temporary condition," Bathilde assured her.

"What became of my silvery gown?"

"I placed it in a clothespress for safekeeping."

"I want you to wear it. On your wedding day." Myrte hadn't mentioned matrimony since her tortured parting from Etienne Lavigne.

"The bodice is too roomy for me, and the skirt far too long."

"You can alter and hem it."

"When the time comes, you will do it for me."

Her companion drew a breath, as if to reply, but was seized by a coughing fit.

"Should we go in?"

Myrte shook her head. "I'd rather see the hives."

"The shortest way to the meadow goes through the woodland."

Horses' hooves and laborers' feet had worn smooth pathways that wound through the forest, branching off in different directions. To the cultivated fields of rye and barley, or to the village and its church, or to the vineyard where grape clusters ripened in the early autumn warmth.

Myrte halted. "Who whispers to us?"

"It's the leaves rustling."

The older girl studied the treetops before pointing out, "There's not the slightest breeze. It was a voice, I'm certain of it. There's another one!"

Bathilde stood still, listening.

"I'm not able to make out the words. Can you?" Myrte bent low to press a palm against the damp earth. "I feel their movement here. How active they are."

"Who?"

"The *samovili*. They're impatient for nightfall."

"We should turn back, before you swoon from the

heat." Bathilde reached down to touch Myrte's forehead, expecting it to feel feverish, but the flesh beneath her fingertips was cool.

"I'm so very cold. Aren't you?"

This reply alarmed her. "You mustn't get chilled again."

"I still hear them calling to me, but I don't know how to respond. I can't understand their strange language."

"You're overtired. We shouldn't have come so far." Bathilde hooked her arm through Myrte's. "Exertion has disordered your mind. Let's go to the music room, and I'll play a calming tune while you rest."

"Must we leave?" Myrte's tone was plaintive. "I like it here."

"Perhaps we can return tomorrow."

Myrte offered no resistance, letting Bathilde lead her away from the shadows and back into the light. Before they reached the portal in the curtain wall, she looked over her shoulder.

"I can't hear them any longer."

You never did, Bathilde thought. You imagined those voices.

In private, she told Sophie, "Myrte behaved oddly during our stroll, and her cough sounds much worse. I believe we ought to send for the physician again."

Myrte, calm and smiling, showed signs of somnolence during the second examination of the day. She made no protest when offered a vial of liquid, and obediently sipped from it.

Bathilde, waiting outside the chamber, described to the doctor what had occurred during the stroll through the forest.

"That must have been distressing for you," he said. "Mademoiselle Vernier suffers from a derangement common to her malady. This development is the clearest evidence yet that her condition is irreparable. You should prepare yourself for worse to come. The next stage of the disease will bring increasing lethargy, with significant loss of breath. As the lungs become more inflamed, her coughing will intensify and produce blood. Her constitution is greatly impaired, and the decline will be swift. Her demise will be peaceful."

Her eyelids flickered. "She's dying? That can't be possible. Before the summer, I never knew her to be ill. She's stronger than you realize, I'm sure of it. Haven't you some means of curing her ailment?"

"No longer," he said dolefully. "Her relatives should be apprised, as they will be wishful of seeing her again before she—" He cleared his throat. "I advise you to get a message to them. Without delay."

Papa hadn't communicated with Bathilde for weeks, not since informing her of the great victory he and Turenne had achieved at the Battle of Arras, against the troublesome and traitorous Prince de Condé and Spanish forces. When a letter came informing her of his inability to host a hunting party, citing his military duties, she had mixed feelings. She'd looked forward to his arrival and cherished a secret hope that the Marquis de Brénoville might accompany him. But bringing company into the house would be an inconvenience when her days and nights were entirely devoted to Myrte. Her introduction to her betrothed would not take place this autumn, and she must wait a while longer to find out whether he liked her portrait. She trusted that Monsieur Mesny had given it to his cousin last month, on his birthday, as promised.

Her harpsichord was moved from the *salle de musique* to Myrte's room because her tunes generally had a soothing effect. Down in the kitchen, the cook exerted himself to provide dishes that not only nourished, but pleased the palate of one whose appetite diminished with each passing day.

Waking from a long slumber, Myrte declared, "I despise him. He's responsible for my weakened state."

Bathilde look up from her book of devotions. "Dwelling on the past will only make you sad."

"Don't tell me what I shouldn't do," Myrte snapped. "If I wish to spend my last hours and final breaths cursing Etienne to perdition, I shall. He deserves it."

This wrathful pronouncement troubled Bathilde far more than the eerie calm that had preceded it. Wishing to distract her friend and soothe her roiling anger, she was relieved when Giselle Durand arrived with a basket of purple and green and golden grapes. The survival of game birds, rabbits, and deer was assured, but the usual seasonal activities proceeded. The vineyard workers were active from morning till dusk, the threshing had begun, children gathered fallen chestnuts, and youths with long sticks knocked down more from the towering trees.

"Uncle Pascal thought the sick lady would like to have these. Hilaire and I picked the nicest ones." The vineyard-keeper's niece glanced towards the fourposter bed. "It's a fine harvest. He says the summer rains caused no harm to the crop, and the last of it will soon be carried to the village. Will you and the prince attend the celebration?"

"He's with the army, but I shall be there. Have you heard who's being crowned queen of the vintage?"

The girl shrugged. "It's supposed to be a secret. If anybody knows, they aren't telling."

"One day your turn will come," she predicted.

"That's what Hilaire tells me. What an honor it would be—for me and my family."

"Who's come?" Myrte mumbled, struggling to sit.

"Giselle brought this luscious fruit for you." Bathilde carried the basket to the bedside. "Will you have some?"

"Later. When I'm able to swallow."

She placed the basket in view of the bed, hoping that the very sight might spur Myrte's flagging appetite. "Have you kept up with your reading?" she asked Giselle.

"Maman says learning is frivolity and a waste of time, when I could be at the spinning wheel or stirring the stewpot. Hilaire teases me when he catches me with the book on my lap. And Uncle Pascal needs my help with the grape-picking."

With weightier matters on her mind, Bathilde accepted the futility of her teaching project. "You owe all your obedience to your mother and your uncle. Colder weather is coming, perhaps then you'll have more leisure," she said absently, directing her attention to Myrte, who had slipped back against the pillows.

A letter arrived from Françoise, filled with entertaining descriptions of her life as a Parisian matron. Myrte, wan and listless, displayed no interest in accounts of carriage rides with Madame Fouquet or their promenades in the Luxembourg Gardens. Her gaze remained fixed upon the bed's canopy as Bathilde read out illustrious names of those who frequented the Scarrons' popular dinners, the dishes they were served, and their witty or scandalous utterances.

"All boasting and vanity," she commented. "She doesn't mention churchgoing or dispensing charity to those who lack her advantages."

"Consider all her past hardships and struggle. It's no wonder she revels in her good fortune."

"Given her husband's age and infirmities, she must already be choosing her next one. A nobleman, probably. Like yours."

To prevent Myrte from sinking deeper into depression, Bathilde asked, "Shall I play for you?"

"Not now. My head aches."

"Because you haven't eaten. Why not try one of the cordials Sophie prepared to ease your cough? She distilled this one from myrtle leaves. And here's juice of cherries stirred into brandy. Perhaps you should have both."

Myrte took a few sips of each liquid before returning the glass. "You're dressed for an outing."

"It's the last day of the grape harvest. I'm riding to the village, but I'll not stay long. I promise." She reached down to smooth her friend's cheek. The skin was nearly as colorless as the bedsheet and so wasted that the bones underneath protruded. Myrte's black hair streamed over the pillow, dull and tangled. When Bathilde returned, she would ask if she might comb it.

Pierre Jousson, the grandson of her *maître d'hôtel*, whose family members filled several household positions, served as her personal page. She found him with Lune, already saddled, waiting in the stable yard. The hounds in the kennel, aware of activity, responded with a chorus of barks.

"Shall I follow, princess?"

"That won't be necessary." She craved solitude.

Guiding her mount along the woodland path, she recalled Myrte's conviction that she'd heard the *vili* whispering to her. During their convent years, they often had joked about Amalie's superstitious belief in the spectral creatures who supposedly roamed in the night, vengefully pursuing any male unfortunate enough to encounter them.

From childhood they had been taught that the soul lived on beyond death and were told of the miracles performed by the saints. If those teachings were indeed true, wasn't it just as plausible that unquiet spirits might rise from the earth at midnight, and descend into it as daylight appeared? Or, she wondered, eyeing the squared steeple of the parish church and the graveyard, did she commit sin by considering the possibility?

Pascal's cart, laden with the last load of fruit, arrived from the vineyard, escorted by grape-gatherers. The forester's son Hilaire, impersonating the wine god Bacchus, was mounted on the donkey. His loose linen tunic hung low over his breeches, and his shaggy head was bound with yellowing grape leaves. As his neighbors cheered, he hoisted a tankard and drank from it.

Pascal approached a pretty young woman, the innkeeper's daughter, and crowned her with a wreath of vines and flowers and rye stalks, designating her harvest queen. Barrels of *pineau* were rolled from her father's tavern into the street, and the people lined up to fill their cups with the potent liquid. The fiddler struck up a tune, and Hilaire sought Giselle as his partner. Surrounded by their friends, they capered about, hands on hips as they hopped from one foot to the other, linking arms as they skipped together, then formed a circle with the other young people.

Their dance was entirely different than the ones Bathilde had learned. They moved so joyfully, with dizzying speed, unhampered by their lightweight garments. Watching, she envied them—and wished she could join in their fun. But she was unfamiliar with the simple steps and knew that none of those lively young men would approach and take her hand. Her status was too far above theirs, and she regarded them across a great chasm carved by centuries of feudalism.

Berthe Durand, Giselle's mother, offered a warm welcome. Women of all ages crowded around to speak to her or show off their offspring. Several older children took turns stroking Lune's muzzle.

"A toast to our princess!" Pascal cried.

Another one followed, honoring her absent father.

She accepted a flagon of *pineau,* returning it after a tentative, throat-searing sip. Realizing that at some point the parish priest had prudently retreated from an increasingly raucous celebration, she decided to make her way home. With a last glance at Giselle's merry face, she directed Lune out of the village and set out on the public road, choosing it over the forest path where Myrte had suffered the strange spell that marked the final stage of her illness.

Passing between the pillars at the entrance to her demesne, she spied the soaring towers, rising skyward. By far the dearest and most familiar of all de Sevreau possessions, she regarded it as her true home, cherishing it all the more in the knowledge that her residence was temporary. How many more harvest celebrations would she witness before Papa summoned her to Paris, to take her rightful place at court?

Pierre helped her dismount.

"After settling Lune in her stall, you and the grooms may go to the village. There's drink and dancing, and pretty damsels in need of partners."

She crossed the moat bridge and proceeded through the courtyard to the door that opened onto the *salle basse.* Spying the bowl of grapes on a table, she plucked one and squeezed it. The dusty skin was slightly firm, with just enough give to indicate perfect ripeness. Placing it in her mouth, she bit down, savoring its sweetness.

Footsteps sounded on the staircase, and she looked around. Sophie paused halfway down, clutching the rail.

"My dear child, Père André is here, preparing the items he needs to administer last rites. Before Myrte falls into a stupor."

Bathilde, her limbs frozen, pressed her palms against the table's solid surface. "Is her condition as bad as that?"

"An hour ago, a great agitation came upon her. She's thrashing about and cursing her lover. This is not my first deathbed vigil, and these are signs she has reached the critical period."

She hurried to the sickroom, praying that her friend would be alert enough to recognize her. The window curtains were drawn together, and the only light came from a branch of candles and the flames in the fireplace.

Myrte's dark head turned, and her dry lips moved to form a smile. "I begged them to let me remain until you returned. I wanted to see you again and bid you farewell before they take me away."

"I'm here," Bathilde murmured. "I'll not leave you."

With sudden fierceness, Myrte said, "We'll punish him for treating me cruelly. How you will suffer, Etienne Lavigne, for betraying me. When you plead for mercy, you'll receive none." She struggled to raise a fist. "I'll soon have the power to bring about your destruction. The *samovili* will help me do it."

Bathilde took up the ewer and dampened a cloth. Placing it over her friend's brow, she said, "This is a time for prayer. Père André is coming, you don't want him to hear you saying such things. Not while you wait on the very threshold of heaven." She pressed a rosary into the limp hand.

Myrte's body stilled. "I don't deserve to enter. Purgatory is my destination." Her fingers closed on Bathilde's wrist. "You will pray for me. Won't you?"

"Endlessly."

The portly priest entered the room and began laying out the elements for communion. He prompted Myrte to make a brief, whispered confession of sinfulness and granted absolution, making a cross in the air, and placed the host on her tongue. As he anointed her brow with the holy oil, she closed her eyes.

Without changing from her riding clothes, Bathilde sat by the bed, observing the erratic rise and fall of Myrte's chest as she labored to draw in air. The faint color receded from her parched lips, which gradually took on a blue tinge. With a final sobbing gasp, her struggle ended.

From another part of the house, a clock chimed the midnight hour.

With the female servants' help, Sophie shrouded the body before placing it in a simple wooden coffin sent over from the village carpenter. Footmen and grooms bore it downstairs to the chapel, where Bathilde and her cousin took turns keeping a prayerful vigil for the rest of the day and throughout the night. Because the Verniers had fled the district, she took it upon herself to make decisions about the burial, and she covered all the expenses.

Unwilling to consign Myrte to an unmarked pauper's grave, she asked Pascal and Hilaire to dig one close to the forest, in a remote and grassy section of the parish cemetery. After the interment, she paid the stonecutter for a cross, and with her own hands planted sweet-scented myrtle on one side and a *Quatre Saisons* rose on the other, to bloom in perpetuity.

She took comfort from these ways of serving and honoring her departed friend. A less pleasant duty awaited—clearing the clothes press of Myrte's belongings. She sent them to the Ursulines, with a message requesting prayers for their former pupil's soul. The plainer garments could be offered to the poor, and the elaborate ones could be picked apart so the rich fabrics and trimmings could be used to decorate ecclesiastical vestments like the ones Myrte had embroidered.

She directed a brief letter to Madame Vernier in Parthenhay.

Lastly, she wrote Françoise.

Taking up her quill, she dipped it into the ink, and formed three words. Her vision blurred as she stared down at the stark, black letters.

*Myrte est Morte.*

# Part II: Giselle

*1659-1660*

*Tant la mort sut pressée à prendre un corps si beau!*
*Et ces roses d'un jour qui couronnaient sa tête,*
*Qui sépanouissaient la veille en une fête,*
*Se fanèrent dans un tombeau.*

So much was death in a hurry to take on
such a beautiful body!
And those one-day roses that crowned her head,
That bloomed the night before in a *fête*,
Withered into a tomb.

—Victor Hugo, *Fantomes*

# CHAPTER 14

Françoise tipped the decanter towards Bathilde's glass to refill it. "Can you confirm that the king gave Marie Mancini a pearl necklace?"

"I've seen her wearing it. He purchased it from his aunt, the Queen of England, who needed the money more."

"Everyone says he's desperately in love, and eager to marry her. Even though her looks aren't much above average, and not at all the fashion."

"She's attractive in her own way," Bathilde replied. "He certainly finds her so. They're besotted with each other."

"No doubt the cardinal and the Queen Mother plan to remove her to a convent to get her away from the king," Françoise predicted. "If he weds the Spanish Infanta, she won't want his discarded sweetheart lingering at court. I'm not at all sure she'll welcome your presence either," she added with an arch look. "I've heard that you're his preferred dancing partner."

"When he's trying to avoid being paired with his cousin, Princess Henriette, who has achieved precedence

over all the noble ladies of the court," Bathilde acknowledged. "The death of the usurper Cromwell might enable
her brother to reclaim his realm, which improves her
chances of becoming Queen of France."

"If our king won't dance with her, he isn't likely to
marry her."

Bathilde put down her empty wineglass.

"Must you go?"

"One of His Majesty's physicians is visiting Papa
today. I need to hear what he says."

Françoise accompanied her to the door of the *salle*.
"I don't see enough of you." She kissed each of Bathilde's
cheeks. "You should come later in the day, when you'll
meet some of the most fascinating people in Paris."

"I will try. We have so many engagements elsewhere."

"At the Louvre, you mean." Françoise didn't bother
to conceal her envy.

"Justine, pray fetch my cloak and let the coachman
know I'm on my way down."

Her servant, waiting in the passage with Françoise's
maid, scurried away to do her bidding.

Thus far, Bathilde had visited the Scarron house in rue
Neuve-Saint-Louis in the morning, wary of mixing with
the scandalous folk who gathered there later in the day.
She sensed that Françoise cultivated her for her connection to the royal family rather than from true fondness.
Each visit to her friend's yellow salon resulted in an hour-
long interrogation about the king, his mother, his habits,
and lately, his thwarted romance with Marie Mancini.
It wasn't as though Françoise lacked credible sources of
information.

The Hôtel de Sevreau, situated in the Marais between
rue Saint Antoine and the River Seine, was one of several
mansions that replaced the gardens of the demolished
hôtel Saint-Pol, in rue Saint Paul. Outwardly less imposing

than grander residences nearby, its interior was lavishly adorned.

Exactly a year ago, in the Battle of the Dunes, Papa had received wounds serious enough to curtail his military career. But he wasn't missing out on any action, for Turenne's triumph over the enemy had persuaded the King of Spain to seek peace. Cardinal Mazarin was actively negotiating the terms. One expected outcome, a marital alliance between King Louis and his double-cousin, the Spanish Infanta, was his mother's most cherished desire. In private conversations with Bathilde, he expressed resignation if not enthusiasm about his eventual fate. He remained under the spell the bewitching Marie Mancini had cast but recognized his duty to his nation—and to his determined, devoted parent.

Because Bathilde's marriage didn't depend on diplomatic agreements or a papal dispensation, she expected to reach the altar before her royal friend. She, too, accepted the inevitability of marriage. Her protracted spinsterhood made her a frequent target of jests from his brother. Philippe, Petit Monsieur, hadn't outgrown his habit of mockery.

She found Papa in his library, his quill moving swiftly over a page of the manuscript recording his battlefield exploits.

"Sit by me," he invited her, "while I impart unhappy tidings."

"Has the physician been here?"

"Not yet. What I must tell you isn't about me, but it does affect you. The Duc de Rozel died a few weeks ago, in Normandy. His son writes his regrets at the necessary delay to your marriage. I shall pen a letter of condolence, in both our names. He's much occupied with necessary business and unable to join us in Paris at present. You must wait to gain the privilege of sitting in the Queen's presence, on the *tabouret* stool, like the other duchesses. And to become one of her *dames de compagnie.*"

A role that wouldn't suit her, although she refrained from declaring her reluctance. "My time with the Ursulines, and at the château, didn't prepare me for a position in Her Majesty's household. After all these months I'm still uneasy when we appear at the Louvre or the Palais Royal for grand celebrations and ballets and plays."

"You'll find Fontainebleau more to your liking, when we join the court there this summer. It has extensive gardens."

Papa was two years shy of fifty, but his graying hair and the whiteness of his short, neat chin whiskers added years to his true age. Although his health and physique had benefitted from years of army life, its more recent rigors had taken a toll. His face had lost the color imparted by hours spent in the saddle, and his stride was halting. A surgeon had successfully extricated a bullet from his side, but the leg broken by falling from his charger would never be perfectly straight or painless. Neither of these battle souvenirs concerned Bathilde as much as the fever that ebbed but inevitably returned.

She was excluded from the lengthy examination of her parent, conducted by *le premier médecin du roi*, but he was willing to discuss his conclusions with her. Monsieur Vallot's eyes were kind and wise, and he bore himself with a confident air.

"I find the prince in reasonably good form," he informed her, "considering what he has survived." He took a sip of the claret she served him. "A surgeon could re-set his leg. But it's not worth the danger of causing one or more bones to protrude through the wasted skin, for that could lead to gangrene. The area where the blade pierced his body has healed well enough."

"And what of the feverishness that comes upon him?" she asked.

"Ah. That is another matter."

"A serious one?"

"Let us hope not. Marsh fever is a remittent or periodic condition, an unwelcome and inconvenient souvenir of his service in the Spanish Netherlands, where the land lies so low and swampy. Apparently, the malady first struck your father while engaged in the Siege of Dunkirk, or during his recovery from his battle injuries. He described a similar ailment that prevails among his tenants in the Marais Poitevin."

"Our region is very wet." The ground couldn't adequately absorb all the water flowing into it from the Sèvre and many smaller rivers all around. Because of these conditions, ditching and dike-building were constant occupations. "Is there a cure?"

"None that I know. To reduce the symptoms when they occur, I recommend Jesuit's powder, ground from the bark of a tree that grows in Peru. Spanish missionaries learned of its efficacy from the native inhabitants. For years, quantities of it have been imported to Spain and France from South America. I credit it with preserving our king's life some months back, when a mysterious and very severe illness brought him close to death. I procure my supply from an apothecary brother, resident in a Jesuit community here in Paris. I'll send some to you, with instructions on how to administer it."

"I'm grateful to you. And to His Majesty, for your services. He knows how much my father regrets no longer fulfilling his responsibilities as a Marshal of France."

"Any accomplished soldier who has repeatedly experienced the dangers of battle is entitled to a peaceful retirement. I pray that the prince has many years left to enjoy his. I assure you I'll do what I can to make that possible."

If only, she thought, I could have discovered an antidote for Myrte's consumption, and a means of restoring her will to live, long enough for her shattered heart to mend.

Wilfride Mesny had no special attachment to Paris or to the royal court, but he was returning there from a château cast into mourning by its master's death. Like the countryside, the capital city looked its best arrayed in May colors. And his cousin could at last present himself to his promised bride and finalize the provisions of the marriage contract.

The past five years had done nothing to diminish Wilfride's memory of a winsome thirteen-year-old. He'd often thought of her, throughout various military campaigns, interspersed with brief stints in foreign courts. His responsibility for maintaining Albin's wardrobe and the security and transport of his possessions meant that he'd had constant access to the oval miniature. Surreptitiously studying the girl's supremely sweet countenance and hazel eyes, he recalled her concern that Albin might be prejudiced against persons with red hair.

Lacking a permanent lodging in the city, they took the very first one that satisfied Albin's requirements. The *appartement* consisted of two floors in a spacious house near the hôtel de Soissons, former residence of Marie de Medici. Conveniently close to the Louvre and the Palais-Royal, it had stabling for carriage horses and the ones coming from Normandy and a sleeping loft for the groom.

"It will do," Albin declared on completing his examination of the premises. "Drawing room, dining room, bedchambers, kitchen. The furnishings aren't the finest, but more comfortable than a requisitioned farmer's cottage or an encampment at the edge of a battlefield."

"True," Wilfride agreed. "What about servants?"

"A female to cook for us and clean. A biddable lad to stir the pots and perform scullery tasks. Perhaps a man to take on duties of valet and footman—help us dress, carry messages, and do whatever else we ask of him."

"A modest establishment," he observed. "For a duke."

"There's no point wasting money to put on a show, when all my acquaintances are aware of my circumstances. I know what I owe my name. And though I care very little for appearances, or expectations, I mean to uphold the Bertrand honor and dignity. Therefore, my friend, I ask that you locate a barber and bid him attend me in the morning. I can't present myself to the Prince de Coulon and his daughter looking like I crawled here from the Cotentin." Albin grabbed a fistful of shaggy brown hair.

"When do you go?"

"Tomorrow, if it suits their convenience. I'll send the groom to their *hôtel* to inquire." With a merry smile, Albin added, "Your cousinly support will be necessary when I embark on my terrifying excursion."

"You've naught to fear from the princess," Wilfride assured him.

The momentous day arrived. In the morning, Albin received a close shave and an inch was trimmed from his long, brown locks. That afternoon, he changed into a pristine white shirt with billowing sleeves and black breeches in the very latest style. He extended his arms so the manservant could help him into a stiff coat fashioned from gray silk. Wilfride, as meticulous in his preparations as the duke, wore plainer attire that was similarly new.

"These shoes cramp my feet. I dislike the color of the ribbons. And the heels are too high."

"Wear a different pair," Wilfride told him.

"That would spoil the effect." Albin set an elaborate hat on his head and reached for a pair of fawn-colored gloves, heavily embroidered. "The princess is friendly with Louis, who dresses very fine. And with Philippe, whose lavishness casts his brother—and all others—into the shade."

"If you assume she'll judge you by what you wear, you're mistaken. You're no monarch, or a prince of the blood. You haven't even been a duke for very long. She received her education in a convent school and spent her recent years in the Poitou countryside."

He'd rarely witnessed this self-consciousness in a man who was frequently the recipient of admiration and accolades. He regarded it as comforting evidence that Albin wanted his princess to like him. Not that he doubted she would. Young women always did.

"Ought I to take her a present? Will she expect one?" Albin removed his hat and fumbled with the amethyst pin that held its plume in place. "She could have this."

"Leave it."

Albin crossed to a table where he'd piled a dozen or more books he'd brought from Château Rozel. "Latin. Greek. Girls don't read ancient languages, do they? Ah, here's a volume of Ronsard's verses."

Wilfride remembered her dismay at receiving Albin's miniature because she had nothing to send him in return, until the completion of her own portrait. "You'll find plenty of occasions for gift-giving after you discover her tastes."

To protect their attire from street grime, they set off in the de Rozel coach, decrepit but serviceable.

Soon after they passed the ornate church spire of

Saint-Jacques-de-la-Boucherie, Albin spoke up. "I wonder if she's had a bout with the smallpox since you saw her. Her face could be scarred."

"If she'd suffered from a disease that dreadful, her father would have mentioned to you."

Which of us is more nervous, he wondered, Albin or me?

The footman who admitted them to the de Sevreau mansion in rue Saint Paul led them up a staircase and scratched at a paneled door. Opening it, he announced, "The Duc de Rozel. And Monsieur Mesny."

# CHAPTER 15

The Prince de Coulon greeted the cousins from his tall-backed chair. His weak leg was propped on a low stool. The two females, one young and the other above middle-age, stood at one of the tall windows.

Although Princess Bathilde's complexion was still fair and her lips rosy, she didn't quite resemble the girl who had entrusted Wilfride with the oval miniature he often examined. Her auburn hair was held in place by jeweled pins. She was slightly taller, a difference in height that could be explained by the satin shoes peeping from beneath her hem. The blue gown flattered her slender form. She wore a necklace of the palest sapphires mined by the Portuguese and the Dutch, and matching stones dangled from her ears.

At Albin's approach, she extended her hand. He kissed it, a politely formal gesture that might or might not carry a deeper meaning. This roused a peculiar sensation in Wilfride's breast, a mix of elation and envy. He wished he could see his cousin's face to read his expression.

Madame de Sevreau made a polite inquiry about their journey.

"The coast of Normandy is a great distance from

Paris," she said. "Farther away even than Château des Vignes, where we had the pleasure of receiving you."

"The marquis and I are accustomed to long journeys," he responded. "The duke, I should say."

Albin had moved to the prince's chair.

Aware that the princess had turned her attention to him, he managed to say, "I am happy to see you once more. And your father, whom we last saw before he received his injuries."

"In recent years, you and the duke have spent more time with him than I," she replied with a smile. "He hasn't admitted it, but I can tell he misses his soldiering days. Do you, Monsieur Mesny?"

"Not yet. Too many responsibilities to contend with at Château Rozel."

"Of course. My condolences on the loss of your relative. I regret that I shall never know him."

Albin returned, bearing a glass of wine for his betrothed. "Your father tells me Château des Vignes produced this vintage."

"It's well-aged," she responded. "Every year, cartloads of barrels come from the estate. There are stacks and stacks of them in the cellar. And *pineau* as well as wine."

"I can arrange for calvados to be delivered from my château, if the prince would like it."

"I'm sure he would."

"My vineyard is not as extensive as yours. We produce only enough wine for home consumption."

Wilfride hadn't imagined that their initial encounter would involve a dialogue about agriculture. In retrospect, he regretted advising against bringing the book of poems. It would probably have inaugurated a conversation more revealing of the couple's personalities. A literary discussion would be preferable to their stilted discourse about crops. He wondered whether he should have declined to come, because the princess graciously, generously granted him equal attention. Albin deserved the whole of it, and he none at all.

Their conversation had shifted to the ongoing peace negotiations between France and Spain. Albin referred to the proposed marital alliance between King Louis and the Infanta, assiduously promoted by the Queen Mother, at which point an awkward silence descended. His mention of matrimony seemed to discomfit the princess.

Madame de Sevreau intervened. "The king invited Bathilde to perform a duet with him in a concert tomorrow, in the Salle des Gardes. Would you care to accompany us?"

"With pleasure."

"Monsieur Mesny as well," the princess added.

"Monsieur Molière's troupe will give a command performance for the royal household. If you aren't otherwise engaged, and are willing, we'd be grateful to have your escort to that as well. I worry that two such events, very close together, will be too fatiguing for the prince."

"We would be honored," Albin replied smoothly. "Having experienced all manner of spectacles and operas and concerts in foreign lands, we welcome opportunities to sample the entertainments available here."

Princess Bathilde said, "After frequently being forced from the city by the Frondeur sieges and rebellions and disruptions, the king and his brother enjoy hosting and participating in plays and ballets." A flush colored her cheeks when she added, "Papa wishes to discuss important matters with you, *monseigneur.* I pray you will excuse us. We have a social engagement."

Albin's face fleetingly revealed his surprise. "Of course, princess." His brown eyes followed her as she took leave of her parent and followed Madame de Sevreau.

"Come near," the prince invited them. "And sit."

Wilfride positioned two chairs near their host.

"We meet again in very different circumstances. As far as I can tell, both of you survived our various skirmishes unscathed. As you see, I was less fortunate."

"Through our combined efforts, and those of many brave men, we achieved a considerable victory," Albin acknowledged. "Cardinal Mazarin will make treaty with our enemy. After years of warring, France and Spain will arrive at a stable peace. After—how long?"

"Decades. The fighting began when I was Bathilde's age, and long before either of you were born. I met her mother shortly before I entered the fray. By the time I marched into Germany, I'd become a father." Shaking his head, the older man declared, "I've regretted that my service to the late king kept me far from home and family, for extended periods. You embark upon matrimony at a promising time."

Albin smiled. "Negotiations between us will be easier and more amiably conducted than those of Mazarin and his Spanish counterpart."

"Indeed. Your father and I discussed the terms in a general way, but you will require specificity. I haven't yet instructed my lawyers to revise the initial draft of the marriage contract. First, I should hear your thoughts."

"I appreciate your consideration, but I've no intention of making demands. Nor am I in a position to do so. My inheritance is merely moderate."

"Upon marriage, your finances will undergo a significant transformation. Our de Sevreau fortune derives partly from my seigneurial properties, extensive and productive. Wine and wheat and wood at des Vignes, and much more of the same at Château Clément. *Fruits de la mer*—the mussels, langoustes, and fish taken from the waters near Esnandes—are mine by manorial right. Some of my farmers are intent on producing a new breed of cattle that can thrive in the marshy areas. The receipt of monetary rents is consistent, and most of the tenants are diligent in delivering my lawful share of their produce. However, as you know, there are years of fair harvests, and years of meagre ones."

Wilfride and Albin both nodded. A frigid winter, an excessively rainy spring, drought in summer—any or all of these in combination could have a detrimental impact on the livelihood of landowners, laborers, and the peasantry.

"If my ancestor from the royal House of Capet hadn't been illegitimate, I might be ruling France. The possessions I inherited provide an income that far exceeds my expenditures, and my principality is intact. Though my late wife had no estate of her own, she brought a large dowry which I've never needed to access. By preserving the greater portion of my wealth, I've been able to expand rather than decrease it. Though I live well, I eschew the pomp and display that drives any number of noblemen into debt—or to seek the largesse Monsieur Fouquet seems particularly eager to provide. For obvious reasons."

Albin nodded. "Purest altruism seems an unlikely motive. He seeks to gain power over them."

"My greatest treasure is my daughter," the prince continued. "During her childhood and the years with the Ursulines in Niort, she had very little understanding of her position, the duties associated with it, and the privileges it conveys. That's why I removed her from the convent when I did. Despite her youth, she has become a dedicated and experienced chatelaine."

"Having conversed with her, even for such a brief time, I'm not surprised to hear it."

"Her children will be Bertrands. Her eldest son will inherit your titles, not mine—unless the king desires that and makes it possible by writ. Therefore, as we settle matters between us, I mean to defer to your wishes. The sole exceptions being the amount granted to Bathilde for her personal use, and her widow's portion, should she outlive you. We need not restrict her ability to freely choose her own clothing and horses and jewels and gifts to others."

"You'll get no argument from me on that point."

"I didn't expect to," the prince said, smiling. "We shall require the services of *notaire* de Châtelet to draw up the contract according to Paris custom, after we've conferred about the complexities—the dowry and settlements and such. If you prefer that your estate should be divided in accordance with the legalities prevailing in Normandy, I won't object, though I believe they are less favorable to widows. I therefore intend to convey property at the time of the wedding. Château des Vignes will become yours, held jointly with Bathilde. And perhaps this house."

"You are most generous."

"In due course, you will both inherit Château Clément and the Poitiers residence. I have the right to designate my successor to the salaried court offices I hold, which I will gladly relinquish to you in my lifetime. If you'd rather not fulfill the duties, which are almost nonexistent, I advise you to sell the posts to other men and use the proceeds as you choose." He nodded his satisfaction with these plans, then said, "As for you, Monsieur Mesny, you also benefit from this alliance, do you not? When a master rises in the world, so does his—remind me, what exactly is your position?"

Before he could reply, Albin said, "Cousin, companion, comrade in arms."

"And *secrétaire*," he clarified, "as needed. Or *écuyer*."

"What a busy fellow."

"Only to the extent that Albin—the duke—requires me to be."

Albin thumped his shoulder. "Hard life, isn't it?"

Chuckling, they exchanged glances.

"And how are you related?"

"Our grandmothers were sisters," Albin explained. "Mine died years too soon. Wilfride's had a certain way of baking spiced apples that I greatly missed during my years in the Jesuits' school."

"My stomach will soon be grumbling," said the prince. He patted his doublet. "It already does. You must stay to dinner. We can continue our conversation over roasted pheasant and whatever dishes the ladies ordered to tempt my appetite."

Wilfride had to wait until they were jolting through the streets in a carriage with an uneven wheel to learn Albin's opinion of Princess Bathilde.

"When I received her portrait, I thought her a pretty creature. How long ago was that?"

Wilfride turned away from the carriage window. "Five years. Almost to the day."

"Quite unsettling, to discover that my future duchess is extremely lovely."

He stared. "You sound disappointed. I can't think why."

"There's a risk in having a wife who looks like that. Especially if she frequents the royal court and is singled out for particular attention by the king himself. Louis partners her in the dance. They play music together. They're riding companions."

"The same can be said about any of his mother's attendants and most of his female relatives. Princess Bathilde lives under her father's protection and has her cousin for a duenna."

"The trouble comes when the king takes a bride of

his own. It's a royal tradition, populating the palace with *dames de compagnie* admired by the monarch. Duchesses always top the list of candidates."

"If you have such scant faith in your lady's honor, it's to your discredit. What makes you think an innocent creature like that would ever betray you, with the king or someone else?"

"Nothing specific. Apart from her being a beauty." Albin leaned against the padded seat-back, frowning. "Who is too closely connected to the royal household for my comfort."

"Count your blessings," Wilfride replied. "You're betrothed to a charming, very attractive young woman, who will provide you with an enormous fortune and numerous estates."

"And, in time, heirs to all of it."

Wilfride had long avoided any thoughts of the inevitable result of the virile young duke's coupling with his delectable duchess. He couldn't let them intrude now.

Albin didn't fall in love with her today, he realized, shamefully aware of an emotion akin to relief.

And I did.

# CHAPTER 16

Françoise's question tumbled out the instant Bathilde and her cousin entered the crowded yellow sitting room. "What did you think of him?" she whispered and leaned in to hear the answer.

"I've not decided."

"I don't believe you."

"We spoke but briefly before I departed."

"I'm astonished you bothered to come at all," her friend declared. "How could you tear yourself away from a reputed paragon?"

Ever sensitive to her discomfort, Sophie interceded, saying, "Not only is the duke personable, he showed a proper sense of the occasion. Not overly reticent or restrained. Nor excessively familiar."

"How soon will you become Duchesse de Rozel?" Françoise inquired.

"It's probably being decided at this very moment. Papa prefers to have the ceremony in the cathedral in Poitiers, where he married my mother and where she's buried. With the archbishop presiding."

"Your duke is unlikely to object to that. Describe him."

Bathilde conjured her revised vision of her future

husband. "His hair and eyes are brown." And much darker than his portrait had suggested. "He has quite a noble profile. He dresses well, though less luxuriously than other courtiers."

"His manners are excellent," Sophie added.

"I wonder whether he's got a mistress."

Bathilde stiffened. "If he does, he's not likely to inform me."

"I can ask certain ladies who might know. Very discreetly, of course. Ninon de l'Enclos discovers all the intrigues in town, almost before they begin."

Sophie put a finger to her lips. "Pray do not stir up gossip about Bathilde and the duke. It's in poor taste and can be terribly destructive. They're barely acquainted."

Françoise, not at all abashed, replied, "I shall guard my tongue, Madame. I forget that after her months in Paris she hasn't yet adopted our sophisticated ways." She leveled her bright blue eyes at Bathilde. "When do you see him again?"

"Tomorrow, at the Louvre, where His Majesty and I are performing duets on guitar and harpsichord. The duke indicated that he'll accompany us to the next play at the Petit-Bourbon."

"I shall look for you there. I'm most eager to see him, and I always enjoy Molière's plays. His theatre occasionally presents my husband's works. And he comes to our salon, with that wraith of an actress who appears to be his current bedmate." Françoise changed the subject by saying, "I do envy you those gems. Are they sapphires? How clear and light they are."

Bathilde laid her fingers over her necklace. "They belonged to Myrte. She insisted that I keep her jewels."

"Poor creature."

Drawing their visit to a close, she and her cousin descended the staircase.

Sophie murmured, "What a motley crowd the Scarrons attract."

"All the most interesting people in Paris, Françoise claims." Bathilde, who regarded the court as dull and staid, was increasingly tempted to accept her friend's repeated invitation to attend nightly gatherings.

After exchanging words with the duke, she wondered about his response to their initial encounter. Was his view of her favorable, or had she failed to meet his expectations, whatever they might have been? She liked him well enough to hope they might become friends, as their acquaintance and familiarity increased. But she was wary of letting her own feelings become engaged to the point of vulnerability. After helplessly witnessing Myrte's anguish, she greatly feared the potency of romantic love.

"If ever you bestow your heart on another," King Louis said to Bathilde, "be prepared for suffering as well as elation." His fingers moved up and down the neck of his guitar, and he lightly plucked the strings to produce notes in a minor key. "Even if the object of your affection returns it in full measure."

Their rehearsal completed, they remained in the Salle des Gardes, conversing in low voices while palace servants arranged rows of chairs for the audience. Bathilde usually stood at the harpsichord, and had to familiarize herself with sitting before a keyboard set so much lower than she was accustomed to playing. She also felt dwarfed by the quartet of giant marble caryatids whose heads supported the musicians' gallery above.

The immense chamber intersected with the bedchambers and anterooms of the king and his mother. It had a long and storied history as the site for royal weddings and funerals of prior centuries and was also a venue for balls, ballets, and theatrical and musical performances. Bathilde's father remembered dancing with her mother beneath the high, barrel-vaulted stone ceiling.

"There's nothing I like more than playing my music," Louis went on, "or hearing Marie read from her Italian books. And riding with her and walking in the gardens. Cardinal Mazarin prefers that I attend dull meetings of the council, but all power and authority belong to him. After he makes up his mind on any matter of importance, he consults my mother, for form's sake. Only afterwards does he tell me of the decision. There's hardly any point in my being attentive to what's said by the ministers, or reading through the stacks of papers their secretaries produce."

His uncharacteristic antipathy towards the cardinal, she suspected, had more to do with resentment at criticism of his romance with his chief minister's niece.

"He doesn't yet know that I declined to wed the Princess of Savoy because I mean to marry Marie. I must declare my firm intentions soon, before he finalizes his plan to match me with Spain's Infanta. He has been a father to me, a tutor, an advisor. I won't believe he's cold-hearted enough to force me into marriage with a stranger and pitch me into everlasting unhappiness and regret. What's the use of being King of France if I can't marry the person I adore? Who adores me."

Bathilde had no answer to that question.

"Marie's tenderness towards me when I fell deathly ill last year was additional proof of her devotion. I'm twenty, no longer the child the cardinal and my mother raised together. I've led troops into battle. I rose from what was supposed to be my deathbed. I know my own mind. I shall be a better ruler with the wife of my choosing by my side. Her lack of dowry makes no difference to me, or her being an Italian. So was my grandmother—a de Medici noblewoman, not a princess. Yet she was deemed worthy of becoming Queen of France."

Many people, Bathilde knew, believed that the cardinal had imported his bevy of alluring nieces from their native land for the express purpose of temporarily ensnaring Louis, to draw him out of his shyness and provide harmless experience with females. If that had been his design, it succeeded all too well. Statuesque Olympe, the plainest of the sisters and the first to stir the young king's passions, reportedly shared his bed before her uncle married her off the Comte de Soissons. Volatile, black-eyed Marie, slightly more attractive, might have been destined for a nunnery. But her time at court softened her rough edges and refined her manners, and maturity improved her looks. The combination of her energy, her superior intelligence, and her fondness of music and literature sparked the king's interest, and over time, kindled his passion. Both were prone to extremes of emotion and wept together as often as they laughed.

"We must play well tonight, *ma chère*. I devised this concert for her pleasure." His voice drifted into silence. Abruptly waking from whatever dream had deprived him of speech, he went on, "And your performance is certain to delight de Rozel. How do you get on with my friend Albin?"

"We met for the first time yesterday."

"If he should be derelict in paying his attentions to you, let me know. I'll have words with him."

Amused by his regal insistence that he could command the duke to pay court to her, she said, "Please don't. He appears to be a proud and dignified gentleman." At this early stage of their acquaintance, she found that combination of qualities attractive and appealing.

"He'd better prove himself worthy of you. After

Marie, you are the lady most dear to me. It would be far harder to endure my present situation if you were not my confidante."

"Is not Signorina Mancini's affection sufficiently comforting?"

"Not as long as her wily uncle pursues the Spanish marriage. Like you, Marie is a rarity. She truly cares for me as a man—not as a monarch. Both of you are virtuous and honorable and selfless. And you share my interests. All the others seek my favor, and offer theirs, in hopes of obtaining a higher position or great riches. They're hardly better than the shameless strumpets who parade themselves in the street. I've expressly ordered that they be seized and confined to the Pitié-Salpêtrière hospice until they repent of their lewdness and immorality and swear to lead clean lives. Tempted as I am to do the same with certain ladies in this court, I accept the impossibility."

His declaration reminded her that at his birth, coming after years without a dauphin, he'd been referred to as Louis Dieudonné, the God-given heir to France's throne. Firm in faith, yet fallible despite his title and role, he clearly felt subordinate to Cardinal Mazarin. To claim Marie Mancini as his bride, he'd have to resist the constraints imposed by his minister and his mother, and rebel against both of them.

Their audience that evening included members and officers of the three royal households—the king's, his brother's, and the queen's. Cardinal Mazarin kept watchful black eyes on Marie Mancini and her lovelier young sister Hortense. Bathilde's father sat between Cousin Sophie and the Duc de Rozel, who had brought Monsieur Mesny. A wave of joy washed over her at the realization that her small family group had expanded. The gentlemen's presence gladdened her as much as it heightened her nervousness. The duke, in court dress, looked particularly imposing—and exceedingly handsome.

She and King Louis ran through their repertoire of tunes by French and Italian composers, making no detectable mistakes. When they finished, the king surprised her with an announcement.

"To honor Princess Bathilde, who generously participated in this collaboration, I offer a piece from the province most dear to her. The *Bransle de Poitou*."

She remained in her chair, her face growing warm from self-consciousness at being singled out in this way. While his fingers drew on the guitar strings, she forced herself to smile in appreciation.

A week later Bathilde returned to the Salles des Gardes for a performance by Monsieur Molière's players. Her chair was so close to the duke's that her bare shoulder, exposed by the low curve of her lace-edged bodice, brushed against the upper portion of his black velvet sleeve. A familiar fragrance emanated from the fabric, indicating that lavender had been used to ward off moths and mustiness. Aware that they received close scrutiny from the rest of the audience, she maintained an impassive face each time he addressed her and made sure to include Monsieur Mesny or Cousin Sophie in their conversation.

The troupe's first presentation, a short burlesque, featured the actor du Parc, better known as Gros René, whose bulk enhanced the humor in his broad depiction of a schoolboy. In Molière's farce *Le Médicin Volant*, its author took the role of Sganarelle, an impudent manservant. He agreed to impersonate a physician to assist his master's romance with a young woman who feigned illness to avoid a forced marriage to an older gentleman of her father's choosing.

His effective caricature of a medical man amused Bathilde. From her encounters with the doctors who treated Papa, she recognized the obvious self-regard and officious tones when making learned pronouncements and prescribing remedies.

On meeting his patient's concerned parent, he grasped the man's hand and felt for a pulse.

"It is my daughter who suffers, sir. Not I."

"No matter." Molière's mobile features took on a serious expression. "The blood of a father and his daughter are exactly the same. By the deterioration of your blood, I can know what malady affects your poor child."

This foolish declaration brought forth a high-pitched hoot from Philippe, the troupe's patron. Bathilde saw the king's shoulders shaking from mirth, and he exchanged a smile with Marie Mancini, seated beside him.

Sganarelle's ruse succeeded, and in the final scene the loving couple received permission to marry. Taking their bows, the seven players were rewarded with enthusiastic applause.

"I enjoyed that," Bathilde said.

The duke offered her a smile, saying, "A familiar situation, no doubt inspired by the Italian *commedia del'arte*. With the addition of uniquely clever dialogue."

King Louis left his gilded chair and approached them. Marie followed several respectful paces behind. As her large dark eyes settled on Bathilde, her expression lacked any sign of warmth or friendliness.

Jealous, she realized. Doesn't she know she has no cause to be?

"A diverting entertainment," the king commented. "If my brother pays his players by the laugh, they will receive a heavy purse for this night's work. De Rozel, my felicitations on your betrothal to the princess, whom I hold in the highest regard. She is too modest to tell you so, but it's true. On the next fine day, Signorina Mancini and I shall ride out to Vincennes to inspect the creatures in the menagerie Monsieur Colbert has established for me. I invite both of you to accompany us."

Bathilde looked to the duke to judge his reaction. His expression revealed nothing.

"My riding horses haven't yet arrived from Normandy," he replied.

"You may choose any of the mounts in my *écurie*. Princess Bathilde has a favorite, I know. A gray, somewhat larger than the one I taught her to ride in Poitiers. Nine years ago, when the Frondeurs were running rampant through this city."

"I'm content to do whatever pleases the princess," the duke declared. "And satisfies Your Majesty."

"Excellent. We will ride together again, with companions more charming than we had when leading our troops into battle."

The duke inclined his head.

Bathilde sensed his unstated reluctance to join in the excursion. Accepting the king's invitation meant going against her betrothed's inclination. Unable to decline, she hoped she'd never again feel trapped between these two opposing forces.

# CHAPTER 17

*November, 1659*

"So, poor Marie Mancini has been banished from the court. Is it true she received a spaniel puppy as a parting gift?"

"With a silver collar identifying her as his mistress. The king showed it to me."

"The puppy's mistress, or His Majesty's?"

"His love for her is pure. He intended to wed her."

"I heard she received more jewelry."

"The de Medici pearl earrings the Queen of England used to wear before Cardinal Mazarin purchased them from her. Now his niece possesses them."

"And the monarch's heart, not that it does her any good. Let us hope her disappointment doesn't affect her as fatally as Myrte Vernier's did."

This remark stirred the ache that recurred whenever Bathilde heard her dear friend's name. "Signorina Mancini's prospects are far better. Her uncle will see to it that she has a dowry large enough to ensure a brilliant marriage."

Throughout the summer, the Queen Mother and Cardinal Mazarin had conspired to part the lovers, successfully persuading Louis to renounce his Italian inamorata. Sacrificing his happiness, he'd fulfilled his mother's and his minister's great plan to bring two antagonistic nations together as allies through the Treaty of the Pyrenees. Having accepted his unwelcome destiny, he set out on a tour of his realm, stopping in distant provinces and cities as he made his way to the border of Spain, where he would marry the Infanta Maria Theresa.

"You never bring your duke to our dinners," her friend continued. "As I don't attend royal functions, I despair of ever seeing the pair of you together."

"You shall, if you attend the next performance at the Petit-Bourbon theatre."

"Catherine de Brie has a significant role. She was telling me about it before you arrived. But she was strangely secretive and wouldn't reveal details of the plot."

Leaving Sophie to deal with Françoise, who was particularly annoying today, Bathilde chose to seek out the actress, regaling several ladies with tales of the mishaps she'd suffered as a performer in provincial towns.

"We were never sure," the young woman concluded, "whether city officials would welcome us or bar our entry." Turning towards Bathilde, she curtsied and said, "An honor to have you in our midst, princess."

"You've been missed by the audiences during the weeks before and after your confinement."

"I delivered my daughter a month ago. As my figure improves, my portrayal of young virgins won't appear quite as improbable as it did prior to her arrival. When I return to the stage in our new comedy, I shall be very tightly laced."

"Is this one of Monsieur Molière's devising, or by a different author?"

"His." In a confidential tone, the actress added, "It's

quite a novelty, and the title alone might provoke contro-
versy in certain circles. This very one, in fact."

"You intrigue me. Let us sit together, and I shall try
and pry it out of you," she said, moving to a yellow-up-
holstered settee in the alcove, safely beyond the chattering
circle gathered around the vivacious Madame Fouquet.

"The piece is a satire," Catherine de Brie explained.
"Two young ladies from the provinces seek to establish
themselves in Paris, intending to pass as the sort of clever,
witty, amoral females who congregate here. By coming
to Madame Scarron's, I'm able to study the type I will
portray in *Les Précieuses Ridicules*. I worry that these
fashionable creatures might recognize themselves as the
objects of Jean-Baptiste's mockery. He aspires to amuse,
not to anger, but could suffer by offending persons of
prestige and power."

"None will dare to express displeasure if his new
work finds favor with the audience."

"The possession of a Paris theatre and royal patronage
may well require Jean-Baptiste to moderate his barbs."

"Not too much, I hope, or his comedies would lose
much of their appeal." Dropping her voice, Bathilde
added, "The nuns instructed us never to flaunt our learning. The *précieuses* I've encountered take themselves so
seriously that I understand why Monsieur Molière is
tempted to hold them up to ridicule."

"Their notions of romantic love are high-minded and
pristine, unsullied by the agonies of unrequited affection
or the vagaries of the human heart."

The discontent underlying this comment raised doubts
about the nature of the de Bries' marriage. It belied her
assumption that commoners, unlike young women of the
aristocracy, were free to choose a spouse based on mutual
attraction and compatibility.

"I became a wife out of love—but not for my husband.

I followed my parents' profession—they were players—and when I joined Jean-Baptiste's company, I was blind to the danger he posed. After his parting from Madéleine Béjart, he mooned over Mademoiselle du Parc, too intent on attracting a rich lover to welcome the devotion of a struggling player-manager. He sought consolation from me, and I willingly provided it. But I'm no fool. I made a pragmatic decision in accepting Edmé's marriage proposal. He's more than twenty years my senior, but as his wife I acquired the semblance of respectability. And he secured his place in our company by wedding the manager's favorite. He doesn't berate me, not much, if Jean-Baptiste seeks to—to be with me."

Bathilde pitied this woman, loving a man who used her for his pleasure, wed to another who used her as a shield against professional failure.

I couldn't accept that situation so rationally, she reflected. But I'm unacquainted with passion, and the physical intimacies that women and men enjoy.

Not that Sophie had withheld information. She'd calmly described what took place in the marriage bed, which sounded equally exciting and terrifying. The novels Bathilde read and the plays she'd seen presented violent, unconquerable emotions experienced by lovers either temporal or mythological. Françoise's association with her fashionable guests had made her just as fluent in gossip as they were. She always knew which lady was mistress to which gentleman, and who sought a new paramour. But despite the ring on her finger, she remained a virgin, the untouched wife of a man too deformed to consummate their union. Whether she regarded her purity as a burden or a relief, she didn't say. Her modest and unadorned gowns were not as revealing as those of her salon visitors but didn't prevent gentlemen from ogling her and flirting.

Monsieur Molière's troupe had established itself in the *grande salle* of the Petit-Bourbon, a former palace adjacent the Louvre. In years past a venue for court masques and tournaments, it was the site of the famous *Ballet de la Nuit,* staged in celebration of Cardinal Mazarin's return and the final defeat of the Frondeur rebels. King Louis had shown Bathilde a gleaming gold costume he'd worn to personify Apollo the Sun God, and gave her a detailed description of the elaborate sets and stage machinery.

Members of the bourgeoisie had crammed into the *parterre* below, and aristocratic ladies and their spouses—or lovers—filled the *loges* that ran along three sides of the theatre. A few had claimed chairs at the sides of the stage. Bathilde and the Duc de Rozel, accompanied by her cousin and his, occupied seats in the first raised tier. Either the manager himself, his players, or their partisans had spread the word about the debut of a fresh farce, because Pierre Corneille's familiar, outworn tragedy would not otherwise draw this large a crowd.

*Cinna* was set in Rome during the rule of Augustus Caesar. In high-flown verse, the title character promised his beloved Emilie, daughter of a man recently executed, that he would avenge her loss by assassinating the emperor. After learning of the plot against him, Augustus pardoned Cinna and spared his life. His offer of clemency and rewards to the conspirators, and the young lovers' joyful reunion, drew tears from the most hardened cynics in the audience.

"An affecting conclusion," Sophie sighed, pressing her handkerchief to her eyes.

Unable to speak past the lump in her throat, Bathilde nodded.

The duke commented wryly, "I was mistaken in my

belief that there could be a final scene as incomprehensible, or as unlikely, as the one in Corneille's *Le Cid*. Obviously, the same author penned this piece in homage to our king. It presents a powerful ruler surrounded by enemies and traitors, who treats them with magnanimity and benevolence."

"You sound as though you disliked it."

He turned brown eyes upon her. "To begin with, the princess declares her love for a man of lower status. She then tries to marry him to another in hopes of eradicating her own affection for him. Highly improbable. The substitute lady, already enamored of the commoner hero, spurns a nobleman's courtship. Absurd."

Softly laughing, Bathilde said, "Never fear, *monseigneur*. I'll not reject your suit in favor of an inferior."

"I'm vastly relieved. But what if a certain superior should become my rival? Unlike Rodrigue in *Le Cid*, I'd not be able to avenge my honor by challenging him to a duel. I'd risk being marched into the Bastille."

"It seems you've got someone in mind," she said, focused on his finely chiseled profile. "May I know who?"

"I'd best not say. In case I'm mistaken."

"Assuredly, you are." She averted her face, lips pressed firmly together. Had her acquaintances, or strangers, been gossiping about her? She'd given them no reason to do so.

Studying the rows of aristocratic faces in the opposite tier, and the ones at the back, some of them heavily coated with *maquillage,* she wondered why anyone would stir up false stories about her—and whom? At the Scarrons' salon, she seldom strayed far from Sophie's side. Whenever a gentleman approached, she behaved circumspectly. Her reputation, if she had one, was that of a convent-bred provincial, living with her invalid father, visiting her married friend, and attending court functions at the king's invitation.

Servants rushed about the stage, positioning house-hold furniture—chairs, footstools, tables, and a folding screen. Lastly, they added the statue of a classical figure, apparently made of plaster rather than stone, for they carried it effortlessly.

Monsieur Molière advanced to address the audience.

"Our humble troupe is flattered by your reception of a renowned author's great tragedy. We are now embold-ened to offer an original work, which, if it meets with approval, will later be performed for the amusement of our monarch, the greatest in power and prestige that this world has ever known. And for Monsieur, our esteemed patron. We poor players ask only that you good people excuse any perceived defects in *Les Précieuses Ridicules,* recently written and rehearsed."

His listeners expressed approval of this preface by loudly applauding as he retreated to the wings.

Two actors, Du Croisy and La Grange, sauntered onto to the stage, complaining to their host about the treatment they received from the pretentious young ladies they courted. After their exit, Madeleine Béjart and Catherine de Brie entered as cousins. These overdressed *précieuses* derided their visitors for proposing to them without demonstrating the gallantry and courtliness they expected from Parisian suitors. Their opinions of court-ship were obviously influenced by Madame de Scudéry's novels, and they referenced heroes and heroines from her popular romances *Artamène* and *Clélie,* familiar to every female in the audience, and some of the gentlemen.

Béjart, as Madelon, tossed her head and said to her parent, "Marriage shouldn't take place unless the lover has expressed beautiful sentiments, sweetly and tenderly and passionately. He develops a passion for a lady he meets at church, or while promenading, or in her father's house, but carefully conceals it from her. When at last he declares his love, he does it in private. On a secluded garden path."

The duke whispered to Bathilde, "I must remember this."

She was startled by an involuntary shiver of anticipation. The possibility of hearing him express affection for her, in any setting, was gratifying. Though also unsettling.

"The maiden becomes angry," the actress went on. "She blushes. She dismisses him. Eventually he draws from her a similar confession. Their fathers find out and are furious. Masquerades and kidnappings result. Such rules cannot be ignored. To offer marriage without following them is simply vulgar."

Her comment drew titters from the ladies and bellowing laughter from their male escorts.

Catherine de Brie stepped forward to tell their uncle, "Indeed, my cousin states the truth. Those gentlemen came to us in hats without plumes, and no ribbons decorating their clothes. Their frugality and lack of fashion is disgusting."

When their guardian accused them of folly, his use of their baptismal names offended them. After they expressed their desire to choose new ones, he exploded with rage, vowing they if they failed to accept their suitors, he would send them to a convent.

The moment he stormed off, Madelon declared, "I cannot be *his* daughter. Someday I shall discover myself to have been born into a far more illustrious family."

The spectators responded to Monsieur Molière's satire with glee. Yet most of them, Bathilde reflected, were as affected as the two female characters and no less preoccupied with the appearance of tastefulness.

The playwright was carried onto the stage in a sedan chair. Ostentatiously plumed and ruffled and beribboned, he presented himself as a marquis. An entranced Madelon sought to impress him with her supposed knowledge of high society, the literary arts, and music. She accepted his boasts at face value, until he declared he was capable of composing tunes despite never having been taught any notes.

"How is that possible?"

"Oh, people of quality know everything, without ever having learned anything."

The actress waited for the laughter flowing from the balconies and the *parterre* to subside, then said knowingly, "But of course." And the audience laughed all the more.

The marquis pointed out the intricacies of his attire, insisting that they sniff his scented gloves and perfumed wig. The ladies' servant interrupted his raptures to announce the arrival of another nobleman—a *vicomte*, their visitor's closest friend. The marquis hailed him as a courtier and valiant comrade-in-arms. The gentlemen proceeded to detail their war wounds and battle scars. The talk turned once more to literature, and the marquis stated his intention of writing a poem.

Regretfully, the vicomte said, "I wish I might do the same. However, my poetic veins are depleted from the massive bloodletting I've lately undergone."

Bathilde held her hand over her mouth to prevent an immature burst of giggling.

Musicians and neighbors were called forth to participate in an impromptu ball. The return of the two suitors cut the revelry short, and they struck the noblemen with their canes.

"What's the meaning of this?" Madelon asked, outraged.

"So, ladies," La Grange retorted, "you receive our servants more warmly than you did us. And encourage them to make love to you at our expense."

"Your *servants*?"

The pair of *précieuses* moaned about being victims

of deliberate deception, prompting the uncle to bellow, "Ridiculous creatures, your folly and idleness and extravagance will bring even more mockery upon us. Those pernicious amusements—your novels and ditties and songs and sonnets—I wish them all at the devil!"

The closing speech prompted foot stomping and cane banging powerful enough to shake the floorboards. Bathilde winced at the noise.

"Most amusing," her cousin commented as the comedians took their bows. "Though the tragedy's formal language is more to my liking."

"Why, Sophie, are you a sentimental *précieuse?*" she jested.

"You know perfectly well that I am not."

"Myrte would have enjoyed the farce, and Monsieur Molière's jests." Turning to the duke, Bathilde told him, "My dearest friend, from my very first day at the Ursuline school. She didn't share her wealthy merchant family's ambitions or her mother's condescension. If she'd come with us to Paris, she would have relished the playwright's disdain for the *salonnières* and *précieuses.*"

"Did she not accept your invitation?"

Sophie answered for her. "Mademoiselle Vernier died of consumption."

"And heartbreak," Bathilde added. "After her father lost his fortune and her dowry, the lawyer she wanted to marry abandoned her."

"A lovely girl," her cousin added reminiscently. "Hair like a raven's wing, and the bluest of eyes."

She fell silent, recalling her friend's misery in her final days, and the solemn burial that had taken place five years ago in grape-picking season. Which girl had been designated this season's harvest queen? Giselle Durand, perhaps. At sixteen, she was exactly the age for it—unless she'd already wed her young swain Hilaire, the forester's son. Bathilde had entrusted her with the care of the rose bush and myrtle growing beside Myrte's grave. She resolved to pen a brief, friendly letter to the girl she'd taught to read, although she wouldn't receive a reply. Her lively pupil had always been too busy—or disinterested—for writing lessons.

Deprived of Myrte, she wished for a sympathetic someone with whom to share her qualms about marrying a man who had chosen her for her fortune and because of the longstanding friendship between her father and his. Pragmatic Sophie might not fully understand. Françoise, who had married solely to obtain her freedom from Madame Neuillant, was now too worldly to sympathize. Besides, her parlor was a haven for those who traded in gossip. Bathilde carefully guarded her secrets and withheld her opinions when visiting the Scarrons' dwelling.

In the six months that she'd known the duke, he had been unfailingly polite and appropriately attentive. When she and Papa and Sophie had passed the summer at the royal Château de Fontainebleau, he'd occasionally visited her there. Her most frequent dancing partner and riding companion, he'd pleased her by loaning several texts on such sober subjects as history and religion and willingly discussed them with her. She ought to find contentment in his friendship, yet she couldn't quite vanquish a hope of it developing into something more. One day.

With a glance at Monsieur Mesny, she asked, "What did you think of the new comedy?"

"I see it as a warning to all who serve the whims of a nobleman. I would never dare to assume my master's identity and title."

"Nor can I imagine any situation that might prompt me to surrender them," the duke responded, with a smile.

# CHAPTER 18

Albin's opinion of Paul Scarron was low, and neither the author nor his literary friends drew him to the celebrated *appartement* in the house on the rue Neuve-Saint-Louis. Wilfride knew he'd come in hopes of finding Princess Bathilde. They both had.

She was resplendent in a purple velvet gown, the rich material cascading from her narrow waist and overlaying a lavender underskirt. The single plume on her flat cap was attached with Albin's amethyst pin, which he'd given to her during Christmas. The long feather curved down around her exposed ear and trembled when she nodded in acknowledgement of whatever Madame Scarron had said to her. Soft candlelight lent her smooth cheek a creamy quality and drew out the russet color of her hair.

He forced himself to look away.

In another part of the room, Monsieur Molière exchanged *bon mots* with their host. To gaze at Scarron was to confront a creature so monstrously deformed that he scarcely looked human. His oversized head hung permanently to one side, and the emaciated, twisted body had to be tied to his wheeled chair to keep it from sliding to the floor. He could move only one arm and used its claw-like hand to wield his pen and cutlery and hold a glass to his lips. Scarron's chest, compressed by his angular frame, struggled to draw breath. But for all that, he was a merry fellow, flinging quips and quaffing his wine.

His young wife regarded Albin with the same admiring expression Wilfride had seen on countless female faces—though never on Princess Bathilde's. His cousin dressed well, his manners were impeccable, and he excelled at saying exactly the right thing at the right time.

Wilfride was the only person present who knew certain truths about him. Albin was a reluctant bearer of his father's title. He grumbled at the necessity of putting on finery for peacocking, as he called it, at court. He spent his leisure hours reviewing his diary of the past several years with the intention of producing a memoir of his military experiences. Not out of vanity, but for sons and grandsons who might someday read it, and perhaps make use of all he'd learned from soldiering.

When prompted, he acknowledged his good fortune in obtaining the hand of the exquisitely lovely princess, whose refinement and intelligence were revealed in her every utterance. He praised her as a fine dancer and a talented harpsichordist and admired her skill as an equestrienne.

Wilfride, deeply and desperately in thrall to the future Duchesse de Rozel, kept his feelings to himself. Until now, the courtly love traditions of past generations and the concept of adoration without reward had seemed pointless and pitiable. Suffering in secret, he hoped—and expected—that an alliance forged from one party's need of fortune and property, and the dictate of the other's parent, would develop into one of mutual affection.

Paul Scarron tapped a fork against his wineglass, commanding silence. "Let us hear the latest verses our friends have produced for this Feast of Saint Valentine. Rhymed quatrains, sonnets, pastorals, or odes."

Monsieur Molière stepped forward and from memory recited a love poem to a lady he addressed as Cathos.

The actress Catherine de Brie, standing beside Wilfride, ducked her head. Her cheeks were pink, and a flush had spread across her thin chest.

The playwright surrendered his place to a youthful vicomte, whose hands shook as he held up the paper on which his verses were written. He swallowed twice before announcing shakily, "For my first public reading of my work, I beg your indulgence." In a tight, nervous voice, he proceeded with his composition.

From the first stanza, Wilfride recognized Princess Bathilde as the subject. Other heads turned in her direction as the poet identified his subject as a daughter of a heroic *maréchal*. Her beatific smiles were more intoxicating than the wine of a princely vineyard. A beloved child of the muses, she delighted all who heard her music-making and witnessed her gracefulness in the dance. A beauty with hair glossier than satin and eyes that shone like gemstones.

Relieved by the polite applause, the author bowed first to the company, then to the inspiration for his every simile and metaphor.

"Who shall be next?" Scarron inquired. "Come forward, Boileau. Let us judge the fruit of your labors to determine whether you, like your brother Gilles, deserve a place in the *Académie Française.*"

The young gentleman, very plainly dressed, intoned, "In Celebration of a Court Beauty."

Each of the ladies in the salon eyed him attentively, as though in expectation that she might be the subject.

*"I can no more my muse constrain,*
*Conceal my thoughts, or hide my pain.*
*No hope of favor, or of fame,*
*Commands the praise that I proclaim.*
*When I behold thy glorious face,*
*I sigh at having lost the race,*
*To call thee mine and claim thy heart,*
*And curse the aim of Cupid's dart."*

Facing the princess, he bowed low.

Albin's frown told Wilfride that these lyrical tributes found no favor with him.

Before their host could call for another presentation, a man stood up and waved a scroll bound by a red ribbon.

"You, Lully?" Scarron said in surprise. "I didn't guess your gifts had taken a poetic turn."

The king's musician, a Florentine, approached Princess Bathilde. Kneeling, he said in Italian-accented French, "Your expertise on the harpsichord compelled me to compose this sonata for the keyboard. Although *Le Tendre Coeur* is my creation, His Majesty pays my salary and also deserves recognition as a giver."

His remark drew laughter.

Accepting the roll of paper, the princess thanked him.

In silken tones, Madame Scarron told her, "On another occasion you must perform it for us. My friends, supper is laid out in the dining room. Scarron will lead us, if one of you will be kind enough to push his chair."

Wilfride suspected her of curtailing the entertainment out of jealousy, and from concern that no flowery tributes to her charms were forthcoming. During the accolades offered to the princess, her forced, false smile proved that praise of another female, even a friend of many years, dented her pride. Gentlemen visitors were obviously expected to extol Madame's charms more than those of her guests.

To the princess, she said, "The gentlemen set you on a pedestal and exalt you because you are a wealthy aristocrat. As a married *bourgeoise* of limited means, I'm regarded as a prospective mistress. I could identify several men here who wish to provide my husband with an heir not of his making. Which would be certain evidence of my infidelity, for everyone is aware of how limiting his infirmities are."

"Françoise, you know better than anyone that romantic recitations like that are part of a social game. My betrothal is known to all. Before year's end, I'll be married."

"And after you become a duchess, you can expect an even greater tide of poetic effusions. Come, Madame de Sevreau. Bathilde."

But the princess didn't join the group pouring into the dining room. She un-scrolled her music and carried it to a sconce on the wall.

Striving for lightness, Wilfride asked Albin, "How does it feel to be so envied?"

"Poor Boileau. The inanity of his verses surprised me. I'm a great admirer of his brother."

"Whose translation of Epictetus," said the princess, looking up from Lully's score, "is excellent. The younger Monsieur Boileau's rhyming couplets were simplistic, I agree. But he meant well. As did the others."

Accepting this as a rebuke, Albin replied, "Their recognition of your qualities does them credit, of course."

To smooth troubled waters, Wilfride said, "The gentlemen would eagerly exchange places with you, Albin, if they could. And Princess Bathilde, every lady longs to be the recipient of such laudatory verses."

"But I do not," she replied, with a sharpness he'd

never heard. "I come to see my friend, Madame Scarron, and because Cousin Sophie enjoys the wit and word play. I do not compete with the *salonnières* for attention, either in dress or in speech or with written words. I would rather read books and see plays that appeal to my own tastes, not those that are temporarily the fashion. Though I admire the royal gardens, each time I stroll along *allées* of the Jardin du Luxembourg or at Fontainebleau, I wonder how my own plants are faring. And the mud of Paris carries a stench, which that of Poitou does not."

She resumed her study of Lully's composition.

Albin stared as if seeing her for the first time.

"Why did the *notaire* spend the entire afternoon with you?" Bathilde asked her father.

"We were completing revisions to my will."

"Should I send for Monsieur Vallot? Are you feeling unwell?"

"Not at all. His fever powder is effective. And though this frigid weather worsens the ache in my mangled leg, I can alleviate the pain somewhat by siting near the fire. I'm not dying from these inconvenient maladies. I simply decided to make a necessary alteration to the document."

"If you've disinherited me, the Duc de Rozel will be disappointed. And quite cross."

"I should think you would be also."

She stroked the top of his head. "It would make me wonder what I'd done to displease you."

"Your inheritance isn't affected in any way, I assure you. One detail has troubled me. The late Duc de Rozel and I agreed that if I should die before your twenty-fifth birthday, he would serve as your guardian for as long as you remained unwed."

"But I won't be. His son will be my husband."

"Nevertheless, as a contingency, I chose to designate the king as your guardian—with his permission. Fear not, I don't mean to expire before your wedding day. I have every intention of being present." He reached for her hand and held it to his whiskered cheek. "I look forward to seeing you become a duchess in Poitiers cathedral, where your mother and I spoke our vows."

"There's no better omen for my future happiness."

Speaking those hopeful words, she wanted to believe they were true.

# CHAPTER 19

*Saint-Jean-de-Luz, May, 1660*

Somewhere on the frontier between Toulouse and the town where the king's union with the Infanta Maria Theresa would be sanctified and consummated, Bathilde was able to define the peculiar, unfamiliar emotion that had blossomed after leaving Paris. It was accompanied by the fear that a word or glance might lead the Duc de Rozel to interpret feelings that he might not want her to have.

For years he and Papa had battled the Spanish, and both were determined to witness the royal marriage that would solemnize and secure a peace. Before departing for the border, Bathilde consulted Monsieur Vallot, more concerned about possible harm to her parent's health than the latest postponement of her own wedding day. The physician advised his patient not to overtire himself and never to take a step without the support of a strong cane. He also provided an ample supply of Jesuit's powder. The onset of mild spring weather, he added, ensured smoother roads and few delays.

To further ease her concerns, Papa purchased a grand and luxurious new coach. Lined with dark blue velvet, its

spacious interior could accommodate four people comfortably, and there was a padded footrest to support his
weak leg. On a sunny morning, they boarded it, accompanied by Sophie and the duke. Monsieur Mesny, Justine
the maid, and Pierre the page—temporarily elevated to
role of valet—rode in the duke's carriage, which also
carried their baggage.

A journey of several weeks, it transpired, was an
excellent means of establishing a relationship with one's
future spouse and obtaining knowledge of his personality
and preferences. Bathilde discovered that the duke wrote
in a diary every day. He tended to be silent in the morning
and talkative in the evening. He preferred certain foods
but uttered no complaint on being served something he
liked less. He relished wine and brandy, and sampled the
varieties that prevailed in the places where they lodged
for the night. Before bedtime, in a low and sonorous
voice, he led the household in evening prayers. Bathilde,
kneeling between Papa and Sophie, tried to focus on the
words and not the dark brown head bent over the well-
worn missal.

From the time they joined the king at Avignon, they
attended nightly banquets and balls. The duke's adequacy
as a dancing partner grew into proficiency, until his
talent nearly equaled that of His Majesty and Monsieur.
Whenever their hands joined, his grasp was firm and
reassuring. Although he was no musician, as she was, he
timed his steps perfectly with the tune. And his way of
gazing back at her, when the dance required them to face
each other, brought a flush to her cheeks and trapped her
breath in her throat.

She revealed things about herself, too. Her habit of
tapping out the notes from harpsichord tunes on her
lap when boredom struck during their long hours on
the road. How her feet ached after a night of skipping

and hopping through the *courante* in heeled shoes. That whenever she got the chance, she would examine every inch of any garden she encountered.

Arriving in this coastal town near the border of Spain, they discovered that certain details about the possession of territories had not been settled to the satisfaction of the negotiating parties. The ministers serving the interests of their respective monarchs spent days in discussion, and reports of their disputes led to rumors that there would be no marriage at all. Cardinal Mazarin, despite an untimely and inconvenient recurrence of his gout, was unrelenting in pursuit of this long-sought victory.

The queen, diligent in her religious observations, visited convents by day and at night sought amusement from the band of Spanish comedians performing in the town. Although Bathilde couldn't understand their dialogue, their physical antics and close study of Her Majesty's reactions told her when to laugh.

To avoid the fierce southern heat, she and Sophie ventured out during the early hours. They strolled the riverside, welcoming any breeze that wafted off the water. They sometimes met King Louis riding back into the town after reviewing the troops that had accompanied him.

On a morning when her cousin was otherwise occupied, Bathilde's maid Justine accompanied her on her walk. Skiffs and white-sailed fishing boats dotted the serene waters, reminders of the region she'd known in childhood. Her sense of calm was disturbed when the band of horsemen thundered past. Louis, seeing her, halted and dismounted, handing his reins to his *écuyer.*

He swept off his hat, beaming as he inquired, "Did you hear the happy tidings?"

"I hope the day of your marriage is settled at last," Bathilde replied.

"No fresh news about that. But I've received

dispatches informing me that England's Parliament will recall my cousin Charles Stuart and let him succeed his late father as king. Thus, our alliance with that nation is strengthened. Tonight, we celebrate with a grand *fête*."

"We'll have far greater cause for rejoicing when your marriage takes place. Is there nothing Cardinal Mazarin and your envoys can do to hasten it?"

His smile slipped away. "I believe the Almighty intervened to cause the delay. I've not yet fully recovered from being forced to part from Marie last summer. The most painful episode of my life, as you well know."

She inclined her head in acknowledgment.

"And after so much suffering in support of the cardinal's great cause—and my mother's—I'm not yet a husband." He pressed his gloved hands together as if praying. "I mean to be a good one. Dutiful. And faithful."

For a king, this was an extraordinary pronouncement. His predecessors, notorious for their amours, lavished titles and palaces and riches on their mistresses. And though she wanted to believe him capable of maintaining his singular ambition, she was skeptical.

Still pondering his declaration, she and her maid returned to the merchant's house her father had requisitioned, at great expense. Any number of residents had surrendered their dwellings to the horde of courtiers descending daily upon this sleepy Basque town.

In the parlor the duke was polishing a leather scabbard with a cloth. The exposed rapier lay across the colorful tapestry table covering.

Looking up, he said, "A short time ago, your father and Madame de Sevreau went to the queen's lodgings. You were included in their invitation."

All too familiar with the formality and tedium of Her Majesty's *lever,* she chose to remain. This was a rare and fortuitous opportunity to be alone with him.

"Doesn't your manservant, or your cousin, perform that task for you?"

"I always do it myself. It's no hardship."

She touched the crest embossed on the sword's hilt. "A rose for de Rozel."

"Not the manliest of emblems, I know."

"You wouldn't say that if you'd ever tied an unruly rose to a *tuteur,* or pruned one. They are hardy and resilient. With dangerous thorns." Pressing her finger on the narrow blade, she said, "I imagine you've used this to slay enemy soldiers."

"It would serve the purpose, if I needed to eliminate someone. But a marshal's daughter ought to know the difference between a rapier worn for dress occasions and the type used in battle."

"Papa won't speak to me of his years in the army. He says I can read about them in his memoir. But not during his lifetime." She gripped the handle and lifted the weapon. "I've wondered how soldiers reconcile their obligation to kill with God's commandment against it."

He balled the fabric and tossed it onto the table. "Murder in any circumstances is a mortal sin. One that I repent of, unfailingly. Our church instituted the sacrament of penance, which alleviates guilt. To some extent."

She focused on dust motes dancing in sunlight that leaked through gaps in the shutter. "I shouldn't have pried into your private concerns."

"Look at me."

Meeting his gaze, she saw the upward curve of his mouth.

"You may ask me anything you wish, Bathilde. At any time."

The proxy marriage uniting King Louis and the Infanta Maria Theresa took place on the Spanish side of the River Nivelle, in Fontarabia. The Queen Regent sent members of her household and a few favored friends to witness the ceremony. At her father's urging, Bathilde accompanied the Duchesse de Navailles, the half-Spanish Madame de Motteville, Madame Colbert, and the others who boarded the boats King Philip had provided. Floating past the Isle of Pheasants, a narrow slip of land rising from the water, she saw the elongated pavilion where the two nations conducted treaty negotiations. The French ladies were taken to a house of reception and served chocolate and biscuits before being driven to the church for the nuptial mass.

King Philip, dressed in black, personified regal dignity and formality. His young daughter, her face full and fair, bore a striking resemblance to the Queen Mother. A monstrosity of a cap topped the enormous blonde wig she wore, and her short, squat figure was disadvantaged by her attire. The broad, flat-fronted farthingale beneath her white satin gown wobbled with every step as she approached the Spanish nobleman standing in for the French King. The Bishop of Pamplona presided over the mass and the exchange of vows.

Bathilde's foray into Spain lasted no longer than a day.

Two days after the proxy wedding, at the *palais de conference* on the Isle of Pheasants, the Queen Mother met her niece, now her daughter-in-law, and was reunited with the brother she hadn't seen for more than four decades. Neither Bathilde's father nor the duke cared enough about this family ceremony to attend, and they had to wait two days more to witness the signing of the treaty, Cardinal Mazarin's great triumph, which also took place on the island.

On their return, Papa climbed down from the carriage, supported by his cane. "It is done," he told her. "De Rozel can tell you about it. The event was longer than I anticipated, and more wearying. I need to sit and catch my breath."

When they gathered in the parlor, the duke said, "The pavilion is divided down the middle. There's a French side, carpeted in crimson velvet, and the floor of the Spanish side has a Persian rug of gold and silver. At either end are facing doors—one for us, one for the Spaniards. After King Louis and his uncle King Philip swore oaths on a Bible, their secretaries of state read the official draft in each language."

"Were the terms greatly altered?" she asked.

"Yes, and all to the benefit of France—as Cardinal Mazarin desired. Our sovereign has become the most powerful in all of Europe. Which is to say, the entire world. We are formally granted our spoils of war: the Spanish possessions we seized in Flanders. And much more. The entire province of Artois. And the Mediterranean territories, Roussillon and Cerdagne. France receives half a million gold *écus* as the bride's dowry. But a peaceful future is beyond price."

His voice heavy with weariness, Papa said, "Indeed it is. All that bloodshed. Cities destroyed. Countless fine soldiers and innocent citizens killed. May God have mercy on us."

"Amen," said the duke.

The following afternoon, the young woman newly named Marie-Thérèse bade farewell to her father and her country and was escorted over the border by her bridegroom and his mother. So began her permanent exile from the life and land she'd always known. Only five of her fellow Spaniards would accompany into French territory—a confessor and a physician, her chief lady in waiting, and two others.

The royal retinue gathered in the Queen Mother's apartments to be presented to the king's consort. The Duchesse de Navailles, her *dame d'honneur,* had already banished the unwieldy farthingale and saw to it that Queen Marie-Thérèse was dressed in the French style. The young bride's eyes were a bright, clear blue, her nose was large, and her lips were full. She bobbed her bejeweled blonde head as each of her new subjects approached, until withdrawing to her own chamber to rest before supper.

"How hard it must be," Bathilde commented to the duke, "knowing she'll never again see her father, and the only people and places she knows. In a few days she must go through another marriage ceremony, and then she will live out her years in a foreign land and unfamiliar court."

"The inevitable fate of royal wives. All of them."

"She doesn't speak French. And few of us know her language."

"I thought all your pity would be directed towards your dear friend Louis, forced into wedlock with a simpleton of a girl who can barely communicate with him. You care for him a great deal, I know. And he for you."

"That is true."

"Have you ever been in love, Bathilde?"

Not until recently, was her silent response. Avoiding his scrutiny, she said, "I doubt you'd willingly answer that yourself."

"As I've said, you may ask me whatever you please. And will receive an honest reply."

She had many questions, but none of them touched on his past. Until she had a clearer sense of his feelings, hers would remain unspoken.

# CHAPTER 20

*June, 1660*

On the morning of the requisite religious rite and mass that would sanctify the marriage, Bathilde's father declined to go to the Queen Mother's residence, the point of departure for the French contingent.

"I'm interested in only one nuptial ceremony," he told her. "Yours."

Entering the parlor, the duke responded, "Name the day, sir."

"While the pair of you are at church, I will carefully consider. You'll have an answer as soon as you return."

"Your daughter, I see, has arrayed herself in a peacock's colors."

"But I do not strut like one," Bathilde retorted, smiling at him. Her turquoise silk bodice and gown, adorned with deep blue ribbons and gold lace, opened in front to reveal a moss-green petticoat. She wore Maman's pearl necklace with the matching earrings Papa had given her in Poitiers, the day she learned she would be the duke's bride. A pearl-encrusted net confined her chignon, and her face was framed by the short, curling tendrils dictated by the popular mode.

"The grace of your movements is always sublime, princess."

"You wouldn't say that if you'd seen me struggling to keep my balance on a ladder at rose-pruning time. Or driving the geese from the riverbank where they spend the day foraging."

"You're giving de Rozel the impression that we don't employ enough servants," Papa said. "Be off, now, or you'll be late."

From the royal lodging they processed across a tapestry-carpeted bridge to the fortress-like church, where courtiers packed themselves into the nave. Ascending to the gallery, they failed to find two places together. The duke insisted that she take a vacant one in front, near the balustrade, so she could see the dais and the altar.

The Queen Mother's face shone with happiness as she took up her position. King Louis had never looked more handsome to Bathilde than he did in his plain suit of black velvet and dark wig of cascading curls. She prayed that he could be content with his shy, plump bride, who couldn't refrain from casting admiring glances at him as they faced each other beneath a canopy. On this occasion, Marie-Thérèse wore a cream petticoat-gown beneath a purple velvet robe embroidered all over with golden *fleurs-de-lis*. A coronet perched precariously at the back of her golden head.

The ceremony, conducted with great solemnity and reverence, lasted for hours. By its conclusion, Bathilde was desperate to escape the heat created by a multitude of bodies pressing together and dozens of lit candles, and she could no longer endure the lingering smell of incense. Loud tolling from the belfry directly above produced a sound so loud that it reverberated within her chest. After descending the narrow stair, she found a crush of people blocking her way, so she turned and followed a side aisle to a smaller door near the sacristy.

Exulting in her release, she drew in deep breaths of fresh air that carried the smell and taste of the sea, familiar from her early years at Château Clément. A welcome gust cooled her damp brow and lifted the little curls clinging there. By walking into the breeze, she could satisfy her urgent desire to see waves and sand.

"Bathilde! Wait!"

She paused, allowing the duke to catch up to her.

"You shouldn't wander the town without an escort. Where are you bound?"

"To the ocean, *monseigneur.*"

"I wish you'd call me Albin."

Reaching up, she tugged at the pearly cage to remove it. With a sigh of relief, she shook out her curls. "That's better."

"I agree. What a lot of hair you've got."

"And such an unfashionable, squirrely color. A legacy from my mother." She gazed towards the water. "Spending so many weeks near the coast has made me miss my birthplace. I remember how Papa placed me at the front of his saddle, and I held tight to the pommel as we rode to a ribbon of a beach, rockier than this one. At low tide, we watched men haul in oysters and mussels. And scallops, which appear on our de Sevreau arms. The land there is flat, covered with vineyards and wheat fields."

"He tells me your Château Clément is as grand as any royal residence."

"I was very little, so it seemed enormous to me. Maman had a beautiful *salle de musique.* She placed a stool in front of her harpsichord and let me strike the keys at will. To her well-trained ear, the sounds I produced must have been painfully unmelodic. But she never lost her patience." On the verge of tears, she averted her face.

"How old were you when she died?"

"Eight. When Papa placed me in the convent school, I was the youngest pupil." She brushed the moisture away from the corner of each eye. "I must be wearier than I realized. Too much hectic activity in recent days."

"For the past month," he corrected her. "You've not said it yet."

"What?" she asked absently staring at the stretch of pale strand that separated them from the rippling blue sea beyond.

"My name."

"Albin Maurice Laurent Bertrand. Marquis de Brénoville. Duc de Rozel."

"I don't need to hear all of it." He moved closer. "My château lies at the very edge of Normandy, on the channel side of the Cotentin Peninsula. The sand there resembles powdered gold."

When, she wondered, would he take her to his home? She feared that he intended to live mostly in Paris, near the court, and supposed they'd spend more time in the royal palaces than at their own provincial residences.

"You seem distracted. Still thinking of your girlhood days?"

"Of the future."

"Our future?"

She nodded.

"Then we should return to your father and discover what decision he's made about it."

Sophie, correctly guessing they were ravenous, offered wine and almond biscuits. "The cook has boasted all day about the fine, large *merlu* she got at the fish market. She's preparing for our dinner in the Basque style, with spices and a saffron sauce."

Bathilde sat down across from her father. "If you envision a wedding as crowded and long and tiring as the one we've endured, I'll plead with the duke to elope with me."

"When you hear my thoughts, you might be even more tempted to do so. Both of you."

Her hand remained poised over the tray of biscuits. "Oh?"

"I've neither the stamina nor the inclination to accompany the bridegroom and his bride all the way to Paris, stopping at every sizable city and royal château along the way. Which is why at first light tomorrow, I'm departing for La Rochelle, to await the king. I'll remain until he completes his inspection of its garrison and the fleet. Then I shall go to Château Clément and spend the summer there."

Her heart jumped on hearing this. "After we dine, I'll tell Justine to begin packing."

"No, Bathilde. Not yet. You and Sophie and de Rozel will remain with the royal party. You should be present for the grand procession when the king and his queen enter Paris. Something to tell your children about. And your grandchildren."

"I'm sure they'd rather listen to your tales of soldiering, Papa."

"Only the boys," said the duke, who had moved behind her chair. "We'll surely have a daughter or two."

"In the autumn, we will gather at Château des Vignes. Where, God willing, I'll feel well enough to host a hunting party. A grand ball will precede your marriage at Poitiers Cathedral. Where you choose to go afterwards, dear children, you will have to decide for yourselves."

A delay of four months—it felt like an eternity. She twisted around for a glimpse of the duke's face. It was frustratingly impassive.

"While in Paris, Bathilde," Papa continued, "you will acquire your trousseau, without counting the cost. De Rozel, I keep funds on deposit with a banker there. Too many noblemen who lack means seek and receive financial assistance from Nicolas Fouquet, one of Mazarin's officials. He readily supplies them with whatever they require. I'd rather you didn't put yourself under any obligation to him. Or to Mazarin, either."

"I don't care to be beholden to any man," the duke replied. "Though my inheritance isn't large, I'm able to manage on my income. At present, I have no debts, nor do I expect to incur any."

After their dinner, Papa summoned the page Pierre, who served as their torch-bearer as they made their way to the evening reception at the Queen Dowager's house. Marie-Thérèse wore another of her new French gowns, white satin and silvery lace, which revealed the full bosom and thick waist previously obscured by her farthingale and the velvet mantle she'd worn earlier at the church.

Bathilde, rising from a curtsy, heard her say to her aunt, *"Esta princesa es hermosa."*

In a whisper, the duke translated. "You are a beautiful princess, she says."

"You understand Spanish?"

"A little."

King Louis stepped onto the balcony. Reaching into the velvet bag a servant held, he tossed fistfuls of commemorative coins. The townspeople below gleefully scrambled to catch them and retrieve the ones that landed in the street.

His brother Philippe approached Bathilde and the duke, saying, *"Mes amis,* I trust you won't spend a full week yoking yourselves together, as the king and his bride have done."

The duke replied, "Our ceremony will take place privately, Monsieur. In Poitiers."

"Ah, yes. That's where the princess discovered that her father chose you for her husband, de Rozel. Oh, the questions she put to us! Naturally, we told her how extremely handsome you are." Monsieur pursed his lips and angled his black head. "Well, I did. And I spoke truly, didn't I, princess?"

She nodded, amused by the duke's evident discomfiture.

"The bridegroom and his bride," Monsieur continued, "will very soon withdraw to the chamber prepared for the consummation. Our mother suffered the ordeal of being deflowered in full view of people and priests. She will see to it that this couple performs their marital and royal duty in complete privacy."

"How—how considerate of her," Bathilde managed to say. She couldn't bring herself to look at the duke.

Until lately, she would have viewed a four-month postponement of her wedding night as a reprieve. As her affection for her future husband had increased, apprehension about the intimacies of marriage had receded, to be replaced by curiosity tinged with anticipation.

"Allow me to partner you in the *menuet*," Monsieur said. "As the second most important gentleman in France, it's my right to claim the fairest of all the titled ladies in the room."

"Stop pacing," Wilfride said crossly. "You'll wake the others."

Albin returned to the table and picked up his wineglass. "She hasn't admitted it, but I'm certain she loves someone. Why else is she so solemn when we're together? It can't be Monsieur. He flirted with her—as he does with every attractive person, female or male. They danced together, more than once. But it's common knowledge that his amorous tastes aren't directed towards ladies. So is his habit of dressing in women's garments and painting his face."

"He's no threat," Wilfride concurred.

"Louis could be."

"He's married now. And the entire court believes he still pines for the Mancini girl."

"He might regard the princess—*my* princess—as a source of consolation."

"Every day, for more than a month, you and she have passed many an hour together. From your way of looking at her, and the tone of your voice when speaking to her, I can tell that your heart has been touched. More than you want to admit."

"I admire her. Respect her. Compared to other females who flock about the king, whom I shall not name, she's sensible and rational. Better educated, too. She's polite and unfailingly pleasant towards me. That should be enough. Yet I'm constantly seeking a modicum of proof that, to some extent, her heart is engaged."

"Why wish for her love, if you feel none for her?"

After a brief struggle to produce an answer, Albin said, "I'm no great believer in it. From all I've observed, it's a fleeting condition. Impermanent."

"Not for everyone." His feelings for Princess Bathilde, he felt certain, would endure for his entire life, to his last day. And beyond, if human emotions survived in the afterlife.

His cousin had subsided into thoughtfulness, staring at the dregs in his glass. Eventually he said, "I confess, I'm fond of her. Isn't that akin to love? Burdening her with unwanted affection could be a mistake. With lasting consequences. I mean to fulfill the wishes of our fathers, friends who recognized the numerous advantages of an alliance between their offspring. So do I. Apparently, Princess Bathilde also does. If she objected, the prince wouldn't be so keen to have me for a son-in-law. I've rarely seen a man so devoted to a daughter."

Wilfride acknowledged the truth of it. "She's the living memorial to a woman he will never cease to mourn. There's your example of lasting devotion."

"Yes, but few marriages are founded on that sort of attachment. The majority of aristocratic wives and husbands appear to despise one another."

"Granted. But you wouldn't wed someone distasteful to you, or who couldn't tolerate you. No matter the size of her dowry or her future inheritance."

"Well, having obtained a bride who is impeccable in every respect, I'll not spoil any chance of mutual contentment with a declaration she might not wish for."

A convent upbringing and an innate reticence, Wilfride supposed, might be obstacles to fuller understanding between the engaged couple. But not, he trusted, insurmountable. Impatient for the day when they arrived at a recognition of how well-matched they were, he also dreaded it.

# CHAPTER 21

Traveling day and night, the cavalcade made rapid progress to Roquefort. The town contained few residences that could accommodate the royal retinue, so its members sought lodging in any available house, however humble or remote. Monsieur Mesny scoured the area and secured space in a dairyman's stone dwelling in a village near the town. Its only bedchamber was large enough for Bathilde, Sophie, and their maid. But the duke and his cousin and Pierre had to fashion makeshift beds in the parlor, using blankets and pillows the farmer's wife provided.

"Your father wouldn't have been at all comfortable here," Sophie said, as she and Bathilde settled onto a thin feather mattress in need of re-stuffing.

"He should've let us go with him to Château Clément. He's not as strong as he thinks he is and will probably overtire himself."

"The servants there will coddle him, you may be sure."

She turned on her side, trying for a position that would induce sleep. After a warm day, this upper room felt stuffy, even with the window partly open. Listening to her cousin's soft breathing, she hoped the duke and his companions weren't suffering downstairs in the parlor.

A loud rumble jolted her awake. She was briefly aware of an odd motion as the entire bed shuddered.

Sophie sat upright. "What is happening? Was that a thunderclap?"

From her pallet, Justine cried, "The floorboards shifted."

Voices elsewhere in the house indicated that others were aware of the strange occurrence.

A sharp knock made Bathilde jump. "I'll go," she said, leaving the low bedstead.

She opened the door to find the duke, fist poised to rap once more. His long brown hair was wildly disheveled, and he wore only his nightshirt. Holding his chamber stick nearer her face, he asked, "You suffered no harm?

"I've never known such a peculiar sensation."

"I have—once. In Italy. Not as powerful but just as startling."

More disquieting than the earth's movement was the sight of him in a state of undress. And her awareness that her thin linen chemise didn't entirely cover her chest or conceal her bare feet.

This is how we'll appear to one another on our wedding night, she thought. And every one thereafter.

"I thank you for—for coming," she stammered. "And I'm relieved that you're unhurt. Should we be prepared for another earthquake, do you think?"

"Our host says they are common in this vicinity. This house is built from stone, and he assures me that it has withstood more than one tremor through the years. Any that follow the initial one would probably be less violent. I expect you'll sleep through them. Rest well, Bathilde."

She watched his candle's glow fade with his progress

along the passage, vanishing completely as he descended the stairs.

For a long while she lay awake, dreading a second event, but eventually slumber claimed her. She woke when the shutters were drawn to let in the morning light. Sophie moaned faintly on rising and rubbed her spine to alleviate an ache.

"Wherever we lodge tonight," she said, "I pray for a bed far softer than this one."

The next long stretch of roadway carried them to Langon on the Garonne, a broad riverway. Its aldermen provided boats for the journey by water to Bordeaux. The king and his two queens, members of the royal family, and the visibly ailing cardinal, boarded a magnificent vessel. Bathilde and Sophie, the duke and Monsieur Mesny, followed.

The deck was surrounded by a gilded balustrade, and the interior cabin had walls draped in crimson velvet and a domed ceiling lined with red damask. Their Majesties seated themselves in throne-like chairs on a dais and passed the time in card games while the courtiers assessed the newlyweds' relationship from a respectful distance. Bathilde wondered how they could bear being under constant observation—waking, dining, walking, sitting on the convenience, retiring to bed. Even if they were accustomed to it from birth, they must sometimes yearn for privacy and solitude.

Following a successful and apparently satisfying consummation, Louis had decreed that he would never sleep in a separate room from his queen while they traveled. His uxoriousness and devotion to the necessary duty of siring an heir to the crown pleased his mother and priests. His attendants, especially the more licentious ones, could hardly comprehend that spousal fidelity might actually become the fashion rather than the exception.

And what was the Duc de Rozel's preference, Bathilde wondered. Would he expect always to share a bedchamber with his duchess?

Four large flatboats, rowed by men in blue livery, pulled the royal barge up the river in the direction of the coast, and a number of smaller vessels followed in its wake. From the cabin's broad window, she watched the barge carrying a party of violin players, and the skiffs floating behind it. After an uncomfortably speedy journey by coach, rattling over public roads, Bathilde relished this smoother, slower passage. Nearing Bordeaux, they met a large convoy of boats, churning up ripples and waves. Trumpeters blasted on their horns, the piercing sounds mingling with the resounding din from exploding cannons.

She and Albin—the name by which she thought of him, despite never uttering it in his presence—stepped onto the deck. The riverbanks and the quay were packed with citizens eager to welcome their monarch and his bride.

"How gratifying for the king, to receive acclaim from his people," she commented. "Much of his reign has been plagued by rebellion."

"And this is only the second major city of his tour," he replied. "He'll be sated from all the accolades by the time we enter Paris."

Paris.

Nearly every young woman longed to be there, but she did not. Crowded, dirty streets and an impoverished populace contrasted with the splendor of palaces and mansions, and damage the Frondeurs had inflicted detracted from the city's beauties. But purchasing fabrics and trimmings for new court gowns, in accordance with Papa's wishes, wasn't as dismaying as what she would face after her marriage to Albin. Either at the Louvre or at Fontainebleau, or in whatever residence the king preferred at that time, she'd make her first appearance as a duchess. All the ladies would inspect her attire and her jewels, and probe the secrets of her bedchamber—and her bridegroom's performance there—with sly, intrusive questions.

She clutched the gold-painted balustrade, her mind clouded by premonition.

"I've rarely seen such a mournful face." Albin placed his hand beside hers.

"I'm contemplating the future."

"Never with any pleasure, I've perceived." His voice grew low and soft as he told her, "Don't be afraid. Not of me. There's no cause for it, you know."

Assuming he alluded to marital relations, she wondered how he'd guessed her thoughts. "I do know," she said, truthfully. "But I dread the preparations. Visiting cloth merchants and ribbon sellers and shoemakers. And worse, all the court rituals that come after the wedding."

"I thought females took pleasure from the material aspects of being a bride. What an unusual creature you are."

"As you've said, or implied, on other occasions."

"If you allow me, I can provide a solution to one difficulty. During my years of roving, I purchased Venetian velvets and Florentine brocades. Fine Flemish lace from Bruges and Brussels. I've got an entire trunkful of silk woven in Lyon. All these luxuries are stored at Château Rozel, unused. My mother didn't live long enough to enjoy them, and my father couldn't afford the making of new garments and hangings. From a desire to see my duchess sumptuously clothed, I bestow all the fabrics and embellishments upon you."

"That's extremely obliging of you, and I'm grateful." To prove it, she added, "Albin."

He lifted her hand to his lips and held it there. A stream of pleasure flowed from the crown of her head to the very tips of her toes.

After reviewing his ships at La Rochelle and dining with the Prince de Coulon at Château Clément, the king rejoined the two queens at Saint-Jean-d'Angély. Presenting Bathilde with a letter, he told her how much he admired the house and grounds.

"Did Papa appear to be well?"

"Most definitely," he assured her. "He was in good spirits, too, and bold enough to request that his sovereign serve as his courier. Having completed my assignment, I anticipate a handsome gratuity."

"I've no coins upon me, Your Majesty."

"Then this will have to suffice." He leaned close to press a kiss on her cheek. With a glance at Albin, he said, "A brotherly act, *mon copain,* and no cause for that grim face."

He didn't mention his secret, sentimental pilgrimage to Château de Brouage, Marie Mancini's place of exile and the site of their last farewell. One of his attendants told another, who shared the tale with somebody else. This gave rise to a rumor that he'd wandered the beach, sobbing out his heartbreak over the loss of his one true love.

Albin and his cousin continued the journey by horse but never ventured far from the coach carrying Bathilde and Sophie and the two servants. The royal caravan, bound for Poitiers, would sweep through Niort without halting.

"But I intend to," she announced. "Long enough to visit the Ursulines."

She directed the driver to the convent in rue Crémault. When she rang the bell beside the gate, the portress who appeared was a stranger. Only her black veil and white scapular and dark woolen habit were familiar.

"If Mother Superior is receiving, please inform her that Bathilde de Sevreau requests an audience."

She watched the woman cross the courtyard and enter the door of the nuns' side. The girlish chatter coming from the cloisters whisked her backwards through the years to the days she and Myrte and Françoise had hurried out of their schoolroom and into the fresh air.

She made her way to the familiar *parloir* to wait for Mother Superior, who soon appeared. Advancing age and heavy responsibilities had added lines to the face on the other side of the grille.

"Dear child, the sight of you is an unexpected blessing. And an opportunity to express our gratitude for the money and gifts we've received."

"I couldn't pass through the town without stopping. I'm on my way to Paris with the king and his bride and the Queen Mother. My own wedding takes place this autumn, in Poitiers."

"We shall pray often for your happiness." With a backward glance, she added, "Here is Soeur Céleste, eager to greet you." The blue-veined hand came up to draw a cross. "God go with you."

Soeur Céleste's pretty face, also older, filled the shadowy area behind the bars. Her beatific smile was unchanged. "When the portress said our dear little princess had returned, my heart was warmed. Though no longer little, I see."

"I often think of you, and the sisters who were here in my time. Tell me, who tends the garden?" She couldn't bring herself to ask whether Amalie was still living.

"One of our postulants has a great love of growing

things. Amalie, in her last months, had strength enough to advise and prepare her for the outdoor tasks." After they crossed themselves, the nun went on, "I don't receive letters from Madame Scarron as often as I used to. If you see her, let her know I give thanks daily for her return to our beloved church."

Bathilde nodded. Françoise was no longer diligent in the practice of her faith, eschewing confession and disregarding all fasts and feasts and holy days of obligation. But she remained true to her marriage vows, fending off the male admirers eager to seduce her, though more from fear of stirring up scandal than dread of eternal damnation.

As her coach carried her away from the community where she'd spent so much of her youth, the soaring steeple of Église Notre Dame resurrected the sad recollection of standing at its door with Myrte, in the rain, waiting and watching for Etienne Lavigne. Her friend's anguish and despair had roused sympathy, but being unacquainted with romantic yearning, she hadn't fully understood its power—or the danger it posed.

To find love, she realized, is to risk losing it.

# CHAPTER 22

*Poitiers, June, 1660*

A fter weeks of carriage travel and many nights in unfamiliar houses in strange cities, Bathilde had a profound and unexpected sense of homecoming when she arrived at her father's *hôtel particulier*. She introduced the servants to Albin and commended them for their diligent care of the property. At his request, she showed him the reception rooms and the private chambers, and he insisted on viewing the cellar and the attic and stable.

"As you see, this is even grander than the one in Paris," Bathilde acknowledged. "And it has a large garden, which is why I like it better."

Fish and fowls had been purchased to augment the quantity of fresh food sent from Château des Vignes, and in her father's absence, she sat at the head of the table for the first time, as mistress of the household. After dinner, she led her guests to the *salle d'assemblée*. Sophie sat at a small table to pen a letter to Papa. Monsieur Mesny stepped into the garden to stretch his legs. Albin, instead of going with him, asked her to play the harpsichord. Its keys stuck from the summer humidity and disuse, but after running through some scales she produced a sufficiently melodious sound.

She slept soundly throughout the night in a bed she knew well from prior visits. There would be no midnight encounters with Albin here, for he and Monsieur Mesny had rooms in a distant part of the house, in the magnificent suite once occupied by the Queen Mother.

In the morning, Justine appeared. "Shall I bring *déjeuner* to you here, princess?"

Although the suggestion appealed to her, Albin's presence prevented her from giving in to laziness. "Did Madame de Sevreau have hers?"

"More than an hour ago. She's with the cook, ordering the day's meals. The Duc de Rozel went early to attend the king's *lever.*"

No need to leave her bed yet. "Bring up some of the fresh strawberries, if we didn't eat them all yesterday. With cream. And bread. With plenty of butter." From her own cows, the ones she'd often seen grazing the flat meadows at Château des Vignes.

After eating, she washed and dressed, and informed Sophie that she meant to visit the cathedral.

"To pray for Maman. Would you care to come with me? We might be in time for midday mass. It's close by, and the weather is fine enough that we can walk."

Her cousin replied, "That sounds pleasant, after all the hours and days in the carriage."

Country people from villages beyond the city walls had brought their produce and their wares to the small market in front of the cathedral. Servants and housewives inspected items on offer, haggling over prices. Well-born females wore masks over their faces to guard their complexions from the searing summer sun.

Built to honor St. Pierre, the centuries-old cathedral of golden stone served as a cool, shaded refuge from the summer heat. Bathilde and Sophie followed a side aisle to the south transept, pausing when they came to her mother's tomb. Kneeling together on the stone floor, they silently prayed.

When they rose, Sophie said, "I wonder whether the king will bring his bride here, as his father did during his wedding journey. You can see Louis XIII and the Queen Mother in the painting behind the tabernacle, commemorating their visit."

"Your servant said I'd find you here."

Startled to hear Albin's voice echoing against the stone pillars, Bathilde whirled around.

"My dear," Sophie murmured, "I've just remembered I have a need of embroidery silk in a particular shade of green. Perhaps the duke will escort you home."

The quirk of his lips showed his awareness of her cousin's ploy to grant them privacy. "I regard it as my duty, Madame. And my only hope of not getting lost, as the princess knows the way. Which I do not."

Beaming at him, Sophie departed.

"I thought you were with the king," Bathilde said.

"Wilfride and I left the *lever* as soon as we could manage it without drawing notice or causing offense. A tedious process to undergo, and a greater hardship to observe. He offered us a commentary on his bride's eagerness for—an activity I shan't mention in this holy place. It won't be long before the kingdom is blessed with a dauphin or dauphine." He ran his hand along the edge of the table monument. "Marie-Madeleine Elisabeth de Sevreau, Princesse de Coulon. Your mother." After reading the rest of the Latin inscription, he said, "With her infant son, Clovis."

Bathilde nodded. "The lost heir to Papa's titles, and most of his properties."

"Are more of your relatives interred here?"

"Generations of them lie beneath us, in a catacomb."

His gaze shifted upwards to the vaulted ceiling before taking in the tall *gothique* windows along the wall, letting in light from outside. "A splendid place to spend eternity."

"And to think a foreign king built it. Henry II of England, who married a Queen of France. They're both depicted in the crucifixion window above the altar." Leading him that direction, she was keenly aware that in a few months she and Albin would stand where her parents had, to speak their vows before the archbishop. "The couple kneeling at the very bottom, with the cross between them. King Henry on the left side, Queen Alienor of Aquitaine on the right."

"I've never seen such a masterpiece in colored glass, or one with such an abundance of Biblical images. It would take the rest of the day to interpret them all."

She smiled. "With your Jesuit schooling, I'm sure you could. But your neck would get very tired."

He rubbed it, saying, "Already I feel the ache. But it's worth every twinge."

To her he looked more handsome than any artist's depiction of the angel Gabriel. Of impressive height, long-limbed and strong-featured, he personified the chivalric ideal. A nobleman of unblemished reputation, a brave soldier and a dedicated scholar. These qualities were admirable, but it was her personal observations and her experiences of his character that had won her heart. His haste to assure himself of her safety during the earthquake. His use of her given name, and his repeated request that she address him by his. His awed appreciation of their surroundings.

Familiarity had fostered a connection, a closeness, and she was about to impair, if not destroy it.

As they walked along the nave towards the broad

doorway, he provided an opening. "At what time do we depart on the morrow?"

Slowly, deliberately, she responded, "You may decide for yourself. Because I won't be going on to Paris."

Throughout his stay at Fontainebleau, when not in the presence of king and court, Albin was dispirited and increasingly irritable. By the time he and Wilfride arrived at the royal Château de Vincennes, on the outskirts of Paris, he'd descended into despondency. Contending with this rare gloominess required care and caution, and Wilfride tried mightily not to give offense by word or deed.

"It's obvious why she returned to Château des Vignes," his cousin said. "To avoid me."

Wilfride reminded him, not for the first time, "She wanted to have all in readiness for her father's arrival. And to be present for the grape harvest."

"Which doesn't start for weeks. Those were convenient excuses to cover the real reason for her desertion. I hoped—I believed—she was beginning to care for me. She called me Albin. Once."

"So you've told me." Repeatedly.

"All through the spring and summer, I awoke with the certainty that we'd be together. In the carriage. At meals. We were able to converse freely, at court events and in private. In all my life, I've never missed anyone as I do her. Not even my family, when I was first at school."

"You realize what this signifies."

"I'm enamored of a lady who doesn't—or cannot—return my affection." Albin tugged at his boot, struggling to remove it. He flung it into the corner of the room, narrowly missing the table leg.

"You're betrothed to her. After speaking your marriage vows, you'll be forever bound."

For more than a year he'd hoped and he'd prayed that the princess would capture Albin's heart. His cousin's obvious distress saddened him, but the necessity of offering consolation was even more agonizing. They found themselves in similar yet contrary situations. They both yearned for a lady whose love was elusive. Only one of them could rightfully possess it.

# CHAPTER 23

"I often wonder what became of Mademoiselle Vernier's sweetheart." Giselle smoothed the edge of the pillow-case she hemmed. "And whether he loved her."

"Not as faithfully as she loved him," Bathilde answered.

"Before she died," the girl said solemnly, "she cursed him and swore she'd haunt him for breaking her heart. The ghost girls who roam the forest from midnight till dawn will help her punish him. Now she's one of them."

"In her delirium, she recalled a fable we heard during our schooldays, from a lay sister who lived in foreign places." Winding a length of silver lace around her hand, Bathilde added, "I'm sure my friend is with the angels."

She needed no reminder of Myrte's visions in the day before her death, and her conviction that the spectral *samovili* invited her to join their nightly pursuit of untrustworthy, faithless men.

"But everyone knows about the spirits who prowl throughout the woodland," Giselle said matter-of-factly. "They rise up from the graves in the churchyard."

"Don't let Père André hear you say that," Bathilde

reproved her. "Our souls don't remain earthbound. They ascend to heaven, unless they're first consigned to purgatory. Or descend into hell."

Although she rued her companion's lack of education, religious and secular, she had accepted that Giselle was perfectly satisfied with a life devoted to household tasks and vineyard work. Cheerful and exuberant, she was the most popular maiden in the village.

"Have you heard who will be named queen of the vintage? It must be your turn this year."

Giselle's brown head dipped down. "That's what Hilaire tells me. But nobody really knows who'll be crowned with the wreath until the very last day, when the final cartload of grapes rolls into the village. In olden times, they say, the Prince de Coulon chose the queen, who was always the girl he most desired. That night, he took her into his bed."

She wished Giselle's version of local history was no more than a cautionary tale dreamed up by mothers and fathers to instill virtue and prudence in their daughters. But she had no illusions about masculine behavior or disreputable ancestors. Therefore, it was probably true.

For decades Cardinal Mazarin had been the primary force in the realm, advisor to the Queen Mother and a second parent to her son. His increasing lethargy and recurring ailments led both of them to doubt his survival. Monsieur Vallot, summoned to the royal château of Vincennes, tried every possible remedy and regularly bled his illustrious patient, whose demise could destroy his established reputation as a superior physician.

In the privacy of his circular tower closet, shortly before the formalities to follow in the *chambre de coucher,* King Louis confided to Albin and Wilfride, "In childhood I saw my father only on ceremonial occasions. At his death, I was expected to mourn him, and I did. But I never really missed him, because I had the cardinal as my guardian and my guide. I'm therefore dreading a far more significant loss."

"Is His Eminence's condition so dire?" Albin asked, gesturing to Wilfride to refill his glass with cordial.

"Vallot and the other medical men try to raise our hopes of a recovery but cannot conceal their unease. The cardinal knows he can count his life in months. After his demise, an event as difficult to contemplate as it is inevitable, I want no chief minister. That is his advice and my inclination. But I will need counselors. You, my friend, might be one of them." Smoothing the white ruffle that extended to his knuckles, he said, "In the midst of sorrow, we also have cause for joy—an unexpected love affair within our court. My brother Philippe intends to follow you and the princess to the altar."

Behind the king's back, Albin glanced at Wilfride with raised brows, signifying surprise. "To whom goes the honor of becoming Madame, Duchesse d'Orléans?"

"Our cousin Henriette, whose brother's coronation as King of England raises her status within the family, and her suitability. The marriage will strengthen the alliance we formed in the last years of the Protectorate. My mother always regarded her niece almost as a daughter. And my aunt would have liked her to become my bride, although during their penniless years, matching her with me or Monsieur wasn't possible."

"You could barely tolerate her," Albin reminded him.

"I do now. She has blossomed. Henriette and Phillipe will make a lovely couple. Though I shouldn't wonder if they sometimes quarrel over which of them should wear a particularly fine ribbon or length of lace."

A valet came forward to set the black, curly wig on the king's half-bald pate.

"After she becomes Madame," Louis went on, "she'll require *dames d'honneur*. The future Duchesse de Rozel will be a leading candidate for the position. Your lady has been and will continue to be one of our court's brightest ornaments. You're the envy of all men."

Although Albin's expression told Wilfride that he didn't favor this plan, he responded with characteristic diplomacy. "If she should receive the appointment, it would of course convey great prestige."

"And I shall provide you with a comparable position of merit, *mon copain*. Perhaps more than one. Never let it be said that we separated a bridegroom from his bride."

Albin waited until they retired to their own apartments, on the opposite side of the square-shaped courtyard, to vent his displeasure.

"Bathilde, naturally, will welcome the opportunity to serve Monsieur's wife, if that royal hermaphrodite goes through with this marriage. And by accepting a position on His Majesty's council, I'd become what I never wished to be. A courtier."

"Which you already are," Wilfride pointed out. "Or we wouldn't be here."

"I'm not captive. I hold no office of state, and nor do I care to. I've no title apart from the one I inherited and need no other. I'm satisfied to serve my king through friendship. I attend his ceremonies and entertainments at will, not because I'm required to do so. My experience of court life began when I left my Jesuit school and accompanied my father to the Louvre. In recent months, my longstanding distaste has been replaced by strong aversion."

"If you reveal it," Wilfride observed, "you'll draw the

displeasure of your former commanders—the king and the Prince de Coulon."

"I know. By the time I left His Majesty's militia for the prince's regiment, I regarded him as a second father and valued my close association with an experienced and highly esteemed *maréchal.* As a result, I'm about to enter into an arranged marriage with his delightful daughter, who will very likely bestow her heart on another man someday. But to lead the life I most despise while it happens—" He shook his head.

"You'll accustom yourself. You must," Wilfride insisted. "You've grown tired of never staying in one place longer than a few days and nights. You're bored by seeing the same people all the time, in so many different palaces." Aware of rising frustration, he made no attempt to contain it. "How would you rather live? Do you even know?"

Albin's head came up, revealing a frown. "If I did, it wouldn't matter. Not at all."

# CHAPTER 24

Nearly every day, as the weather allowed, Bathilde mounted Chardon, a gray gelding with a coat like thistledown, and rode over the many hectares of her estate. She assessed the condition of the crops ripening in the fields and the grape clusters dangling from the rows of vines. And on a hot, dry day in August, she visited Pascal's house in the village to inquire about the expected timing of the harvest.

"Picking is likely to begin late next month. We've already begun sharpening the vine knives, and making sure all the baskets are in good repair." Excusing himself, he reached for his hat and left the cottage.

Bathilde asked his sister. "Why haven't Giselle and Hilaire announced their marriage? You and your brother should be making ready for their wedding."

"The little *chaumière* next to us stands ready for them," Berthe Durand replied. "We've cleaned and furnished it. Every evening Hilaire stops by to press her for an answer, impatient for the priest to call the banns in church. But she hasn't accepted him."

"They've always been so close, almost inseparable. I thought it was a settled match."

The other woman resumed her knitting. As her

needles rapidly formed another row, she said with regret, "Giselle says she doesn't care for him the way a bride should for her bridegroom. Don't ask me what she means by it. I've no idea."

"That must distress him."

"She knows he's a hardworking fellow who's known her from infancy and will treat her well. Shouldn't that be enough? Alas, no. She declares that she won't marry unless she's in love, so much that she could die from it. Mind you, there's no rival. Not in this village or anywhere nearby. Besides, plain people like us don't seek romance when choosing a spouse, any more than the nobility does. How on earth did she come by such a foolish notion?"

From Myrte, thought Bathilde. Giselle, a witness to her rapid decline towards death, believed the sole cause was her lovelorn state rather than a rampant disease of the lungs. "I agree, she ought to accept Hilaire instead of waiting for another swain, who might never appear. If you think it would help, I could speak to her."

Berthe clasped her hands together. "Your words will carry more weight than those of a mother. Or an uncle."

"There's something else I can do," she realized. "When my father arrives, we'll be joined by friends and acquaintances for a hunting party. Our gamekeeper has grown old in the years since the last gathering, before my mother died. Hilaire has been at Valère's side, learning all he knows about the game birds and stags and rabbits, and he's familiar with every inch of the forest and fields. As the assistant gamekeeper, with a salary and livery and all the necessary items to carry out the responsibilities, he'd have higher status and an income. Might that persuade Giselle?"

"If anything could," Berthe acknowledged. "She yearns to dress well and wear pretty trinkets."

"I'll speak first to Valère. I doubt he needs

convincing—he'll probably regard it as a favor. He looks on Hilaire as the son he never had."

Finding another useful strand to weave into her plan, Bathilde added, "You and Pascal rely on Giselle to cook and sew and tend the fowls. After she's wed and in her own home, she'll be quite busy. If you find a village girl to be your servant, I'll pay her wages."

The older woman dropped to her knees and lifted Bathilde's hem to kiss it. "If you succeed in making this match, I will never cease to be grateful."

"From her earliest years, I've been fond of Giselle. Like you and her uncle, I desire her happiness and security. I'd be very sorry if she lost her greatest chance of attaining it."

At four o'clock, well before dawn, the valet helped a yawning Albin dress in the red uniform coat he'd acquired with his recent appointment to the light horse brigade. Only members of the nobility noted for their superior horsemanship served in the king's guard. He would ride ahead of the newlyweds as they entered Paris.

"My hat, if you please." Albin turned to Wilfride. "I'm told our position will be somewhere in the middle of the procession."

"I shall watch for you."

"It's not too soon to be off, if you want to claim a good viewing place. I shall meet you—eventually—at the Prince de Coulon's *hôtel*."

Going to the stables in near-darkness, Wilfride mounted Albin's second-best charger. After leaving the palace grounds, he rode through Vincennes, its populace already stirring, and passed under the triumphal arch erected at the city gate. Beyond, coaches clogged the highway to Paris. A large crowd had assembled at Porte Saint-Antoine, and people shouted to him, asking how long before the king and queen would appear.

His destination was his and Albin's old lodging near the Louvre, which had stabling for the horse. Its rooms smelled stale from many months of disuse, and he flung back the shutters and parted the casements to admit fresh air. Removing his clothes, damp with sweat, he bathed and changed into clean garments. They, too, smelled musty, but he couldn't remedy that. Borrowing one of his cousin's less ornate hats, and taking a spyglass, he headed into the busy street. He walked over to the Prince de Coulon's *hôtel particulier*, offered to Albin for his use while in Paris, where he hoped to get breakfast.

"A servant came here a short time ago," the major domo told him, "to say that Madame Scarron invites the duke to view the spectacle with her and her friends at the Hôtel d'Aumont."

"He's riding in it, so I shall go in his stead. After I've eaten."

When he'd satisfied his ravenous appetite, he followed the directions the prince's factotum had given. At the next much grander *hôtel,* a servant guided him to an upper *salle* teeming with people, only one of whom knew him.

"I'm pleased to see you again, Monsieur Mesny," Madame Scarron greeted him. "Is the duke unable to join us?"

"When you see him, he'll be with His Majesty's guards."

"A great pity Princess Bathilde is missing this remarkable event." The young matron's bosom rose and fell with her sigh.

Churchmen led the procession—archbishops and bishops and priests and monks who carried crosses and chanted as they passed along the street. Cardinal Mazarin, too ill for a public appearance, had sent his household attendants and dozens of baggage mules. City officials came next, then members of the Paris Parlement. After a group of young pages marched by, a long line of carriages bearing various important people rolled past.

The red coats of the light horse brigade were easy to spot. Albin and his comrades trotted along in advance of the many officers and gentlemen of the royal household— the passage of this group lasted an hour and was followed by the smaller contingent that served Monsieur.

"I see the musketeers," Madame Scarron announced. "And the Duc de Navailles, my godmother's husband, leading the cavalrymen." She watched in silence for a while.

The eruption of excited cheers from afar alerted them to the king's presence.

"Oh, how magnificent he is," Madame breathed.

Wilfride lifted his spyglass to examine the royal canopy. Behind it, King Louis, in a pearl-studded costume decorated with fluttering ribbons, sat astride a prancing charger. The shouting grew louder with the appearance of a golden chariot drawn by six gray horses. Queen Marie-Thérèse, its sole occupant, was decked out in a rainbow of colored jewels that shimmered in the sunshine.

Many hours later, Albin joined Wilfride at the Prince de Coulon's *hôtel*.

"I've endured enough ceremony these past few months to last my lifetime," he declared. "My head hurts abominably. After an entire day in the saddle, I had to sit and listen to countless prayers and lengthy addresses touting the king's magnificence and his queen's beauty and virtue. Much time for thinking—and forming a plan for our amusement."

Wilfride was relieved to see his cousin's grin. "What is it?"

"We're not expected at Château des Vignes for more than a month." Albin came over to pound his shoulder. "Let's go adventuring!"

# CHAPTER 25

Françoise Scarron's latest letter contained hardly any personal information, apart from a mention of her husband's increased sufferings, but it held more news of the royal family than *La Gazette*. Monsieur's infatuation with Princess Henriette of England had persuaded his mother to consent to a betrothal. Cardinal Mazarin, barely alive, remained at Vincennes, without hope of recovery. Several paragraphs described Queen Marie-Thérèse's entry into Paris. There was a single brief reference to the Duc de Rozel, who had ridden in the procession.

Bathilde, at Sophie's urging, had summoned Giselle Durand to help out with plain sewing. With many guests expected for the hunting party, there was a great need for bed linens, and some items for the trousseau weren't yet finished.

"You must regret not being there," the younger girl said when Bathilde finished reading Françoise's description of Their Majesties' splendor and the citizens' enthusiastic welcome. "To see all the buildings hung with tapestries and banners, and the streets strewn with flowers and herbs. And the duke riding his horse. You could've worn one of your beautiful new gowns and danced with him. Have you chosen the day of your wedding?"

"The feast of St. Maurice of Carnoët, the thirteenth of October. At Poitiers Cathedral."

"That's not so many days away."

"What of yours? Your mother tells me Hilaire grows impatient."

"We've quarreled."

"About what?"

"He's jealous." Blushing, Giselle added, "I have an admirer."

"Someone in the village? Do I know him?"

"Nobody does. Last week he stopped at the well to draw water for his horse. He walked to the vineyard to watch the grape-cutting, and heard there was a lack of workers. He offered to help, which won my uncle's favor. His name is Louis. He's the handsomest, politest man I've ever known."

Bathilde doubted that Hilaire had any cause for concern. The remarkable newcomer wouldn't remain long. It wasn't unusual for itinerants to assist with the harvesting of fruit or barley or hay, but they soon moved on.

Giselle gathered an armful of new chemises and petticoats and carried them to the clothes press, then crossed to the window. The slanting afternoon light illuminated her pretty face and burnished her brown hair. "The laborers will soon make their way home. Last evening a fiddler played for us, and Louis danced with me. Perhaps he will again."

"Be sure to dance with Hilaire as well. He's your suitor and has the approval of your family."

Giselle approached her to ask shyly, "Might I please have some of the blue ribbon and a length of bobbin lace for the new gown I'm making for the festival of the vines? It has a bodice of blue cloth, and I sewed the skirt from the whitest linen I've ever seen. Uncle Pascal bought it for me when he went courting his sweetheart in Niort."

Bathilde sorted through her collection of trimmings and handed over the requested items.

"This is more than I need."

"Keep it. For a matching cap, or a new bonnet."

"I want to look nice for Louis," Giselle confided. "I like him very much."

No harm can come from liking, thought Bathilde. She's young, with an affectionate nature, and courted by someone she's known all her life. In her place, I'd probably enjoy a handsome stranger's attentions. For a few days.

"Do you think you'll be happy with your duke?"

"I believe so," Bathilde replied. "Although I'm not entirely sure whether he will be happy with me. There are many similarities between us, I've discovered. But one significant difference." Albin, by accepting a commission in the king's guard, had tied himself to the royal court from which she'd chosen to separate herself.

"He's not old and ugly, I hope."

"He's about five years older than I am. And extremely good-looking."

"I'm glad. Everyone is eager to see him when he comes. And excited about your marriage." Curtsying, the girl said, "I thank you for the trimmings, princess."

"I'll be there for the festival, to see you in your finery," Bathilde told her.

A little while later, Sophie entered the room and announced, "Monsieur Mesny is here. My dear, I scarcely recognized him!"

She rose. "He came alone? The duke isn't with him?"

"Apparently not. I received no explanation."

Since their parting in Poitiers, she hadn't received any letters from her future husband. Her only knowledge of his activities came from Françoise's pen, in that single line about his appearance in the royal cavalcade. She supposed he'd remained in Paris, with the court. Was he as eager for their wedding day as she was? That question, she knew, she couldn't ask his cousin.

Unable to feel at ease in a situation where he'd previously been comfortable, Wilfride forced his spine into rigidity. He thrust out his chin for the servant who carefully scraped away the thicket of beard that had obscured much of his face during weeks of rambling through the provinces with Albin. Outwardly calm, inwardly he seethed with frustration and wrath. The secret he'd carried into this château weighed upon his conscience. He couldn't banish his fear that the truth he so carefully concealed would be detected. Or revealed.

After the man left the room with his razor and bowl and cloth, Wilfride gazed at his reflection in the glass. The paler flesh below his cheekbones and over his chin contrasted with the tanned portions above.

Bored and jaded by many months dancing attendance on the king, Albin had rushed away from Paris, intent on finding amusement. He had, in the oddest ways and in some most peculiar places.

Throughout their journey to Normandy, they had lodged in the guest quarters of various abbeys, ancient stone buildings with inhabitants devoted to prayer and worship and study and work. His cousin's monkish tendencies had been evident in the company of Jesuits, but between those stops he reverted to vagabond ways. They spent several days traveling with a troupe of actors. Albin, uninterested in performing, relied on logistical skills developed in the military to arrange the transport of wardrobe and properties as they moved from town to town. At Cherbourg, on the northern coast of the jutting Cotentin peninsula, he decided to join the crew of a fishing boat. Every day for a full week, he had hauled in nets teeming with flounder, langoustines, and crabs, with a set of brawny fellows who were unaware that the merry volunteer was an aristocrat, a cavalry officer, and a king's companion. Wilfride remained on shore, fretting that someone would recognize Albin. Rounding the peninsula, they spent several nights at Château Rozel, where the duke had cast off his disguise.

To Wilfride's dismay, his cousin had entered Poitou incognito. Giving in to a final, fleeting urge for adventure, he acquired a lodging in the small cottage beside the vineyard keeper's house, provided in exchange for his assistance with the grape harvest. His whimsical and risky masquerade as the commoner "Louis," practically under the nose of his betrothed, tried Wilfride's patience to the breaking point.

His reunion with the princess he dearly loved was bittersweet. Throughout dinner, he had to feign ignorance about his cousin's exact whereabouts and present activities. Worse, Albin wanted him to slip out of the castle later and make his way through the darkness to the village for a conspirators' conference.

And I'll have to watch him flirt with that pert, pretty coquette who hangs on his every word, he grumbled to himself, clenching his teeth in frustration.

She lived in the house beside Albin's temporary abode. Her name was Giselle.

"When I become lord of these lands," Albin declared, "all these good people will remember the days I worked alongside them."

"And how you danced too often with that girl," Wilfride retorted. Reluctantly he'd responded to his cousin's urgent request for fresh body linen. "What am I to do with this?" he asked, holding up a discarded shirt, damp with sweat.

"Madame Durand will launder it, if I ask very nicely. She hasn't been uncivil, but I can tell she dislikes me."

"Handing over soiled garments isn't likely to improve her opinion," he said wryly. "What difference does it make whether she likes you or doesn't?"

Albin avoided his gaze. "Everybody wants to be liked."

"That's no answer. She would be wise to keep her daughter close."

"You imply that she has cause to mistrust me."

"If you had sisters, you'd know that youthful, impressionable females can spin much meaning from careless words and gestures. You do that girl, and the princess, a grave disservice by maintaining your disguise. Mark my words, the truth will come out."

"Cease your carping," Albin grumbled. "I happen to enjoy picking grapes in the sunshine and exchanging japes with the locals. And at day's end, dancing with the fairest girl in the village."

"What of sleeping in a hovel? Eating common fare instead of the delicacies served at the de Sevreau table?"

"Join me in the vineyard. You might find you enjoy harvesting, and drinking *pineau* with the other fellows."

He had to go. Not from any eagerness to perform manual labor, or to disport himself with the common folk, but to keep watch on his cousin and ensure that he didn't get himself into worse trouble.

# CHAPTER 26

*October, 1660*

Bathilde gazed raptly at the pup wriggling from excitement at being released from the confines of a coach. A female, she had a white body with a contrasting black mask and ears and a prominent oval dot marking her forehead. At the base of her tail there was a corresponding black patch, and faint ticking was scattered along her back and sides.

"How thoughtful of the king to send her."

The royal courier handed over the leather lead attached to the dog, and a letter.

Reading it, she announced to Sophie and Monsieur Mesny, "Her name is Blisse, from a litter produced late last year by a pair of His Majesty's white and black hunting dogs. She came from a place called Versailles." She knelt down to caress the pointed muzzle. A pink tongue darted out to lap at her fingers. Engraved on the silver collar were the words *My Mistress is Princess Bathilde*.

"An unusual wedding present," Sophie commented.

"His Majesty sent another," the courier informed them.

In comparison to beautiful Blisse, anything else would

seem insignificant. Bathilde picked up the pup. With her arms full, she couldn't accept the casket being presented.

"Take it, Sophie. Open it for me."

"Here's a proper bridal gift," her relative declared. "Diamonds. Necklace, earrings, brooch, hair combs—and a ring. They come with a note in his own hand. He expects to see you wearing these when you appear at court."

"They're exquisite." She turned to Monsieur Mesny, standing beside her. "Which do you suppose I prefer, Blisse or these brilliants? His Majesty knows, I'm sure." Bestowing a smile on the royal messenger, she added, "Stay and take refreshment, while I pen a letter of gratitude."

She placed Blisse on the grass and reached for the casket.

After writing her note and sending it off with the courier, she took her pup into the garden. Watching Blisse trot through the *parterre,* she hoped the king didn't expect her to place his offering among the pack of de Sevreau hunting hounds. She had no intention of kenneling Blisse with the other dogs.

"I won't make a killer of you," she murmured, gently tugging the length of leather. "You shall stay near me by day, and at night you'll sleep on a cushion in my bed-chamber. When I go walking or riding or travel in the coach, you'll be at my side."

Hearing light footsteps, she whirled around to find Françoise Scarron observing her.

"Most noblewomen keep tiny spaniels, easily carried and cradled in the lap."

"Yet another delightful surprise! But my dear, why are you in black?"

"Last week Monsieur Scarron was delivered from his earthly agonies."

Bathilde crossed herself. "I'm sorry."

"After initial indecision and great reluctance, in the last hours he accepted the blessed sacrament from a priest's hand. His funeral took place the following day. I was the only person in attendance." She stood stiffly within Bathilde's sympathetic embrace. "I had no opportunity to write. I left our house in rather a rush, with only my clothing and a few personal possessions. All the furnishings and hangings, Scarron's pictures, and any other items of value will be sold at auction to pay his creditors. His cousin very kindly loaned me her lodgings at a convent. I must avoid Madame de Neuillant until next month, when I turn twenty-five. On that day, I shall attain complete freedom from her guardianship."

"Her son, the governor of Niort, is joining our hunting party. We expect him tomorrow."

"Do not, I beg, mention that you've seen me, or that I'm staying with my Tante Louise and Uncle Benjamin at Château de Mursay. I came to Poitou to collect my baptismal document. The Paris lawyers handling Scarron's estate—what little there is—require it. I'm hopeful of obtaining some part of my marriage portion once his debts are paid. But the matter will probably take a long time to resolve. What of you, are you now a duchess?"

"Not quite. I wish you might attend the ball, and my wedding in Poitiers next week. Although you probably wouldn't care to at such a sad time," she concluded, stroking her friend's black sleeve.

"I do mourn for Scarron. Even in his feeble state, he was a fascinating companion. People marvel that I remained faithful to a man incapable of being a true husband, in every way. I'm that rarity, a virgin widow." Eyeing the puppy, Françoise asked, "Your dog is quite young."

"The king sent her, with a casket of diamond jewelry. Will you stroll with us through the wood, to Myrte's burial place? I'm determined to exercise Blisse into a state of prostration."

The trees showed hints of more vibrant autumn color to come. The pup's black nose tracked scents left by the wild creatures that roamed the forest. Excited by the red squirrel darting from branch to branch, she emitted a high-pitched whine, and Bathilde reined her in before she could give chase.

"Wandering these pathways is a favorite pastime," she said. "Although I shall curtail my excursions as soon as the hunting begins."

"Are you a huntress?"

"I shrink from bloodshed. I'll be rising early to see the huntsmen depart. I'll graciously welcome them back when they return. But how I dread hearing the descriptions of their activities."

They emerged from the dimness and arrived at the bright and open place marked with the solitary stone cross. Pink blossoms adorned the rose bush growing beside it.

Bathilde said, "Amalie gave me three of these *Quatre Saisons* plants before I left the Ursulines. I moved one here, where it thrives. I believed the myrtle was too tender to survive the severe cold of winter, yet it does. Someone has been picking it." Examining the shaggy shrub, she counted several places where a sprig had been taken.

"During our schooldays, Myrte and I spent hours together, yet never became close. I still find it hard to believe that a girl so strong-minded died from heartbreak."

"It weakened her. But she was also quite ill."

"Fidelity is a virtue too few gentlemen possess. Can you trust that your duke won't respond to the longing glances the court ladies cast at him?"

Staring at the church steeple in the distance, Bathilde replied, "If he strays, I daresay he'd be discreet enough not to provoke unpleasant gossip. I doubt I'd ever learn of his lapses." She leaned down to grasp the pup's metal collar and gently pulled her away from the rose canes.

"Concealment would deprive him of the opportunity to do penance and obtain forgiveness," her friend said. "You should demand that he be shriven before making his vows."

"The state of his conscience is his affair, and his confessor's. If he has one."

"Where does that music come from? I hear a violin."

"Our villagers make merry after a long day of grape-picking. You must take some fruit with you. This season's crop is abundant, and we have plenty to spare."

After silently praying for their departed friend, they returned to the château.

On reaching the *salle-basse,* Bathilde untied the strap to free her pup. It followed her until it came to the staircase. Halfway up, she heard a mournful cry and turned to see Blisse helplessly pawing the bottom step.

"Come," Bathilde urged. The young dog managed an awkward but determined ascent. After giving praise, she said, "In no time, you'll be racing up and down."

She took Françoise to the antechamber where her new possessions were stored, soon to be packed into trunks for her journey to Poitiers. And afterwards—Paris?

"Justine," she said to her *fille de chambre,* "go to the kitchen and ask someone to fill a basket with the choicest grape clusters for Madame Scarron."

"Yes, princess." With a wary glance at the pup, the servant said, "I hope it won't harm your lovely things."

Elaborate court gowns and delicate underclothing were strewn over chairs. Velvets, satins, and length of lace not yet used were piled on tables and chests.

Françoise ran her hand across silver tissue overskirt.

"I shall have garments this fine, as soon as I'm out of mourning black."

Giving voice to a fresh thought, Bathilde said, "Cousin Sophie tells me that after I'm wed, I'll need a lady companion. I'm sure that's her way of indicating her wish to remain here as chatelaine in my stead." She didn't admit that it was also her wish to stay at the château. "Perhaps you might agree to fill the position."

"Me? My dear Bathilde, my situation isn't so desperate that I'm a candidate for your charity. I mean to find myself a bachelor, or a widower, to marry. I won't lack for suitors, but my next husband must be rich and well-connected. I've had my fill of poverty and philosophers and poets."

Even if her friend's expectation of receiving honorable proposals rose from vanity, it was firmly grounded in truth. Her dark curls, fair complexion, and rounded figure could make a convert of any man guided by the popular preference for golden-haired ladies.

"Cardinal Mazarin cut off Scarron's pension from the Queen Mother," Françoise went on. "Certain friends of mine will petition her to transfer it to me. It's not much, but any amount would be welcome." Crossing to a long bench, its surface covered by silver boxes and ebony caskets of various sizes, she lifted each lid to inspect the contents. "More rings than you've got fingers. Enough bracelets to cover each arm to the elbow. Ah, the diamonds." She held the necklace up against the light to make the stones sparkle. "Grand enough for a monarch's consort. Or mistress. At His Majesty's assemblies, you'll arouse even more jealousy wearing these than you already do."

Bathilde's education at the Ursuline school, subsequent years here at the château, the months in Paris with Papa, and their summer travels with the royal retinue—all had been planned as preparation for her future as a duchess. Within days, she would acquire a husband, the king's friend, who relied on her to carry out the required and desired duties. Just as she'd tried throughout her life to please Papa, she wanted to satisfy Albin's expectations. But at what cost to her own comfort, and with how much sacrifice of her preferences?

Aware that her dog had placed its dark, damp nose alarmingly close to a pair of silken sleeves, she moved to intervene.

It wasn't necessary. The thud of hooves and the rumble of wheels drew Blisse to the window. Bathilde joined her there, and saw her father's carriage coming over the stone bridge.

# CHAPTER 27

"I've kept my uncle's horses idling long enough," Françoise said. "Don't let that little beast trip us going down the staircase."

Blisse paused on the landing and sat on her haunches, uncertainly studying the steep decline.

"I'm not waiting for you," Bathilde said, and picked her up. Unable to hold the banister rail, she took slow, cautious steps in order to maintain her balance. Reaching the bottom, she placed Blisse on the polished floorboards.

Her father, supported by his cane on one side and his valet on the other, limped into the *salle basse*. Not bothering with the formality of a curtsy, Bathilde rushed forward to kiss his whiskered chin.

Bowing to her guest, he said solemnly, "Madame Scarron, my condolences. You've suffered a recent bereavement, I see."

"My husband has been in his grave less than a week." To Bathilde, she said, "We shall meet again, in Paris. In the meantime, you may direct letters to the convent. Petite-Charité."

"I will," Bathilde assured her.

"A pity," Papa said, as soon as they were alone, "that your school friend lost her husband. One wouldn't say it in her presence, of course, but she's well rid of that scamp Scarron."

"Françoise was devoted to him, in her way," she replied, "but he left her in desperate straits. She must settle all his debts and will have to sue in court to receive any inheritance she's entitled to. She's hoping for a stipend from the royal purse. We should write to the Queen Mother in support of her request."

He pointed his stick at Blisse, who had ceased sniffing his boots and stood at the fireplace, watching the flames. "Why is that animal in the house and not in the kennel?"

"Because Blisse belongs to me, not to you. King Louis sent her as my wedding present. She comes from a place called Versailles."

"A hunting lodge favored by His Majesty's father. I knew it well when I was younger. The red deer herd there provided us with excellent sport. I wonder if we'll be as fortunate here." Clapping his palm against his thigh, he called, "Come to me, little one. I encountered your forbears, many years ago." Stroking the black and white head, he smiled at Bathilde. "Look at those paws—she'll not stay this size, you know."

"Your chamber has been readied these three days, Gerard," Sophie informed him. "The guests arrive tomorrow."

"And I'm here in time to welcome them," he responded. "More warmly, I might say, then you've greeted me, *madame*." With a grin at Bathilde, he added, "So high and mighty. Does she have the effrontery to supplant me as master while I'm in residence?"

"Don't be absurd." Sophie took his arm, saying fondly, "You look in need of a dram of cognac, and a basin of hot water for your feet."

He bussed her cheek. "Indeed I am. Help me up these

stairs." Before going, he said to Bathilde, "Let de Rozel know that I've brought the marriage contract."

"He hasn't yet arrived," Sophie informed him.

"He'd best not tarry, or he risks missing out on splendid weather for the chase. We can't depend on it to last."

Albin's accommodations in the thatch-covered *chaumière* reminded Wilfride of the hardships of their soldiering years. At Château des Vignes, he was the recipient of gracious hospitality and slept in a soft bed and had servants to wait upon him. But he couldn't enjoy those luxuries, dreading that he would be called upon to explain his wayward cousin's prolonged absence. No one had questioned it, possibly assuming the king required the duke's presence at court. Neither had the prince or the ladies inquired about his evening excursions, when he came over to the village in hopes of persuading Albin to give up his pointless masquerade.

"Our horses," he said, ducking to pass through the low doorframe, "reside more comfortably in the Prince de Coulon's stable than you do here."

"It's not so bad. Besides, I'm in the vineyard most of the day. If you come with me tomorrow, you can use my extra knife. It's freshly honed."

Grudgingly responding to this invitation, early the next day he joined Albin. Armed with a sharp blade, he worked his way down a seemingly endless line of trellised vines, slicing off heavy grape clusters. Men and women loaded wicker baskets of fruit onto carts pulled by shaggy Poitevin donkeys. Hours of labor stiffened his arm, and his back ached from constant bending. Albin might relish this change from aristocratic life, but Wilfride was painfully aware that less than a league away, the princess waited patiently for her absent bridegroom.

"There's that fellow Hilaire," Albin grumbled from the opposite side of the vine. "Always searching out Giselle."

"Why shouldn't he?" Wilfride responded. "He courts her with the intent of making her his wife."

"But she hasn't accepted him as a husband."

Because, it was obvious to Wilfride, she expected a proposal from the visitor she knew only as Louis. Whether she was merely flirtatious or truly enraptured, he couldn't tell. Somehow, without exposing his eccentric cousin as a duke in disguise, he must make clear to her the futility of any marriage hopes.

After the sun dipped low behind the parallel rows, weary workers made their way home to drink and dine. The younger folk gathered around a bonfire in the village center. Casks of the local fortified wine were breached, and the male revelers—Albin among them—held their cups beneath the stream of liquid. A fiddler struck up a tune, his bow sawing the strings, to start the dancing.

Albin reached for Giselle before Hilaire could claim her. They joined the circle to skip and hop around the leaping flames. Watching their uninhibited performance, Wilfride recalled the many occasions when his cousin had partnered Princess Bathilde in a stately *allemande* and the lively, precise *courante*.

Someone handed him a tumbler of the dangerously potent *pineau Charentais*. He sipped it tentatively, unlike Albin, slaking his thirst with great gulps.

Flinging an arm around Giselle's waist, his cousin drew her away from the crowd, onto the path between her uncle's cottage and the smaller one adjacent. When he tried to steal a kiss, she ducked to evade it. She bent to pick a daisy from the clump growing beside a rustic bench. As they sat together, she playfully pulled off individual petals in the loves-me-loves-me-not game, until Albin seized it and tossed it aside.

The presence of guests transformed Château des Vignes from Bathilde's quiet countryside retreat to a smaller version of a bustling royal palace. It was filled with distant cousins, some of whom she recognized only by name, and she relied on Papa or Sophie to explain precisely how she was related to them. They had come from La Rochelle and Poitiers, or other places to the north and the south, bringing servants and horses and, in the case of one exalted female, a parrot whose frequent screeches provoked Blisse into growling.

Papa's duties as host to the gathering left Bathilde's urgent desire for private conversation unfulfilled. She could no longer put off revealing to him her firm reluctance to live at court. As much as she wished he could be the one to inform Albin, she knew it would be too cowardly a request for a marshal's daughter.

I have to do it, she realized. For myself. And for Albin, who deserves to enter our marriage knowing the full truth.

He'd repeatedly told her she could ask him anything, which surely meant she could also tell him everything. He was a good man, with an easy temperament, so she didn't greatly fear that her confession would rouse his anger. If she could make him understand, they might be able to find a compromise. But she needed to choose exactly the right moment to raise the subject.

Each carriage that failed to deliver him lowered her spirits. The marriage contract, pages of legal language concerning property and inheritance and contingencies, awaited his and Papa's signatures, a prerequisite to the ceremony at Poitiers. Monsieur Mesny had assured her that Albin would appear in time to participate in the hunt, well before the day appointed for the banquet and ball.

But he was not there on the mild, misty morning when the riders and horses and hounds first congregated in the stable yard. Bathilde maintained a tight grip of the woven leather lead attached to Blisse's collar. The dog raised her voice in unison with the baying hounds, as if disappointed not to join in the pursuit of their quarry.

For the next two days, Bathilde supervised the packing of her trousseau, frequently pausing at a window in anxious expectation of Albin's arrival. On the final day of the chase, she decided to wear her riding attire, a dark green velvet gown with a coat that extended almost to her knees. Justine bundled her hair into a chignon and bound it with a net fashioned from black cords. After adding the gold and crystal chain she'd worn when sitting for her miniature, Bathilde took up her plumed hat and a pair of leather gauntlets and went downstairs.

Her garments prompted her father to ask if she'd be participating in the afternoon sortie.

"I'm riding with you only as far as the village. I want to see the final cartload of grapes brought in, and I'll stay for start of the harvest celebration."

"If the stag eludes us," said her father, "we'll meet you there."

"Promise me you'll take no risks. I prefer a wedding next week in the cathedral, not a funeral."

"You think me feeble, but thus far I've managed to remain on my horse."

Bathilde paused at a table to inspect the *Quatre Saisons* roses she'd cut this morning and placed in a Chinese blue and white bowl. Bright pink and still fresh, she gathered them up and tucked them into the front of her jacket. "For Giselle," she told Sophie. "To bring her luck."

Before guiding Chardon across the stable yard, Bathilde heard a faint, plaintive whine. Blisse watched her departure from an upstairs window, nose pressed against the pane.

She accompanied the riders and the eager hounds over the bridge, along the drive, and between the tall stone pedestals topped with the de Sevreau shield.

Papa conferred with Valère and Hilaire, and called to his head huntsman, "We'll follow the road to Bois des Cerfs." He pointed the direction with his crop, then led the way at a pace faster than Bathilde liked.

She turned her horse in the opposite direction. A large group had left their houses and workshops, gathering in the village center to watch for the last cart.

Dismounting, she led Chardon into the gap between the two Durand cottages and looped the reins over an iron hook attached to one wall. Feeling something beneath her foot, she glanced down and discovered she'd trodden on a wilted daisy blossom. Several white petals lay scattered in the dirt, pulled from the faded golden center. She smiled to see evidence of the familiar, age-old game of determining a sweetheart's devotion. Myrte had sometimes played it as they sat together in the château garden, softly chanting, "Etienne loves me. Etienne loves me not."

She hoped the girl who plucked the daisy received the answer she desired.

# CHAPTER 28

Berthe Durand greeted her with pleasure. "Can I fetch wine for you, princess?"

"Thank you, yes." Handing the roses to Giselle, Bathilde said, "You've not visited me for many days."

"I've been helping my mother in the house and the *potager*. At night, after my friends and I finish our tasks, we dance." Holding up the bouquet, she spun on her toes.

Berthe returned with a beaker. She told her daughter, "You'd best change into your new gown and pin up your hair."

After Giselle entered the house, Bathilde asked, "The visitor you mentioned when last we met, is he courting her still?"

The woman sniffed derisively. "He amuses himself. After today, there'll be nothing more for him to do round here. Come, sit at the table."

Giselle reappeared and happily showed Bathilde how she'd sewn the lace to her sleeves and trimmed her white skirt with the blue ribbons she'd bestowed. One of the pink roses was tucked into her blue bodice, and she'd placed the rest in her hair. Kneeling, she stroked Bathilde's riding habit. "It's the color of the dark moss that grows in the forest, and feels exactly the same." Leaning close, she murmured, "Louis kissed me this morning, when we met at the well. If he asks me to wed him, I'll say yes."

Berthe shook her head. "We know nothing about him."

"He's handsomer than Hilaire," Giselle declared. "He dances well. And dresses better than anyone else."

To divert her, Bathilde said, "No matter which suitor you marry, you should have something special to wear on the day." She removed her hat and lifted the necklace over her head.

The girl put her hands behind her back. "Oh, I couldn't accept. This is too fine for me."

"Nonsense. Here, let me put it on."

"I thank you." Giselle kissed her hands, then started capering again. "I wish the harvesters would come. I want to dance all the night long."

Berthe grasped her shoulder, forcing a stop. "Hopping about like that, you'll do yourself a mischief. Save your strength for later."

"I feel only half alive when I'm not dancing."

Bathilde said, "If you come to my ball this evening, you'll see dances very different to the ones you know."

"How can I? This is my best gown, and I know it's not grand enough."

"I'll send over a pair of silken ones, for you and for your mother. Wear the necklace. And bring both of your sweethearts," she teased.

Distant shouts and laughter alerted them to the approach of the donkey carts, laden with the last baskets of fruit. Children raced to meet them, and the maidens clustered together, each one hopeful of wearing the crown fashioned from grape vines and flowers. The *notaire* stepped forward and handed it to Bathilde, inviting her to place it on the head of the designated queen of the vintage.

"Who receives it?"

"Mademoiselle Durand."

People of all ages formed a ring around the pair of them, and a cheer went up as Bathilde placed the wreath on Giselle's bowed head. She bestowed a quick kiss on each blushing cheek. "A happy day for you."

"I pray it will be even happier," the girl confided breathlessly.

The fiddler struck up a tune, an invitation to the young men and women to choose their partners. The boy dressed as Bacchus, in a long smock with grape vines wound around his head, came forward and asked Giselle to dance.

Before accepting his outstretched hand, she asked, "Did you see Louis, is he still in the vineyard?"

"He was drinking *pineau* with the men, until his friend came. They went away together, but I don't know where."

"You can't return to the village," Wilfride insisted. "Haven't you heard the hunting horn? This foolishness must end. At once."

Albin blinked up at him. With a grimy hand, he shaded his eyes from the midday sun. "Why?"

"The Prince de Coulon and his guests could pass by here at any moment. If Princess Bathilde is with them still, she'll see you."

"I promised to dance with Giselle."

"She'll have plenty of partners. You shouldn't have kissed her."

"I couldn't help myself."

"Or fondled her."

"She let me. She's quite free with her favors."

"They're not free. She has expectations."

Albin nodded, muttering, "She said if I asked her to wed me, she would."

Horrified, Wilfride stared down at him. "You didn't?"

"Don't remember." Albin rubbed his forehead. "No. I can't."

"You've wronged Princess Bathilde, who deserves all your loyalty." He dared to add, "And your love."

"I know. I *know*. What am I to do?" Albin gazed helplessly up at him.

"Take yourself to the river and bathe. It will sober you. I'll return to the cottage for the rest of your things. Wear my coat, and wipe the mud from your boots before you go to the château. By the time I meet you there, that beard had better be gone."

Wilfride pulled him up from the ground. He watched Albin long enough to make sure he didn't stumble and fall, then rushed along the path leading from vineyard to village, where a bonfire blazed. A group of men had circled around it, to quaff wine or the devilishly potent *pineau.* Young people cavorted to the music of the fiddler, a piper, and a drummer, their pounding feet bringing up clouds of dust.

He found the Durand girl and her mother standing outside the small cottage with the young gamekeeper—who had drawn a rapier halfway from its leather scabbard.

It belonged to Albin.

"Here's the crest, you can clearly see," Hilaire said. "This is the property of a gentleman—or an aristocrat. Your precious Louis is a thief."

Giselle inspected it. "He could have received it as a gift. Or a reward. Perhaps he found it lying in the roadway. We saw the nobles pass by on their way to the château. One of them might have dropped it."

"You delude yourself. On the day he arrived, he rode

a horse as fine as any in the prince's stable. Likely he stole it also. What became of it? I believe he sold it to some unsuspecting person."

The girl shook her head. "He's no criminal."

Madame Durand said, "I pray to God, my child, that you'll be spared suffering. Let us take this weapon to the château. The owner is surely a guest of the prince and princess."

The moment had come, Wilfride realized, to intervene.

"As it happens," he told them, "I'm on my way there." He reached for the rapier, his hand closing over the rose engraved at the top of the handle, the de Rozel heraldic emblem.

Hilaire refused to relinquish the weapon. "I mean to discover what manner of man has been living among us. If he's a nobleman's lackey, we might see him at the ball."

"What makes you think you'd be admitted?" Wilfride asked.

"The princess invited us," Giselle replied.

How like her, he thought, ever charitable and considerate. Refuting her good intentions made him feel both disloyal and brutish, but he had to do it. "I doubt she meant for you to mix with the grand company."

"You're wrong, *monsieur*. She knows I like to dance." The girl lifted a portion of the chain around her neck. "She gave me this."

"You misunderstood," he insisted.

"She sent silk gowns for us to wear. Mine is pink and my mother's is brown." Giselle frowned at him. "Aren't you acquainted with Louis? I've seen you together in the vineyard. Where is he? He didn't return with the others."

"I'm not sure," Wilfride said, truthfully. "Won't you give up that blade? I'm willing to restore it to its owner, without causing any trouble for—for Louis."

Hilaire shook his head. "We shall see to it ourselves."

He could do nothing more. Except collect Albin's belongings with all possible speed and leave the village without anyone noticing he had them.

Wilfride watched the dancers until Giselle and her mother entered their cottage, accompanied by the suspicious young man. He stepped inside the *chaumière*, muttering curses at his cousin for leaving his rapier where it could be found, and Hilaire for intruding without permission. A careful survey assured him that the remaining possessions hadn't been disturbed. A single trunk, secured by a lock, contained velvet and silk garments unused during these weeks of nomadic living. And the gemstone ring Albin had purchased before they'd left Paris, for his princess.

Wilfride had to warn him that his imposture was perilously close to being exposed. And, somehow, he must prevent Giselle and her mother and Hilaire from entering the château.

# CHAPTER 29

At dusk Bathilde took Blisse into the garden. Pierre, like all her servants, was too busy completing tasks related to the evening entertainments.

"Hurry," she murmured as the pup sniffed at the ground. "If I don't soon dress, I'll be late to my own banquet."

Within the past hour, the duke's trunk had been delivered by cart, and he would soon follow—if he hadn't already. Casting her hopeful gaze towards the upper windows, she found those of the chamber that Albin would occupy. A man's shadowy figure was visible. He placed a hand on the glass pane, as if reaching out to her.

She turned and hurried towards the nearest doorway. Clutching her skirts, she moved swiftly up the steep spiral staircase, with the dog following behind. Albin stood at the top, framed by the stone arch, wearing shirt and breeches and hose, but without a coat. Or shoes.

Blisse paused, front legs on the last step and her rear legs on the one below. The white fur at the back of her neck rose.

"Greet him politely," Bathilde told her. "Before long, he'll be your master." To Albin, she said breathlessly, "Welcome to Château des Vignes."

"I'm relieved to be here." His sober tone and bleak expression seemed to belie his words. "Is there a place where we can speak privately, with no danger of interruption?"

Taking him to her *salle de musique,* she said, "The king sent Blisse as a bride gift. You'll have to accustom yourself to her presence, for she cannot bear being separated from me."

"I hope she accepts me as readily as I do her." He stroked the black spot on the dog's forehead. "Part of your dowry, is she?" Looking up at Bathilde, he said, "As you know, I bring nothing into our marriage but my title, my reputation as an officer, and a single property in Normandy. I trust you don't regard them as insufficient."

Boldly, she declared, "I do. For I desire a great deal more."

"At this late date, amending the contract agreed by your father and me would cause further delay to the wedding."

"What I crave requires personal negotiation between us. It cannot be stated in legal language."

"Go on."

"First, I'd like to know how you envision our life together, after we're married. What your expectations are. Your hopes. Where you mean for us to live."

He angled his head to one side. "In Paris, I suppose. Or at Fontainebleau. Anywhere the king chooses to be. You'll likely be given an important position in his consort's household. He wants me to serve on his counsel of advice. Though initially reluctant to accept the appointment, I've made up my mind to do so. I shall tell your father, when I see him."

"You don't want to be the king's counselor?"

"I fully intend to adapt myself to your wishes. At certain times of the year, we'll—"

"But you don't know my wishes."

Her interruption obviously startled him. "I've made assumptions, guided by my conversations with the prince. I see now that I should've inquired about your preferences. I want to hear them."

"If you promise to tell me yours. With complete honesty."

He nodded.

She searched for the words that would accurately convey her convictions. "I've always been an obedient daughter. Occasionally at the cost of my contentment, I confess. As determined as I am to be the sort of wife—duchess—you require, I must also to be true to myself. And I want you to understand what I mean. Only, it's difficult to express."

"Try," he urged.

"My greatest hope is that you'll be able to—that in time you can learn to accept that I'm quite unlike Papa. He's majestic and illustrious and grand. I am not, and never will be, however hard I try to emulate him and fulfill his wishes. I don't aspire to be a great lady, flaunting myself at the king's court. I've no interest in becoming a *dame d'honneur* to his queen."

"Do you say that to please me, because I've admitted my reluctance to serve in the royal household?"

"No. It's the truth."

"Then I shall speak as plainly as you asked me to. I cannot abide court life," he declared vehemently. "The constant striving for superiority. The ceaseless sycophancy. I see now that I should've made it clear to you weeks ago. But I was fearful of alienating you and thwarting your ambitions."

She laughed softly. "I have none. I was schooled in a convent, remember? Peace and quiet and useful pursuits are more meaningful to me than parading in my finest clothes and jewels, in a palace where gossip and scandal are common currency. I feel most content when I'm here. And I know I'd be just as happy at Château Clément. Or in Normandy. Anywhere, as long as we're together. Because I care for you, Albin. More than I imagined possible."

"I've longed to hear you say it."

"Have you?" she whispered.

"I admit, on the day we met I didn't think in terms of feelings—yours, or mine. My only emotion was relief that you turned out to be lovely and mannerly. That was sufficient, I thought. Later, encountering you at Madame Scarron's salon, among all the shallow *coquettes* and preening *précieuses,* I admired your intelligence as well as your refinement. I began to envy your many admirers their gift for gallantry and their crackling wit. What's more, the king favors you to the extent that I regarded him as my rival."

"Never. Oh, Albin."

"All these weeks since we parted in Poitiers, I've missed you, with a longing I've never known. Or imagined. May I kiss you?"

"I wish you would."

She went joyfully into his embrace, meeting his lips.

Drawing back, he smiled down at her. "That is a surer seal of our bond than scrawling my name on a document. I'm in love with you, Bathilde de Sevreau."

"And I with you, Albin Bertrand."

"For how long have you known?" he asked.

"Before we reached Saint-Jean-de-Luz. And you?"

"It began to be obvious to me while we were there. The day of the king's wedding, when I followed you down to the shore. In Roquefort, my feelings became a great deal clearer, during the earthquake. I was desperate to find you and make sure you weren't frightened—or injured. In Poitiers, I was on the verge of a declaration. But when you chose not to go with me to Paris, I realized you weren't ready to hear it. And feared you might never be."

"I wanted that, for by then I knew the depth of my affection for you. But we were being watched as closely as the king and queen. I'd grown uncomfortable with everyone constantly observing us whenever we talked and dined and danced. I've wanted to be with you. Exactly like this."

They kissed again, more feverishly.

Blisse, stretched upon the carpet, thumped her tail.

"She approves," Bathilde murmured.

His palm cupped her cheek, then moved to his mouth to stifle a yawn.

She smiled. "Bored?"

"Overtired. Before I finish dressing, I'll rest a while—if I can. But I won't leave until you swear to me that this is no dream."

"If it is, I want never to wake."

After a day of vineyard work, Wilfride thankfully put on formal garments—not that he expected to stir Princess Bathilde's admiration. He never appeared to advantage at Albin's side.

Handsome Albin. Fortunate Albin.

He visited his cousin's bedchamber, intending to warn him about the danger of being revealed as Louis the grape-gatherer.

"No more beard," he observed. "Good to see the whole of your face once more."

Beaming, Albin rubbed his smooth cheek. "I am myself again. Rather, a better, much happier version."

"Your drenching in the river improved your mood."

"It helped. Though not as much as hearing Princess Bathilde profess her love for me. Our hearts are fully engaged. Our desires are in concert. We arrived at a true understanding. You may felicitate me."

"I do."

This affirmation came at a cost. For months he'd hoped that a mutual regard would develop, believing that the two people he loved best deserved to love one another. He should rejoice for them, with them. And he was trying to. But Albin's revelation did make him ache inside.

"I must attend to other matters," he managed to say. "Before the banquet."

It was even more imperative that he intercept the girl and her mother and the gamekeeper and send them away. He didn't want them to see Albin and accuse him of stealing his own sword.

He charged down a back stair, motivated more by his concern for the princess than for the miscreant. He was determined to prevent her discovery of Albin's foolish impersonation and extreme carelessness in dallying with a girl so far beneath him. And he couldn't let Giselle find out she'd had been deceived by the Duc de Rozel until he was safely married. She would eventually, it was inevitable. But if her suitor had his way, she'd also be wed by the time she learned the truth.

"Giselle?" a harried kitchen maid repeated. "Yes, I know her. She delivers baskets of fruit for the princess, and sometimes helps with the sewing. No, I've not seen her tonight. She'll likely be at the festival in the village."

"If she does come, keep her here and send someone to inform me. Do you understand?"

"Yes, *monsieur.*"

Going to the great hall, he accosted a footman. "You,

there," he called. "Who's responsible for admitting invited guests?"

"The porter, *monsieur*. But he stepped away to have his dinner."

"Let him know that if the Durand women and the gamekeeper turn up, they cannot be permitted to enter. No matter what they say, they are not to step over the threshold. Is that clear?"

"As you wish, *monsieur*."

He'd almost reached the door to the garden when Madame de Sevreau, splendidly attired and bejeweled, hailed him.

"The prince is asking for the duke. Do you know where he is?"

"In his chamber, when last I saw him."

"When the servant called to him, he didn't respond."

"I'll find him," Wilfride offered, barely concealing his reluctance to delay his mission.

# CHAPTER 30

"The diamonds from the king are exquisite," Bathilde acknowledged. "But tonight, I prefer these." She handed her mother's pearl necklace to Justine, who moved behind her to fasten it around her neck and added the matching earrings she'd received from Papa. Her shimmering gown of blue and gold brocade, she hoped, would find favor with the person responsible for her soaring spirits.

"Princess." Pierre stood on the threshold. "The prince requests your presence in his private chamber."

"I can do nothing more," Justine told her. "You are perfection."

The family apartments were clustered in the same wing, and Papa's suite was near her own. He wasn't alone.

Albin, dressed in black velvet trimmed with silver lace, came forward to take her hand. "We've signed the marriage contract," he told her. "You and I are as irrevocably bound as human law can make us."

"And in less than a week," Papa added, "the archbishop will do his part. My children, I offer you my blessing on your betrothal, before we celebrate it with our family members and friends. I shall be present to welcome our guests to the banquet. After the dancing begins, I mean to withdraw—quite discreetly. Several days of hunting has depleted my limited strength. De Rozel, I designate you as host of the festivities, in my stead. Not too great an imposition, I trust."

"None at all. I deem it an honor."

"And you don't mind that the document we lately signed burdens you with the care of my daughter?"

Smiling, Albin's fingers pressed Bathilde's. "That is my privilege. Never a hardship."

"Seeing the pair of you happily conjoined pleases me more than I can express. Let us go down," Papa said, "and open our revels."

They entered the *salle à manger* together, Bathilde between the two men. Tapers flickered in the *candélabres* lined up on the long table and in the *lustres* overhead. Guests surged forward to offer felicitations—relatives, neighbors. Her mother's great-aunt addressed her in the loud, heavy tones of one whose hearing had faded long ago.

"You're acquainted with my sister Suzanne," Niort's governor reminded her. "The Duchesse de Navailles, *dame d'honneur* to Queen Marie-Thérèse."

"I first met Madame Scarron's godmother in Poitiers, when I was a girl. We were often together during the summer, while traveling with the king." She refrained from mentioning Françoise's recent visit, as requested.

Sophie's cousin, a stately female, conveyed the good wishes of family connections living in a town close to Château Clément. "Everyone in the vicinity is eager to be presented to the Duc de Rozel. Do you expect to go there after you wed him?"

"We've not decided," she replied. Nor had they discussed it. "Sometime before Christmas, perhaps. I look forward to being there once more. For so many years I've lived elsewhere."

Papa, she knew, intended to pass the winter there, and she trusted that a lengthy period of rest would improve his health—his earlier admission of frailty troubled her. If she and Albin followed him, she could ensure that he didn't overtax himself. For the duration of this nuptial season, he'd temporarily abandoned the military memoir, and looked forward to resuming his painstaking work on his return to the grand château in Aunis. During this blessed peacetime, he said, officers and soldiers currently serving would benefit from reading about wartime exploits, and the veterans would enjoy reliving them.

Bathilde's appetite often failed her at banquets. During this one, her heart was beating an ecstatic rhythm at the memory of kissing and being kissed by Albin. In a little while they would dance together. Perhaps tomorrow he would touch and caress her. Within days, she would experience the pleasures awaiting her in their marriage bed. Contemplating future intimacies, she studied the angles of his cheek and jaw, the gleaming brown hair. She recalled the strength in the arms that had enclosed her, and the firmness of his broad shoulder when she'd rested her head against it.

As footmen carried in trays of fruit and cheese, Albin suddenly rose and drew her from her chair in a proprietary move that was immensely pleasing. He led her down a passage and into a tower chamber, guiding her away from the door before he cupped her face with his hands. He tipped it up for his kiss.

"I can't help myself," he told her.

"You needn't apologize."

"Must we wait to marry? The contract is signed. There's a chapel downstairs. At any time, we can send for the village priest."

"Papa's heart is set on the cathedral," she reminded him. "If we insisted on altering his plan, I'm sure he'd consent. But he'd be terribly disappointed if we don't speak our vows in the same place where he and Maman did."

"Then we shall comply with his wishes. I'm too grateful for his fatherliness, and his decision to entrust his precious daughter to me."

"We'll be together every day till then. Whenever we wish."

"Not quite." His fingers traced the curve of one breast. "Of all the capital virtues, patience proves most problematic. By comparison, sobriety, charity, diligence, humility, and kindness seem much easier. Usually."

"You left off chastity." She lifted her brows. "I wonder why."

"If I were a philanderer, Bathilde, I wouldn't be so eager for our wedding—and what comes immediately after. I feel as though my life truly began when you said you love me."

"So did mine, saying it. And hearing the same words from you."

"If we don't leave this room now, I'll be tempted to hold you here the rest of the evening."

"I wouldn't mind," she assured him. "But Papa and our guests wait for us to open the ball."

They moved to the *grande salle* and claimed the center of the room, the musicians' signal to begin the *allemande*. They had often performed these steps in front of the king's watchful courtiers, but on this night her enjoyment was far greater. During the *courante* that followed, she was intent on the intricate footwork and didn't notice Papa's absence until the end of the dance.

"He told us he'd retire early," Albin pointed out.

"Even so, I should make sure he's weary and not unwell."

She moved quickly across the *salle,* hoping no one

would detain her, but her attention was drawn by raised voices from the antechamber. Peering inside, she saw Monsieur Mesny with Giselle and Berthe Durand, and Hilaire—holding an unsheathed sword.

Giselle took it from him and carried it to Bathilde. "Do you know who owns this?"

Inspecting the rapier's hilt, she recognized the floral emblem. "It belongs to the Duc de Rozel. How do you happen to have it?"

"It was in the cottage where my—where Louis lives."

Pointing at Monsieur Mesny, Hilaire said, "Princess, this man tried to drive us out, knowing we came to expose his friend's thievery. I believe he works in league with Louis, as an accomplice."

She looked to Albin's cousin. "I'm confused. Are you acquainted with a person who stole your cousin's blade?"

"You needn't concern yourself, princess. This is a misunderstanding."

"I'm extremely concerned." Pitying Giselle, clearly distressed, she said gently, "If this is proof that your Louis is disreputable and untrustworthy, you'll not be in the mood for gaiety. Let your mother and Hilaire take you home."

In a faint voice, the girl replied, "I no longer feel like dancing. But I would like to watch." She fingered the necklace of gold and faceted crystal that Bathilde had bestowed.

"Then do. And you must stay for the supper that will be served later."

Giselle didn't respond. She stared straight ahead, eyes wide and mouth gaping.

Bathilde followed her gaze. Albin, in the doorway, extended his hand.

"The *sarabande* is next, and I know you enjoy—"

Abruptly his expression altered and his arm fell to his side.

"Louis, I hardly recognize you."

"No common thief," Hilaire muttered. "No commoner, either."

"This is the Duc de Rozel. Our marriage takes place next week."

"No, no," Giselle protested. "That's not possible. He's my sweetheart."

Comprehension dawned. Dazed and numbed by her young friend's plaintive words, Bathilde turned to Albin. He regarded her silently, a flush staining his cheeks.

His gaze shifted to Giselle. "The princess and I have been promised to one another for the past six years," he told her.

Several curious guests had gathered near the door. To prevent their entry, Monsieur Mesny closed it, muffling the music and voices on the other side.

"We picked grapes together. Every night you danced with me."

In a subdued voice, Albin went on, "My behavior in recent days gave a false and unfair impression."

Giselle's astonishment swiftly turned to anguish. Her shoulders sank, her brown head drooped. She curled one hand into a fist and with the other plucked at the air. "He loves me, he loves me not," she warbled. "He loves me. Not. He never did."

Bathilde recalled the daisy on the ground, half its petals missing. "Oh, Giselle."

"I entreat you to pardon me. Tell me how I can make amends."

At his approach, Giselle shrank back, gasping, "Don't touch me!" She pulled the pink roses from her hair, so violently that she dislodged the pins holding up her long brown tresses.

"Believe me, I meant no harm." He faced Bathilde, saying softly, "To anyone."

Unable to find adequate words of sympathy, or consolation, she led the trembling girl to the row of chairs against the wall and made her sit.

Rocking herself back and forth, Giselle wailed, "Louis is no longer mine. I've lost him. Mother didn't want me to dance. This sun makes me so hot. The grapes were ripe. You placed one in my mouth. We laughed, sitting together in the shade. If you ask, I will say yes." She babbled on, her speech veering from calm coherence to frantic delirium. Her fingers shook as she removed the necklace and dropped it into Bathilde's lap. "I'm grateful for your goodness to me, but I need this no longer."

"Keep it. I want you to."

"I cannot," Giselle replied and let it slip from her hands. She rose jerkily and rushed over to Hilaire, tugging at the sword he still held. His grip loosened and it fell to the floor with a loud clatter. Lifting it by the pointed tip, she arched herself over the raised blade.

Albin rushed over and seized it before she could impale herself. He passed it to his cousin, who slid it into the scabbard.

Giselle staggered towards Berthe and fell into her arms, sobbing. "The pain, it's more than I can bear."

"We'll take you home." The woman brushed away the tears and stroked the tangled hair. "I'll give you a calming *tisane.*"

"It won't heal this ache." Giselle touched her breast.

Wrenching herself out of her mother's embrace, she ran frantically from one corner of the room to the next and back again, as if seeking an escape. Each time she passed Albin, he tried to catch her, but she moved too swiftly. Halting at a window, she pounded the glass as though desperate to break through, until Hilaire pulled her away.

"I feel nothing now," she said faintly, unclenching her fists. "I fade away."

Bathilde approached her. "Let me take you to a chamber, where you can lie down."

With a piercing shriek, Giselle stepped back, arms flailing. "Help me! Save me! The girls in white are here, they fly at me. They'll take me away, to dance in the forest forever." She shuffled her feet, her steps fast and frantic.

Her cries had penetrated the solid door. Someone turned the handle and tried to push it open, but Monsieur Mesny pressed his shoulder against it.

Hilaire gripped Giselle's forearms. Shaking her, he said forcefully, "We must go. Now."

Ignoring him, she said to Bathilde, "I wish you all happiness with Louis. I bless you." With outflung arm, she gestured at Albin. "Never again will I see him. I do forgive him. And bless him, too."

Myrte cursed her betrayer, thought Bathilde. Giselle offers absolution and a blessing. Each, in her delirium, spoke of ghostly females. The imagined appearance of the *vili* was regarded as a premonition of—

"I'm dying." Giselle flattened her palm against her heart. She turned to Bathilde and Albin. "When I'm gone, both of you must pray for me." She drifted back to the window, and whatever she thought she saw beyond it made her smile serenely. As she sank to the floor, pink silk pooled around her inert form.

Berthe laid her hands upon her daughter's chest, seeking signs of life. Unable to detect movement, she moaned in agony and collapsed onto the body.

No one spoke until Bathilde said to Albin, "Leave us. This is no place for you."

Until awakened by her maid's footsteps, Bathilde was unaware that she'd slept at all. At some unknown hour, she'd reached her bed. For a very long time she'd lain there, stunned by sorrow and weakened from weeping. Her wretchedness was made worse by the knowledge Giselle's demise resulted from an impetuous and benevolent invitation to her ball.

"I didn't mean to disturb you," Justine murmured. "I came for the dog, knowing she'll want her food."

"I should go to Papa." In a faint voice, she added, "And find the duke."

"He departed at dawn, with his man. Off to Poitiers, I expect, to make ready for your wedding. Such a strange, sad morning this is. I've come from the chapel, where the servants are praying over poor Giselle. You'd think her a bride, lying peacefully in the white silk robe you chose for her, with the roses in her hair and a myrtle branch in her hands."

Bathilde recalled wandering in her garden, sometime after midnight, gathering greenery.

"Everyone wonders what caused her to drop and die so suddenly."

"A weakness of the heart, her mother said. The same malady that took her father."

Berthe Durand wanted no scandal attached to her daughter. She'd forced Hilaire to swear he would never reveal the cause of Giselle's rapid descent into derangement and death.

What, Bathilde wondered, does Papa know? Before going away, did Albin confess his role in bringing about a tragedy?

Leaving her bed, she stepped onto the balcony. Golden autumnal light spread itself across the garden, making the dew sparkle in the grass. October could not have produced a more perfect morning, one she might have spent strolling the *parterre* beside the man she loved, listening to him beautifully, eloquently express his love for her.

Whatever his purpose in leaving, or his destination, he'd deserted her at a time of great need. And he must also require comfort, knowing the great damage he'd done—however unintentionally.

Bathilde recalled the distant childhood days she'd spent with Giselle, occupied in simple games, largely unaware of their difference in status. Later, on her return from the convent, she'd taught the young villager to read and loaned her a book. Giselle had amused Myrte by dancing to harpsichord tunes, and helped nurse her through decline and early death, never expecting to share her fate.

Entering the mysterious, liminal space between life and whatever came after, both of Bathilde's friends had received a visitation from the spectral *vili*, the deserted brides who flitted through the night forest, torturing any man who had the misfortune of rousing their vengeance. Their state as described in legend seemed akin to purgatory—but far worse, with no prospect of release or redemption. Had they lived long enough, they might have forgiven their faithless sweethearts, as Giselle had *in extremis*.

Whatever Albin did to make her believe he was marriage-minded, Bathilde reflected, his declaration of love for me was sincere. He accurately described the journey from mild admiration to appreciation to possessiveness to longing. Because I followed a parallel path, I know he spoke the truth.

From across the room, Justine said, "Even when distressed, you shouldn't be so careless with your jewels. If

I hadn't seen this on top of your *armoire,* it might have rolled over the edge and been lost."

"I placed the pearls in my casket. I'm sure of it."

Justine moved to her bedside and held out a ring. "Keep it on your finger. There's no safer place."

She took it, without admitting she'd never seen it before.

The large, table cut beryl gleamed greenish blue, as though the colors of the sea and the sky were stirred together. Its setting was gold, and tiny rose garlands were engraved along the shank.

While she slumbered, Albin had entered her room. She didn't know whether this was intended as a love token, a symbol of their approaching union, or his parting gift.

# Part III: Bathilde

## *1661-1664*

*Je les vois! je les vois! Elles me dissent: "Viens!"*
*Puis autour d'un tombeau dansent entrelacées;*
*Puis s'en vont lentement, par degrés éclipsées*
*Alors je songe et me souviens . . .*

I see them! I see them! They say to me: "Come!"
Then intertwined around a tomb they dance,
Then slowly go away, by degrees eclipsed
So I dream and remember . . .

—Victor Hugo, *Fantomes*

# CHAPTER 31

*Château Clément, April, 1661*

On the cusp of a New Year, after an absence of nearly half her life, Bathilde returned to the property her late father had loved more than any other.

Several weeks before Christmas he'd suffered a setback, and it soon became apparent that the brave *maréchal* wasn't robust enough to win his final battle. After laying him to rest with her mother in Poitiers Cathedral, she decided Château des Vignes was too closely associated with bereavement—Myrte died there, then Giselle, and so had her only parent. And though Albin lived, she'd lost him also, either temporarily or permanently.

The day she arrived at this grand château close to the sea, she'd taken on numerous and daunting responsibilities. With capable Sophie at her side, as well as an experienced and knowledgeable major domo, and servants glad to welcome a de Sevreau mistress after so long without one, her initial concerns vanished. Papa had been their benign and respected master, and Maman was fondly remembered by those whose tenure stretched back far enough to have known her.

Receiving visitors, learning the local residents' names

and titles, inventorying supplies, and approving orders of provisions had occupied her throughout a grim winter. Persistent freezes and frequent showers had proved disastrous to the field crops, threatening farmers and laborers with ruin. During her months of mourning, Bathilde prayed for better weather, on their behalf and hers. She'd devoted herself to the study of stone fruit cultivation, to better understand the extensive production of apples, pears, peaches, apricots, plums, and cherries. She commissioned updated maps designating each of the groves and the varieties grown in them. Grapes grew on these lands in far greater quantity than at des Vignes, for this was a region noted for its wine production.

A change of season restored her optimism and instilled a much-needed sense of renewal. Spring was declaring its presence with increased birdsong and bursts of color to brighten even its dreariest days. With each cluster of blossoms that opened on the branches, hopefulness dawned.

Wandering the orchards on a mild morning, she was surrounded by profusely blooming trees in various shades—pure white, palest pink, deeper pink—and the hum from the bees was constant. She wished Papa were present to join in her admiration of the spectacle. But she was not alone.

"Blisse, come to me."

Diligent training had fostered unfailing obedience in her young dog. Nearly a year old, Blisse responded to her call and followed her every command. During their rambles through the demesne, Bathilde kept her close, inhibiting the instincts of a creature with a sharp eye, bred to track scent. The estate abounded with rabbits, squirrels, and moles. Red deer emerged from the woods to graze at dawn and at dusk. But before turning homeward, she always allowed Blisse a brief period of freedom to explore at will.

Her relationship with her dog, closer than she'd known with any of her horses, was a consolation in this uncertain time. Blisse's constant presence was a gift. Her trust and complete dependence provided Bathilde with a fresh and meaningful purpose. They shared a bedchamber, and on a wakeful night, the deep, steady breaths coming from the cushion in the corner had a soothing quality that eventually lulled her into slumber. Whenever grief swelled, drawing tears that couldn't be contained, she held fast to the warm body and lovingly stroked the soft fur until she recovered her composure.

A distant flash of white gave assurance of her companion's return.

"Clever girl," she praised the panting dog, whose facial contortion exposed bright teeth, giving the impression that she smiled back.

The walk back to the château took them through the formal gardens. The oval pool's smooth surface mirrored the blue sky overhead. Water rose from a fountain at the center of a circular basin. Like everything else, the long *allées* and broad *parterres* had been created on a scale far more impressive than the place she'd left. At Château des Vignes, she'd willingly and eagerly busied herself among the flowers and in the *potager*. Here, intimidated by the expertise of the head gardener, his younger assistant, and their several underlings, she assumed they would regard any suggestion from her as meddling.

Much of the original medieval fortress established by her de Sevreau forbears had been razed several generations ago. Her grandfather, in his later years, commissioned a design for its replacement from a son of royal architect Jacques Androuet Cerceau, a Protestant follower of Palladio the Italian. Constructed from creamy Charente limestone and adorned by skilled Huguenot artisans from nearby La Rochelle, it stood three stories tall and was roofed in dark gray slate. Because the basement level sat partly above ground, the kitchens and cellars had ample light and curved vaulted ceilings like those of the main floor above.

Each time she approached the house from the garden, she looked up to the lofty room where, nearly two decades ago, she'd entered the world. Ascending the shallow steps between a pair of pediments, she paused to study the flat capstones that topped the twin plinths—ideal platforms for statuary.

"Blisse, would you pose for a sculpture?" She reached down to touch the black dot on the dog's forehead. "Seated exactly as you are. You'd have to keep still long enough for sketches to be made."

After informing Sophie of her plan, she said, "There will be a stone carver in La Rochelle who could do the work. The designs for the château were bound together in a leather volume, it's in the library. I should be able to identify the man who produced all the classical statues in those niches between the front windows."

"He'll be long dead," her cousin pointed out.

"The son or grandson could still be carrying out the trade."

"While you were out, a letter arrived. It bears the royal seal. You'll find it on the *escritoire.*"

The wax disk confirmed the sender's identity, for it bore the arms of France: a shield, surmounted by a crown and decorated with three *fleurs-de-lis*, held by a pair of winged angels on either side. She pried it loose and unfolded the page.

"Well?" Sophie prompted.

"This isn't the king's handwriting," she reported. "He dictated it to one of his secretaries."

"And?"

"The queen is with child and expects to be delivered

before Advent. He invites me to join them at Fontainebleau, where they will remain until autumn. Monsieur is there with his bride, Princess Henriette—Madame, as she's called now. His Majesty promises merriment and pleasure. Balls, plays, ballets, sport."

"That sounds most pleasant. There's no finer place to spend spring and summer than Fontainebleau. Your father would approve."

Throughout her life, Bathilde had sought to please him. The knowledge that she'd nearly always succeeded tempered some of her sorrow at losing him. In the aftermath of his untimely death, she'd grown increasingly conscious of her own preferences and desires. And from long association with the assertive Sophie, she was just as resolute in carrying them out.

"You can be sure Gerard wouldn't want you hiding yourself away any longer."

Bathilde eyed her reproachfully. "I'm not hiding."

"Then you'll accept this invitation?"

"I'd rather not. But for the next five years, the king is my guardian. Even though he requests my presence, it's his to command. If you go with me, I won't mind quite as much."

"I wasn't asked. Nor do I fancy all that activity. Or the company. The court is a youthful one now. I'm an older lady, untitled, with very few acquaintances in the royal household, apart from the Queen Mother. I shall remain here, quite contentedly. You'll have Justine to wait upon you and bear you company, and young Pierre Jousson as your page." Sophie paused before asking, "Does the king offer any information about the Duc de Rozel?"

"None."

"Perhaps he means to bring about a reconciliation."

She placed the letter on the desk. "I don't see how he could. The duke's only communication, in the months since we last saw him, was addressed to Papa and arrived after he—after the funeral. He indicated that he'd be departing on a foreign mission to a country he didn't name. He hasn't sought release from our marriage contract. He may not be aware that only the king has the power to free us from it."

"Do you want that?"

She twisted a loose curl around her forefinger. "There's too much I don't know. But I shall raise the subject while I'm at Fontainebleau. To the king, this is an insignificant matter. He has more important affairs to manage. Cardinal Mazarin is gone. He's ruling France without the advice and guidance he's had his whole life."

"Let us pray that he will do it well. And wisely."

"Amen to that," Bathilde murmured.

Although she accepted the necessity—and possible benefits—of abandoning Clément in this season of beauty and growth, her spirits dipped as she began the preparations to travel across the country. She directed Justine to pack lavish gowns that had languished, unworn, since her final days at Château des Vignes. Papa's spacious traveling coach, rarely used since his funeral procession from Château des Vignes to Poitiers and her journey to this house, must be made ready.

She climbed two flights of stairs to an attic room that stored a collection of items either infrequently used or never needed. While she searched for her trunks and *coffres,* Blisse explored the unfamiliar space, darting around discarded pieces of furniture and sniffing faded cushions. Sunlight from a rectangular window struck an object Bathilde had never seen.

The cradle, fashioned from a dark, heavy wood— walnut, she supposed—had a peak like a church spire at the head, carved with roses. Grasping the edge, she rocked it several times, aware that she'd been the last babe to lie here. Her brother hadn't lived long enough.

How long, she wondered, will it remain empty? Will I ever place a child of mine and Albin's here? Our son would inherit all the de Sevreau property and possessions accumulated over the centuries, along with the various titles and hereditary offices held by Papa. If we had a daughter, I would tell her stories and teach her to play the harpsichord, as Maman did me. I'd kiss and cuddle them both, and make it possible for them to lead lives of their choosing—not of mine, or their father's.

Before opening her letter from Louis, her plans for the future had been savoring the abundant pleasures Château Clément offered. She didn't relish the prospect of leaving this comfortable refuge while her gardens exhibited their springtime glory. She longed to see blossoms on all those unknown varieties of roses lining the *allées* and clambering over arbors. But as she'd admitted to Sophie, she couldn't decline His Majesty's invitation. Papa's last will and testament spelled out his authority as her guardian. Because she would be a royal ward until her twenty-fifth birthday, should she remain unwed, she wanted to discover how much liberty, if any, the king would grant her. He might insist that she live at court, regardless of her wishes. He had the power to revoke her marriage contract and marry her off to another nobleman. Lonely spinsterhood—and this empty cradle—would be preferable to an alliance with a stranger.

An added complication was the inescapable fact that she loved Albin. His weeks toiling in her vineyard would have amused her, had it not resulted in so much misery. She'd read the contrition in his face when Giselle had declared him to be her suitor Louis, and his apologies had sounded heartfelt. And after that endless night he'd vanished, surely burdened with guilt and grief that Bathilde might have eased.

We're legally bound, she reminded herself, unless and until he repudiates the marriage contract he and Papa signed and sealed. If he does, and I die a spinster, the *vili* will come for me. Our marriage would save me from that sad fate. If there's truth in Amalie's legend, as my jilted friends believed, they would dance him to death for abandoning me.

The king knew Albin's present location, and could be aware of his intentions with regard to matrimony. She would therefore travel to Fontainebleau.

# CHAPTER 32

Bathilde's entourage, considerably smaller than her father's had been, consisted of her maid, a page, the coachman and a groom, a man to drive the mule-drawn baggage cart, and her dog. Before Palm Sunday, they broke their journey at Château des Vignes. Her attachment to it endured, tempting her to linger there until Easter and beyond.

She had no relative or friend to listen when she played her mother's harpsichord in the *salle de musique*. She missed Papa, whose heel would strike the floor as he kept time. Sophie's favorite chair stood empty. Myrte wasn't there to raise her glorious voice in song, and Giselle no longer skipped and danced about in response to a lively tune. Blisse, Bathilde's only companion, lay curled at her feet, nose to tail, sleeping soundly.

During her earlier tenure as chatelaine, she'd raised Monsieur Jousson's eldest son to the position of assistant *maître d'hôtel*. The father had always intended to retire if he outlived his master the prince, and therefore his son had assumed his duties. This change created no disruption in the management of the household and the keeping of accounts. Bathilde had already provided the senior Joussons with an alternative lodging on the estate.

On Maundy Thursday, after mass, she made her way to the graveyard to prune the roses and myrtle and marguerite daisies she'd planted by the pair of stone crosses. Someone had raked away the leaves deposited by winter winds. Although she needed to cut away a few sparse, leafless fronds from the myrtle bush, it had survived the colder months and was remarkably—quite miraculously—green and vigorous.

Berthe Durand was passing through the burial ground. She stopped at a fresh grave to pray before approaching.

"It must be you," Bathilde said, "who tends this place."

"As my daughter did before me. I've come to tell you about poor Hilaire, if you haven't yet heard."

"He's unwell?"

"Dead, princess." She pointed to the mound of earth not yet covered by grass.

Bathilde crossed herself. Another tragedy, in this place where too many had occurred. "How?" she asked.

"In his sorrow over Giselle, he drank overmuch. Wine. *Pineau.* One night, wandering about in a stupor, he tumbled into the river. Valère found his body the next morning, by the bridge. Superstitious folk said the ghost maidens, those men-murderers, seized him and threw him in. Others believe he went into the water intending to drown himself. But Père André declared it an accident and let us bury him in hallowed ground."

"I will go to his parents. There must be something I can do for them."

"Pascal and I mourn for him as we do for our Giselle. And we bear the shame of knowing her carelessness and vanity caused offense to our prince and princess."

"Oh, no," she protested. "Don't say such a thing, or believe it. She did no wrong."

"I warned her, often, that no good would come of

her affection for a stranger. So did Hilaire. She was too headstrong to heed us."

"Misunderstandings were responsible for what happened, more than any human fault or frailty." She'd told herself this since last autumn, and speaking the words to another helped to convince her of their essential truth.

"During the night, as I sat vigil over my girl, the duke came into your chapel and knelt to pray. He didn't speak, but I saw that he was sorely grieved. Whenever he returns, he'll not be recognized as the grape-gatherer. I told no one. Nor did Hilaire, not even during his drinking bouts."

Albin must have gone to the chapel before or after leaving the ring in Bathilde's bedchamber. A good and righteous gesture, and one that comforted her—as it had Berthe.

"My brother," the woman went on, "intends to wed a Niort girl he's had his eye on. Years younger than he, and of an age to bear children. I can tell she expects me to defer to her. And though I'd never make trouble, I wouldn't care to find myself in the position of servant where I've been mistress. It may be that I shall move into the *chaumière* meant for Giselle and Hilaire."

"I'll take you into my household," Bathilde offered. "To do the same light work as you're accustomed to. Spinning and weaving. Sewing and mending. You'll have lodging and meals and wages."

"Wouldn't my presence be a reminder of heartache?"

That response gave her pause. Brushing away a stray rose leaf that clung to her sleeve, she replied, "I could ask the same question of you."

"The duke would be discomfited to see me about the château, of that you can be sure." Berthe sighed. "I came to this village when I married. I'd leave it, if I knew where to go." She gestured towards the newer of the two crosses.

"To escape everything that happened last autumn. But this harsh world has nothing to offer a widow."

"The Ursulines in Niort would welcome you kindly. As a lay sister."

"Not without a dowry. I'd be living on their charity, which doesn't suit me any more than remaining with Pascal and his bride."

"I'll provide the necessary funds for your entrance."

"I suppose," the woman said heavily, "there's little else left for me to do, besides live out my years on my knees, in prayer."

"You possess all the domestic skills that the sisters practice, and teach," she pointed out. "They'll be useful in the convent or the *pensionnat* or the day school. You would live comfortably, among congenial companions. You might even find acquaintances among the nuns. Your relatives and friends could visit you there. Please accept my offer, for my sake, as well as your own. It would be a consolation to me, securing your future."

"Then I shall."

"I'll write Mother Superior, and Père André can send her a letter confirming your good character. And I'll take you there myself, when you're ready."

"On the day my brother marries, I'll go. The banns have been cried at a Niort parish, but the ceremony must wait till Lent is past."

Bathilde spent the rest of Holy Week busily. She penned her message to the convent and collected items for Berthe to carry into her new life—woolen hose and thick petticoats to wear beneath the plain habit she'd be given, and a pair of sturdy leather shoes. When she raised the lid of a huge wooden chest, she found the remnants of silks, satins, and velvets left over from her trousseau. She decided to donate them to the nuns, for making and adorning ecclesiastical vestments.

Two days after she and her servants observed Easter in the chapel, she and Berthe set out for Niort. At Église Notre Dame, where Myrte Vernier had met with heartbreak, they witnessed Pascal's marriage. After the couple exchanged vows, Bathilde presented the awed bride with a handful of coins and large piece of point lace. She then took Berthe, quivering with nervousness, to rue Crémault. As soon as the older woman carried her *coffre* over the parlor threshold and into the convent, Bathilde passed a heavy purse through the grille.

Mother Superior accepted it, saying, "Let us hope that Madame Durand will find peace and solace here, after the losses you recounted in your letter. What of you, my child? You have suffered greatly since our last meeting. Since learning of the prince's death, I've prayed mightily for his soul's repose. Take solace in the knowledge that he is with God."

"I do."

"And you have the prospect of marriage, another source of comfort."

"The king, as my guardian, will decide my future. He commands me to join him at his summer court."

"Please remember us to the Queen Mother and offer our thanks for her generosity to us in years past." She murmured the traditional farewell blessing, and with a shriveled, palsied hand she formed the sign of the cross.

The day after Bathilde's twentieth birthday, she departed for Poitiers, arriving at dusk. She passed a fortnight at her *hôtel particulier,* unoccupied since the week of her father's interment. At her direction, the servants unshuttered the tall windows and opened them to let in mild spring air, freshening the rooms. She selected bedding to take with her to Fontainebleau—a goose down mattress and pillows, and fine linen pillowcases and sheets embroidered with the de Sevreau scallop shells. Before leaving, she visited the tomb in the cathedral, praying for her parents and for Albin, wherever he might be. She pleaded to her own Saint Bathilde of Chelles for fortitude and a forgiving spirit.

Along the route from Poitiers to Orléans, where she would spend a night and rest her coach horses, she encountered distressing poverty and destruction. In some locations, the ravages of the Fronde wars—crumbling city walls, scarred town halls, burned out dwellings—hadn't been repaired. Roadside beggars and village peasants wore tattered garments, too many lacked shoes. At each convent, she dispensed gold *louis d'or* for their relief. Everything she witnessed firmed her determination, already strong, to be a careful steward of her lands, and considerate of the needs of the people who lived and worked on them.

The Château de Fontainebleau, ten leagues from the capital city, was the most palatial of all the royal residences. The birthplace of the king's father, it had a rich history and had been improved and embellished through the centuries. Its present owner would no doubt demand funds from Nicolas Fouquet, the superintendent of finances, to continue that tradition. She found it unchanged from the days she and Papa had searched stone carvings and plasterwork for the recurrent salamander emblem of their ancestor King Francis I.

Her rooms were located in one of the sections that formed the Cour du Cheval Blanc. From the windows on one side, she could view the courtyard and the horseshoe-shaped staircase at the palace's entrance front. On the opposite side, she saw formal gardens and a long *allée* of pine trees. Beyond them lay the vast glassy pool known as the Carp Pond, dating from Henri IV's reign.

She slept well in the unfamiliar bed, supported by her own well-stuffed mattress, her head resting on pillows she'd brought from her Poitiers house. She spent the next morning supervising Justine and Pierre as they rearranged furniture to her liking. With the maid's assistance, she changed into a jade green gown and made her way to the Queen Mother's apartments, situated on the western side of the Cour de la Fontaine.

Ushered to a *salle* hung all around with tapestries, she was received by the senior attendant. The half-Spanish Madame de Motteville was familiar from their many encounters during the king's wedding journey to and from Saint-Jean-de-Luz. A bevy of attractive young ladies was presented in a flurry of names that Bathilde despaired of remembering—redheaded Mademoiselle Bonne de Pons and a pair of cousins from the La Mothe-Houdancourt family.

"We are desolated at the loss of your father," said the Queen Mother. "I can think of no man as admirable, as brave, and yet as humble as the noble Prince de Coulon."

"Your Majesty's good opinion meant a great deal to him," she answered. "He was proud of serving the late king, and the present one. In his final days, he expressed regret that he left no son to succeed him as a supporter and defender of the monarchy."

"How like him. But you are with us, and just as dear. We thought this the most advantageous location for the queen to await her confinement. Quieter and cleaner than Paris, with plenty of good air and open spaces. The king wants you to participate in the many entertainments he and Madame have devised. This afternoon, a *fête champêtre*. In the evening, a concert of music beside the Grand Canal. All this gaiety is exhausting. But these young people are devoted to their pleasures, as you will discover."

# CHAPTER 33

Because the *fête* took place outdoors, Bathilde saw no reason to leave Blisse closed up in the bedchamber. She took her page Pierre along, to supervise the dog and restore her to their quarters should she became unruly from excitement. Leading them down a staircase, she met a blonde, blue-eyed girl who looked at her hopefully, as though she might be a deliverer of salvation.

"I thought I knew my way back to my room," the pretty stranger told her. "But I'm utterly lost. Again."

Bathilde said apologetically, "I'm only familiar with my own suite, some reception rooms, and the royal apartments."

"What a beautiful dog! Oh, I suppose I ought to curtsy—if you visit Their Majesties, you must be import-ant. I'm Louise. I'm the newest *fille d'honneur* to Madame. My father, Seigneur de la Valliere, fought in the wars."

"I imagine that mine—the Prince de Coulon—would have known him. I'm Bathilde de Sevreau."

Louise smiled in recognition. "You're the princess the king has spoken of. I wish I had a room in this part of the palace. Mine is under the roof. At night, I hear mice scratching behind a wall."

"That must make sleeping difficult."

"Not really. Madame stays up till the early hours, strolling in the torchlight with the king, and playing cards and dancing. By the time I return to my bed I'm exhausted. What's your dog's name? How old is it?"

"Blisse. The king gave her to me last autumn. She's exactly a year old"

"His Majesty must regard you with great affection." The soft voice was tinged with wistfulness.

"I've known him since childhood. Last year, when I lost my father, he became my guardian."

"There's no one on earth more wonderful, is there? Like a hero from mythology. Apollo, the Sun God. Or Hercules."

In Bathilde's estimation, Louis was in every respect fully human, but she expressed agreement. "Do you know where I might find him?"

"In the grove, where it's shady. With Madame. It's so hot that I came inside to get my fan."

"I suggest you find a palace servant to help you locate your chamber."

"Yes, thank you. I will." Louise dipped into a swift curtsy, and continued up the staircase, limping slightly. Observing her progress, Bathilde noted the different heights of her heeled shoes, obviously intended to correct a halting gait—not quite successfully.

Long tables were arranged in the Grand Jardin, their white clothes barely visible beneath platters of *charcuterie, patisserie,* and *confiserie.*

Monsieur stepped away from a group of his handsome hangers-on and declared, "Princess Bathilde, we're relieved to see you safely arrived, though later than expected. My brother is most eager to welcome you. And include you in our revels."

"Your Highness, I offer sincere felicitations on your recent marriage."

He responded with a careless shrug. "Old Mazarin had the bad manners to die on the same day my cousin and I received the papal dispensation permitting our union. Two weeks later, my brother lifted the mourning requirement, allowing us to dress in splendor for our betrothal ceremony and the exchange of vows. But our wedding lacked the pomp we witnessed in Saint-Jean-de-Luz."

Aware of how best to please him, she said, "I'm sure you both looked magnificent."

"So we were told." In daylight, his *maquillage*—thick white paint daubed with rouge—gave him an unnatural appearance. The delicate lips, colored vivid red, parted once more as he said, "I give you warning, there's a plan afoot to give you a position in Madame's household, as one of her attendants. First as a *fille d'honneur,* and a *dame* after your marriage. I can't imagine de Rozel would object."

He spoke in expectation of her becoming a duchess at some time in the future. It occurred to her that Albin might be present.

Before she could ask, he went on, "That color is a good choice for you, but the style of the gown is too plain. It wants embellishment. Not at all in the mode, I regret to say."

Although his criticism cut her, she responded with a smile. "The only one my maid could prepare in time. No goffering iron to crimp the flounces on my finery."

"Tell her to send your things to the royal laundry."

"Thank you, Monsieur. I shall."

"Your animal, however, lends a certain distinction."

"A present from His Majesty."

"Ah, yes. A fair copy of those white and black hounds he breeds for the field."

"Blisse, make your *reverence* to this Prince of the

Blood." With a hand gesture, Bathilde directed the dog to bow down.

Monsieur clapped his gloved hands. "Well done! Ah, but it's good to have you among us again, *ma belle*. You've missed much scandal since we last saw one another. Marie Mancini recovered from her disappointment at losing my brother, or pretended to, and wed her admirer the Prince of Colonna. Henceforth she will reside in Rome. Jean Colbert, who served as Cardinal Mazarin's deputy, is in greater favor with the king than Nicolas Fouquet, who mopes about the place because he hasn't yet been named chief minister. One would think he'd be satisfied with his position as controller of finances. He has access to all the money in our treasury, down to the last *livre*."

She forced herself to attend to the rapid flow of gossip that erupted from his cherub mouth, fighting her urge to search the crowd for a certain tall figure, last seen leaving the *petite salle* at Château des Vignes.

"The king will complain if I monopolize you," Monsieur said. "Come, come, I shall take you to him."

"I don't see the queen," Bathilde commented as he ushered her away from the throng.

"Spaniards cherish their sleep, and at this hour she keeps to her rooms. Her condition makes her sleepier— and lazier—than ever. Forget I ever said that. Even stuck in your distant province, you will have heard we have great hopes of a dauphin arriving late in the year."

"All of France rejoices at the prospect."

"As do I, believe me. I've no wish to wear the crown. From what I've observed, ruling this nation is a tremendous nuisance. Mazarin's wars depleted our treasury. Our soldiers, those who survived, are weary and disheartened, and the navy needs building up. Bishops compete for influence. No matter how late he reaches his wife's bed, my brother rises ridiculously early. After he completes his toilette and his devotions, he meets with his council until noonday mass. Then he works again until the hour of public dining. Later in the afternoon he meets again with advisors and receives petitioners. He participates in evening entertainments, and as soon as they conclude he resumes state business. He's very rigid in maintaining his schedule."

Bathilde found the king enjoying what must be a rare period of leisure in a shaded grove, drinking wine with Madame and one of her ladies. He stood, smiling as he watched her progress across the lawn. He wore a black wig, lustrous and long, but unlike his brother he eschewed cosmetics despite the faint smallpox scars marking his face.

Reaching out, he pulled her up from her deep curtsy, and pressed a kiss upon each cheek. "The privilege of a guardian. I'm a relation as well, though I can never recall exactly where our bloodlines meet. If your father were here, he could enlighten us. I join with you in mourning his untimely loss. As monarch, I have need of such wise heads as his. But even more, I valued his friendship."

"And he yours, Your Majesty."

"Mademoiselle Blisse has fared well in the months since I parted from her."

Bathilde commanded the dog to bow to her former master. "I keep her as a companion," she explained. "She isn't trained to the chase."

"No? You're no huntress, I perceive. But I know you to be a skilled rider. You had an excellent instructor."

They exchanged a smile, each recalling their youthful excursions in Poitiers.

"I mustn't linger, but I wish you to become better acquainted with Madame." He cast an affectionate glance at his sister-in-law.

By virtue of her marriage to Monsieur, Henriette,

Duchesse d'Orléans, ranked third in the hierarchy of royal ladies, after Queen Marie-Thérèse and the Queen Mother. Not yet seventeen, lovely in her unique fashion, she had milky skin and dark hair arranged in long ringlets on either side of her head.

Gazing up at Bathilde, she said, "The king says you're as fond of gardens as we are. You must let him know your opinion of his plans for improving these grounds."

"Only if it is sought, Madame."

"Nonsense. You two are friends, are you not? And you're his ward. I never hesitate to share my thoughts with him, on any subject."

"You have the advantage of being His Majesty's cousin. And, by your marriage to Monsieur, a beloved sister."

"That she is," the king declared. He seized Henriette's hand and carried it to his lips. "I regret leaving you, but matters of state await me. We shall meet again this evening, for a concert by the water. Lully will conduct his latest composition."

Bathilde accepted a seat beside Mademoiselle de Pons and accepted a glass of wine.

"We're making plans for a ballet," Madame told her. "Only we haven't decided whether to use the grand salon or the Galerie des Cerfs. What do you think?" Without waiting for a reply, she said, "Well, we have plenty of time to decide. You will please us—the king and me—by taking one of the speaking roles. I will instruct you. He commends your dancing, so we'll be sure to make use of it as well."

"As with riding, he tutored me in the art. At school I learned the rudimentary steps, but he was my first male partner."

"Oh, how I should have liked to attend a school! Did you enjoy it? What did you study?"

"Religion. History. Geography. Latin. Languages. Music. We embroidered church vestments and sewed garments for the nuns and the pupils to wear, and those that were given to the poor. I helped tend the garden."

"It sounds delightful. You must have made friends there."

Bathilde answered softly, "I had a special one. From my first day at the *pensionnat* she looked after me, and we were inseparable. Until she died."

"How terribly sad. I should think it's better to have had such a companion, even though you lost her, than not to have one at all. I've lived apart from my brothers and sisters since I was born, with only my mother to console me when my cousins here in France treated me unkindly. As a married lady, I can have as many friends as I please. Ladies *and* gentlemen."

# CHAPTER 34

*May, 1661*

"He's in Vienna."

Louis made this announcement while walking with Bathilde in the Jardin de la Reine, their first opportunity to be alone together since her arrival. Ever the gallant, he slowed his long stride to accommodate her shorter steps.

"Did he ask to go, or did you banish him?"

His glove, embroidered with silver thread, batted away her question. "A harsh word, *ma chère amie.*"

They paused at the fountain's edge, watching Blisse lap from the pool surrounding the bronze statue of Diana. The Roman goddess carried a quiver full of arrows over her shoulder, and a deer stood beside her. Four long-eared, life-sized bronze hunting hounds were seated at the edge of the pedestal.

Studying them, Bathilde said, "I'm tempted to commission a pair of similar statues in stone, modeled on Blisse, for the entrance of the Château Clément gardens."

"Let me make a gift of them," he offered. "It would be quite appropriate for me to do so, as the giver of the life model. Monsieur Larembert can come here from

Paris to make the necessary drawings. His workshop will produce the sculptures and send them to your château on completion."

"Your Majesty is always generous."

"My initial wedding gifts were premature. I owe you another—or will, in time." He took her by the wrist and turned her to face him. "You very neatly shifted the subject from Albin. You must be curious to know why he's sojourning in Austria and adjacent lands. I sent him there to assess the condition of the emperor's army after three decades of constant fighting against our troops. Precisely the type of mission your father might have undertaken. But de Rozel has sufficient military experience and an expertise in documentation. I'm eager to hear an explanation of why he willingly removed himself to a foreign court. I can only surmise the pair of you quarreled."

"It wasn't that. Not exactly."

"A change of heart?"

"Not on my part. As for his, I've no reason to believe so."

"You're entirely too circumspect. If you dislike my prying, I must point out that as your guardian, I have a right—nay, the responsibility—to determine how matters stand between you and the man to whom you are pledged."

She halted and looked directly into his face. "Until you told me about Vienna, I knew only that he'd gone away from France. I've received no letter from him. He didn't send an acknowledgment of Papa's death. As we're no longer at war, I assume he's in no danger."

"None whatsoever. Apart from the grave risk of being bored senseless at Leopold's court. Like me, the emperor is a musical fellow, and that's all I know to his credit. I find the Hapsburg rulers to be a dull and charmless breed, utterly devoid of verve and spark. My Spanish queen has confirmed that opinion."

"You should be thankful Her Majesty isn't of an excitable temperament," Bathilde said mildly. "Better for her, and the babe she carries."

"I'm well satisfied with my bride. To you, I can confess that her affection for me far exceeds mine for her. I've recently discerned in her a troubling tendency towards jealousy. My mother is her confidante—and my tormentor."

They could hear a leather ball repeatedly striking the inside walls of the Jeu des Paumes, where a pair of players on the court competed with one another.

"I can't imagine you've given the queen cause for jealousy."

"Only because you've not been with us long enough. It's my deepest joy and my worst misfortune to be consumed by a forbidden love."

"But Monsieur told me that Marie Mancini is in Rome, too far away to distress your wife."

"I think of her no more. I allude to a person nearer to me by blood. And lately, through marriage."

"Madame?" She tilted her head, marveling, "And to think you might have wed her, if her brother had reclaimed his crown sooner than he did."

"Cardinal Mazarin would never have countenanced my union with Henriette. For him, achieving peace with the Spanish and bolstering our treasury with the Infanta's dowry were too important. At the time I was traveling to Saint-Jean-de-Luz to sacrifice my desires to Mazarin's and my mother's ambitions, my cousin Charles was sailing across the channel to begin his reign. His waif of a sister meant nothing to me. And though I didn't favor her marriage to Philippe, it wasn't because of a secret *tendresse*. That developed quite recently. Most unexpectedly."

"Does she return your feelings?"

"She enjoys my company, and I hers. We amuse one another. Our tastes in music and authors and poets are highly attuned. Her mind is lively, her manners perfect. In recent weeks we've been inseparable, in defiance of my mother's remonstrations." His dark eyes narrowed. "How did we come to speak of my love affair instead of yours?"

"You felt the need to unburden yourself," she told him frankly.

"I have done. It's your turn."

"There's little to say that you don't already know. I am betrothed to the Duc de Rozel. He's in Vienna. He has no idea I've come here."

"At any moment, I can recall him. All it takes is a word from you."

"Or he could seek your permission to return. But he has not."

The king offered her a half-smile. "What a pitiable pair we are. You, at least, have cause for hope. It's otherwise with me. I am a devout Christian. A faithful husband—by the accepted definition of marital fidelity. I'm determined to become the greatest and the strongest ruler France has ever known. Mine can be a glorious reign, one of achievement and innovation and certain victory, should we be drawn into any wars. These ambitions lift my spirits in my dark, despairing hours."

"Is that enough to content you?" Bathilde asked.

"It can be." He nodded, adding firmly, "It *must* be."

Enlightened about the object of His Majesty's regard, Bathilde closely observed his encounters with Madame and noted his courtiers' reactions. When he played love songs on his guitar, he kept his eyes on her. Whenever he floated along the Grand Canal in his gilded barge, she sat at his side. Monsieur alternated between watching them intently from the gravel path by the water's edge or set out in a smaller vessel with the Chevalier de Lorraine. The Queen Mother and Marie-Thérèse, riding through the grounds in an open carriage, pretended to be unaware of the various dramas taking place on the mirror-like surface. Bathilde learned that this appearance of unconcern was feigned.

Her long acquaintance with the king's mother ensured her admission to the *lever* and entrance to her apartments at all hours. She spent part of every morning in the tapestried antechamber, in the company of the Queen Mother and her close companion Madame de Motteville. When seized by the need to speak candidly, they dismissed Mademoiselle Bonne de Pons, little Charlotte de la Mothe-Houdancourt and her cousin Anne-Lucie, and the rest of her *filles d'honneur*.

"I know you to be a recipient of the king's confidences," the queen told Bathilde "And I have decided to trust you with mine. I'm sorely troubled by his attentions to the person with whom he spends his leisure hours. His behavior is a source of distress to his wife, who feels neglected. How am I to comfort her? And Monsieur is so unpredictable. I live in dread that he'll make a scene in response to the disgraceful flirtation—there's no more accurate word for it—between his bride and his brother."

More than a flirtation, Bathilde reflected. Not only had their attachment destroyed harmony within the royal circle, it threatened to bring scandal upon the court. And it adversely affected the king's relationship with the young woman who would bear their first child.

"You may rely on His Majesty to be careful of his reputation," she pointed out. "He'd never do harm to another. Especially a virtuous young woman, his near relation, who is recently wed."

"He has always been overly susceptible to a certain type of femininity. That Mancini girl, who lacked beauty, had it. Her uncle, the cardinal, suspected her of employing dark arts to ensnare my son. He intended to marry her and made no secret of his wish. Now, after less than a year as husband to my sweet niece, who adores him, he's sighing over my other niece. Whose marriage to Monsieur took place but two months ago."

Madame de Motteville said soothingly, "I agree with the princess. The king won't allow his feelings to sway him into impropriety."

"Even the appearance of it is offensive. I heartily wish Madame were better served by the young ladies she keeps about her, for a flightier set I've never seen. Gossip and games and fashion and pleasure-seeking—that's all they care for. Has the king spoken to you about joining her household? She should have a companion as level-headed as you, with more maturity than she possesses. You're several years older than she."

"Monsieur did mention such appointment," Bathilde admitted. "I assume the decision rests with his wife."

"If the king commands her to accept you, she cannot refuse."

"She might resent my being forced upon her," she pointed out. A convenient excuse to shield her reluctance.

"Not if you first win your way into her good graces. I'm confident you can do so. Promise me you will make the effort."

The request posed a difficulty. She had no desire to attach herself to the court. Her experiences last year, throughout the king's summer progress through France before and after his wedding, affirmed her distaste for serving and satisfying the whims of royalty. *Filles d'honneur* were young girls of the minor aristocracy, close in age to their mistress, placed by ambitious relatives in an environment where they could capture a matrimonial prize of higher status. Unlike sophisticated Françoise-Athénaïs de Tonnay-Charente or simple Louise de la Valliere, Bathilde had borne the title of princess from birth. She was entitled to a large inheritance and a signed marriage contract required her to wed a duke. What would be the advantage, she asked herself, in becoming one of Madame's attendants?

She had nothing to gain by it. But, she acknowledged, nothing left to lose.

# CHAPTER 35

*June, 1661*

Although discussion of Bathilde's prospective appointment as a *fille d'honneur* lapsed, she was nonetheless admitted to Madame's circle of close companions. On the hottest days, she participated in bathing parties in a secluded forest stream, escorted by a cadre of noblemen. She was included in evening carriage rides through the Hermitage, to a place where a collation would be waiting beneath the trees. Boat races took place on the canal and torchlit violin concerts in the Cour de la Fontaine. These amusements, ordained and devised by the king, were presented in Madame's honor and arranged for her pleasure.

Later in May, not to be outdone by these impromptu, informal gatherings, Monsieur hosted a formal ball. Afterwards, at his mother's urging, he took his wife to her mother's château at Colombes, removing her from his overly attentive brother's orbit. The king celebrated their return with an even grander ball and opened the dancing with his sister-in-law. The two queens watched their graceful movements and fond glances with evident dismay.

The next day, Madame demanded that Bathilde

accompany her to an urgent audience with the Queen Mother.

"She can't upbraid me if you're present—or not as much as she would if I went to her alone." Tossing her ringlets, she declared, "She's forgotten what it's like to be young and happy, as she was when the Duke of Buckingham fell passionately in love with her and vowed his eternal devotion. We've all heard the tales. His son, the present duke, paid extravagant court to me in London last year. His attentions were most flattering, but as my mother constantly reminded me, I was already promised to Philippe. All members of the Villiers family are incredibly beautiful and dangerously seductive. They're perpetually involved in scandals. My brother Charles is dallying with one of them, a magnificent creature called Barbara."

Bathilde wanted to warn her that insouciance would not serve her well with a mother-in-law who rigorously followed and enforced the same protocols imposed upon her as an Infanta of Spain. Her fondness and care for the young queen were firmly founded on their identical upbringing and their shared blood.

"My dear Henriette," the Queen Mother began, "you have grown excessively thin, and your color is much too high. All the dancing and hectic activity late into the night is injurious to your health. Monsieur is as concerned by it as I. You would do better to model yourself on Her Majesty and spend your hours restfully."

"But I have not the same cause for care as she does," Madame replied. "Perhaps, if ever I find myself in a similar state of expectation, I shall choose to be less active than I do at present. As Princess Bathilde can attest, I am not able to lounge away the days or spend hours napping or retire when the night is young. Because the queen keeps to her rooms so much, His Majesty relies on me to confer with him and assist in devising our entertainments. We've begun rehearsing the first of two ballets to be presented in coming weeks."

"I regret that Fontainebleau has not turned out to be a calming summer retreat for you. I shall advise Monsieur to take you to his palace at Saint-Cloud, outside the city, for the remainder of the season."

"If that is your wish, Your Majesty may of course broach to the king the subject of our removal," Madame said silkily. "And he can say whether he wishes us to go."

"I shall also consult your mother," her aunt declared more forcefully. "Perhaps she has more influence upon you than I do. You may leave me. And I urge you to carefully consider the ramifications of your behavior."

For the duration of this interview, Bathilde had spoken not a word. If she made a comment that pleased one combatant, she would alienate the other.

On escaping the chamber, Madame scoffed at her censorious mother-in-law's effort to control her.

"The king will object to our being sent away—to Saint-Cloud, or anywhere else. It's tiresome, being constantly bombarded with criticism. My husband expects me to dress as extravagantly as he does and exert myself to delight the court. But if I draw attention away from him, he becomes peevish. And he's growing jealous of my attachment to the king. Why, I cannot say. It doesn't affect my devotion to Monsieur in any way." Madame blinked her eyes several times, as though to clear them. Her head drooped and slender white fingers gripped the stair rail. "Dear me," she whispered, "I do feel odd. I wonder why?"

Bathilde took her to a bench on the landing. "Sit here until the faintness passes."

"My head aches, so fiercely." She swallowed hard. "All week I've notice a burning in my throat, like bile. I had no taste for food this morning. It must be hunger that unsettles me."

Observing the rapid beat of the pulse in her throat, Bathilde wished this princess weren't so highly strung and volatile. "If you let me take you to your rooms, I shall request that one of His Majesty's physicians attend you."

"I'm better now." Madame stood and smoothed her cherry-colored skirts. "I thank you for going with me to face the dragon. I wish we had a role for you in *L'Impatience*. I saw several performances during the winter and am familiar with Signor Buti's libretto—it's written in Italian and French. The king and Monsieur will repeat their parts, as will the gentlemen of the court. De Guiche, Villeroy, Saint-Aignan, and the rest. The female characters will be performed by professionals, who dance and sing well. But I'll make sure you receive a notable part in the *Ballet du Saisons*, de Bensérade's next creation. With music composed by Monsieur Lully, of course."

"If it pleases Your Highness," Bathilde said soothingly.

"There are vine-gatherers, men and women. But you're too noble to appear as a commoner. I will portray Diana, and my ladies will appear as my nymphs. You shall be one of them. I will speak to His Majesty about it, although he's certain to endorse all my suggestions. We're of the same mind about everything. He denies me nothing I wish for."

"My mother is making my days a misery," Louis complained to Bathilde.

They wandered through the island garden surrounded by the Carp Pond. A short time ago the ballet had concluded, but he hadn't yet changed from the costume he'd worn as the character Amour, and garish paint covered his face.

"It's Madame's seventeenth birthday, yet my parent— her aunt—could hardly bring herself to be civil. For many a year she showed great kindness to Henriette, defending her whenever Philippe and I mocked and teased. Nowadays, she offers nothing but reprimands. To both of us."

"You know why," Bathilde said.

"I do. Of course, I do. And she's correct in saying I've behaved carelessly, imprudently. Henriette also." He drew a long breath. "She's carrying a child. No one outside the immediate family, and our physicians, are aware. My brother is ecstatic, he longs to be a father. He can be confident of his paternity, for it would be many times a sin for me to lie with his wife. But people will gossip. How do we prevent it?"

Madame glided towards them, a shimmering goddess in a silvery gown. Fixing her large eyes on the king, she moaned, "You cannot imagine my suffering since my mother arrived from Colombes. She pretends that she's here to mark my birthday and to make sure I take care of myself. And this babe." Her palm grazed her belly, not yet showing signs of her condition. "But she has joined the campaign to separate you and me. I'm being mercilessly criticized for my conduct, every minute of every day. Even worse, I'm in danger of being banished!"

"Impossible. By whose authority?"

"Your mother's. She wants me to accompany her on a visit to the old Duchesse de Chevreuse at Dampierre. With Monsieur. Can't you stop it?"

"I could. But I won't."

"Oh, you are too cruel!" Turning to Bathilde, she said, "I thought he'd ceased his unkindness towards me. When I was his gawky, impoverished cousin, his mother commanded him to partner me at a ball. 'I do not like to dance with little girls,' he said." She turned her accusing eyes towards the king.

"Because I recalled an impromptu dance with another young princess. It ended badly." With a smile for Bathilde, he said, "You recall our first meeting at your father's house in Poitiers. And how Philippe laughed at us while we twirled helplessly about the *salle.*"

"I haven't forgotten."

Madame intruded on their reminiscences. "I dread what people will say when I announce that I'm with child. Those who are jealous of my popularity will accuse us of—of gross immorality. They won't dare malign you, but I shall be fair game."

"I made a similar observation to the princess. We'll have to find a means of warding off false and vicious innuendo."

"While I'm away, you should pretend to transfer your attentions to another lady. There are plenty who would willingly, gratefully receive them. Starting a flirtation with somebody else is the best way to disarm our critics."

"With whom?"

"Any of the *filles d'honneur.*" Madame studied Bathilde. "Or, even better, one who is aware of the scheme and consents to participate in it. Princess, will you help us?"

Hastily she said, "I cannot. He's my guardian. I'm pledged to marry his friend." If Albin should ever hear that Louis had courted her favors, even in a meaningless fashion, he would be outraged.

"Oh, very well. Someone else, then. Anyone. Bonne de Pons?"

The king shook his head. "I wouldn't dare. She serves my mother."

"All the better. Her Majesty will notice. Though I

suppose it ought to be one of my ladies, so you can remain at my side and continue your visits to my apartments."

"What about that beauty who has made such an impression among the gallants? Mademoiselle de Tonnay-Charente."

"Definitely not. I don't trust her."

Bathilde repressed a smile at this waspish retort, essentially an admission that she also mistrusted the king. Statuesque, fair-haired Françoise-Athénaïs was stunning and alluring, admired for her perfections of face and figure.

"Mademoiselle de Chemerault might suit," Madame suggested. "The La Valliere chit doesn't stir much interest in the gentlemen and isn't the type to convincingly lure you into an *affaire*. Pretty enough but very shy. No sparkle."

"Must I choose now? I'll arrange for each candidate to sit by me at banquets. I'll partner them in the dance. I'm an excellent actor, you told me so earlier tonight. By the time you return from Dampierre you'll hear that I've become utterly infatuated with a young lady of the court."

"I depend upon it. And none but the three of us will know your true purpose."

"Correct," he answered.

# CHAPTER 36

### July, 1661

L ouis resembled a great bee, constantly darting from one female to another. This impression was visually enhanced on the days he wore his favorite black velvet coat, trimmed with gold lace, and the yellow ribbons dangling from his black breeches. The young ladies he singled out responded languidly to his compliments and smilingly partnered him in the dance, but didn't appear to take him seriously. Nor did they allow matters to proceed any farther in private than they did in public. His mother continued to lecture him about his preference for Madame, and his queen's tearful recriminations proved that his feigned interest in the *filles d'honneur* was unpersuasive.

On a showery morning that postponed outdoor activities, an excess of girlish chatter drove Bathilde into Henri IV's Galerie des Cerfs for silence and solitude. Its flat, wood-beamed ceiling belonged to an earlier age, and the name derived from the stag heads—she counted forty—hanging on the walls. Fashioned of plaster and painted brown, they were crowned by genuine antlers and attached to plaques inscribed with the date of the creature's demise. The room was also decorated with an extended bird's-eye-view mural of royal residences—Fontainebleau, Chambord, Saint-Germain-en-Laye, and Amboise.

She moved among classical busts and bronze statues, attempting to identify their subjects. While sympathetically studying Laocoön and his two sons, writhing in agony while giant serpents mauled them, she heard footsteps.

"Don't gaze too long upon that group, or you'll have nightmares," Louis told her. "What's more, this was the scene, four years ago, of a bloody and gruesome murder." He pointed to the floor. "Here is where Marquis of Monaldeschi lay dying, skewered by Queen Christina's assassin."

Averting her gaze, she said, "Papa told me about it."

"When I arrived days after, I was shown the bloodstains. Even Mazarin, regarded by the majority of my subjects as a devil, was shocked by the Swedish queen's brutal revenge against her former favorite. And her complete lack of repentance. We ought never to have let her stay here." He shook his head. "A peculiar woman. As difficult as it is to rule a nation, I cannot conceive of why any monarch would abdicate. Where's Mademoiselle Blisse?"

"She came into heat over a week ago and is confined to my bedchamber. My page Pierre is guarding her virtue."

"A sensible precaution. One wouldn't want one of the ladies' little lap spaniels to mount her, amusing though it would be to observe. When she's old enough, I propose that we place her with my purest white hunting dog. We might create a novel and highly desirable, breed. Would you permit it?"

"If that's Your Majesty's desire."

"One of them. I was searching for you so I could tell you the other."

"At this hour, you should be diligently reading reports and reviewing accounts."

"I decided to spend the morning furthering our secret plan. Before I could succeed with Mademoiselle de Pons, her parents took her away. Today I watched that coquette Mademoiselle de Chemerault rehearse her part in the new ballet. Afterwards, I took her into a secluded place and tried to kiss her. She rebuffed me."

"That must be an unfamiliar occurrence."

"Which I hope will not very soon be repeated. Let us leave this gloomy chamber. I've something to ask you and would rather do it in a place that isn't associated with so much violent death."

He led her out of the gallery and into a small, windowless interior room containing one table and no chairs.

"The pretty creatures of my court have provided a pleasant distraction from the hardest decision I've faced since becoming France's ruler. I've determined what I must do, though not when it must be done. If only your father had lived longer, to advise me. I've got Colbert, but it's not strictly a financial or administrative matter. Le Tellier will counsel me about how I might employ the army in my plans. I fear it may come to that."

"And Monsieur Fouquet. He appears eager to fill the cardinal's place," she pointed out.

Her comment drew a frown. "Excessively so."

"What of your mother?"

"I've revealed just enough to know we aren't in agreement about how I should proceed. My trust in you is complete, and infinite, and I regret that I'm unable to confide in you to the extent that I should like to."

"True authority has no partner," Bathilde responded. "That's what Papa said when he made me chatelaine at a very young age. His advice proved even more helpful to me as mistress of Château Clément, a far greater responsibility."

"For power to be absolute, it cannot be shared. I thank you for that reminder. As usual, the prince was correct." Now he was smiling. "On to my other dilemma—and for that, I crave your assistance. De Pons ran away. De Chemerault turned away. When Madame returns, she'll discover all my efforts to find a substitute love have failed."

"Because your interest isn't engaged. Neither is your heart."

"Ah, there you are mistaken. Both have quickened, and in an unexpected way." His bare hand moved towards her, and his palm cupped her cheek. "Why not you, Bathilde? Henriette thought of that before I did."

For several heartbeats, she gazed up at him uncertainly. "I hope you're jesting."

"My affection for you is boundless. And I believe you care for me."

"As my king," she murmured. "And my guardian."

"That's the perfection of it, don't you see? In that role, I can be near you whenever I choose, with justification. In public. Or in private. Even when I visit your bedchamber."

Shaking her head, she said, "What you suggest is impossible. It would destroy my reputation and impair my relationship with your family."

"You can rely on me to be discreet. In view of my courtiers, I'll be as attentive to you as Madame wishes me to be. Not a soul will know how we conduct ourselves in private. Every great king of France had a legendary romance. Charles VII and Agnès Sorel. Henri II and Diane de Poitiers. Henri VI and Gabrielle d'Estrées."

"I tell you, there will be no history of Louis XIV and

Bathilde de Sevreau. All these months you've been faithful to your queen. Why would you break your vows and imperil your mortal soul?"

"Because without passion, life is insupportable. I married a princess who has the misfortune to love me. I cannot love her. My infatuation for my brother's wife, attractive and charming and compatible, has revealed my deepest desire. Henriette and I cannot go on the way we have been. I don't need my mother, or my confessor, to tell me. My conscience is just as insistent as they are. But kingship is a lonely state. Much more now than at any time since Mazarin's death. Must I deny myself the comfort of true companionship? Of mutual regard? Of bodily pleasure?"

She yearned for those things just as much as he did. But not with him, or from him. Unable to deflect him with that stark truth, she said calmly, "I'm promised to the Duc de Rozel. He is your friend."

"I'll free you from the betrothal. Or allow your marriage go forward as a means of obscuring our *affaire.*"

Resenting his assumption of her compliance, she said sharply, "You cannot believe that I'd favor either of those suggestions."

"Why not?"

"I'm in love with him."

Her admission startled him into momentary speechlessness. "I see. But does that half-Jesuit war hero cherish you in the way that I would? As you deserve?"

"He did, on the day he and my father signed our marriage contract. We shared a few joyful hours together before everything went wrong for us. I'll not tell you exactly why, or how, but mistakes were made, with fearsome consequences. I was deeply wounded, in my heart and my pride. And angry, at times. But in my despair and regret, I never ceased to care for him. I still yearn to be his wife. Even though, as I've told you, he left me without saying farewell."

"That astonishes me. Albin is always mindful of the appropriate courtesies."

"Have you ever heard about *samovili?*"

"Not that I recall."

"To put it simply, they're the ghostly spirits of young women who were jilted before their marriage day. After midnight, the *vili* rise up from underground regions to hunt for deceitful men and force them to dance until they also die. You may think me foolish and fanciful, but to save Albin—and myself—from that dire destiny, we must be wed."

"I'm not sure whether you're serious." He rubbed his forehead. "What am I to do? On her return, Henriette will expect me to be pretending to chase after some shining ornament of my court. She mentioned another lady, didn't she? The blonde girl with all the names."

"Louise de la Baume le Blanc. The late Seigneur de la Valliere's daughter."

"That's the one. Shy. Walks with a limp. All golden hair and scant wit. Apart from her ability to converse with me in my own language, she strikes me as all too similar to my wife."

"Louise adores you." This was no exaggeration. "She's the sweetest and the gentlest of the girls I've met here. She is a fine horsewoman and an excellent dancer. What's more, you'll find that she listens more than she speaks. Madame, you will agree, has not that gift. She's too eager to demonstrate her cleverness and wants always to be the center of attention. Sometimes, at your expense, and your brother's."

"How observant you are, *ma chérie*. It's you I should be sending on foreign missions."

"I wouldn't mind," she said, smiling. "Provided the destination is Vienna."

"Very well, I shall find out whether your praise of Mademoiselle La Valliere is warranted. And I'm doubly grateful to you. You've just provided what might prove to be a solution to my great problem. I'll say no more— in every palace, the walls have ears." He took both her hands in his and drew them to his lips for a kiss. "You are a marvel. And the one man in all Christendom I will admit to envying is the Duc de Rozel."

# CHAPTER 37

"I'm sincerely obliged to you," Madame told Bathilde, "for encouraging the king to devote himself to Mademoiselle Louise. She's pretty enough to please his eye, making his attentions believable, and she's young—we're the same age. While absent from Fontainebleau, I worried that he might turn to you. He makes no secret of his high regard, and I suppose you could win his heart with hardly any effort. No longer being first in his affections would be unbearable for me."

Unsettled by how close she'd come to the truth, Bathilde replied, "If you are satisfied with the outcome, I am glad. Pray excuse me, Madame. Monsieur Larembert has come to make drawings of my dog—for a pair of statues."

"And what a worthy object of his artistry she is. I shall save a place for you when we gather for Monsieur Molière's new comedy."

Bathilde and Blisse met the sculptor at the Diana fountain. He measured the dog from nose to rump and forehead to paw, standing and seated, and sketched her from every angle. He scribbled notes, documenting the length of her ears and her tail.

"A noble beast," he declared, "one who might have

hunted with the gods and goddesses. As soon as your statues are finished, I will inform His Majesty. It's my understanding that they're to be delivered to a château well to the west of here."

"Near La Rochelle."

"We carefully pack and crate our works, that no damage occurs during transport. If you desire, we can send a man to set the statues properly on their supports."

As a reward for submitting to the examination, she took Blisse into the Jardin des Pins for a run. Louis and Louise strolled there, his dark head close to her fair one and her arm intimately twined with his. This surprised her, for they were cautious and circumspect in the presence of the royal family and the courtiers. He danced with her only after partnering all the ladies of higher rank. While hunting, he seemed more intent on his four-legged than his two-legged quarry, although he complimented Louise on her management of the energetic, high-spirited mount she preferred.

Absorbed in their conversation, they didn't notice her until the dog raced past them.

From the moment he spoke his wedding vows, the king had been faithful to his queen. He was diligent in making his confession and attending daily mass. But Bathilde knew, because he'd admitted it to her, how he strained against the bonds of fidelity and honor. He'd expressed his need of a female who could stir and satisfy passions. Yet sweet, sensitive Louise was an unlikely candidate for royal mistress. Retiring and humble, she was extremely devout, just as dedicated as he to her devotions. And so naïve that she was slow to realize when gentlemen were flirting with her.

The two widowed dowager queens, permanently clad in black, departed for Vaux-le-Vicomte, taking their increasingly discontented children. At their return, they expressed astonished admiration of Monsieur and Madame Fouquet's splendid château and the magnificent gardens André Le Nôtre had created. Entertainments included banquets and a ball, and a performance of Molière's *L'École des Maris*. Their enthusiastic praise of the new comedy convinced the king to summon the troupe to Fontainebleau, where they achieved similar success.

The courtiers had rehearsed the *Ballet des Saisons* indoors while a stage was being built in front of the Carp Pond. On its premiere night, Bathilde stood at her bedchamber window and watched the lighting of all the lanterns strung between the trees. A thousand blazing torches transformed darkness into a semblance of daytime, and the lake and canals reflected the flames.

"That gown," Justine commented, "reveals as much of what's under it as your nightshift does."

Bathilde plucked the sheer green fabric of her costume. "All the nymphs are wearing one just like it. I mean to hold my flower basket over the parts of me that I'd rather not show."

"Don't stand with light behind you, or the lack of petticoats will be obvious."

As they had repeatedly rehearsed, she and nearly a dozen sister naiads emerged from a glade, scattering loose petals as they made their way to the stage. Its curtain parted to reveal Madame, as the huntress Diana, draped in an approximation of a classical robe. A silver crescent crowned her head, she carried a bow, and a quiver of arrows was strapped to her bony shoulder. During her speech, her attendants danced.

Bathilde offered a brief warning about the danger of entering the woods alone, where a satyr lurked. Louise de la Valliere spoke of springtime beauty. They withdrew to make way for the next group of performers,

Flora—portrayed by a man—with a troupe of noblemen dressed as gardeners.

The king had taken on the role of Ceres, goddess of the harvest. His retinue consisted of Comte de Saint-Aignan, the composer Lully, and others, as grain reapers in tunics, brandishing scythes.

"With my own hand," he declaimed, "I happily sow on this earth enough to provide for all mankind."

Led by the Comte de Guiche, male and female grape gatherers entered. Their flowing silk garments bore no resemblance whatsoever to the simple, serviceable garb worn by the people who labored in Bathilde's vineyards. Monsieur, elaborately dressed in velvet, had rouged his lips and placed black patches on his white-painted face.

The spectacle went on and on, with speeches long and short. A professional dancer, Mademoiselle de Verpré, performed a solo *sarabande*.

For the final tableau, Bathilde and the other ladies reappeared as white-draped muses, led onto the stage by the Duke of Beaufort as Apollo. Lovely Frances Stuart, aged fourteen, trod upon her train.

"Forgive me, princess" the girl whispered. "It was an accident." Born in Paris to a Scottish family, she was a favorite of Madame's and a member of the English queen's household.

Trumpets sounded, heralding His Majesty's return. He wore a different costume as Spring, the season of new birth and of beauty. Individuals representing Health, Peace, and Prosperity surrounded him.

Marianne Mancini, only thirteen years old and the youngest of Mazarin's nieces, warbled, "This petite muse is not inferior, with mind and breast already formed." She blushed so fierily that Bathilde pitied her, and her embarrassment amused the spectators.

Enthusiastic applause assured the courtiers and the

professionals, the composer and the librettist, of a grand success. Madame stepped forward in triumph, exulting in the outpouring of praise. She failed to notice, as Bathilde did, that the king had fastened his admiring gaze upon Louise de la Valliere.

Bathilde never knew who informed Madame that the king was enamored of Louise. Perhaps she realized she'd been supplanted without being told. Members of the court, recognizing Mademoiselle de la Valliere as the king's new *amante*, exerted themselves to befriend her. Her prominence was confirmed when Nicolas Fouquet, the superintendent of finance, singled her out, offering effusive compliments.

Madame sought consolation from the handsome and scandalous Comte de Guiche, rousing Monsieur's ire. Doubly jealous, as the husband of one party and the admirer—some said lover—of the other, he drove the comte from court, with the king's assent.

Returning from a nightly excursion for Blisse's bodily comfort, Bathilde met the Comte de Saint-Aignan in the upper passage.

"This wing is a giant rabbit warren," she greeted him. "Do you seek someone who lodges here?"

"I've been given temporary shelter here myself, having loaned my chamber to a fond couple whose need of it is greater than mine. It's an inconvenience to them, galloping off to that place miles away, the late king's hunting lodge at Versailles." He wagged his head, jostling his wig's cascade of fair curls. "Ah, but I have broken my promise of discretion. I beg you to forget what I just said."

If the lovers borrowed a courtier's bedchamber, they had become physically intimate—or soon would be. Was Louise aware that her romance with the king had grown out of a casual flirtation instigated by Madame? Bathilde hadn't expected a girl so firmly religious to surrender her virtue to any man, regardless of his title or position. Her own role in this seduction, and the potential ruin of her friend's reputation, shamed her. She had inadvertently and unwittingly served as a procuress for royalty.

She told the comte, "As a confidante of the person to whom you refer, I am just as careful to guard his privacy."

"No member of my family would refuse a monarch's request," he informed her. "My sister, a professed nun of Montmartre Abbey, broke her vow of chastity to become Henri IV's mistress. Eventually he discarded her, but as recompense he made her abbess of the place from which he abducted her." Stroking his prominent nose, he added, "I knew your father well, many years ago. One of our finest officers, respected as such long before becoming a marshal of France. A great loss to the kingdom. And, of course, to you. In the prime of life, wasn't he?"

"He hadn't yet turned fifty."

"Curious, isn't it, how some soldiers live on to a great age, and others die far too soon."

"He was severely wounded in battle and contracted a recurring fever in the Low Countries. Despite his physicians' efforts, his health was never fully restored."

"I detect a resemblance between you and your mother. We rarely saw her at court. I gather she favored the rural life."

"A preference I inherited," Bathilde confessed.

# CHAPTER 38

"You ought to go with me to Fontainebleau," Wilfride said. "You want to, even if you won't admit it."

Avoiding his stare, Albin replied, "I can carry out my orders without visiting His Majesty's pleasure palace. I'm entrusting you with delivery of the documents I've produced. I intend to stay where I am."

"You hate Paris," he retorted. "The château is but ten leagues from here. Your best horse could get you there before nightfall. The coach, even sooner."

"Listen, and heed me. Louis entrusts me with an extremely important and highly confidential undertaking, for France's benefit. It must be conducted in complete secrecy. You'll be staying in Avon village, at an inn. Take great care to disguise your appearance and draw no attention to yourself. When you arrive there, send a message to the king informing him that a former soldier and friend of mine wishes to wait upon him at a convenient time. He receives petitioners in the morning, but to conceal your presence I imagine he won't see you until the evening—possibly quite late. You will give him my report." Albin handed over a thick letter, several sheets folded together, tied with string and sealed with wax in several places.

"Don't be surprised if Colbert is with him. He's aware of my activities."

"That's the extent of my mission?"

"You might be asked to return with additional instructions, in writing."

"You ought to receive them in person. I can't understand why you refuse to go."

Albin picked up the latest copy of *La Gazette*. Brandishing it, he asked, "You've read this?"

He nodded. "Every word."

"Then you saw the paragraph naming His Majesty's guests. One of them in particular."

He meant Princess Bathilde. "Her presence is sufficient justification for your going to Fontainebleau. No one will question your joining her there, or be at all surprised to see you."

"She mustn't discover I've returned from Vienna. Not yet. The king doesn't want anyone to know."

Wilfride stretched out his legs and crossed his ankles. "When she sees me, she'll realize you're in France."

"You won't let that happen." After a period of silence, Albin added, "For the time being, I must set aside personal matters."

"Even though it's an opportunity to explain what happened with that peasant girl?"

"I need no reminder that I caused the death of Bathilde's friend. She lost her father not long afterwards, and for all I know, my actions contributed to his decline. I placed my signature on a contract of marriage. She is my promised wife." Albin concluded bitterly, "Her willingness to have me for her husband is doubtful."

Last autumn, after leaving Château des Vignes, a repentant Albin had cloistered himself among the Jesuits to do penance. Precisely what that entailed, he hadn't revealed to Wilfride. The mission in Vienna must have felt like yet another process of mortification, in a secular setting. Observing the Habsburg emperor's troops on maneuvers and assessing fortifications was a tedious responsibility, but he seldom complained about it. He consumed a moderate amount of Austrian wine. At social gatherings he rebuffed overtures from females of his own class and ignored the night strollers who accosted him in the streets. And he unfailingly rose in time for morning mass.

Before departing for Fontainebleau, Wilfride offered to convey a letter to the princess.

"I can manage it without revealing that I'm lodged so near to the royal château. Write to her, Albin. Assure her that you mean to fulfill your pledge."

"Not until the king's plan is concluded to his satisfaction. If he wishes to inform you about it, he will. I'm sworn to silence."

"You received Lieutenant d'Artagnan of the musketeers, who spied for Mazarin. I gather he's also involved."

"I congratulated him on the birth of a second son," Albin said.

"You're a marvel of discretion."

"Which is why His Majesty has charged me with this burdensome and inconvenient business. May I soon be done with it."

Wilfride arrived in Avon village in garments plainer and more somber than usual and secured a room in a small lodging house. He carried a case that held the spyglass his cousin had used to survey the Austrian troops. If asked, he would profess to be connected to the improvements being made in certain areas of the royal gardens.

"If you've ever wished to glimpse our king," said the

man who served his dinner, "you'll get a chance tomorrow. He and his mother will pass by here on their way to the Carmelite priory. After twenty years of barrenness, she prayed there for a son. God gave her one. Then another. They say she pays the abbot a handsome sum in remembrance of the miracle."

He'd already sent his groom to the château to inform the king of his presence, but hadn't received a response by the time the procession entered the village. Later in the day, the expected message came. When he presented himself at the regal residence, he was taken directly to His Majesty's private closet. As Albin predicted, Jean-Baptiste Colbert was also present for his interview. Noted for his brilliance and shrewdness, he'd served Cardinal Mazarin for a decade. Only Nicolas Fouquet possessed greater power.

Rising from his bow, Wilfride said, "This isn't my first time of seeing Your Majesty this day. I witnessed your morning ride through the village."

"I was making my way to Église Carmes des Basses-Loges. My mother and I offered thankful prayers for my queen's excellent health as we await the birth of the next dauphin of France."

Colbert commented, "The Almighty has been generous in another respect. Fouquet, in the belief that higher office awaits him, has decided to surrender his post as attorney general. A development germane to the matter we've entrusted to the Duc de Rozel."

The king had finished breaking the many wax seals and unfolded the pages covered with Albin's precise handwriting. Completing a cursory review of the contents, he told Wilfride, "Colbert and I should study this report more carefully before sending your cousin's next instructions. Just now we must attend to other pressing demands. This evening I attend a violin concert on the terrace of the Jardin du Tibre. You may join the company if you care to."

From a certainty that Princess Bathilde would also be there, he made no commitment. Fearful of inadvertently drawing her attention, he resolved to avoid the château except when the king expressly demanded his return. But after nightfall, he was unable to suppress his urge to be near, even if he couldn't see her or speak with her.

Venturing into the early darkness, he pulled his hat low over his brow and drew his cloak closer. He strode along the quiet streets, leaving the village for the adjacent palace grounds, following the faint strains of music to the wall enclosing a courtyard.

She's there, he told himself.

He imagined her as he'd seen her at concerts or attending performances in the Petit-Bourbon theatre or during her own betrothal banquet. She would be sitting perfectly still, hands folded in her lap, and her lips slightly curved in a smile of appreciation or amusement. His understanding of the term "heartache" had never been so profound. She'd couldn't belong to him. He'd accepted that fact years ago. Albin had won her love, prior to her discovery of his vineyard escapade and the resulting tragedy. What her present feelings for him might be, neither of them knew.

The violins fell silent, and remained so, signaling the conclusion of the concert. As the courtiers' applause drifted over across the high stone barrier, he turned away and retraced his steps back to his lodging house.

He spent the next day exploring the countryside on his horse, returning to the inn at intervals in case further communication had arrived from the king. It had not. He passed the evening in his room, penning letters to each of his four sisters in Normandy, which he'd neglected to do since returning from Vienna.

The next royal summons directed him to attend an evening ballet performance, with assurances that His Majesty would meet with him afterwards. He could neither refuse this command, nor suggest an alternative time or location. Mounting his horse, he rode to Melun, the nearest sizable town, to acquire garments suitable for a court function and to do everything possible to alter his appearance.

Beardless for the first time since reaching manhood, with his moustache clipped and thinned in imitation of the king's, he returned to Fontainebleau. Judging that a mask would only make him conspicuous, he relied on the barber's efforts, a full brown wig, and the largest *chapeau* he'd ever worn. His new dress coat had a standing collar, and he covered himself with a cape as black as the night, with a pocket deep enough to hold the spyglass.

He found the stage and claimed a chair in the back row that provided an adequate view of the platform and the lake. Craning his neck, he searched the audience for the princess. Queen Marie-Thérèse, her pregnancy concealed by her full skirts, sat with her mother-in-law. Her eyelids drooped as though she was succumbing to drowsiness.

The gentleman beside him commented, "I've seen this delightful ballet once before. I enjoyed it immensely. The female players' pulchritude will enchant you. Bensérade's verses never impress me, and Lully's tunes are as you might expect."

"You're a more astute critic than I," Wilfride acknowledged. He had come because the king required him to.

A tableau formed by what appeared to be a grouping of fauns and an opera singer's high-pitched warble failed to stir his interest. When Monsieur's bride wafted out of the wood, appareled as the goddess Diana, she was accompanied by a troupe of youthful beauties clad in flowing green draperies. In a voice sweet and clear, the princess on whom he'd bestowed his heart recited several lines. All too soon, she exited with the others. Hoping to catch another glimpse of her, he paid closer attention to subsequent scenes. The king and his brother obviously relished performing, and looked magnificent.

Princess Bathilde returned as one of several muses surrounding Apollo. This time she was arrayed in white and carried a gilded lyre. As her fingers grazed its strings, he caught the flash of a gemstone. Drawing out his spyglass, he directed it towards her hand and identified the ring Albin had purchased from a Paris jeweler. Wilfride couldn't imagine how she came to possess it, for his cousin had never mentioned giving it to her.

The players assembled on the stage to take their bows. The spectators dispersed, some entering the palace, and others—couples—drifting in the direction of the gardens and groves. Unsure where his meeting with the king would take place, Wilfride searched the crowd for Monsieur Colbert.

His gaze landed on Princess Bathilde, in close conversation with the sovereign. In their flowing white costumes, the pair resembled a god and his goddess, altogether superior to ordinary mortals in their status, wealth, splendor, and grace. Observing their exchange of fond glances, he recalled his cousin's past suspicion about an intimacy between them.

The king placed a hand upon her bare shoulder. She smiled up at him and nodded in response to whatever he was saying.

Wilfride needed no more evidence to conclude that Louis was intent on seducing Albin's future bride. Or worse, had already done so.

# CHAPTER 39

*August, 1661*

Beyond Chartrettes, Bathilde urged her mount into a faster pace so she could catch up to Louise. With a hand gesture, she signaled her desire to halt.

"We shouldn't arrive in advance of the royal party. Let's wait here and rest our horses.

"Very well." Louise, ever agreeable and extremely biddable, never voiced an objection.

After a mid-afternoon departure on this oppressively warm day, the king's cavalcade made slow progress towards Bois-le-Roi, where it crossed the bridge over the River Seine. Nicolas Fouquet, whose château Vaux-le-Vicomte lay fewer than seven leagues from Fontainebleau, was hosting a grand *fête*, and his invitees reportedly included every aristocrat and person of importance in the realm—and elsewhere in Europe. Bathilde and Louise had preferred to travel by horse instead of in the stuffy confines of a coach. Their servants and baggage followed at the rear of the long procession of carriages and other riders.

"I require your advice," the younger girl said, "on a

perplexing point of etiquette. You know exactly how to behave in every situation."

"Not yours, Louise. The king was never my lover," Bathilde said. Nor would he ever be.

"I know that. I wasn't implying that he had been. Because the queen stayed behind, and won't be constantly watching us, I fear he'll be too attentive in the presence of other people. He abandoned all discretion after Monsieur Fouquet made me so uncomfortable."

Through a female emissary, the superintendent of finance had offered Louise thousands of *livres* as payment for information about His Majesty. Later, concerned that she would tell the king about the bribe, he had approached her himself to deny involvement in any plot.

"I had to tell him what happened. I love him too much to let harm come to him through a person he trusts. No, *used* to trust. He accuses Fouquet of an ulterior purpose, in addition to enlisting me as his paid spy—purchasing my favors. That may well be so. My concern is that the gossip about me, and His Majesty, will increase if his minister's effrontery becomes widely known."

"His wife's presence will prevent him from bothering you," Bathilde assured her.

"How I wish Madame had stayed at Fontainebleau and not insisted on making this trip. Although her pregnancy isn't as far advanced as Her Majesty's, she is the one who is unwell. She assumes the absence of both queens will make it possible for the king to devote himself to her, as he used to do. He'll always admire her, he says, but he offered his heart to me. If everyone becomes aware of it, I'll be even more mired in scandal."

She couldn't avoid it, but Bathilde wouldn't add to her friend's distress by saying so. Though he might strive not to unsettle his increasingly jealous consort by flaunting an affair while she carried the heir to his crown,

Louis would have his own way. If he decided to publicly acknowledge Louise as his mistress, he would do it
without compunction.

"His reputation won't suffer," Louise went on. "Mine
already has." She threaded the reins through gloved
fingers. "Here's another dilemma. During the lottery the
Queen Mother held in her rooms, the king drew the best
prize—a pair of bracelets studded with diamonds. I know
Madame expected to receive one, or both, but he gave
them to me. Should I wear them tonight?"

Turning the mater over in her mind, Bathilde decided,
"It would please him to know you appreciate the gift.
And because he presented the bracelets when others were
present, nobody will be astonished."

"Madame will dislike it."

"She's too proud, and too wise, to reveal her true feelings. All summer, a great worry has weighed upon the
king's spirits. That, I'm certain, is why he sought distraction and amusement in her company. It wasn't enough to
content him. From you, he receives a tenderness that he
sorely needs."

In certain respects, the ladies were opposites. Henriette
sparkled, brimming with energy and bright wit, and she
craved the prominence denied by her youthful poverty.
Under her husband's influence, she'd become increasingly
artful in the arrangement of her hair, and had a talent for
choosing fashions that flattered her thin frame. By contrast, Louise glowed. Her pure complexion required no
*maquillage*, and she arranged her thick blonde hair in the
simplest style. Her mode of dressing, never ostentatious,
suited her slender figure. From natural shyness, and lately
because of her romance with the king, she didn't draw
attention to herself.

Hearing an army's worth of hoofbeats, Bathilde said,

"Here comes the troop of musketeers—His Majesty won't be far behind. Let's remain here until he overtakes us."

The armed guard charged past, their short blue cassocks fluttering, and the silver and gold crosses embroidered on the fabric glittered in the bright sun. They were soon followed by the king's open carriage, which he shared with a duchess and a pair of countesses. The Queen Mother and Monsieur traveled together in a closed vehicle. After it, Madame's horse-drawn litter passed by, its curtains drawn.

Bathilde and Louise waited for the dust clouds to settle before urging their horses to follow. The route converged with the busier, more crowded road from Paris, further delaying their arrival.

The recently completed Vaux-le-Vicomte stood upon a raised foundation, surrounded by a square moat, and the château appeared to be floating on the water. Bathilde had never seen one so perfectly, symmetrically situated. Its roof was a series of peaks, and behind them rose a large slate-covered dome topped with a tall cupola. Formal gardens and more water features were visible in every direction. Her impatience to explore the grounds designed by Andre Le Nôtre exceeded her curiosity about whatever lay within the pale stone walls.

She and her friend guided their mounts into the stream of carriages flowing across a bridge that spanned the moat, which brought them into the vast forecourt. Nicolas Fouquet stood at the imposing entrance with his wife, only two months past the birth of their son. Stepping out of his carriage, the king addressed a comment to the finance minister, who bowed with exaggerated courtesy. The couple ushered their royal visitors inside their mansion.

Louise joined Madame's ladies, and Bathilde searched the busy throng for Justine and Pierre. A footman conducted them up one side of a double staircase to the upper floor and a broad passage that stretched all the way across the building. The king's suite, the man informed them, was directly below Bathilde's elegantly painted and furnished room. She didn't dare to lie down on the ornate bed in her riding habit, or before washing away the dust that had penetrated her every pore.

A page delivered water and a soap ball, then brought a decanter of white wine and a tray of fresh fruit. She drank and she nibbled. Knowing the planned entertainments would last all night and into the early morning, she tried to sleep. But her thoughts were chaotic, darting from the king's mysterious problem to Louise's scruples, and back again. Belatedly it occurred to her that Albin must have been invited, since no one bearing the title of duke would be excluded. The possibility of encountering him here destroyed any chance of peaceful rest.

Twisting the beryl ring around her finger, she considered whether she should leave it in place. This only tangible—and personal—connection to Albin was as significant to her as the legal document bearing his and Papa's signatures.

Justine helped her put on the same turquoise and gold lace dress she'd worn last summer for the king's wedding, when Albin had teased her about decking herself in peacock colors. As her maid fussed with the dark blue ribbons, tying bows at her shoulders, elbow, and wrist, she recalled her conversation with him on the shore at Saint-Jean-de-Luz, and how he'd urged her to address him by his name.

"Shall I pin your hair in the usual way?" Justine inquired.

She nodded absently.

The same page who had waited upon her earlier led her back down the staircase to the vestibule, and into an oval-shaped room he referred to as the *grand salon*. It had a high, domed ceiling and a floor paved with black and white marble. The windows lacked glass panes, admitting fresh air, as did the open doors. Stepping onto the terrace, she discovered that the praise Monsieur and Madame had lavished on the gardens after their June visit hadn't fully conveyed their magnificence.

Guests were touring the grounds in open horse-drawn chariots, and Madame's litter, carried by four footmen, traversed a broad *allée*. The king and his brother stood beside a circular pond with their host and hostess.

When Bathilde joined them, Madame Fouquet welcomed her and said, "One of my very dear friends is particularly eager to find you. I'm sure you remember Madame Scarron."

"I shall be glad to see her again." Her correspondence with Françoise had faltered in recent months.

Madame Fouquet returned to the house to supervise preparations for the festivities to come.

Her husband interrupted his monologue long enough to acknowledge Bathilde. "I've been telling His Majesty that I acquired three local villages, some as far away as five leagues, to divert the rivers and streams that supply my moat and ponds and canals. I employed nearly a thousand laborers to level the landscape by digging and filling baskets of earth and moving it about. The basins were excavated and these walks and turf laid."

"The result is sublime," Monsieur declared. "Well worth the effort and expense."

"I'm flattered to receive the admiration of such a renowned connoisseur. The entirety of Vaux-le-Vicomte has been created for occasions such as this. These marble fountains and statues were produced in Italy."

"The golden figure prominently placed on the distant knoll, who is it meant to be?"

"Hercules. Le Nôtre, in his brilliance, arranged the perspective to make it seem that the statue returns our gaze. Permit me to escort Your Highness to a carriage. It will take us to the grotto so you can view it at close range."

The king did not go with them.

He turned to Bathilde. "Last year I came here with the queen, prior to our entry into Paris. On that occasion, I saw only a hint of the miracles my own artisans Le Vau and Le Brun and Le Nôtre would produce." He studied the imposing domed façade. "All of this stone was quarried at Ravières, shipped to this site by river barge. And the builders completed their work in little more than a year. You, I know, prefer a garden to any other place. Our surroundings must enchant you."

Detecting the note of envy, Bathilde pointed out, "Monsieur Le Nôtre is employing the same artistry and skill on your behalf, at Fontainebleau."

"Where he'll never achieve the same grandeur. Not enough space. Too many antique structures. He can improve, yes. And alter, to some extent. But for a project of this scope, there must be an expanse vast enough to fulfill the vision and the design. And an endless supply of money," he added darkly.

A hearty burst of masculine laughter nearby made her whirl around.

"He not here," said the king. "Nor will he be."

"Your Majesty is entirely too perceptive."

"Your hopeful expression revealed your thoughts. Be comforted, for Albin is no farther from you than Paris. He was bidden to these festivities but unable to attend."

"I gather you've communicated with him. Or he with you."

Without confirming her surmise, he asked, "Did you and Mademoiselle de la Valliere enjoy your ride? I imagine you confided the secrets of your hearts to one another along the way."

She repaid his reticence about Albin in kind. "I'd be a poor friend to share her confidences with another. But you might as well know her reluctance to wear the bracelets you gave her. I assured her that a demonstration of her gratitude would be entirely proper."

"I applaud your finesse." He brought his gloved hands together gently, hardly making a sound. "Fouquet claims he's got more than a thousand orange trees lining these walks and terraces. Would you care to join me in counting them?"

He jested. She could tell by the quirk of his mouth.

"It grieves me to disappoint you, but I'd rather not."

"I wish I wore a diamond or some other valuable jewel to give you. I've not forgotten that I'm greatly in your debt."

"For what?"

"Suggesting that I seek out the sweet mademoiselle for whom I feel the most profound *tendresse.*"

"You did give me a box filled with brilliants, for a bride gift. As I'm unwed, I ought to return them."

"Certainly not. And I shall find a way to repay you for my present happiness, do not doubt it."

"I desire only your trust. And your friendship."

"*Ma chère,* both are eternally yours."

She acknowledged his fond words with her deepest curtsy.

# CHAPTER 40

Louise was innocence personified in a white taffeta gown patterned with gold stars and a headdress fashioned from white flowers and lustrous pearls. She extended lace-gloved hands to Bathilde, exposing the glittering bracelets that encircled her wrists.

"Madame was watching you and the king," she whispered. "Be aware, she's peevish today and taking it out on everyone."

At the lottery stalls set up along the *allées,* tickets were offered with no payment required. Each could be redeemed for a prize—weaponry for the gentlemen, jewelry for the ladies. Fouquet, beaming with pleasure at the accolades his gardens and gifts received, announced he was giving a horse to every member of the king's entourage.

Louise, an avid equestrienne, seized Bathilde's arm. "I don't know how I shall afford to keep another one. But I can't bear not to accept."

A line of open carriages delivered the privileged guests to the extensive range of brick and stone buildings that formed the stable court.

"The horses live in a château of their own," Bathilde

commented. Another feature that would stir the king's envy.

An army of grooms brought forth a string of glossy, perfectly proportioned animals. The courtiers applauded appreciatively as they were paraded around the courtyard and turned around so every feature could be judged. Each guest was asked his or her preference.

Without hesitation, Louise declared, "The black, fifth in the line. It has spirit, I can tell by the way it holds up its head."

"I like the gray beside it. An excellent match with my other mounts." Guessing her companion's intent, Bathilde grasped her elbow. "You mustn't go near them, or you'll smell of horse for the rest of the night."

"I was forgetting that. You're right, of course."

One of the vehicles carried them from the stables to the forecourt. Before ascending the front steps, Louise paused to ask, "Have you noticed the squirrels?" She pointed at the roundels in the frieze running across the upper part of the façade. "I see them everywhere. Carved into the stonework. Painted on the walls."

"It's the emblem in Monsieur Fouquet's coat of arms."

"We have a rearing lion, half white, half black. What's yours?"

"Three scallop shells. Representing *the fruits de mer* taken from the waters between Esnandes and the outflow of the Sèvre-Niortaise."

Throughout the banquet, two dozen violinists performed new airs composed by Lully. Floral arrangements and dishes of bite-sized delicacies covered the tablecloths. The royal guests ate from solid gold plates, the courtiers had silver ones, and the several hundred diners of lower status were fed on fine porcelain. Servants trooped in with great platters heaped with food—roast meats and game birds of every variety, vegetables stewed in sauces or baked into pastry, silver cups filled with *sorbet*—and lastly, nuts and fresh exotic fruits. Monsieur and Madame Fouquet moved through the rooms, greeting friends and acquaintances and accepting their compliments.

The evening's first entertainment was the debut of *Les Fâcheux,* a new *comédie-ballet* by Molière. The company followed paths lined with orange trees, the white blossoms perfuming the night air, to the stage erected in an ever-green bower. As the musicians began the overture, water jets rose high, drawing gasps, and a giant shell parted to reveal Madeleine Béjart. Naiads with long, streaming hair slipped out from behind the rocks to dance while the actress recited a prologue in praise of the king. They were joined by dryads, fauns, and satyrs.

Éraste, the main character of the play, desired to wed Orphise, but his courtship was impeded by numerous bores and pedants, many of them portrayed by the versatile Molière, whose speeches drew repeated laughter. Catherine de Brie excelled in her part as a young woman stubbornly engaged in a long-winded dispute with her sweetheart on the nature of love and jealousy. Dance interludes took place between each of the three acts, during which the fauns and satyrs ran into the audience, presenting each lady with a sparkling gem.

"Can this be a genuine diamond?" Louise murmured.

Bathilde replied. "Monsieur Fouquet would never lay himself open to ridicule by handing out stones made of paste."

When the king congratulated Molière on his latest success, the author's mobile face expressed his pleasure. "Sire, I spent but a fortnight composing and rehearsing the piece. Deficiencies will be remedied."

"If you will entertain a suggestion, I can offer one. The greatest of bores are the hunting men, who drone on and on about their exploits during the chase—whether or not the outing succeeds. You might consider including a character like the Marquis de Soyécourt."

"No consideration is required. Not being a sportsman myself and knowing none, this excellent notion didn't occur to me. I am indebted to Your Majesty. Should you ever command a repeat performance, I hope you'll find that my satire of a verbose huntsman is apt."

"In a week's time, you must present the revised piece at Fontainebleau. We'll be less distracted by eruptions of water and too large a crowd."

The next diversion, a mock battle between two miniature galleons, drew the guests to the Grand Canal. At the conclusion of the contest, an enormous mechanical whale floated out of the darkness, its head spouting flames. Fireworks soared heavenward, rockets and squibs lighting the black sky so brightly it could have been midday, showering sparks that were extinguished on hitting the water. Drumbeats thundered and trumpets blasted throughout the display, and at its conclusion, carefully positioned illuminations bathed the entire façade in light.

A ball was the unsensational epilogue to these pyrotechnic feats. In this château, unlike most, all the reception rooms were located on the ground floor. People flowed from one to another to the next, commenting on the magnificent decorations—the gilding, the furnishings, the tapestries.

The frown that occasionally flitted across His Majesty's countenance had become fixed. Bathilde watched him stride purposefully across the *grand salon* to address his mother. As they exchanged words, her expression of annoyance matched his. She shook her head at him as though he were still a boy-king under her influence.

Well before Françoise Scarron cornered her, Bathilde was fatigued into a state of near incoherence.

"I assumed that by now you'd be the Duchesse de

Rozel," her friend commented. "Instead, I discover that you're His Majesty's ward. He must be impatient to hand you off to your duke."

She deflected this inquiry with a jest. "You imply that he finds me a troublesome charge." Dismissing the subject of matrimony, she inquired, "Do you often forsake your convent lodging?"

"I reside there no more. My pension from the Queen Mother has been a godsend, enabling me to live comfortably and independently. As a widow, I've money enough to purchase the luxuries that were beyond my means as Scarron's wife. This isn't my first visit to Vaux-le-Vicomte, for Madame Fouquet's kindness is unequaled. In Paris, at Maréchal d'Albret's, I became acquainted with Mademoiselle Bonne de Pons and Mademoiselle Athénaïs de Tonnay-Charente, who serve Madame. You must know them."

She simply nodded, unwilling to admit that she liked neither very much.

"You cannot imagine their dismay to be passed over for the insipid de la Valliere creature. No one expects that *amour* to last."

"Tell me about yours."

"What have you heard?" Françoise's response was swift and sharp.

"Nothing at all. I simply assumed you must have an admirer. If not several."

"I have learned, to my great regret, how dangerously persuasive a libertine can be. Ninon de L'Enclos invited me to be her guest in the country for the summer, and her former lover was also with her. A courtesan is a bad influence, I can attest. But I've freed myself from that unwise liaison."

Françoise stepped away to pursue a more distinguished personage, leaving Bathilde to ponder this third

departure from the path of virtue. Françoise, after resist-
ing the Ursulines' efforts to turn her into a Catholic, had
apparently surrendered her virginity to a philanderer.
Devout Louise, despite her great dread of mortal sin, had
become a king's mistress. And Louis, faithful to his queen
for longer than anyone expected, had allowed a mixture
of lust and sincere love to overcome his scruples.

The Comte de Guiche was partnering Louise in a
*courante.* He was one of several gentlemen who had cautiously singled her out, not as a rival to the king, but in
compliment to the lady who enjoyed his favor. Because
one of her legs was shorter than the other, her ankle and
knees suffered if she danced too long. When the music
ended, she joined Bathilde.

"By now you must be as fatigued as I am. Shall we
withdraw?"

The watchful king pursued them to the library, his
heeled shoes striking the black and white floor tiles.

"Fouquet is far too busy to have read many of the
items in this collection," he commented. Like Bathilde,
he eyed the array of bookcases enviously. Constructed of
warm, perfectly matched wood, they extended almost to
the height of a ceiling decorated with gilding, hovering
cherubs, and painted panels. The central medallion featured a soaring eagle.

Louise, standing before a wall tapestry, pointed at
the center. "Another squirrel." The red creature stood
on hind legs with front paws extended, as if reaching for
something.

"A bold and pesky animal," the king commented,
"noted for gathering and hoarding. My superintendent
of finances makes no secret of his ambitions, emblazon-
ing his motto quite prominently. *Quo non ascendet?"*
He glanced at Bathilde and said, "You're a learned lady.
Translate for Mademoiselle Louise."

"I believe the phrase means, 'How high might I climb?'"

"It reminds me of an encounter I had with a young squirrel in the forest near my hunting lodge of Versailles. Striving to reach a tall oak's topmost branch, he misjudged the distance and fell to the ground. He landed on his back, stunned and immobile."

Louise's blue eyes widened in concern. "Did it suffer?"

"I feared it was dead, until its eyes blinked. As I gently stroked the belly with my crop, one paw jerked, altering my decision to hasten its death. I handed it over to my gamekeeper, who tucked it into his bag. After the creature recovered from its temporary stupor, the man gave it to his children for a pet. It soon became a nuisance, climbing the furniture, greedily devouring food from the larder. I therefore provided a sturdy cage for its confinement. By far the best method of dealing with a troublesome squirrel."

Bathilde detected the undercurrent of deeper meaning—or purpose—beneath the anecdote. In her weariness, she made no attempt to interpret it.

"I've seen more than enough opulence and spectacle," he went on, "and will depart very shortly. I wish you both a peaceful rest. Do not, I insist, ride back to Fontainebleau. Your own horses haven't rested long enough to make the journey so soon, and those you received from Fouquet are untried. I'll order him to return you to me safely, in one of his many carriages." As he left the room, the clock chimed the hour of two.

Bathilde returned to her bedchamber and nudged Justine, sleeping in a corner chair.

"Did you and Pierre watch the fireworks?" she asked while the maid removed layer after layer of clothing.

"We did. The noises were so loud I was almost

jumping out of my skin, and I feared this grand place would be burned to ashes. Never did I see such sights."

"Nor I."

While Bathilde slept, she dreamed she was observing a band of laborers as they felled trees and harrowed rough ground and uprooted wild shrubs. Their excavations roused female spirits, all veiled in white, who surged up from the ravaged earth. Rising out of ditches and furrows, they soared towards the men, driving them into a river, while Bathilde stood helplessly by, horrified by the scene.

"Princess." Justine squeezed her shoulder. "Do you have a pain? You cried out so sharply."

"I was trying to escape from a nightmare."

Even in her wakeful state, visions of wrathful *vili* haunted her.

In the morning, she was glad of the king's directive that she and Louise should travel back to Fontainebleau by coach. She'd had too few hours of slumber and doubted her ability to remain in her sidesaddle.

# CHAPTER 41

Bathilde reviewed her letter to Cousin Sophie twice before sealing it. Her faithful account of what occurred at Vaux-le-Vicomte included a description of the house and grounds, the horse she received, and a few words about Françoise, but not the king's vexation during the grand *fête*.

Since their return to Fontainebleau, he'd treated Monsieur Fouquet with affability, giving no outward sign of the displeasure she had sensed during conversations in the garden and library. His determined effort to demonstrate that he was untroubled by abundant evidence of his minister's extraordinary wealth and taste convinced her that he was, and very much so. She didn't doubt he raged inwardly at the accolades his finance minister continued to receive from admiring, fawning courtiers. They sought out Fouquet to praise his château's sumptuous decorations, his generous patronage of the nation's great artists, his innovative entertainments, and the costly gifts he'd bestowed upon them. Behind his back they debated whether he'd be punished for flaunting his riches before the monarch, and speculated about their derivation.

As though to keep his companions too busy for gossip, the king revived the popular *Ballet du Saisons*—again. He summoned Molière's troupe to Fontainebleau to perform the latest version of *Les Fâcheux*. Comedies in French or in Spanish were presented in the queen's apartments, from which she rarely stirred.

In these final days of summer, Bathilde felt the seasonal pull of Château des Vignes. Nearly a year had passed since Giselle's death, and Albin's disappearance, yet she believed she could find comfort in a place familiar and dear. More importantly, her presence would assure the people on the estate and in the village of her care and concern.

Never doubting that the king would consent to her plan, she nonetheless waited for an advantageous moment to declare it. Long hours in the saddle usually put him in a mellow mood, so she chose a day that he and Louise spent in a chase that took them all the way to Versailles.

"I cannot permit it," he stated firmly. "You're going with me to Nantes. I've decided to attend the meeting of Brittany's parliament, and my retinue will include only a few select persons. My brother. Saint-Aignan. Turenne. A few others. My chief counselors—Le Tellier, Colbert. This morning, Fouquet and his wife departed. Tomorrow, we follow them."

She regarded him in dismay. "I'm honored to be included in that illustrious company, but I'm returning to Poitou."

"Impossible. Nantes first. We'll be there no more than a week. Then you may go wherever you wish."

"Please grant me the freedom to do it now."

"Your reluctance forces me to remind you that I have double authority over you, as king and guardian. I don't intend to order your compliance, unless that's the only means of obtaining it."

"You can compel my obedience," she acknowledged. "But that wouldn't be a friendly act."

"Neither is pointless and futile obstinacy."

"Whenever Papa directed me to do something," she said, "he presented the justification for it."

"Believe me, Bathilde, I wouldn't ask this of you if it wasn't important."

Accepting the inevitable, she inquired, "Which ladies accompany you?"

"Turenne's wife, I expect. Madame Fouquet has obtained a house not far from the castle. You—and your dog—will have my hardiest horses to draw your carriage. I'll provide transport for your baggage and servants. They must immediately prepare for departure. I'll arrange the transfer of your riding horses to your château in Poitou."

That evening she took her leave of Queen Marie-Thérèse, whose pregnancy had increased her size and drawn her emotions to the surface. She shed tears at parting, although they had seldom interacted or conversed.

The Queen Mother smiled upon her. "You go with my prayers. And I assure you that at the proper time, the king will explain why your presence is essential to him."

Her knowledge and sanction diminished Bathilde's dread of potential harm to her reputation.

She had no need to inform Louise, already aware of the king's planned departure though not his purpose.

"How I shall miss you. No one, except His Majesty, is as kind to me. I hope it won't be long until we meet again."

Bathilde had resolved never to return to court, but she knew better than to admit it to the king's mistress. "I'm confident you will prosper in the meantime."

They kissed cheeks before parting.

In the morning, she descended the horseshoe-shaped stone stair at the château's front entrance to board her coach. Pierre opened the door for Blisse, not only an experienced passenger but an eager one, before he climbed up beside the driver of the baggage cart. One of the king's mighty chargers was saddled and waiting at the head of an entourage that included a larger contingent of musketeers than usual. Bathilde was thankful to travel separately from him. Other ladies had warned that he maintained a desperate pace and disliked stopping for any reason, including extreme bodily discomfort.

They halted in Orléans, long enough for a change of horses, and kept to the highway throughout the day and late into the evening, passing the night at Saint-Dyé-sur-Loire. The king rose at dawn to attend mass, and resumed his journey. At Onzain, he broke his fast and exchanged his sweating mount for a fresh one. He dined at an inn outside Amboise before proceeding to Tours. When the cavalcade bypassed the road leading south to Poitiers, Bathilde felt frustrated and trapped, miserably aware of her subordinate status. She deplored her inability to return to the place she regarded as her refuge.

They stopped short of Nantes, passing the night at Ancenis, a few miles from the city. In the morning, Louis instructed Bathilde to proceed there ahead of him, and deliver his orders to the castle's governor and its steward.

The former seat of the dukes of Brittany, now a crown possession, was a moated fortress not far from the River Loire. Bathilde was taken to the suite of rooms designated for a monarch's consort. The elegant curtained bed was a welcome sight after three days of hurtling across the country and passing two nights in roadside hostelries.

In the morning, as she dressed, she learned of the king's arrival. At midday he summoned her to the ramparts, to observe and hear a lengthy welcoming salute from the canons on the castle grounds and a ship moored in the river. When the guns fell silent, he offered his arm and escorted her inside.

"My finance minister and his wife came from Orléans

by water," he told her. "Unfortunately, Fouquet has succumbed to the same fever that has attacked any number
of my musketeers. Today you will call upon his wife to
deliver my hearty wishes for his rapid recovery. They
occupy the Hôtel de Rougé, which belongs to their friend
the Marquise du Plessis-Bellière. I'm providing a sedan
chair for your use. And a town coach."

"That comes as a great relief," she said, smiling up
at him. "I've been wondering whether I'm your guest, or
your prisoner."

"Neither. I hereby confer upon you the position
of chatelaine. I must leave you to meet with Le Tellier
and—and another gentleman. To discuss various matters,
including those related to my conference with the provincial parliament."

The chairmen delivered her to a palatial dwelling situated on the banks of the River Chézine, a tributary of
the Loire.

"How considerate the king is, sending so many distinguished emissaries to express his concern about my
husband's health," Madame Fouquet said. "Earlier
today, Monsieur Brienne came on the same errand. He
found Monsieur in bed, shaking all over from his ague.
But the doctor says it won't last long."

"That will be a relief to His Majesty."

A servant carried in a tray with two glasses of cordial
and withdrew.

"Comfortable as this house is," said her hostess, "it
lacks the magnificence of Vaux-le-Vicomte. I hope you
enjoyed your time there, brief though it was."

"An occasion that will forever linger in my memory."

"Do you think the king was pleased?"

Cautiously, Bathilde responded, "Everyone was."

"I intended to invite him—and you—to sail with us
over to Belle-Île, our island possession. The fortifications

there would interest him, and he could review the troops. I'm sure you'd enjoy seeing the local peasants in their curious garb. Alas, my husband says it's such a long distance from the coast and doubts His Majesty has time to spare for the excursion."

Later, the king questioned her about her visit. "Did she say anything more about Belle-Île?"

"Only what I've told you. I didn't know Monsieur Fouquet owns an island."

"Not only did he purchase it, he has fortified it and established a personal army there. He claims to have done so in order to provide a necessary defense against a naval assault and invasion."

"But we have no enemies," she asserted. "The years of warring are past, and we're at peace with neighbor nations."

"Long may it last." He faced her, saying, "I rely upon you to cultivate a very close friendship with Madame."

"I shall do my best." Compared to his other requests— or demands—it was not objectionable to her.

The finance minister's wife welcomed Bathilde's overtures, responding to every invitation, and readily reciprocating. To avoid the fever running through the city, they rode through the nearby countryside in the king's coach. For exercise, they promenaded along the riverside.

On the morning of His Majesty's birthday, the canons sounded again in his honor. He informed Bathilde of his intention to spend part of the day in hunting, before his daily consultation with the council.

"Fouquet recovered from his indisposition and attends our meeting," he added. "A visit from you at the same time will be pleasing to his wife."

This wasn't merely a suggestion, Bathilde perceived, but a command. She set out in a *chaise à porteurs*. The streets were unaccountably crowded with soldiers, some mounted on horses, others on foot. Her sedan chairmen had to maneuver past the throng to reach the *hôtel*.

Through her forced acquaintance with Madame Fouquet, she'd discovered several common interests— music, books, and gardens—and they had a mutual friend. When Françoise Scarron's name eventually came up in the course of conversation, Bathilde learned the identity of her former lover.

"The Marquis de Villarceaux. Master of the royal hounds. His affair with Ninon de l'Enclos was notorious. Though his passion for her faded after she bore his son, they're inseparable. The pair of them caught poor, pretty Widow Scarron in their net of intrigue. Though she claims to have escaped, I'm not entirely convinced."

"At your château, she mentioned an *affaire*. It ended, she told me."

"She's very careful to give the impression of being more virtuous than she is. For some time, I feared my husband might seek her favors. He is overly susceptible to attractive young ladies, but I trust her not to respond to any inducements he might offer." Madame Fouquet tipped her head to one side. "Oh, yes, I'm aware of his infidelities. As I cannot alter his behavior, I have accepted it. His respect and admiration, and the multitude of luxuries he provides, are my consolation. My position is secure, which none of his mistresses can claim. What is it, Gaston?"

Her servant, palpably uncomfortable, replied, "Several gentlemen ask to be admitted."

"I am at home to anyone. You may send them in."

Albin entered the salon, followed by a musketeer.

Seeing him so unexpectedly, Bathilde could scarcely breathe, or utter a single word.

"Madame Fouquet," he said, bowing. "We've come

to conduct you to the waiting carriage. The king orders your immediate removal."

The woman stared at him in confusion. Rising, she asked, "Did my husband send for me? Has his fever returned? I did warn him it was too soon to leave his bedchamber."

"Monsieur Fouquet has been arrested."

"Arrested?" she repeated.

"He's being taken to Angers as we speak, where he'll be confined until his trial."

"Am I to follow him?"

"No, *madame*. Limoges was chosen for your place of exile."

"I refuse to go."

"I bear a *lettre de cachet,* signed by His Majesty. My men have orders to search the entire house and remove all documents."

Finding her voice, Bathilde said, "Albin, you cannot treat her like a criminal, whatever wrong her husband committed."

He turned to her, his expression stern. "This is none of your concern, princess."

His coldness, and the use of her title rather than her name, cut her to the core.

The soldier approached her. "Come along, now, *mesdames.*"

"No!" Albin barked. "Princess Bathilde will be escorted back to the castle."

Bathilde grasped Madame Fouquet's hand. "I'll plead your cause to the king, I promise."

"It will do no good," the woman replied heavily. "My husband's friends feared this would be his fate. They will assist me in defending him, you may be sure. His mother enjoys the Queen Mother's friendship. As soon as I'm permitted to leave Limoges, I shall join her at Saint-Mandé."

"Your house there has been seized and searched and sealed," Albin told her. "You may take a few servants and whatever belongings they can gather up in the next quarter-hour—this officer will supervise them. Any other necessary items can be sent on later."

"And my babe, my older children, are they to join me?"

"Arrangements will be made for their care."

Until that moment, she had maintained her composure. Clutching a chair-back for support, she said, "I have no money. How am I to live?"

"Gourville is being interrogated downstairs, and will accompany you to Limoges. Apply to him."

Bathilde held out the *louis d'or* intended as a gratuity for her sedan chairmen. "Take these. I wish I had many more."

"I'll not forget your kindness," Madame Fouquet said.

"Princess," said Albin, "you must leave this place."

Very nearly the same words she'd spoken when sending him from the room after Giselle died. Did he remember? Was it intentional?

As her chair passed through the crowded streets, Bathilde reflected on the king's tale of the squirrel that failed to reach the highest bough and tumbled to the ground, and ever after was confined by the bars of a cage. Fouquet's capture had been planned well in advance of his arrival in Nantes. And the king had given himself the birthday present he most wanted.

# CHAPTER 42

"You saw her?" Wilfride asked.

"I did."

"And spoke with her?"

"Briefly."

"How did she appear?"

"As lovely as ever," Albin replied. "No. Lovelier." His tone, softened by reminiscence, hardened when he added, "I followed the explicit order I was given and offered no explanations. That is the king's prerogative. From him she will learn how Fouquet plundered the treasury for his personal use and benefit, and buried his thievery within our wartime budget and expenses. Whether his wife is fully aware of his criminal actions, I couldn't tell. She's in for a difficult time, but she needn't fear His Majesty's wrath. All of it is reserved for her husband."

Wilfride wanted to hear more about the princess, but his cousin's grim tone and expression told him no further details would be forthcoming. "I followed d'Artagnan to the cathedral square," he reported. "He marched Fouquet into the archdeacon's house. A short time later I saw the carriage depart, surrounded by musketeers."

"They'll pass the night at Ancenis. Tomorrow they go to Angers. What happens after that, I can't say. I wasn't informed." Albin shook his head, as though to clear it. "I'm famished. Tell the landlord we want our supper. And whatever is the best Breton wine. Muscadet, isn't it?"

Wilfride hadn't revealed his conviction, based on his observation at Fontainebleau, that the relationship between the king and the princess was more intimate—and scandalous—than that of ward and guardian should be. Was Albin already aware? That would explain his foul mood.

The evening passed without an answer to the question he couldn't bring himself to ask. They dined, they drank, and they discussed Fouquet's probable fate. A tribunal would assemble and the stacks of documents Albin had gathered would be presented as proof of a long history of fiscal misdeeds.

In the morning, the governor of Brittany and members of the provincial parliament, wearing their robes of state, and the bishops, assembled in the king's presence. Wilfride went to the chamber with Albin, and they sat through a number of presentations on trading activity in the port, and certain resolutions which Louis received with grave patience.

At the conclusion of the ceremony, Colbert and Le Tellier beckoned to Albin. After a brief conversation, he rejoined Wilfride.

"They've asked me to review additional papers collected from Fouquet's residence. They're still determining the extent to which he used the embezzled funds to fortify Belle-Île, and to outfit and arm his own ships."

During his cousin's private conference, Wilfride remained at the castle to carry out his own secret mission of discovery. By questioning servants, he collected much unsavory information about Princess Bathilde, all of it confirming that she was, as he suspected—and feared—the king's *chère amie*. Each disclosure increased his disappointment and strengthened his disgust.

He stepped onto the ramparts overlooking the courtyard. Because fewer musketeers were stationed there than earlier in the day, he assumed most of them were at large in the town, detaining as many of Fouquet's associates as they could. According to Albin, the king would scour the nation to obtain additional evidence—verbal or written—of his minister's treachery.

A carriage, its horses guided by a driver wearing royal livery, passed over the moat bridge and through the arch in the ancient wall. A groom followed, leading a fine white charger, its blue saddle cloth embroidered with silver *fleurs-de-lis*. Wilfride took up a position from which he could view the main portal, in expectation of soon seeing the king.

Louis emerged in his riding dress, with cape and boots and spurs. Princess Bathilde walked beside him, accompanied by a white dog. They proceeded to the carriage, deep in conversation, their heads so close that the plumes atop their hats appeared to touch. A footman opened the coach door and the dog jumped in. The princess climbed inside and for several minutes the king stood at the window, continuing to address her. Reaching for her hands, he pressed fervent kisses on them. At his signal the carriage rolled forward. He mounted his horse and followed it.

The king and his attendants galloped past the coach as soon as it crossed the bridge over the Loire. It carried Bathilde southward, halting at the place where hounds and huntsman waited. He would spend the rest of the day pursuing deer in the Forêt Nantaise.

Dismounting, Louis asked Bathilde to leave the vehicle.

Blisse, excited by the dogs' presence and eager to join them, jumped frantically down from the seat. Before she could escape, the king shut her inside.

Moving away from his entourage, he escorted Bathilde to the edge of a flat field of waving golden rye stalks.

"I've angered you, and I heartily regret it. What can I say to restore myself to your good graces?"

"You used me," she said. "Relying on me to distract Madame Fouquet all this week, befriending her while you plotted her husband's arrest. Sending me to her yesterday, to make sure she'd be at home when Albin—when the duke came to seize her."

"I did. Maintaining complete secrecy was absolutely essential. I could reveal nothing of our plot until it succeeded. My gratitude is boundless, for the very great service you rendered to me, and to France, though you were unaware. Hearing your confession of love for de Rozel, I realized I could rely on him to obtain the necessary proof of my minister's treachery."

"How long have you been suspicious about Monsieur Fouquet's deeds? Before we went to Vaux-le-Vicomte, I think."

"Mazarin expressed doubts about the source of Fouquet's fortune, aware that his own accounting system allowed concealment of certain transfers and payments. Even so, he advised me not to turn against Fouquet until I was able to build a firm case against him. De Rozel assisted in that effort. As did others."

"Papa also seemed to doubt his integrity. He warned me—and the duke—never to accept money if he offered it."

"The Prince de Coulon was ever astute. In the spring, I received initial proof that Fouquet was appropriating treasury funds for his personal use. What's more, for years he has provided my courtiers and officials with loans, purchasing their loyalty in the expectation that they would protect and defend him if ever he got into trouble. His grand new château is but one example of how he lavished France's money on himself. He built a fortress on Belle-Île and formed his own army, declaring he did it for our national defense. Not so. Lying beneath the Hôtel de Rougé is an underground waterway that connects to the Loire, near where it flows into the sea. To escape retribution, he could have taken ship and sailed away to his private island."

"Now you will cage your troublesome squirrel," she said, referring to the tale he'd told on the night of Fouquet's grand *fête*. "What happens to Madame Fouquet?"

"Her exile at Limoges will be lengthy, but sufficiently comfortable. Although she was a beneficiary of her husband's greed, I can't accuse her of involvement in his schemes. Nor his mother, a terrifyingly devout woman. But you need not feel any sympathy for Fouquet. He shouldn't have set himself up as a rival to me—his king."

"And for that, he'll land in the Bastille?"

"In the interest of justice, I cannot declare his punishment until a trial determines his guilt. But his ordeal will serve as a warning. I mean to demonstrate very clearly that I possess the ultimate authority in this land. From the time I inherited the throne as a boy, others acted on my behalf. My mother served as regent, but in truth the cardinal reigned supreme. There will be no chief minister in future. Henceforth, all administrators and counselors will know they are subordinate to the crown. I rely on Colbert's meticulous methods of management to balance the accounts, pay the debts, restore the finances, and lower the taxes. If we succeed, poor Mazarin, temporarily interred in the Sainte Chapelle at Vincennes and awaiting his final entombment, will be pleased."

She gazed into the distance as she voiced a question she often pondered. "Do the dead watch us, do you think, and judge us for what we do? Or don't do."

"There's no way we can know, Bathilde."

"I imagine them to be like the saints, though they haven't been canonized. Companion angels. Guarding and guiding us." She thought of Maman and Papa. And Myrte. And Giselle. "Is that blasphemy?"

"You'd best consult the Duc de Rozel, who spent his youth among the Jesuits. He's the theologian. Not I."

Would she ever get the chance? In Madame Fouquet's parlor he'd treated her like a stranger, and she'd detected nothing in his face or voice to indicate that she was foremost in his heart. Or that he regarded himself as her future husband.

The king linked his arm with hers and walked her back to the coach. "Something good came of my visit to Vaux-le-Vicomte. André Le Nôtre's achievements inspired me to create a similar garden of my own—no, a far grander one. Not at Fontainebleau, but elsewhere. I mean to construct a new royal château that will better suit my tastes, in a style of my devising." A sharp yap interrupted him. "Mademoiselle Blisse chides me for keeping you so long."

The dog pawed the edge of the window, her entire body quivering with relief.

"Come springtime," he went on, "she'll be old enough for breeding. I'll choose a mate of similar coloring and send him to you, provided you let me know where the consummation should place. Now give me your word that you won't travel all through the night."

"I've no desire to do so. I shall sleep at Montaigu."

"I return to Fontainebleau tomorrow. As word

spreads of what took place in Nantes, there will be great uproar in the court. And throughout the land." He pressed her hand but didn't kiss it this time. "*Au revoir, ma chère.*" He stepped away to address the coachman. "Proceed with great care. And don't become mired in the soggy Marais."

She didn't tell him that *adieu* was the more appropriate and accurate form of farewell. This road would carry her into Poitou, and her journey would end at Château des Vignes, where she'd be at safe distance from Louis and his courtiers. This time, she resolved, the separation would be permanent. As the horses surged ahead, her sense of relief swelled.

"Freedom," she sighed, caressing Blisse's pointed muzzle.

Wilfride had no desire for dinner, but he reached repeatedly for the cognac bottle.

Albin stared across the table. "If you continue gulping that *eau-de-vie,* you'll soon be stretched out on the floor in a stupor. And there you'll stay, because I'm not dragging you to your bed."

He set down his glass forcefully, shattering its stem and slicing his flesh. With a curse, he wrenched off his cravat and wrapped his hand to stanch the blood. "I don't care."

"For at least a fortnight, you've been sunk in despondency. Isn't it time you told me the cause?"

"Very well." He pushed back the dangling lock of hair that obscured his vision. "Princess Bathilde is lost. To both of us." Uttering the truth he'd concealed for years, he added gruffly, "I loved her before you did."

Albin drew and released several long breaths, absorbing this tortured declaration. "I never guessed."

"Don't be troubled. I do not mean to see or speak to her again." He reached for the cognac bottle and held it to his lips.

His cousin yanked it away. "You've always known we were betrothed."

"I used to be glad of it, caring for you both. No longer." Meeting his cousin's confused stare, he added, "At Fontainebleau I saw her with the king. I couldn't speak of what I witnessed, or its implications, until I was sure, quite sure, that I wasn't mistaken. Today my worst fear was confirmed. What the king has done to her is wrong. But she's not blameless. She gave in to him."

"You aren't making sense. What do you mean?"

"She's his mistress, Albin. His *fille de joie.* For so long she was my ideal of female perfection. Not merely beautiful, but kind to others. Thoughtful. And generous. But I cannot esteem her, knowing her to lack virtue. And decency."

"That's a baseless assumption. I don't want to hear any more of your drunken prattle. You'll regret it in the morning."

Too irrational to heed the prohibition, he went on, "At Fontainebleau, I overheard people discussing the king's dalliance with a court lady. At Nantes castle, I've heard, she occupies the consort's suite."

"Bathilde is his ward. I doubt there's a lady of higher rank in his entourage."

"Earlier today, I saw him kissing her hands—passionately. They rode away together. She in her coach, and he following on his horse."

"Whatever you observed," said Albin, "it led you to a wrong conclusion. You malign her without cause."

"In the past, you harbored suspicions about the two of them. Do you deny it?"

"That was before she—before we—" His hands gripped the table. "Bathilde would never allow Louis, or any man, to seduce her. You claim to love her, and I don't doubt that you do. It's impossible not to. But you've never known her as well as I do."

"Did," he muttered. "She's changed. You ruined her, Albin. Not by seduction, like the king. But you betrayed her trust, dallying with that peasant girl. Her grief and disappointment made her vulnerable to His Majesty's overtures."

"I won't believe it," Albin declared. "If you do, when you return to a state of sobriety, we will have to part ways. Forever."

"For more than a year I've listened to you endlessly declaring that you don't deserve her. Think it no more. The pair of you belong together. A murderer and a whore."

Hearing his own harsh words, he knew he'd gone too far. There was no way to unsay them.

Albin rose and advanced towards him with upraised fist.

He braced himself for the blow. It didn't come.

"Go. I don't care where to. Find my purse and take only enough coins to pay for a different lodging."

"Albin, I shouldn't have—"

"Leave. Spare me the indignity of removing you and tossing you into the street."

# CHAPTER 43

*Château des Vignes, September, 1661*

After an active summer that had taken her, reluctantly, into other provinces, Bathilde was grateful for the familiar calm she found in Poitou. Adverse weather during winter had affected the fields of barley and rye, but the fruit trees and the vineyard hadn't suffered as much as she'd feared. According to Pascal, the grape harvest would be only slightly delayed and possibly less abundant than usual.

Even though Bathilde hadn't asked her to, Sophie traveled from the coast to keep her company.

"I missed you these past four months," her cousin explained. "Besides, unwed ladies of your age are expected to have a duenna. Your guardian would want you to."

Bathilde wasn't so sure. Louis hadn't insisted on one when he whisked her away from Fontainebleau to Nantes.

At twenty, she was four and a half years from complete independence, but she regarded herself as effectively liberated from his control. With a multitude of problems to solve, he'd be far too busy to concern himself about her. He had to restore and improve the nation's finances.

He devoted his leisure hours to his mistress. Within weeks he would become a father.

If he sends for me again, she thought, I'll refuse to go. Punishment for disobedience would be exile from his court—which would be pointless. I've voluntarily exiled myself.

Her unwitting role in Madame Fouquet's removal from Nantes to Limoges had increased her natural distaste for intrigue. She had no desire to return to her *hôtel particulier* in Paris and doubted she'd keep the one in Poitiers. The sums she would derive from selling both would be put towards an endeavor inspired by a recent visit to Berthe Durand at the Niort convent.

Young girls living in the vicinity of La Rochelle lacked a similar academy, and she intended to establish one there. The king, deeply pious despite his fluid morals, was certain to permit the sale of her properties for such a worthwhile purpose, one his mother would also approve. She'd already applied to the Queen Mother for support, either as a co-foundress or as a donor, preferably both. She wrote to the newly appointed Bishop de Laval of La Rochelle, stating her desire to establish an Ursuline community in the vicinity of Château Clément. Nobly born, he was the son of a marquis and the grandson of a Marshal of France. His mother had been a famous *salonnière* in Paris before withdrawing to a convent, and two of his sisters, according to her cousin, had taken vows.

Sophie, impressed by her plan to establish a teaching nunnery, asked how she might lend assistance.

"It's too soon to know," Bathilde told her during their visit to the dovecote, where they made sure the birds had returned and settled for the night. "My next letter goes to Bishop de Palluau of Poitiers. I believe his permission is necessary for sisters from Niort to transfer to a new community. I will seek advice from Mother Superior. And inform our priest at Clément, who would serve the religious community as well as his parish."

"I confess, I'm relieved that you don't contemplate taking the veil yourself."

Bathilde smiled. "My vocation is the care of my people and my lands. I harbor too many questions and doubts about doctrine and proscribed beliefs. If I made them known, no order would accept me."

She was increasingly aware of the changes in her outlook and her ambitions, the result of harsh experience and suffering. The losses over the past several years had taught her to value those she loved, and those for whom her position made her responsible. Like her father, she'd turned away from a demanding monarch to pursue the mode of life she preferred. As to marriage—it was futile to speculate about that. She'd spent nearly a twelvemonth living with uncertainty. Exchanging a few strained words with Albin had done nothing to alleviate it.

"Even if I wished to become a nun, which I do not, I haven't the power to repudiate my marriage contract."

"Nor the intention of doing so?" Sophie wondered.

She loved Albin. She longed for him. In that, she was constant.

Blisse waited for her at the door.

"It must be the hour of her evening outing," Sophie said. "She's as accurate as a timepiece."

The dog bounded ahead, racing for the woodland, and Bathilde followed more slowly. She hadn't gone far when she noticed a myrtle sprig on the path—an occasional occurrence which had no logical explanation. Determined to solve the mystery, she continued to the twin stone crosses at the edge of the cemetery. In the years since she'd planted the shrub, it had grown large and bushy. She soon found the exact spot where the piece she held had been broken off, and places where others had been removed.

By whom? And why?

She called to Blisse, who scampered back to her, nose and paws caked with dirt. "You've been digging for moles. Poor Pierre will have to make you clean."

In the dimness of early evening, her garden took on an unearthly quality. Summer's long days had receded, and darkness arrived with startling abruptness. She didn't linger.

Sophie, the most sedate of females, came rushing at her through the gloom.

"The duke is on his way here."

Bathilde stared. "How do you know?"

"He sent a boy from Coulon to inform us."

She mustered a smile. "Considerate of him, to warn me."

"You'd better change. Your gown is soiled."

"He won't care."

She put off their dinner as long as possible, thinking he might share their meal. After Sophie retired, she sat up until the clock struck midnight, afterwards watching the minutes stretch into hours. Having long past dismissed Justine, she undressed herself and sought her bed.

Its softness couldn't quell her inner turmoil. Either her dream of spending the rest of her life with the man she loved was about to be realized, or else he'd come to free them both from their betrothal. She needed to prepare herself for either outcome.

Blisse stirred, then left her cushion, whining as though in distress. Bathilde heard her low, rumbling growl near the window. Leaving her bed, she saw that the dog had nosed past the thick curtain.

A full moon revealed the garden walls and the shapes

of topiaries within, but nothing more. No servants would be stirring this early.

"You must've heard an owl," she murmured. "It will do no harm to the birds. They're safe in the dovecote, roosting."

From a great distance, she heard the bell in the church steeple ring six times.

Before she let the curtain fall, she was startled by a beam of light hovering over the distant trees. Not a sudden sharp flash of lightning or a flame of fire, but a misty transparency resembling a thin cloud—vanishing as swiftly as it had appeared.

She covered her nightgown with a velvet robe and thrust bare feet into her leather outdoor shoes. "Come," she said, unnecessarily—Blisse followed her every step. They hurried along the passage to the tower staircase, the quickest means of exiting the château.

The faint breeze carried the scent of late blooming flowers. At ground level, Bathilde's perspective was more limited than it had been from her upper window. She no longer saw the strange, pale glow. But Blisse's keener senses detected a disturbance. Her black ears twitched, her legs stiffened, and the white fur rose alone her spine. She ran into the woods.

A gust wafted against Bathilde's face. An invisible hand lightly, gently, swept across her cheek, caressing it. A mysterious yet comforting sensation.

She went after Blisse, urged on by a sudden, sharp yap. The silence within the murky forest was broken again by movement among the trees. A stag or a doe, foraging for acorns or chestnuts, she told herself. She stopped to listen, inhaling the damp, mossy air.

The noise grew louder. Something, or someone, was approaching—rapidly.

Albin stumbled out of a thicket. Seeing her, he

staggered towards her and seized her forearms. "Why are you wandering out here in the dark?"

"I'm not sure. Why are you?"

His hands moved up to grip her shoulders, then cradled her face. "It's really you? Not a figment of my disordered mind?"

"Yes." She took his wrist and squeezed it. "I'm quite real."

"I can't yet tell whether I'm fully restored to consciousness. I've just awakened from a horrific nightmare."

"Where did you spend the night?"

"In the graveyard. Beside Giselle's burial place."

She looked into his face, trying to read his expression.

"While I prayed, I was so overcome with drowsiness that I stretched out on the grass to rest. I'm not entirely certain I was truly asleep when I sensed that I wasn't alone." He shuddered. "I hardly know how to describe what I saw. Females in white garments had surrounded me. Their faces and flesh were as pale and vacant as that moon above us."

"The *vili*," she whispered.

"Their leader approached. An imposing creature whose eyes were deepest blue, with long, black hair. She carried a leafy, flowery wand. As she waved it at me, though she spoke not a word, I knew she was commanding me to dance. I was utterly powerless, and sensed her determination to bring about my death. I felt nearer to losing my life than I ever did in battle."

He could have been describing Myrte—her features, her strong will. Her appetite for vengeance.

"Before I could obey, Giselle suddenly rose up from the ground beneath her cross. The other apparitions formed a circle, trapping us within it. She was my partner in the dance. Whenever I faltered, she supported me." He paused to draw a labored breath. "You must think I've been overcome by madness."

"I had a similar dream," she told him. "At Vaux-le-Vicomte."

"The church bell tolled," he continued. "The spirits flew skyward, all together, but Giselle stayed by me. She smiled and extended her hands towards me. Perhaps in farewell. Or, as I hope, forgiveness. When she pointed in this direction, I realized she was guiding me to the château. To you. And as suddenly as she had appeared, she descended into the earth and vanished beneath the flowers growing there. I'm not sure how long it was before my senses returned. If they have." He rubbed his forehead.

She doubted he had ever heard about the *samovili*. She knew if she sought some rational explanation for his supposed dream, and everything she'd observed since leaving her bed, she wouldn't find one. Down through the ages, people had described their visions, and told of witnessing miracles wrought by the holy saints. Did believing in these occurrences bestow reality upon them, or had they actually taken place? It was impossible to know.

Leaving his embrace, Bathilde followed the path until she found a myrtle branch at the base of a slender chestnut tree. Reaching for it, she was overtaken by dizziness. She grasped the trunk to keep from falling. The rough bark scraping her palm pulled her back to consciousness.

Myrte, on her deathbed, saw the *vili* coming for her. So did Giselle, in her last moments of life.

The pale glow hovering above the treetops matched Albin's description of the ghostly females' ascent. Which of her friends had stayed back, to touch her face?

Blisse, tongue lolling, scampered over to sniff the myrtle.

Albin approached her, saying, "Forgive me for distressing you. I shan't speak of Giselle again."

"We must, Albin. There's so much I need to hear. When you met her, why did you pretend to be someone else?"

"By that time, it was a habit. I cast aside my title and called myself Louis during my weeks of roving the provinces with my cousin, seeking adventure and amusement. That was my temporary, necessary escape from the stifling atmosphere of the court, and the hateful competition for royal favor and position. All the shallowness and false morality. Our marriage, I believed, would place me more firmly in the very sphere I most detested. I admitted that to you, the night of the ball."

"Did you love her?"

"I barely knew her. Her gaiety appealed to me, and I was flattered by her interest. I did flirt with her—recklessly, selfishly, with no regard for the possible consequences. We danced together. Under the influence of that pernicious *pineau*, I saw no harm in kissing her—rather, Louis the grape-gatherer thought it was harmless. My masquerade was coming to an end, and I dreaded resuming that refined existence I'd abandoned. But I never intended to break my pledge to you. When I arrived here, and learned that you returned my feelings, I was happier than I imagined possible. Until the terrible moment when I saw Giselle again. And watched her die, an innocent victim of my deception. As you were."

"Why did you abandon me?"

"You wanted me to go. I heard you say so."

"You mistook my meaning."

"How could I remain, after causing your friend's death? And bringing great grief to her mother, and the young man whose intentions were sincere."

Bathilde crossed herself. "Hilaire didn't long outlive her."

Albin bowed his head. "I've seen his grave." After a brief silence, he continued, "I left behind a love token. I'm glad you wear it."

Looking down at her ring, she asked, "Where did you go?"

"I spent several weeks in a Jesuit community, repenting of my misdeeds and doing penance. When the king ordered me to Vienna to conduct a survey of the emperor's troops and fortifications, I had no reason not to comply. Yearning for you, I was relieved when he recalled me to France. But my desire to proceed with our marriage was immediately thwarted by his involving me in the confidential and extremely complex campaign to bring down Nicolas Fouquet. I spent weeks delving into army accounts and badgering his correspondents to share the letters they received from him. I collected documents and wrote reports. And when I reached Nantes and learned from Louis that you had accompanied him, he forbade me to seek you out."

"Did he tell you that you'd find me here?"

He nodded. "Wilfride saw your carriage leaving the castle. I would've arrived yesterday, but I took a wrong road from Nantes and lost myself in the Marais. So many inconvenient rivers and streams and marshes."

"Did you and Monsieur Mesny travel by horse, or in a carriage?"

"I rode. He didn't come with me." He added, "We've had a serious falling out."

"I'm sure you'll be able to reconcile."

"This is the only reconciliation that matters to me. My reason for coming is to try and make amends for all the ways I've done wrong. And to carry out the provisions of the document that binds us. Though I won't claim to deserve the honor of being your husband, that is my desire. If you're still willing to let me spend the rest of my life proving my worthiness."

"I am," she declared. "After we marry, those ghostly maidens will never trouble you again. As soon as you've had something to eat, and I am properly dressed, we can send word to the priest to meet us in the chapel."

"Keep the nightgown. You won't need it very long. From our very first meeting, in Paris, I've gone alone to my bed. I've no wish to do so again." He leaned down to pick up the myrtle wand. "Your bridal flowers."

She fingered a starry blossom.

As they made their way out of the forest, arm in arm, Blisse trotted ahead of them. Occasionally she paused as though perplexed by their slower pace. While Bathilde and Albin took turns expressing the depth of their love, and the breadth of their hopes, the sun slipped above the horizon, enfolding them in warmth and light.

# EPILOGUE

*Château Clément, May, 1664*

Examining the branch ends of the apple and pear trees, Bathilde found tiny green beads of fruit, the size of her smallest fingertip. Passing through the orchard with Blisse, she stepped around clumps of yellow primroses and buttercups, the blue violets springing up in the shadiest places, pink clover heads, and scatterings of tiny white daisies.

Reaching the formal gardens, she saw Sophie in the *allée,* cutting the last of the tulips and adding them to her basket. Gerard, the year-old Marquis de Brénoville, crawled across a section of lawn to reach Fleur, Blisse's pure white puppy. His twin sister Giselle, equally adventurous, wriggled out of the nursemaid's lap and set out after him, wearing a most determined expression and stretching her little limbs as far as they would extend. Their hands and pristine gowns would be stained by grass and marked with dirt, but they would eat well at dinner and sleep the afternoon away. Trusting the servant to prevent the russet-haired imps from climbing into the basin of the fountain, Bathilde continued towards the walled *potager* at the side of the house, to inspect the strawberries.

She heard before she saw the horseman coming along the drive at a fast trot. An unusual occurrence, she would welcome it if not for the emblem decorating his saddle cloth.

The rider, noticing her, drew on the reins to bring his mount to a halt.

She approached him. "You come from the king?"

"I do, Madame. I bear a letter for the Duchesse de Rozel."

"Your errand is accomplished."

He reached into a leather pouch and handed over the missive. "I'm instructed to wait for a reply."

"Continue to the stables, and a groom will take care of your horse. Someone in the kitchen will give you food and drink."

She ran her forefinger across the hardened wax—red, not mourning black. Relieved that the messenger hadn't brought news of a death, she unfolded and smoothed the pages. She skimmed over the salutation and the warm sentiments embedded in the first paragraphs. Farther down, she came across the names of persons she hadn't seen for nearly three years. They muddled her earlier serenity and cast a shadow over her complacency.

She made her way to the terrace where identical dog statues seated on pedestals gazed unseeingly at the activity in the garden. Bathilde could never pass between them without admiring the sculptor's skill in recreating Blisse in solid stone. The living model accompanied her into the house.

She went to the library. Albin sat at a large desk covered with the books and loose papers he relied upon for writing the military biography based on her father's memoir manuscript and his own diary and recollections.

Originally intended for Papa's grandson and namesake, who wouldn't be able to read it for many years, on completion it would go to a Paris printer who anticipated high demand for the finished product.

"May I interrupt?" she inquired softly.

"The Battle of the Dunes chapter is completed. The prince's detailed observations and description required very little improvement or embellishment. Just as well. This afternoon the Dutch engineer comes with his plans and drawings for our ditching project, so we can begin to drain the marsh near Serigny. Is that my letter?"

"It was written to me by the king's own hand, delivered by royal courier."

Albin grinned up at her. "Louis is sending Blisse a new paramour?"

"It's an invitation. In a few weeks, he's hosting a grand *fête* at Versailles, his new palace. Three full days of entertainment to honor his queen for presenting him with a healthy dauphin, and in acknowledgment of his mother's devotion. But also, though he hasn't shared this publicly, he also honors Louise for bearing his other son. Monsieur is in a similarly happy mood, because his daughter will soon have a sibling. Madame lies in again this summer and is unable to participate in the ballets. The king asks me to perform her roles, and another in a new spectacle devised by Molière and Lully. He'll provide us both with prancing, dancing horses to ride in the carrousel. He wants to show us the beasts in his menagerie. He's eager to hear my opinion of Le Nôtre's achievements— *parterres*, fountains, terraces, *allées.*"

"What else?"

"He's paying all travel expenses for his guests and their attendants."

"I can't tell whether you're truly tempted by this catalogue of delights. Would you care to know my thoughts?"

"Of course. That's why I'm here."

"This self-described Apollo, our Sun King, seeks to reduce any lingering sympathy for Nicolas Fouquet, whose trial drags on. While England and the Dutch Republic wrangle over their sea trade and fisheries, Louis builds up our navy in anticipation of being drawn into the fray. Colbert has stabilized the finances, enabling him to demonstrate his superiority and his refined tastes. And, more to the point, to consolidate his power and influence over his nobles."

Impressed by this reading of the situation, Bathilde said, "When last I saw him, he was determined to establish his authority in every possible way. Don't you think it odd he invites us to his Versailles revels? That he even remembers us?"

"I've been acquainted with him longer than you. If you were merely one of several delectable duchesses in his realm, he wouldn't write in terms of intimacy. He's adamant that you—we—attend these festivities. I can guess why."

"Tell me."

"You represent a rare failure, a lost cause. By now his passion for Mademoiselle de la Valliere must be fading. Who better to replace her than a married woman, formerly of his court, who has already provided her husband with a male heir? When my cousin saw you together at Fontainebleau, and later in Nantes, he was convinced Louis had seduced you."

"So you've said."

That false and insulting assumption had caused Albin's prolonged estrangement from Wilfride Mesny. Yet despite his indignation, he'd generously provided his cousin with the position of steward at Château Rozel in Normandy.

"I could've been the king's mistress," she admitted. "He wanted me to be. Before Louise."

"He told you so?"

"Oh, yes. During my summer at Fontainebleau. In a fashion so charming and gallant that I doubt any other lonely, heartsore young woman would have refused him. But I did. I declared my love for you, and my abiding hope that one day you would marry me. He offered to recall you from Vienna."

"Most chivalrous. Admirably unselfish. Except he didn't. Not until he required my assistance ferreting out Fouquet's crimes."

"None of it matters now."

"If we go to Versailles, it does," he maintained. "My loyalty to the crown does not extend to relinquishing my wife, whose devotion has made me a better, wiser man. I've served His Majesty on the field of battle, from my youth onwards. In peacetime, I traipsed about the kingdom to help him bring down a traitorous minister. What can I say to persuade you that returning to court would be a grave mistake? For both of us."

"We won't go," she said blithely. "You should have guessed that already. I'm too busy here, overseeing our household and as patroness of the Ursuline school. Besides, three years of matrimony hasn't altered my aversion to the royal court."

"Or your regard for me?"

"Oh, my dear, that is altogether different. On the morning we spoke our vows in the chapel of Château des Vignes, I didn't realize I could care for you more than I did at that moment. Yet I do." She wrapped her arms around his shoulders and laid her cheek against his. "And if you put down your pen and go with me into the garden, it's possible that my unwavering affection might even increase."

"An invitation that I gladly accept," he replied, leaving his chair.

Passing through the glass-paned double doors, Bathilde heard the distant tolling of the convent bell, informing the nuns' pupils that they could set aside their books and step outside into the sunshine. The faint, familiar sound evoked memories of her girlhood. As she descended from terrace, her skirt brushed against the myrtle planted in urn-shaped *jardinières* on either side of the shallow steps. Sometimes the distinctive aroma reminded her of past sorrows. On this day, she associated it with the flowery wand she'd held during a hasty exchange of marriage vows, the prelude to her present joys.

# AUTHOR'S NOTE

Story ideas come to authors in various and often unexpected ways. For years, when viewing the classic
Romantic ballet *Giselle,* I couldn't shake questions about
what happened before the curtain rose, and occurred
after it fell. Did Princess Bathilde and Duke Albrecht
know one another well before becoming engaged, or was
it an arranged marriage between near-strangers? The first
version of the ballet ended with their reconciliation, at
the behest of a ghostly Giselle. This knowledge fired my
imagination. Curiosity about their future together eventually compelled me to create it for them.

Professor Marian Smith, dance and music historian,
points out that, "The Titus [1842] and Justamant [mid-
19th century] scores make it clear that Bathilde is a kind,
generous-hearted person; a kindly aristocrat." Dance
critic Alistair Macaulay observed, "To me, the friendship
that quickly builds up between the peasant girl and the
noblewoman is one that transcends class to a remarkable degree." These observations proved inspirational.
And I'm grateful to them for mentioning an alternative staging of the famous "mad scene" that takes place
during Bathilde's ball rather than the village festival. As
my knowledge of the source material increased, I eagerly

explored so many "What if?" questions. Choreographer Alexei Ratmansky, in his highly detailed re-creation of the original ballet, restored Bathilde's personality and her reunion with her wayward fiancé.

Just as I've pondered Bathilde's past and future, I've always been intrigued by the character Myrthe—in my story, Myrte—and the suitor who jilted her. She had to be a female of strength and determination, I decided, in order to become the Queen of the Wilis.

Setting my version of the story firmly in France, in areas I have visited and where some of my ancestors lived, was easily justified. A Frenchman, Théophile Gautier, created the libretto of *Giselle,* and he gave most of the characters French names. A castle and peasant cottages feature prominently in the set design, and France is noted for its splendid châteaux and picturesque villages. Act I of the ballet features a grape harvest and festival—France has vineyards. Love of dancing is a strong theme, and Louis XIV and his court were famous for it. The earliest story ballets were produced in his palaces, and he frequently performed in them.

As for the historical characters I inserted into my narrative . . .

Françoise d'Aubigné was briefly a pupil at the Ursuline convent school in Niort, before marrying Paul Scarron in Paris. Years later, Louis XIV appointed her governess to his illegitimate children by his mistress Athénaïs, Madame de Montespan. Initially alarmed by the widow's temperament and piousness, he grew to value her frankness and her ability to discuss politics, religion, and finance. He ennobled her as Marquise de Maintenon, and under her influence broke with his mistresses. Her power at court increased, and she was equally admired and detested. Youthful experience with the Ursulines led to the founding of Maison Royale de Saint-Louis for girls from noble families without means. She devised the curriculum, which included secular as well as religious subjects, and was actively involved with the instructors, a mix of lay sisters and nuns, and the pupils. After Queen Marie-Thérèse died in 1683, the king and Françoise were joined in a morganatic marriage that he never acknowledged, publicly or privately.

The Sun King was so devoted to his dogs that he commissioned portraits of them. For many years, I have immortalized mine in my fiction. I therefore gave my current canine companion to Bathilde—or rather, I let Louis do so. A decision that turned out to be historically, serendipitously justified. Paintings of the royal hunting hounds by Alexandre-François Desportes include several who look exactly like my Dot, who appears in the novel as Blisse.

At the first Versailles *fête*, which Bathilde and Albin chose not to attend, Jean-Baptiste Molière presented his *Tartuffe,* a comic satire on religious hypocrisy and gullibility. It got him into trouble with the church—though not with his royal patron. During my acting days, I portrayed Mademoiselle de Brie in *The Impromptu at Versailles,* his one-act depiction of his troupe's manner of rehearsing, so incorporating her was a very personal pleasure.

The king's Spanish-born mother, Anne of Austria, lived an increasingly retired life at Val-de-Grâce, the convent she founded. A victim of breast cancer, she died and was buried there.

Louise de la Valliere was Louis XIV's mistress from 1661 until about 1670. She bore five children, two of whom were legitimized and three who died when young. Although her relationship with the king was no secret, it wasn't formalized until after his mother's death, when she became Duchesse de la Valliere. She was never comfortable in her role and was supplanted in 1668 by her showier and more scandalous rival Athénaïs, Marquise de Montespan, who had also served as *fille d'honneur* to Madame. In 1671, without asking permission of the king, she left the court and entered a Carmelite convent. Four years later when she took her vows, Queen Marie-Thérèse attended her veiling. She died in her cloister in 1710, aged sixty-five.

Henriette, Duchess d'Orléans, known at court as Madame, remained a popular but troubled figure, enduring frequent bouts of ill health, miscarriages and stillbirths, and her husband's homosexual affairs. Louis relied on her as go-between to foster good relations with her brother, England's King Charles II. At her death in 1670 she was only twenty-six. Poison was the rumored cause, and there were several suspects, but in fact she suffered from an internal ulcer.

Her widower, Philippe, Duke d'Orléans, took as his second wife Elisabeth Charlotte of the Palatinate, known as Liselotte, whose cleverness and popularity compensated for her lack of beauty. Philippe served as a commander in his brother's European wars and was a connoisseur of art, architecture, music, dance, and handsome male courtiers. He predeceased Louis.

Madame Fouquet, through a secret printing press, produced numerous pamphlets in support of her husband, whose trial lasted for three years and ended with his conviction and imprisonment at the fortress of Pignerol. Madame spent a decade in exile but was eventually permitted to return to Vaux-le-Vicomte, the château where the famous—and fateful—*fête* had taken place. In 1679 she joined Fouquet at his prison, where he died the following year.

During the later years of the 17th century, King Louis and his armies waged war throughout Europe, seizing foreign territories. He exerted firm control over his courtiers, requiring them to take up residence at Versailles. His reign lasted for seventy-two years, and he died in 1715 at age seventy-six. Françoise outlived him by nearly five years.

My acknowledgements are numerous.

I'm endlessly indebted to Hugo, Olya, Nelli, and Yuri. For more reasons than I can adequately convey.

I extend thanks to the Gallica Press crew, as well as to Erin at Hook of a Book for her stellar copyediting skills, Michelle at Melissa Williams Design for stylish formatting, and to Deborah Bradseth for the beautiful cover.

Writing a novel is essentially a solitary occupation, but this writer cannot thrive in complete solitude. My gratitude, as ever, belongs to my husband, who throughout my career has been the very model of an author's spouse. He copes well with my mental absence when I am physically present and uses his impressive logistical skills on overseas research trips. He attends my public speaking events, where he learns everything I never revealed to him about the work-in-progress.

The sisterhood and brotherhood of fellow writers also deserve recognition. Most particularly author Virginia Macgregor, in whose sunny sitting room I began creating this novel. And Paul Brogan, whose stupendous support of my prior novels, interviewing skill, and writing talent has enhanced my life in many ways. My cohort of historical novelist friends and cherished colleagues stretches across the globe, and to name them individually would require another chapter. By this time, after our years of surviving this unique calling, they definitely know who they are. I must also acknowledge those non-writers in my life who miraculously choose exactly the right time to pull me out of my authorly absorption and involve me in walks, cocktails, dinners, and music events.

Lastly, I'm appreciative of the universe of readers, the ones for whom every word of this book was written.

# ABOUT THE AUTHOR

MARGARET PORTER is the award-winning and bestselling author of more than a dozen works of historical fiction. A former stage actress, she also worked professionally in film, television, and radio. Other writing credits include nonfiction, newspaper and magazine articles, and poetry. She and her husband live in New England. Information about her books and other aspects of her life and career can be found at www.margaretporter.com.

9 798985 673494